SLEEPING BEAUTY

Also by Phillip Margolin

Ties That Bind
The Associate
Wild Justice
The Undertaker's Widow
The Burning Man
After Dark
Gone, but Not Forgotten
The Last Innocent Man
Heartstone

PHILLIP MARGOLIN
SLEEPING BEAUTY

 HarperLargePrint

An Imprint of HarperCollins*Publishers*

HarperCollins books may be purchased for educational, business, or sales promotional use. For information, please write: Special Markets Department, HarperCollins Publishers Inc., 10 East 53rd Street, New York, NY 10022.

FIRST HARPER LARGE PRINT EDITION

Designed by Laura Lindgren

Printed on acid-free paper

Library of Congress Cataloging-in-Publication Data is available upon request.

ISBN 0-06-008326-3 (Hardcover)

ISBN 0-06-072681-4 (Large Print)

04 05 06 07 08 BVG/RRD 10 9 8 7 6 5 4 3 2 1

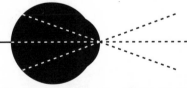

This Large Print Book carries the
Seal of Approval of N.A.V.H.

For my folks,
Joseph and Eleonore Margolin.
I couldn't ask for better parents.

BOOK TOUR

The Present

The bellman Claire Rolvag was looking for was standing next to the box with the keys of guests who parked in the hotel garage. She turned into the long, circular driveway, pulled around a cab, and parked her shiny new Lexus in front of him.

"Carlos?" she asked when he walked over to the driver's window.

"That's me."

"I'm Claire. I'm filling in for Barbara Bridger, just for tonight."

"She told me what you'd be driving," Carlos said as he opened Claire's door. Claire grabbed the book that lay on her passenger seat and got out.

"It'll be over there," he said, pointing to an area at the end of the driveway.

Claire thanked Carlos and handed him a folded

bill, which he slipped into his pocket. He was driving the car to the spot he'd indicated when the doorman welcomed Claire to the Newbury, one of Seattle's finest hotels.

There was a convention in town and the Newbury was packed with laughing, chatting people. Claire shouldered through them until she stood in the center of the lobby. She scanned the crowd. He wasn't there. A bell signaled the arrival of an elevator. Claire cast an anxious glance at her watch, then focused on the group of convention-eers that poured out. For a moment Claire did not see him. Then Miles Van Meter was standing in front of the bank of elevators. His sandy blond hair and blue eyes had been touched up in the color photograph on the back of the book jacket of **Sleeping Beauty** to hide his gray hairs, and he was a little shorter than Claire had imagined, but he was just as handsome in person as he was on television.

The lawyer-turned-writer was in his forties, five-foot-ten, broad-shouldered, and trim. He had dressed in a tailored gray pinstripe suit, white Oxford cloth shirt, and a tasteful Armani tie. Most escorts would have been surprised by the elegance of Van Meter's attire. Male authors tra-ditionally wore sports jackets on their tours—if they wore jackets at all—and damn few brought ties with them. You packed light and opted for comfort when you spent weeks of one-nighters, rising before dawn each day to catch another short flight to another strange city. But Miles Van Meter, a corporate attorney with a large firm of business lawyers, was used to traveling first class and dressing expensively.

Van Meter spotted Claire easily because she was holding a copy of his true-crime bestseller. He guessed that the attractive brunette was in her mid-thirties and would be peppy and efficient, as were most of the author escorts who shepherded him through his appearances in the often unfamiliar cities he visited each day of his grueling, six-week book tour.

Miles held up his hands in a mock plea for forgiveness. "Sorry, I know I'm late. My plane from Cleveland was delayed."

"It's not a problem," Claire assured him. "I just got here myself, and the store is only twenty minutes away."

Miles started to say something. Then he paused and looked at Claire more closely.

"You didn't take me around last time, did you?"

"You're thinking of Barbara Bridger. She owns the escort business. I'm just filling in. Her son came down with the flu and Dave—her husband—is out of town on business."

"Okay. I thought it was someone else. You do this a lot?"

"My first time, actually," Claire answered as they left the lobby and headed toward her car. "Barb and I are good friends and I told her I'd be willing to help if she ever got in a jam. So. . . ."

As Claire shrugged, Carlos spotted them crossing toward him and ran over to open the passenger door for Miles. He knew the drill. She was hired help. Miles Van Meter was the star.

It was a little before seven at night when Claire pulled into traffic. Rain was falling, so she switched on the wipers.

"You didn't do Murder for Fun last time, did you?" Claire asked.

"No. I think I hit one of the superstores, Barnes and Noble or Borders. I'm not sure which. After a few days they all blur together."

"You'll like this store. It's small but Jill Lane, the owner, always makes certain that there's a big crowd."

"Great," Miles said, but Claire sensed that the enthusiasm was manufactured. She knew that her author had been on the road for three and a half weeks, which meant that he was probably sleep-deprived and running on fumes.

"Is your room okay?"

"I'm in a suite with a view. Not that I'll get much use out of it. I've got a six forty-five flight to Boston tomorrow morning. Then it's on to Des Moines, Omaha, and I forget where after that."

Claire laughed. "You're doing pretty well. Barb says that after three weeks on the road most of her authors can't remember where they were the day before." Claire checked her watch. "There's a cooler in the back seat with soft drinks and bottled water, if you want any."

"No, I'm fine."

"Did you get a chance to eat?"

"On the plane."

Miles closed his eyes and leaned back against the headrest. Claire decided to let him relax in silence for the rest of the ride.

Murder for Fun was a mystery bookstore located in a strip mall on the outskirts of the city. Claire parked around back, next to the service entrance. She'd phoned from the car when they were a few minutes away, and Jill Lane opened the back door after her first knock. Jill was a pleasant, heavyset woman with salt-and-pepper hair. She had on a peasant dress and wore a turquoise-and-silver Native American necklace and matching earrings. Jill had retired after a successful career as a real estate broker. Reading mysteries had been her passion, and she'd jumped at the chance to buy the store when the first owner had to move to Arizona for his health.

"I can't thank you enough for coming, Mr. Van Meter," Jill said as she ushered Claire and Miles inside. "And you're going to be very pleased with the audience. We've got a full house. All of the seats have been taken and there are people standing in the aisles between the bookshelves."

Miles couldn't help smiling. "That's very flattering."

"Oh, the book is great. And Joshua Maxfield's appeal put the case back on the front pages. Did you know that Maxfield's two novels have been reissued? They're back on the bestseller lists."

Van Meter sobered.

"I'm sorry," Jill apologized immediately. "That was insensitive of me."

"No, it's okay." Miles shook his head. "It's just that I can't help thinking about Casey when I hear Maxfield's name."

The back door opened into a storeroom/office.

A desk overflowing with paperwork stood next to one wall, and cartons filled with new releases were piled against another. Stacks of books were everywhere. A table stood in the center of the room. On it were several copies of **Sleeping Beauty.** Jill pointed to them.

"Would you sign these before you leave? We've had requests from several people who couldn't make it tonight and customers who ordered off our Internet site."

"I'd be glad to."

Jill peeked through the office door and down the short hall that led to the front of the bookstore. Miles and Claire heard a rumble of conversation.

"Do you need anything?" Jill asked. "I've got a bottle of water on the podium and there's a mike. I think you'll have to use it."

Miles smiled. "Let's do it."

Jill led the way down the hall. Murder for Fun was dark, dusty, and crammed with floor-to-ceiling bookshelves, separated by narrow aisles. The shelves were designated as the homes of "New Arrivals," "Hard-boiled," "True Crime," and other mystery categories by hand-lettered signs, giving the store a homey feel that reflected Jill's personality. A podium was standing in one corner of the store. Several rows of bridge chairs had been set up in front of it. The chairs all held customers, many of whom held hardcover or paperback copies of **Sleeping Beauty** that they hoped Miles would sign.

A rustle of applause greeted Jill's appearance. She walked to the podium with Miles in tow. Claire moved around the edge of the crowd and settled near a musty shelf dedicated to mysteries set in exotic locales.

"Thank you for coming out on this dark and stormy night," Jill said to scattered laughs. "I think you'll find the trip well worth it. Tonight, we are fortunate to have with us Miles Van Meter, the author of **Sleeping Beauty,** one of the most compelling true-crime stories I've ever read.

"Mr. Van Meter was born in Portland, Oregon, and is the son of the late Henry Van Meter, a member of a prominent timber family. Henry took over the family business when his father died but he had many other interests, among them education. Henry founded the Oregon Academy, the elite private school where many of the terrible events recounted in **Sleeping Beauty** occurred. Miles and his twin sister, Casey Van Meter, were educated at the Academy. After high school,

Miles went on to Stanford, his father's alma mater, and Stanford Law School. He still practices business law in Portland.

"As many of you know, **Sleeping Beauty** was originally published several years ago. This new edition was just released with additional chapters that recount the startling events that occurred after the book's initial publication. Tonight, Mr. Van Meter is going to read from **Sleeping Beauty,** then he'll graciously answer your questions. So, please give a warm welcome to Miles Van Meter."

The applause was immediate and heartfelt. Jill stepped aside and Miles took her place at the podium. He sipped some water and arranged his papers while he waited for the ovation to die down.

"Thank you. Receptions like this made it possible for me to go on during those dark years that followed Joshua Maxfield's brutal attack on my beloved sister, Casey. As you might guess, talking about what happened to Casey is not easy. To be honest, writing this book was not easy. But I began this project because I felt that it was something I had to do to keep Casey's memory alive. And I also wanted to keep these terrible events in the spotlight to force the authorities—the police, the FBI—to hunt down Maxfield and bring him to justice—not just for the horrible crimes he committed against my family and the family of Ashley Spencer, but for all the other people whose lives were fouled by his inhuman acts of murder and torture.

"So, I wrote **Sleeping Beauty** and I went around the country, and when I started, I can tell you that I was depressed, because the outlook for Casey was bleak and Joshua Maxfield was still at large. But everywhere I went people like you told me how real my book had made Casey seem, and you told me that you were praying for her. That raised me up in my darkest hours, and I want to thank you for that."

The audience erupted again. Miles looked down at the podium to collect himself. After a moment, the applause stopped and Miles held up a copy of his book, on which was affixed a gold stamp emblazoned in raised letters with SPECIAL EDITION.

"I'm going to read the first chapter of **Sleeping Beauty.** After my reading I'll stay to answer any questions you have and I'd be pleased to sign your books."

Miles opened **Sleeping Beauty,** took a sip of water, and began to read.

"Why do we fear serial killers so much more than other murderers? I believe we fear them because we cannot understand why they kill and torture helpless people against whom they cannot possibly bear any rational form of malice. We know why angry husbands and wives slay each other. We can see a cause-and-effect relationship when a gang eliminates a rival gangster. We feel safe when we know that a murderer has no reason to harm us. But we feel at risk when someone like Joshua Maxfield is at large, because no rational person can fathom what motivated him to perform his horrible acts in the Spencer home one cold March night during Ashley Spencer's seventeenth year on this earth.

"On that fateful evening, Ashley was a junior at Eisenhower High School in Portland, Oregon. She was a pretty, cheerful girl with bright blue eyes and straight blond hair she wore most often in a ponytail. Ashley looked solid and powerful because she had trained hard for years to be a top soccer player. The training had paid off. In the fall, she had been the star of her high school soccer team and first team All-State. After the high school season, Ashley played on an elite club team. Earlier that day, F. C. West Hills had won a close match against a tough rival and the coach had hosted a pizza party for the team.

"Where did Joshua Maxfield see Ashley for the first time? Was it in the pizzeria? Was he lurking in the crowd at the soccer game? The police have examined home movies of the soccer match and the pizza party, and there is no trace of Maxfield in the frames. Maybe theirs was simply a chance encounter on the street or in a mall. In the end, how they met is not as important as the horrific consequences of that meeting for the Spencer family and for my family.

"Sometime around two A.M. Maxfield entered the Spencer home through a sliding door at the rear of the house and crept up the stairs to the second floor. Norman Spencer was sleeping alone in the master bedroom, because Terri

Spencer, Ashley's mother and a reporter on Portland's daily newspaper, was on assignment in eastern Oregon. Norman was thirty-seven when he died. He had taught junior high school for several years and was well liked by all who knew him.

"Maxfield attacked Norman Spencer first, stabbing him repeatedly as he slept. Then he moved down the second-floor landing. Staying with Ashley was Tanya Jones, a slender, African-American honor student, who was All-State honorable mention. Tanya was Ashley's teammate and best friend. They had both scored goals that day, and Tanya's mother had given her permission to sleep over. Ashley's door squeaked a little when it opened. We can guess that the noise awakened Tanya. When Ashley opened her eyes, she saw her friend sitting up in bed, and the silhouette of a man in her doorway. Then Tanya arched back and collapsed sideways onto the floor. Ashley had no idea what had happened to her friend until she leaped out of bed and was hit by Maxfield's stun gun.

"Maxfield was on Ashley immediately. Before she knew it, she was bound hand and foot and Maxfield was carrying Tanya Jones next door to the guest bedroom. Ashley struggled against her bonds but was unable to break them. Moans of pain came from the guest room. The sudden sounds paralyzed Ashley.

"Tanya Jones's autopsy report recounts in detail the horrors that she endured at Maxfield's hands. To Ashley, Tanya's ordeal seemed to go on for a long time, but she probably suffered only fifteen minutes or less. The medical examiner concluded that Tanya was beaten and partially strangled, then raped and stabbed violently and repeatedly. Many of her knife wounds were delivered in a fury after she was dead.

"Ashley lay on her bed waiting to die. Then the door to the guest bedroom closed and Maxfield, dressed in black and wearing a ski mask and gloves, was standing in Ashley's doorway. She believed that he had come to rape and murder her. Instead, after watching her for a few seconds, he whispered, 'See you later,' and went downstairs. Moments later, Ashley heard the refrigerator door open.

"We must assume that Joshua Maxfield temporarily spared Ashley because he was exhausted and famished after raping and murdering Tanya Jones. That would explain why he took a break from his ghastly tasks to go to the Spencer kitchen, where he drank a glass of milk and ate a piece of chocolate cake. Eating the snack would land Maxfield on death row, and writing about it would cause another tragedy."

PART ONE
MIDNIGHT SNACK

Six Years Earlier

CHAPTER ONE

Ashley Spencer's childhood ended the night her father died; the moment before she fell asleep was the last time she experienced unadulterated joy. Ashley and her best friend, Tanya Jones, were still pumped up from their 2–1 victory over F.C. Oswego, a perennial state soccer power. Both girls had scored, and the victory would give them a shot at the top seed at the State Cup. They had gotten into bed after watching a video, then talked in the dark until a little after one o'clock. When Tanya went to sleep, Ashley closed her eyes and pictured her goal, a header that had boomed past Oswego's All-State goalie. She was smiling as she drifted off.

Ashley had no idea how long she'd been asleep when a sudden movement on Tanya's side of the bed woke her. Tanya was sitting up, staring at the open doorway. Ashley, groggy and not completely certain she was awake, thought she saw someone walking toward Tanya. She was about to say something when Tanya grunted, twitched, and toppled to the floor. The man turned as Ashley leaped out of bed, extending his arm like a duelist. Ashley's muscles spasmed as a bolt of electricity surged through them. She fell sideways onto the bed, confused and unable to control her body. A fist smashed into her jaw, and she tottered on the brink of unconsciousness.

Tanya's head rose over the far side of the bed. The intruder was on her instantly. Ashley saw his fists and legs moving. Tanya fell back on the floor and out of Ashley's sight. A roll of gray duct tape appeared in the man's hands. He tore off several strips and knelt next to Tanya. Moments later, he walked around the bed. A black ski mask covered his face. He wore gloves and dark clothing.

A vise-like grip closed on Ashley's throat and her pajama top was ripped open. She made a feeble attempt at self-defense but she couldn't control her muscles. A leather-covered hand squeezed Ashley's breast until she screamed. The man hit her hard before sealing her mouth with a strip of tape. The intruder rolled Ashley onto her stomach and taped her wrists and ankles together. His face was close to her and she could smell his breath and body odor.

Once she was bound, the man slipped his hand inside her pajamas and caressed her buttocks. Ashley bucked and received a blow for resisting. She tried to squeeze her legs together but stopped when he grabbed her ear and twisted. A finger slipped inside her, probing, rubbing. Then the finger disappeared and he lowered himself onto her. Ashley's body trembled violently for a moment more. Then the sexual assault stopped and the oppressive weight disappeared. Ashley turned her head and saw Tanya being dragged into the guest room that was next to her bedroom.

Ashley strained to hear what was going on. Bedsprings squeaked. Tape sealed Tanya's mouth but Ashley could still hear her friend's muffled scream. Ashley was gripped by a fear different from any she had ever known. It was as if a stifling gray fog had settled over her, cutting off her air and paralyzing her limbs.

There were more moans and screams from Tanya, but the man who had invaded her home worked in silence. Ashley's heart was pumping furiously and she couldn't get enough air through her nose. She tried not to think about what was happening to her best friend and concentrated on breaking her bonds. It was impossible. She wondered whether her father was dead and the thought galvanized her. If Norman was dead then she couldn't count on anyone to rescue her. She would have to save herself.

In the next room, the man uttered a primal roar of release and Ashley shuddered. He'd finished raping Tanya; next he'd be coming for her. For a moment, the only sounds from next door were Tanya's muffled whimpers. Then Ashley heard an animal snarl and the sound of a blade slamming into flesh. Tanya made a strangled cry that was followed by silence. The stabbing continued. Ashley was certain that Tanya was dead.

The door to the guest room slammed shut and the intruder emerged, ghostlike, out of the darkness. Only his eyes and lips showed through his ski mask. Ashley's breath caught in her chest. The man savored her terror. Then he whispered "See you later," and walked downstairs.

Ashley collapsed from relief, but the feeling was short-lived. "See you later" meant that he was coming back to kill her. She struggled to sit up and scanned her room for something she could use to cut her bonds. Downstairs, the refrigerator door opened. The thought that he was going to eat something horrified Ashley. How could he eat after what he'd done? What kind of thing was he? The refrigerator door closed. Ashley grew desperate. She was going to be raped and killed if she couldn't get away.

A sound from the doorway brought her around. Something covered with blood was dragging itself across the floor. With a great effort, the thing raised its face and Ashley almost blacked out.

Norman Spencer crawled toward his daughter. There was stubble on his bloodstained cheeks and his hair was in disarray. In his right fist was his Swiss Army knife, the long blade out. Ashley fought the nausea and horror that threatened to disable her and rolled onto the floor. She turned her back to her father and presented her bound wrists. Norman had almost no strength left and he did not speak as he sawed at the tape with feeble strokes. Ashley wept as he worked the knife. She knew that she could not save her father and that he was using all that was left of his life to save hers.

The tape parted. Ashley grabbed the knife and freed her ankles. Then she ripped away the tape that covered her mouth and started to speak. Norman shook his head and jabbed weakly toward the hall to warn her that the intruder might hear. There should have been fear in his eyes since his death was certain, but he looked triumphant as he touched her lightly on her cheek. Ashley shook with silent sobs as she knelt beside her father. She held him. Norman whispered, "I love you." Just the effort of speaking cost him dearly. He coughed blood and a shiver went through him.

"Daddy," Ashley moaned. She felt so helpless.

A plate rattled against the kitchen table. "Go," Norman said, the words barely audible. Ashley knew she had to flee or die. She cried as she kissed her father's cheek. His body trembled, he closed his eyes, and stopped breathing.

Another sound from the kitchen brought Ashley to her feet. If she died, her father would have given his life for nothing. She wrenched open her bedroom window. Wood screeched against wood. To Ashley, it sounded like she'd set off an alarm.

Feet pounded up the stairs. It was a two-story drop to the ground, but Ashley had no choice. She crawled into the chill night air and hung from the ledge. The drop terrified her. A broken ankle would leave her helpless. She felt the strain in her arms. Then she heard a bellow of rage from her room and she let go.

The impact with the ground stunned her. Ashley lay on her back in the wet grass. A masked face stared down at her from her bedroom window. Ashley's eyes locked with the killer's for a moment. Then she was up and running, her breath slamming in her chest, legs pumping, running faster than she ever had before—running for her life.

Ashley sat in Barbara McCluskey's kitchen. Despite a borrowed sweat suit and the heat in the house, she hunched forward as if chilled to the bone. Her eyes, bloodshot from crying, stared blankly at the tabletop. She was so numb that she didn't feel the bruises and cuts that a medic had treated a short time before. Every once in a while she would raise a mug of hot tea to her lips. Sipping the tea took every ounce of strength she could muster.

Ashley's flight had taken a random route through the neighborhood and ended in the bushes in the McCluskeys' backyard. The cold and rain had eventually driven her to pound on her neighbor's back door. While she was hiding, Ashley tried to imagine ways in which she could have averted the horrors that had befallen her father and her best friend. In every scenario the outcome was the same: if she stayed behind she ended up dead. Yet that didn't stop her from feeling guilty for running away.

A policewoman sat beside Ashley. There were other officers in the McCluskey home. Logic told Ashley that the man who had murdered her father and her best friend was long gone. She also knew that she would fear his return every minute of every day as long as he was at large.

The police had set up barricades on either side of the Spencer home to keep away the neighbors and the reporters who stood behind them, staring at the officers moving through Ashley's yard and in and out of her house. Every once in a while, the short, intermittent bark of a siren would signal the arrival of another police vehicle that was working its way through the crowd. Ashley paid no attention to anything that was going on outside. She had too much going on inside her head.

The policewoman stood up. Ashley caught the motion out of the corner of her eye and jerked back violently. She was holding the mug, and tea splashed on the tablecloth. A man was standing next to her. She had been so self-absorbed that she hadn't noticed him enter the kitchen.

"It's okay, Miss Spencer. I'm a detective," he

said, holding out his identification. The detective's voice was calm, and he had a pleasant face. He was dressed in a brown tweed jacket, gray slacks, and a striped tie. Ashley had only seen detectives on TV, and he did not fit the stereotype. He wasn't handsome or rugged-looking. He just seemed ordinary, like her teachers or her friends' parents.

"May I sit?"

Ashley nodded, and the detective took the chair the policewoman had vacated.

"My name is Larry Birch. I'm with Homicide and I'm going to head the investigation into . . . into what happened at your house."

Ashley was touched by the detective's consideration.

"We've called your mother and she's on her way home. She'll probably be here by dawn."

A wave of sadness overwhelmed Ashley as she pictured the life her mother was about to lead. Her parents were still in love. Sometimes they were like teenagers, displaying a closeness around her friends that often embarrassed Ashley. What would Terri do now?

Birch saw Ashley's chest heave as she fought to control her tears. Gently he placed his hand on her shoulder, then went to the sink and returned with a glass of water. She was grateful for the kindness.

"I'd like to talk about what happened tonight," Birch said after a moment. "I know that's going to be rough for you. If you don't want to discuss it, I'll understand. But the more I know, the faster we'll be able to arrest the person who did this. The longer I have to wait for information, the better the chance that this man will get away."

Ashley felt sick. So far, no one had asked her to discuss her ordeal in detail. She did not want to remember her father covered in blood or Tanya's screams. She wanted to forget the sound of the intruder's shuddering orgasm and the way he'd eyed her from the doorway of her room. But she owed it to Tanya and her father to help the police. And she wanted to be safe and would only feel safe when Detective Birch caught the monster that had destroyed her family.

"What do you want to know?"

"Everything you remember. For instance, who was in your house tonight before everything happened?"

"Dad was home and Tanya was with me. Tanya Jones. Is she . . . ?" Ashley asked, irrationally hoping that her friend had somehow survived.

Birch shook his head. Ashley started to cry again.

"She was my best friend," Ashley said with such despair that the detective had to fight to keep his composure. "We were teammates."

"What sport?" Birch asked to distract her.

"Soccer. We both played varsity for Eisenhower and we started for our club team. The team is doing really well. We have a chance to get to the Regionals in Hawaii. Tanya's never been to Hawaii. She was really excited."

"She was good?"

Ashley nodded. "She scored the winning goal today. Her mom said she could sleep over. That's why . . . why she's dead."

Ashley's shoulders shook, but she choked back her tears.

"We fell asleep," she continued after a moment. "I know it was around one. Then I woke up. He was in the room."

"What did he look like?" Birch asked.

"I don't know. It was dark. He never turned on the lights. And he was wearing dark clothes, a ski mask, and gloves."

"Could you tell his race? Was he Caucasian, African-American, Asian?"

"I don't know, really."

"Okay, what about height? How tall was he?"

Ashley thought about that. Most of the times she'd seen him she had been on her back and he'd seemed like a giant, but she knew the angle had distorted her perspective. Then she remembered that she'd been standing when the killer shot her with his stun gun. She closed her eyes and pictured the scene.

"I don't think he was very tall, like a basketball player. I'm five-foot-seven. I'm pretty sure he was taller than me."

"All right. That's good. That's something."

Birch made a note on a small spiral notebook he had opened.

"Can you tell me the color of his eyes?" he asked next.

Ashley strained to remember but it was no good. "I saw them but it was dark and. . . ." She shook her head. "I can't remember the color."

"That's okay. You're doing fine. Tell me what happened after the man entered the room."

Ashley told Birch how the killer had used a stun gun to subdue her and Tanya and how he had beaten and bound them before taking Tanya into the guest room. Then she described the sounds that told her that Tanya was being raped, then murdered.

"Did he do anything to you after that?" Birch asked quietly.

"No. I was certain he would but he didn't. Not then. He would have. I know he would have. But he . . . he. . . ."

Ashley shuddered.

"What, Ashley? What did he do?"

"He went down to the kitchen. I couldn't believe it. He'd just raped her and killed her. I could hear it. And he went to get something to eat. How could he do that?"

"How do you know he ate something?" Birch asked, working hard to hide his excitement.

"I heard the refrigerator door open. Later I heard a dish clatter on the table."

"Okay, Ashley. This could really be important. You know what DNA is, right?"

Ashley nodded. She watched detective shows and read crime novels. And they'd covered genetics in biology class.

"We can get a person's DNA from bodily fluids like saliva. If he ate some food in your kitchen he may have left something on a fork or a glass. Now let me ask you, was anyone at your house last night other than you, your friend, and your father?"

"No."

"And you ate dinner at home?"

"No. There was a pizza party to celebrate our win. My dad came to the game, ate with us, then took Tanya and me home."

"Did you, Tanya, or your father eat anything at home?"

"I don't think Dad did. He's on a diet. Mom would have been pissed that he ate three slices of. . . ."

Ashley stopped. It was too much. Mom was always getting upset when Dad sneaked a cookie or a bowl of ice cream. Now her father was dead and there would never be any more playful bickering about his diet.

"I know this is going to be tough for you, Ashley," Birch said after an appropriate silence, "but I'd like you to come back to your house. . . ."

Ashley looked up, alarmed.

"You won't have to go anyplace upstairs. Just the kitchen. I have to know if you can identify something this man ate, or a glass he drank from, a utensil he used. If you can, we may be able to get him. Do you feel up to it?"

Ashley nodded. It was a chance to do something. The policewoman was Ashley's size. Detective Birch asked her to give Ashley her heavy coat and to pull a car into the McCluskeys' driveway. He wanted to protect Ashley from the elements and the press.

When the car was as near as it could get, Birch led Ashley out a side door. A few reporters noticed the exit but Ashley was in the car before they could bother her. The policewoman turned on the bubble lights and used the horn and siren during the short drive to the Spencer home.

It was still raining, and Birch opened an umbrella over Ashley.

"I won't see the bodies, will I?"

"We're just going in the kitchen," he assured her.

Birch had been in the house earlier and he knew the way to the kitchen, which was adjacent to the stairs that led to the second floor. A photographer was snapping shots of the area. Birch shooed him out of the room.

"Take your time, Ashley," the detective said. "Look around all you want."

Ashley stood in the center of the room and turned slowly before focusing on the kitchen table. There were two folded paper napkins and a small spot of milk. She walked over to the sink. Then she opened the dishwasher.

"This is wrong," Ashley said.

"What's wrong?"

"When we got home Dad emptied the dishwasher. Mom was gone and he wanted the place to be clean when she got back, so he ran a wash before he came to the game. Then he put the dishes and glasses in the pantry."

"Okay."

"Tanya and I had some chocolate cake and milk when we watched this movie we rented. Mom made the cake. Our dirty dishes and stuff are in the dishwasher. We put them in after Dad went to bed. But there's nothing in the sink and no other dishes or glasses or forks in the washer, and I know he ate something."

"Maybe he didn't use a plate or fork," Birch said. "Maybe he ate with his hands."

"No," Ashley said adamantly. "I heard a plate hit the table. It's why I . . . I left my dad. I knew he was done downstairs and was going to come for me. So, where is the plate?"

Birch scanned the room. He noticed that the door to a cabinet under the sink was ajar. The detective was wearing latex gloves but he used a pencil to open the door. A box of garbage bags was lying on its side, and the tip of a new bag was visible. Birch squatted in front of the cabinet, thinking. After a moment, he stood up.

"You're certain that you heard the refrigerator door open?"

Ashley nodded. Birch opened the refrigerator. "Check it," he said. "See if you can figure out what he ate."

Ashley looked inside. A transparent plastic milk container was up front. She studied the level of the milk. Then she looked back and forth among the shelves, searching for something.

"The cake is gone. He took it all and the plate it was on. And I'm certain he poured some milk from this container. It was three-quarters full when we were done. And look. There's some milk on the table. I wiped the table after we ate."

"Good girl. This is terrific detective work." Ashley smiled for the first time since her ordeal started. "I'm betting our man put the plate, the cake, everything that could give us a DNA trace, into one of these trash bags and took it with him."

Ashley stopped smiling. "Does that mean you won't be able to find him?"

"No, Ashley. It just makes our job a little harder."

CHAPTER TWO

March had been unseasonably cold. April made up for the rainy gray days with a profusion of multicolored flowers and vibrant greens that were so bright in the sharp sun they seemed unnatural. Ashley saw very little of the change of seasons. She had loved her father, and the fact that he had died to save her was devastating. The horrible way that Tanya Jones had died compounded Ashley's grief.

Right after the murders, Ashley's coaches, some of her teammates, and several of her friends had stopped by or called. The conversations had been awkward and painful for Ashley. Everyone meant well but they did not know what to say after "I'm so sorry," "We love you," and "Are you okay?" After the first few visits and calls, Ashley stopped seeing or talking to anyone. A few friends persisted for a while before giving up.

The reaction of Todd Franklin, Ashley's boyfriend, had been especially difficult for her. Todd was the captain of the boys' soccer team, which did not do nearly as well as the girls' team. Sometimes Ashley thought that Todd resented the recognition she received. They had started seeing each other early in the year, but Ashley wasn't sure she wanted to keep dating Todd.

They went out mostly with other friends, but they had been alone at parties and a few times at her house after her parents had gone to sleep. She liked making out with Todd. He was gentle and he made her laugh, but he also got mad when she didn't let him go all the way. Ashley just wasn't ready to make love to anyone yet. She thought she would do it with the right guy. Todd just wasn't that boy.

Todd had come over to see her a few days after the attack. The meeting had been awkward from the start. Everyone knew from the stories in the media that Tanya had been raped before she'd been killed, but the same reports had been silent about what had happened to Ashley.

Terri had left Ashley and Todd alone in the den.

They'd sat on the couch where the two of them had made out on several occasions. Usually, Todd was all over her as soon as the door closed. This time, he had kept a space between them and made no move to touch her. He hadn't looked at her directly for more than a second or so, and his conversation was monosyllabic. He made her feel like a leper, and she thought that he'd come to see her out of a sense of obligation, but would rather be anywhere else. Not that she wanted to be touched. Any thought of sex evoked memories of the killer's probing finger and his sour odor. Still, it would have been nice if Todd had shown some sign of affection instead of sitting next to her as rigid as a rabbit poised for flight. After that meeting, Todd had not visited or called again.

Since the tragedy, Ashley had refused to return to school. She stayed in her room or sat in the recliner in the family room watching mindless television shows. Terri Spencer told her daughter that no one was accusing her of being responsible for Tanya's death, but Ashley was certain that her classmates would demand to know why she had lived and Tanya had died.

On the second Friday in April, at four in the afternoon, Terri returned from a meeting with the principal of Eisenhower High School. Ashley's mother was five-foot-three, with large brown eyes, a dark complexion, and straight black hair she wore in a short, practical cut. She had competed in cross-country in college and still had the slender, wiry build of a long-distance runner. When Terri walked into the family room there was a talk show on the tube. She watched her daughter from the doorway for several seconds. Terri was certain that Ashley was using the show as a narcotic and would not be able to tell her a thing about it if she quizzed her.

Ashley's self-imposed exile was frustrating and painful for Terri, who had raised a self-sufficient, confident young woman and now lived with an insecure young girl who had nightmares that kept her up at night and left her so exhausted that she slept away a good part of the day. She had suggested therapy, but Ashley refused to discuss the murders with anyone. Terri was having a hard time dealing with her own grief, but she did not have the luxury of withdrawing from the world. She had to take care of Ashley and earn a living.

Ashley was dressed in sweats, and her hair was uncombed. It took all of Terri's self-control to keep from throwing her into a cold shower. She prayed that her news would break Ashley out of her funk. She attracted her daughter's attention by switching off the set.

"I've got two pieces of good news," Terri said. Ashley eyed her warily.

"I just finished talking to Mr. Paggett. He's going to let you finish your junior year without going back to school. You won't even have to take any exams. He'll give you the grades you've gotten to date. They're pretty high so that's okay."

A look of relief spread across Ashley's face, but Terri showed no reaction. Ashley had always confronted her fears; she was strong, a born leader. That she wanted to hide in her house saddened Terri.

"There's something else. Last week, I received a letter from the Oregon Academy. I didn't want to discuss it with you until I'd talked to Mr. Paggett and the people at the Academy. I met with both of them today."

Ashley sat up. The Oregon Academy was a perennial powerhouse in girls' high school soccer. The private school had repeated as state champion this year and was ranked nationally. Eisenhower had lost to them in the state quarterfinals, but Ashley had scored two goals.

"The Academy wants you to go to their school for your senior year," Terri said, keeping her tone neutral so that Ashley would not see how desperate she was for Ashley to take this opportunity. "They're offering a full scholarship. We . . . we don't have much money. I told them I couldn't afford to send you if I had to pay. But they really want you. You impressed them at States. And playing for the Academy would increase your chances of getting into a top college. The school is A-one academically, and there would be a lot more athletic scholarship offers if you played for a nationally ranked team."

For the first time since the tragedy, Ashley looked interested in something. Terri pressed on.

"And it would be a new start, a change of scenery. You could even board at the school, if you want to. You'd be out of the house, on your own. It would be a little like college."

Terri stopped and held her breath. She knew that she would be terribly lonely if Ashley roomed at the Academy, but she was willing to make any sacrifice to help Ashley heal.

"When . . . when would I start?" Ashley asked.

"The school year begins in September but they have a soccer camp there in the summer. Some of the girls help out. The person I talked to said that you might be able to do that. I think some members of the Olympic team are going to be there."

Ashley shifted in her seat. Terri could see that she was thinking hard.

"You don't have to make up your mind right away. We could visit. You could see if you like the place, maybe meet some of the girls on the team. It's only thirty minutes away," Terri said, desperate to keep the conversation going. "What do you say? We could take a drive out there tomorrow. The weather is going to stay nice. The school is in the country. It would be fun."

"Okay," Ashley said in a voice so small that Terri wasn't certain she heard her correctly.

"Good. I'll call right now and see when they want us."

"That's fine."

Terri nodded, when she really wanted to cry from relief. Ashley was going to shower, dress, and leave the house. After everything that had happened, this was more than she'd hoped for.

CHAPTER THREE

The Van Meters had built Glen Oaks, their country estate, in the late 1800s by clearing several acres of oak, maple, and Douglas fir that ran up to the banks of the Willamette River. A stone wall guarded the perimeter of the estate. On the other side of the wall the road ran through a further buffer of forest that soon gave way to well-tended lawns and flower gardens bordered by pruned hedges. Then the road forked. To the left was an elegant stone mansion. A wide lawn separated the house from the road.

"That's Henry Van Meter's home," Terri said as she took the right tine of the fork. "He founded the Academy. We're meeting with his daughter, Casey. She runs the school."

A boy and a girl on bicycles rode by, and Ashley saw a group of girls sitting on the grass, laughing. The Academy was pastoral and idyllic, the way she imagined one of those English universities like Oxford or Cambridge might be.

They passed some boys and girls playing tennis. Beyond the courts was a large outdoor pool, and beyond the pool was a modern steel-and-glass gymnasium. Behind that was the soccer field. The team was practicing. Ashley stared with longing at the running, shouting girls.

On either side of a grassy quadrangle that was shaded by well-spaced elm trees were three-story brick buildings with white columns and peaked roofs that housed the classrooms of the Academy. Students were talking on the quadrangle and walking back and forth between the buildings. Everybody seemed happy and engaged.

The administrative offices were in another brick building at the far end of the quadrangle. Terri parked next to it in a small lot. The admissions office was on the first floor, and the dean's office was above it. Upstairs, Terri gave the receptionist her name while Ashley looked at pictures of the school that hung on the waiting-room wall. One of them was a black-and-white photograph of a straight-backed, stern-looking man in a business suit standing in the middle of a construction site.

"That's my father, Henry Van Meter."

Ashley turned. A tall, thin woman with clear blue eyes, high cheekbones, and a wide forehead was standing in the doorway of the dean's office. She was dressed in a white silk shirt, a blue pin-stripe jacket, and matching skirt. Her straight blond hair fell to her shoulders, and a pearl neck-lace graced her slender neck.

"He started the Oregon Academy in this build-ing." She pointed at the picture Ashley had been looking at. "That's what everything looked like during the first week of construction."

The woman held out her hand. "I'm Casey Van Meter. You must be Ashley Spencer."

Ashley hesitated, then shook Casey's hand.

Casey smiled. "Actually, I didn't have to guess who you were. I saw you score those goals against us in the quarterfinals of the state championships. I go to all the girls' games. You're very good—but you know that."

Ashley flushed and looked down, embarrassed. Casey laughed. "And modest, too. That's a trait I admire. We don't encourage prima donnas at the Academy."

Casey turned her attention to Ashley's mother. "Hi again, Terri. I'm glad you two decided to look over the campus."

"It was Ashley's decision."

Casey nodded. Then she fixed Ashley with a sharp gaze that was impossible to avoid.

"What do you see yourself doing five years from now, after you've graduated from college?" the dean asked.

"I like science. I was thinking of medical school, but I'm not sure."

Terri was thrilled to hear her daughter talk about the future and she admired the way Casey Van Meter had shifted Ashley's attention there so easily.

"Well, we've got a top-flight science facility. It's the first building you passed when you drove down the quad. We designed it to look like the older buildings but, inside, the labs are state-of-the-art. Would you like to take a look at it?"

"Okay."

"Good. I'm tired of sitting inside on a day like this. We can look around the grounds and end up at the gym. If you'd like, I can introduce you to some of the girls on the soccer team."

"That would be okay," Ashley answered nonchalantly, though her body language revealed her excitement at the possibility of meeting the girls on the Academy team.

Casey held open the door. "Shall we stroll?"

The dean walked beside Ashley as they descended the stairs and left the building. Terri followed, listening to Casey's exposition on the history of the Academy and the school's goals. The dean cut across the quadrangle, stopping her monologue occasionally to say hello to some of the students they passed. They were almost to the street that separated the quad from the academic buildings when a man in a tweed sports jacket and gray slacks hailed the dean.

Joshua Maxfield wore his reddish-brown hair stylishly long and had emerald-green eyes. He was lanky, a little less than six feet tall, and looked trim and fit. Ashley would not have been surprised if someone told her that Maxfield had played tennis in college or ran for exercise.

"Joshua!" Casey said with an enthusiastic smile. "I want you to meet Terri and Ashley Spencer. Ashley is a junior at Eisenhower High School and a top soccer player. We're hoping that she'll attend the Academy for her senior year.

"Terri, Ashley, this is Joshua Maxfield. He's our writer-in-residence and he teaches creative writing. He'll be your instructor if you take the course."

"Joshua Maxfield," Terri said, half to herself. Then she asked, "Did you write **A Tourist in Babylon?**"

Maxfield beamed. "Guilty as charged."

"I thought it was terrific. I'm a big fan."

"Well, thank you."

"I remember **Babylon** so well. When Marion died from the overdose I cried. That scene was so powerful. I just couldn't help myself."

"That's music to my ears, Mrs. Spencer. A writer tries to create real emotions in his readers but we rarely know if we succeed."

"Well, I did cry and I'm not ashamed to admit it. That was a very moving book. Are you working on another?"

Ashley thought that Maxfield looked uncomfortable, but it was only for a fraction of a second. Then he was smiling modestly.

"Actually, I am."

"What's it about?"

"I'd rather not say at this point. I've just started it. I will tell you that it's a departure from my previous books."

"I won't press you. I'm working on my own novel and I don't like talking about it, either."

Ashley hid her surprise while she watched this exchange. Her mother was usually so businesslike. Now she was gushing the way some of Ashley's friends did when they talked about a hunky TV teen idol.

"How far along are you?" Maxfield asked.

"About halfway. I'm a reporter for the **The Oregonian.** They keep me pretty busy. I grab a few hours here and there to work on it. Weekends mostly. It must be great to write full-time."

"I'm very fortunate. You know, when you feel that you're well enough along, I do critique manuscripts for a small fee." Then he paused and pointed a finger at Terri. "Better yet, this summer I'm running a writing group on campus. It's for serious writers who haven't published yet but are working on something." Maxfield fished out his wallet and handed Terri his card. "That's my number, if you're interested. I'm trying to keep the group small. Two people have signed up already so don't wait too long to decide. I'd hate to have to turn you away."

"Thanks," Terri said, as she put the card in her purse.

"Joshua, what did you want to ask me?" Casey asked. Ashley thought she sounded a little sharp.

Maxfield smiled at the dean. "Nothing that won't keep. I'll catch you later." The author turned to Terri. "It was nice meeting you." Then he focused on Ashley. "I hope you're thinking seriously about the Academy. It's an excellent place to go to school." He paused and his smile widened. "Maybe I'll get you in my class."

Maxfield walked off and Casey led Terri and Ashley across the street to the science building.

"Joshua Maxfield," Terri said, smiling. "Have you read his books?" she asked Casey Van Meter.

"Of course."

"**A Tourist in Babylon** was so great." She paused. "How long has it been since it came out?"

"About ten years," Casey answered.

"That's what I thought. And **The Wishing Well** was published the next year. I wonder why he's taken so long to write his third?"

"You can ask him if you decide to join his group. That sounds like a great opportunity for someone working on a novel, to get advice from a published writer."

Casey turned to Ashley. "That's why we asked Joshua to join our faculty. We want our students to have opportunities they don't get in public school. He lives on campus. If you develop an interest in writing, like your mother, you'd be able to consult with him whenever you wanted to. Joshua is very approachable. He loves working with our students."

CHAPTER FOUR

Terri Spencer parked in the visitors' lot of the Oregon Academy. It was the second week in June, and the weather was as sunny as her mood. Ashley had decided to attend the Academy in the fall and the decision had started the process of healing. During the summer she was living in the dorm and working as a counselor in the school's nationally respected soccer clinic. Terri was going to have lunch with her at noon, but she had something important to do first.

Joshua Maxfield's writing group was going to start in two weeks, and Terri had joined it. The members were supposed to submit a writing sample that Maxfield and the group would critique. Terri had brought her partially written manuscript for Maxfield to read. She still could not believe that the author of one of her favorite books was going to help her with her writing.

The Academy had a building for pre-school through fifth grade, another for the middle school program, and two buildings—one for science and the other for liberal arts—for the high school. Joshua Maxfield's office was in the middle of the hall on the third floor of the liberal arts building. The door was closed. Terri knocked.

"Enter," Maxfield said.

This was the first time she had been in a published novelist's workplace, and Terri was uncharacteristically nervous. She opened the door and took a quick look around. Maxfield's office surprised her. A mug of coffee, a half-eaten doughnut, and a neatly stacked manuscript were the only things on his desk. There were no family photographs, no literary journals or books, not even an ashtray.

The rest of the office also had the feel of temporary occupancy. A bare coatrack hid in a corner, and a glass-fronted bookshelf, with very few books, stood near it. The four walls were devoid of decoration except for framed covers of Joshua's two novels, a favorable review of **A Tourist in Babylon** from the **New York Times,** and framed awards that the book had garnered. Other than

Maxfield's desk, the bookshelves, and some chairs, the only other furniture in the room was a small table upon which sat a coffee pot. A few mugs, packets of powdered creamer and sugar, and an open box of doughnuts kept the pot company.

Maxfield was dressed in jeans, running shoes, and a tight black T-shirt that stretched across his chest and showed off his well-defined biceps. He looked amused.

"If you're searching for the tools of my trade—the quill pen, the parchment, my smoking jacket—they're in my cottage. That's where I create my masterpieces. I'd never get anything accomplished if I tried to write here. Too many interruptions and distractions."

Terri looked embarrassed.

"Don't worry. You're not the first person to have that reaction. I've never felt comfortable in an office. Makes me feel like an accountant. You'd like my cottage. It's on the school grounds down by the river. I don't have any animal head trophies hanging from the walls à la Papa Hemingway but the cottage is much closer to the stereotype of a writer's digs, very cluttered and untidy. Maybe I can show it to you someday."

That sounded like a pass, and Terri hid her surprise. If Maxfield noticed her discomfort he didn't show it. Instead, he pointed at the manila envelope Terri was clutching with both hands.

"Is that your magnum opus?"

Terri blushed. "Yes."

Maxfield flicked his fingers, beckoning for the manuscript.

"Let's have it."

Terri handed over the envelope. "It's hard to part with," she said. "Especially when you know that strangers are going to rip it apart."

"No one is going to rip your baby apart. My critique groups are very civilized. And you should look forward to criticism, even when it's negative. One of the rules of good writing is that no one is perfect. Everyone screws up. That's why we have editors. The good ones catch our mistakes before the public sees them in print." He paused. "And not everyone is going to be a stranger."

Terri looked surprised. "Do I know someone else in the group?"

"I was referring to myself. We've been formally introduced. I hope you don't still consider me to be a stranger. Sit down. Can I get you some coffee?"

"Thanks," Terri said, taking one of two chairs

that faced Joshua's desk. Maxfield walked over to the coffee pot and filled a mug for Terri.

"Cream, sugar?" he asked.

"Black is fine."

"Can I tempt you with a doughnut? I'm addicted to sweets."

"I'll pass, thanks."

When Maxfield set the mug in front of Terri, he looked down at her and smiled. It was a warm smile, but something about his proximity made her uncomfortable. She'd received many friendly smiles from men while she was married, but she had not received one from a single man since Norman died. Terri wasn't sure how to respond. She wanted to be friendly, too, but showing any kind of interest in a man made her feel as if she was being unfaithful to Norman. That made no sense but it was the way she felt. She had really loved Norman; she still loved him. You didn't stop loving someone just because they were dead.

"Your daughter . . . Alice?" Joshua asked when he was back on his side of the desk.

"Ashley."

"Right. Has she decided to come to the Academy?"

"Yes," Terri answered, relieved to be discussing a safe subject. "Actually, she's here now. She's a counselor at the soccer clinic."

"I thought I saw her around."

"She's living in the dorm. I miss her at home, of course, but we talk on the phone a lot. She chatters nonstop about the Olympians she's met, the other counselors, and the children she teaches. Working with the young kids has been very good for her."

"I'm glad to hear it. She seems like a very nice young woman."

"She is. It was horrible right after her father died." Terri's voice caught for a moment. Maxfield looked concerned and surprised.

"Was this recently?" he asked.

Terri nodded because she was unable to speak.

"Are you all right?"

"I'm sorry. I still. . . ." She stopped and shook her head.

"I hope you don't think I'm insensitive, but I really didn't know."

Maxfield reached in his drawer and pulled out some Kleenex.

"I'm okay," Terri assured him.

"I'm glad working at the clinic has helped Ashley deal with her grief," Maxfield said. "Maybe she'll take my creative writing class and I can get to know her better."

Ashley had enjoyed eating lunch with her mother. Terri had been so excited about being in Mr. Maxfield's writing group. It was good to see her happy again. She had been so sad since Norman's murder. Ashley knew that she hadn't helped matters by being depressed. She felt bad about the way she'd added to her mother's problems. Terri was always asking how she felt, checking to see if she was sinking back into despair. It could get a little annoying at times, but Ashley knew her mother asked because she cared.

After lunch, Ashley worked with a group of girls age eight to ten on basic skills. She really liked working with the little kids. They were very eager to learn, and so cute. When the clinic ended, she and Sally Castle, her roommate and an Academy starter, slipped into their swimsuits and headed for the Olympic-size outdoor pool.

Sally was a stocky brunette who was always happy. She and Ashley had played on the same club team when they were in middle school, and they were being courted by some of the same colleges. It was possible that they would be college teammates.

Sally's folks had Ashley over for dinner at their big house in the West Hills shortly after they started rooming together. Back at the dorm afterward, Ashley had apologized for being so quiet during dinner. She told Sally how much it hurt to be around a happy family. The laughter and good feeling had reminded her of the way things used to be at the Spencer family table when her dad was alive. Sally had been very understanding, and the two girls had been tight ever since.

Half of the pool had lane lines for lap swimming. The other half was for fun. Ashley and Sally dove in the unlined section and paddled around to cool off. It had been very hot all afternoon, and the water felt great. Some of the boys from the soccer camp showed up, and the play became rowdy. Ashley and Sally didn't enjoy the roughhousing, so they swam closer to the lap swimmers. That's when Ashley noticed a man squatting on the edge of the pool and Casey Van Meter stroking smoothly down the center lane toward him. The man was deeply tanned and wore his long black hair in a ponytail. His black silk muscle shirt and tight-fitting jeans looked out of place among the cheap T-shirts, baggy shorts, and swimsuits that everyone else was wearing.

"Uh-oh," Sally said.

"What's the matter?"

"See that guy at the edge of the pool?"

Ashley nodded.

"His name is Randy Coleman. He's married to Dean Van Meter."

"You're kidding?"

"Here's the good stuff." Sally dropped her voice. "I heard that she met him last year in **Las Vegas** at an **education** convention. Supposedly, they had a wild fling and got married in some Elvis chapel."

"Dean Van Meter! Gosh, she seems so . . . so sophisticated. And that guy looks so greasy."

"Well, she did drop him about a month later but he followed her to Portland. We're members of the country club where the Van Meters go, so my mom is on top of all the good gossip. She says that Coleman is bugging the dean to come back to him because Henry Van Meter had this real serious stroke and he's still sick. If he dies, the dean and her brother will be loaded and Coleman wants a piece of it. And get this, Coleman's supposed to be a professional gambler with ties to the **mob.**"

Casey reached the wall. Coleman tapped her shoulder. She stopped in mid-turn and looked up.

"What are you doing here?" Ashley heard Casey ask. She sounded annoyed at having her workout interrupted.

"We have to talk," Coleman said.

Something about his voice was familiar, but Ashley was certain they'd never met.

"If you received the papers you know that there's nothing to talk about," Casey said coldly.

"Yeah, I got them, but this is all wrong. We belong together, baby."

Casey took a quick look around. A number of the students were watching.

"I'm not going to discuss this here, Randy. In fact, I'm not going to discuss it at all. You can have your lawyer call mine if you've got questions."

Casey turned her back to Coleman and positioned herself to start swimming away from him. When she raised her arm, Coleman grabbed her wrist. Van Meter glared at her husband.

"Release me at once."

"I said we have to talk."

A movement to her right distracted Ashley. Joshua Maxfield was strolling toward the pool.

"Hey, Randy, let her go." Maxfield sounded friendly, not threatening.

"Fuck off, Maxfield. This is between me and my wife."

"Get your hands off me," the dean commanded angrily.

Coleman turned his face toward Casey Van Meter and said, "Listen, bitch," but he never finished the sentence because she lashed out with her free hand and smacked him hard. Coleman reared back to punch Casey but Maxfield was on him before he could strike. Everything happened fast after that, and the action ended with Coleman on the ground, his arm twisted behind him at an odd angle.

"This isn't helping anyone," Maxfield said, still calm and completely in control of the situation. He stood and forced Randy to his feet.

"I'll get you, you fuck," Coleman gasped, obviously in pain.

"Now, now. I'm the last guy you want to threaten, Randy. I had demolition training in the Rangers. Make me nervous and you'll be even more nervous every time you start your car or open your apartment door. Do you want that? I don't think so. So why don't you calm down and leave while the only aches you have to nurse are a sore wrist and injured pride."

Coleman looked unsure of himself. Maxfield inched up Randy's arm until he was forced to stand on his toes.

"What do you say, old chap?" Maxfield asked. "I've got nothing against you but there are kids around here. It's not good for them to see this."

Coleman grimaced with pain and nodded.

"I'm going to let go. Okay? No sneaky punches, promise?"

"Let loose, damn it," Coleman gasped. Maxfield released his hold. Randy cast a furious look at Casey.

"We're not through," he threatened before stomping off.

"Thanks, Joshua," Casey said as she watched her attacker walk toward the parking lot.

"No problemo. These marriage things drive people crazy."

Casey studied Joshua. She didn't look angry anymore, just curious.

"Do you really know how to rig a car?"

Joshua threw his head back and laughed. "Hell no. Remember, I'm a novelist. I lie for a living."

Suddenly, Maxfield and the dean noticed the gawking teenagers. Maxfield held up his hands.

"Everything's cool. You can return to your regularly scheduled programming." He turned to Casey. "Let's go."

"Did you see that?" Sally Castle said, awestruck. "I didn't know Mr. Maxfield knew that Jackie Chan stuff. That was so cool."

Suddenly, Sally noticed her friend's ashen complexion. "Are you okay?" she asked.

"I'm fine," Ashley answered, but she was lying. The violence had made her flash back to the attack in her house. And there was something else, but she couldn't put her finger on it. Was it Coleman's voice? She'd thought that it sounded familiar when she first heard him speak, but now she wasn't so certain she'd heard it before. But Coleman was about the same height as her father's murderer. No, that was ridiculous. A lot of men were the same size as the killer. Mr. Maxfield was the same size, too, and he didn't make her nervous.

CHAPTER FIVE

Terri Spencer rushed up the stairs to the second floor of the liberal arts building, then walked down the hall slowly so she could catch her breath. It was the first day of the writing group, and she was late. When she entered the schoolroom, Joshua Maxfield waved her onto a chair next to a heavyset, bearded man who was seated on the side of a conference table nearest the door. Next to him was an older woman with long gray hair. Across the table were two middle-aged women and a young man.

"Sorry I'm late," Terri apologized. "The traffic was horrendous."

"It's not a problem," Maxfield assured her from his position at the head of the table. "We just got settled. All you missed was a chance to get some coffee and doughnuts and I think we'll still let you do that. What do you say, group?"

Everyone laughed, including Terri. "I'm fine, thanks," she told Maxfield.

"Then we'll get started by introducing ourselves. And I'll begin by telling you a little about myself. I went to community college in Boston after I was expelled from high school. I began **A Tourist in Babylon** in my English class as an essay. My professor encouraged me to turn it into a novel. I thought he was crazy—I honestly didn't think I had any talent—but I decided to give it a try. I transferred to the University of Massachusetts and finished the novel while getting my BA.

"**Tourist** was rejected by several houses before an editor at Pegasus Press was wise enough to discern its merits. The rest, as they say, is history. My first novel was nominated for all of the major literary prizes and was a bestseller. So I know a little about crass commercialism as well as literature.

"**The Wishing Well** was published a year or so later. I taught creative writing at a college in New England for a while but I decided to come west a few years ago and dedicate myself to working with younger students. I've enjoyed my two years at the Oregon Academy tremendously but I like to work with older writers for balance, which is why I conduct these seminars.

"But enough about me. Terri, why don't you tell everyone who you are, where you work, and why you're here?"

"I'm Terri Spencer, I'm a reporter at **The Oregonian.** I know all reporters are supposed to be writing the Great American Novel in their spare time. It's a terrible cliché but it's true in my case. I don't know about the 'great' part but I am halfway through a book and I thought it was time to get some professional help."

"Harvey," Maxfield said, nodding to the bearded man sitting to Terri's left.

Harvey Cox told the group that he was a biotech researcher who had published one science fiction short story and was looking for help with a science fiction novel he was writing. Lois Dean, the older woman, had run across a set of diaries written by an ancestor who had followed the Oregon Trail in the 1800s. She wanted to turn them into a historical novel. Mindy Krauss and Lori Ryan were housewives and bridge partners who were trying their hand at a mystery, and Brad Dorrigan was a computer programmer who had majored in English Lit and spoke earnestly

about the coming-of-age story he had been working on for several years.

"Okay, great," Maxfield said. "Well, we certainly have a diverse group. That's good. It means
that we're going to get different opinions when we
critique each other's work. And that is one of the
things we are going to do here.

"Now let me talk about criticism for a moment.
Each week I'm going to read something that
someone in the group has submitted and each of
you is going to be painfully honest with your
opinions. That doesn't mean that you are going to
be mean or spiteful. The only type of criticism I
expect here is constructive criticism. It's perfectly
all right to dislike something, but I want you to
tell the writer **why** you don't like what he or she
has written and I want you to suggest how the
work can be changed for the better. So think before you speak.

"My job will be to moderate these proceedings
but I'm also going to give you tips that I hope will
improve your writing. When we start each class
I'll spend some time talking about character development, outlining, and other aspects of the
writer's craft. Now, I don't like talking to hear
myself speak. I assume you're here because you
are motivated to improve your craft. So, ask ques-

tions. Remember, in this group there is no such thing as a stupid question.

"And with that introduction, unless there are questions, I'm going to start our first session with a brief discussion of the method I use to develop story ideas."

They took a break after the first hour, and Terri talked to the other members of Maxfield's class. Except for Brad Dorrigan, who took himself a little too seriously, the other aspiring writers were a pleasant group.

"Okay, back to the grind," Joshua Maxfield said when fifteen minutes had passed. Terri carried a cup of coffee to her place. While everyone got settled, she checked the notes she'd taken about developing story ideas.

"I said that we're going to spend a portion of each meeting critiquing each other's writing," Maxfield said. "Tonight, I'm going to read a chapter from a work in progress and everyone will comment."

Terri was nervous that her manuscript would be the subject of the first critique. The other students looked just as worried. Maxfield squared up a short stack of paper that lay in front of him. He picked up the first sheet.

"I am a God. Not The God. I am from one of the lesser pantheons but a God nonetheless. I don't make a practice of announcing the fact, and those that discover my powers never tell. On a balmy spring evening in mid-May I introduced myself to the Reardons of Sheldon, Massachusetts.

"I chose the Reardons because they were so ordinary, the type of people who occupy space while alive and are not missed when they die. Our experience together would be, by far, the most amazing event in their boring lives.

"Bob, a short, overweight man who was losing his hair, was an accountant. Margaret sold makeup at a department store on Main Street. I imagine that she had once been attractive. She still worked hard to keep her figure, but her skin was beginning to wrinkle and her legs were marred by cellulite. Their only daughter, Desiree, was seventeen, a junior in high school. She was of normal intelligence, and her looks were average, but she was physically advanced. I'd caught sight of her when she visited her mother at work. Her tight shorts showed off her taut buttocks and long firm legs. Her T-shirt was cut to display her flat, tanned tummy and sensual navel. Oh how I desired to lick it.

"With my appetite whetted by my first sight of Desiree, I laid my plans. Entering the Reardon home was easy. They were living from month to month and could not afford a security system.

"The master bedroom was down the hall from Desiree's room. I subdued her parents with ease but I did not kill them. I had no interest in Bob but I wanted him to know who had taken his life force. Gods should not work in anonymity. I taped Bob's mouth, hands, and ankles and arranged him on his side so he could watch me play with his wife. After Margaret was bound and gagged, I stripped her naked. Then I left them to contemplate their fate and went to Desiree's room.

"The object of my desire was lying half-covered by a thin sheet. Because of the heat, she wore only a pair of bikini panties and a thin cotton top that revealed her taut nipples and the tops of her firm breasts. I wanted her to experience sheer terror, the appropriate response of a mortal in the presence of a God. I approached her stealthily. Then I clamped my gloved hand across her mouth. Her eyes sprang open and she stared at me with pure horror. The reaction was very satisfying. Her body actually arched off of the mattress as if electricity had coursed through her. I bound her quickly. She was small and no match for my supernatural strength. My arousal was immediate but I restrained myself, rejecting immediate gratification so that our experience would be more intense.

"After caressing various parts of her nude body, I left Desiree and returned to her parents. As Bob watched, I slowly dismembered his wife. He struggled and wept through it all. She screamed as I heightened her pain. It was wonderful and, as a prelude to the main course, thoroughly satisfying. With Margaret on the edge of death, but still conscious, I turned my attention to Bob. His eyes widened when I spoke to him of the journey he was about to take to the next plane of existence. I explained how birth began with pain and how pain was a necessary part of the transition he was about to make.

"My knife was very sharp, and I wielded it slowly and with precision. Each cut would have pleased the most skilled surgeon. Bob stayed conscious even after I opened his belly. He was screaming still when I began to remove his internal organs. It was only when I crushed his beating heart in my gloved hand that he passed from this life to the next.

"I returned to Margaret. Her transition was quicker and less satisfying. She slipped away after I had drained no more than a quarter of her psychic energy. There was an armchair in the room, and I sat on it to gather myself. I had been thinking of Bob and Margaret's passage from life to death as I worked, but now my attention turned to my corporeal body. It was exhausted from its exertions, and I was hungry. I did not want to undertake the most exciting part of my adventure in this condition. I did walk down the hall to check on the sweet Desiree. I could hear her weep from frustration as I approached her door. I assume she'd tried to free herself and found the task impossible. The weeping stopped abruptly when I entered her room. She grew rigid with fear. I watched her from the door, exploring the curves and valleys of her body with my x-ray eyes. Then I stroked her forehead and told her that I would be returning to her soon. After planting a kiss on her cheek I left her room and went to the kitchen. I was famished and prayed that the Reardons liked to snack. I was in luck. In the back of the refrigerator I discovered a carton of cold milk and a slice of apple pie."

Maxfield read with his eyes on the page but every once in a while he would focus on one of the students to gauge their reaction. The faces of the others varied from fascination to horror. Terri had grown pale during the reading, and when

Maxfield read the part where the killer ate the snack in the victim's kitchen, she nearly threw up.

"Any comments?" he asked the group when he finished. Terri tried to compose herself, terrified to show her true emotions.

"That was . . . very gruesome," Harvey Cox managed. "I mean, if the writer was trying to gross me out he succeeded."

"Why **he**?" Maxfield asked.

"It's got to be a man," Cox said, casting a quick glance across the table at Brad Dorrigan. "Women don't write like that."

"That's not true," Lori Ryan protested. "Some of today's women authors write very grisly scenes."

"Let's get back to your comment, Harvey," Maxfield said. "Was this really gruesome? Does the writer describe his murders in detail or leave the details to the reader's imagination?"

Lois Dean raised her hand.

"Lois?"

"Before I say anything, I've got to tell you that I don't like books like this. I don't read them. So I'm biased against it. But I see your point. There are a few graphic parts but most of the violence isn't spelled out."

"Is that good or bad?" Maxfield asked.

"Good, I think," Mindy Krauss answered. "It's like in **Psycho.** You don't really see Norman Bates stab the woman in the shower but you're sure you did see her stabbed. Hitchcock makes you use your imagination."

Maxfield nodded and looked at Terri Spencer.

"What do you think, Terri, more details or less detail? Do you prefer it when the writer leaves nothing to the imagination or when the writer forces you to be part of his fantasy?"

Terri had all she could do to keep from racing out of the room but she made it through the rest of the class, even supplying intelligent answers on the two occasions she was asked a question.

As the discussion droned on, Terri tried to make sense of what had just happened. She told herself that the incident in the chapter was a coincidence, but she knew that was impossible. Milk and cake, milk and pie. It was too close to real life. But there was one possible explanation. Some writers fictionalized real events to make their stories seem authentic. Maybe the person who wrote the scene had read about the killer's snack and used the incident because it was so horrifying. For a moment, Terri felt relieved. Then she remembered the newspaper accounts of her tragedy that she had read. She didn't recall the snack being mentioned in any of them. Had the police held back that information? She had to know.

And who had written the scene that Maxfield read? She was pretty certain that Lois Dean was not the writer. Dean was working on a historical novel based on her ancestor's diaries and she had told the class that she didn't like graphic serial killer books. Mindy Krauss and Lori Ryan were working on a mystery novel, and Lori Ryan had not been upset by the grisly nature of the scene. Lori was even acquainted with women authors who wrote this style of book. But Terri leaned toward one of the men as the author. Which one, though? Harvey Cox had told the group that he was writing science fiction. That left Brad Dorrigan.

When the class ended, Terri waited for the computer programmer. He wore wire-rimmed glasses, and his hair was shaggy and unkempt. He was also thin and, Terri guessed, only five-six or seven—much shorter and less muscular than the killer Ashley had described.

"Interesting class," Terri said.

"I expected more," Dorrigan replied disdainfully. "I assumed that we would be discussing theory, certainly something more advanced.

Outlining, where we get our ideas from—drivel. Maybe Maxfield was a one-shot wonder, like the critics say."

Terri was aware that Joshua's second novel, **The Wishing Well,** had received poor reviews and sold dismally. She thought it was okay but nowhere near the quality of **A Tourist in Babylon.** Joshua Maxfield had been hailed as a new voice of his generation when his first novel was published. Within a year of the publication of his second novel it was rare to find any mention of him.

"What did you think of that excerpt Mr. Maxfield read?" Terri asked.

"Talk about unmitigated crap. Garbage like that is destroying literature. Publishers don't want to read anything with depth and characterization anymore. They're all looking at the bottom line. Dismember a naked woman and they'll give you a million dollars, but write about the soul of man, what makes us human . . . forget it. You should see some of the rejection letters I've gotten from those morons in New York. Do you think Camus, Sartre, or Stendhal would get a book contract today?"

Terri forced a laugh. "I guess you didn't write that bloodbath, then?"

Dorrigan looked appalled. "I wouldn't use those pages to wipe my ass."

Terri caught up with Lori Ryan and Mindy Krauss in the parking lot. "What did you think of the first class?" Terri asked.

"It was great," Mindy answered. "I took so many notes my hand cramped."

"He's such a terrific teacher," Lori gushed.

"That wasn't your mystery he read, was it?" Terri asked.

The women laughed. "Ours is set in a bridge group," Mindy told her.

"Someone is murdering the members and leaving a card pinned to the bodies," Lori said.

"The clue is so clever," Mindy said. "If you make a hand out of. . . ."

"Don't tell the ending," Lori jumped in. "It will spoil it for her."

"You're right," Mindy sighed, frustrated at not being able to reveal the clever solution to their mystery.

Terri said good-bye to the women and got in her car. She started it just as Joshua Maxfield left the building. He was carrying a briefcase and strolling toward his cottage as if he hadn't a care in the world. Terri felt sick. She was fairly certain that none of the members of the class had written the excerpt. Maxfield had told her that he critiqued manuscripts for a fee. The chapter could have been from a manuscript that he was editing. But Maxfield had also said that he was working on a new book. And he lived on the Academy grounds. Terri looked toward Ashley's dormitory. She wanted to run to her daughter and take her away from the Academy and Joshua Maxfield, but Ashley was doing so well. If she took Ashley home she would have to explain why, and that could undo all of the healing that had occurred. No, Terri decided, she would not act until she had investigated more thoroughly. She was a reporter. She knew how to develop a lead into a story; she knew how to nail down facts.

CHAPTER SIX

The Detective Division of the Portland Police Bureau took up one side of the thirteenth floor of the Justice Center, a modern, sixteen-story building located across the park from the Multnomah County Courthouse. Each detective had a workspace separated from the other detectives by a chest-high divider. When the receptionist told Larry Birch that Terri Spencer was in the waiting room, he came out to the front counter and escorted her to his cubicle.

"Sit down," Birch said, gesturing toward a chair that sat next to a gunmetal-gray desk piled high with reports, correspondence, and departmental memos. A picture of Birch with a woman and two small children stood on one corner.

"How are you, Mrs. Spencer?" he asked when Terri was seated.

"I'm okay," she answered, but Birch didn't think so. He thought that she looked drawn, pale, and very nervous.

"How's Ashley doing?"

"Fine. She's going to a new school, the Oregon Academy. I thought the change—you know, starting over in a new place—would help her."

"It sounds like a good idea. And it's working out?"

"She doesn't start classes until the fall, but she's a counselor at a soccer clinic out there, teaching young children. She seems to enjoy it."

"She's a top player, right?"

"All-State. Several colleges are looking at her."

"Well, that's great."

All the time she'd been talking Terri had been shifting nervously in her seat. Birch waited patiently for her to tell him why she wanted to see him.

"I was wondering if there was any progress. If you have any idea who. . . ."

Terri's voice trailed off. Thinking about what had happened to her husband was too hard on her.

"I'll be honest with you, Mrs. Spencer, we have made some progress but we're nowhere near an arrest."

"What does that mean?"

"We asked the FBI in on this and they came up with something."

"What?"

Birch hesitated for a moment. Then he looked Terri in the eye. "You're a reporter, right?"

"Not where my husband's murder is concerned."

Birch nodded. "Okay. But I need to know that you will absolutely not tell anyone else what I tell you."

"Of course."

"The FBI thinks that the person who murdered your husband and Tanya Jones has committed other crimes in several states over the past few years."

"A serial killer?"

"That's what they think. But they have no clue to the killer's identity."

"Why do they think it's a serial killer? What are the common threads?"

"Duct tape was used to bind the victims instead of rope. The FBI has established that the same company manufactured the duct tape used in all of the crimes and they've made a physical match between the duct tape used in a case in Michigan and another in Arizona. For obvious reasons, this is something we're not telling the public."

"Are there any other clues you're keeping from the public?" Terri asked, fighting to keep her tone neutral.

"Why do you want to know that?"

"I don't want to leak anything unintentionally."

"You know the killer ate a piece of chocolate cake at your house?"

Terri nodded.

"He ate a piece of pie during a murder in Connecticut."

Terri felt the blood drain from her face. She averted her eyes. "So only the investigators know about the snack at our house? You haven't released the information to the public?"

"That's right."

"Are they keeping the snack a secret in Connecticut too?"

Birch nodded.

"Where were the other murders?"

"They started in New England about five years ago. Then there were a few in other parts of the country." Birch listed the cities.

"What . . . what does he do?"

"They're like your house, Mrs. Spencer. There's always a teenage daughter. He murders the adults and rapes the daughter before killing her. Ashley is a very lucky young woman. She's the only person who has survived his attacks."

Ashley stayed after the clinic session ended to help a seventh-grade girl with her passing skills. The kid was good, and she would get better because she cared about technique. The girl's mother had waited patiently while Ashley and her student put in an extra twenty minutes. When they were through, she thanked Ashley for taking the extra time to help her daughter. The praise felt good. On the way out of the gym Ashley was wondering if she wanted to teach or coach as a career when a man's voice interrupted her reverie.

"It's Ashley, right?"

Ashley looked up. Joshua Maxfield was standing in front of her. He was dressed in a T-shirt and athletic shorts and looked like he'd just finished a workout.

"I hope I didn't interrupt any great thoughts," the teacher said. "You looked like you were in a trance."

Ashley blushed. "It's okay," she mumbled.

"I'm Joshua Maxfield. I teach creative writing.

We met when Dean Van Meter was showing you and your mother around the school."

"I remember."

Maxfield gave her a warm smile. "Your mother's in my critique group. She says you've decided to come to the Academy in the fall."

Ashley nodded.

"Well, that's terrific. I hope you'll think about taking my class. Your mother's work is very good. Do you do any creative writing?"

"Not really. I mean, I had assignments in school but I don't do any on my own. I'm pretty busy with soccer all year."

"That's right. You're a counselor at the summer clinic. You must be pretty good. Our girls have a good team, don't they?"

"Yeah. They won state's the last two years."

"Are you going to start?"

"I don't know. I hope so."

"I'm sure you will," he said, smiling. "Well, I'm going to hit the shower. It's nice seeing you again."

CHAPTER SEVEN

Terri was shown into Casey Van Meter's office a little after four. The dean was wearing an elegantly tailored black silk suit, and her hair and makeup were perfect.

"Sit down, Terri. I'm glad you dropped by. I'm getting glowing reports about Ashley."

"Thank you. She's having a great time. Living in the dorm with the other girls and working with the children has been a wonder cure."

"I'm glad to hear that. So, what brings you here?"

"I wanted to talk to you about one of your teachers but I don't want the teacher to know that I've been investigating."

"Investigating? That sounds serious."

"It is. But before I tell you anything more I want

to make sure that you'll treat the inquiry confidentially."

"I'm not certain that I can do that without knowing why you're asking. The welfare of our students is paramount."

Terri wasn't sure how to proceed. She had promised Detective Birch that she would keep his confidences but she needed to know more about Joshua Maxfield, and Dean Van Meter might have some of the information she needed.

"I'm in a funny position," Terri explained. "I have suspicions about one of your faculty but I don't want to tell you why, right now, because I don't want to get this person in trouble if I'm wrong."

"Whom are we talking about?"

"Joshua Maxfield. I'd like to know if there's anything in his background that's . . . suspicious."

The dean sighed. She even looked a bit relieved. "You'd find out anyway with a little digging, and I don't want you to think that the Academy is hiding anything. Joshua did not leave his teaching position at Eton College voluntarily. He was forced to resign."

"What happened?"

"His first novel did very well but his second

book was a failure both critically and financially. Then Joshua developed a terrible case of writer's block. He'd been given an advance for another novel but he couldn't write it. A conglomerate bought his original publisher. The new owners demanded that Joshua meet his deadline or return his advance. Unfortunately, he'd spent the money. He was desperate for a job. Eton College was looking for a creative writing teacher. He applied. Joshua's name was still golden in academic circles but he didn't know that so he made an unfortunate decision."

"What did he do?"

"He doctored his résumé. It was totally unnecessary but Joshua wasn't thinking clearly. He claimed that he had an MFA from the Iowa Writers' Workshop when, in fact, he had attended for less than a semester."

"How did the school find out?'

"Joshua was under tremendous pressure to repay the advance. The publisher was threatening a lawsuit. He started drinking and acting erratically. He was depressed, not writing, that sort of thing. He missed classes. Then there was an incident with a student. . . ."

"What sort of incident?"

"She claimed he offered to give her an A if she slept with him. During the inquiry the school discovered the discrepancy on his résumé. He was given the choice of resigning or being fired."

"Why did you hire him if you knew all this?"

"Joshua came to us more than a year or so after he left New England. He was completely open with us about his problems at Eton. He admitted propositioning the coed. He said he did it when he was drunk and depressed after getting another letter from a lawyer about the advance. We felt that it was worth the risk to have a writer of Joshua's caliber on our faculty. To our knowledge, he has not betrayed our trust."

"What I'm concerned about is a lot more serious than lying on a résumé."

Casey looked confused. "Please be more specific."

Terri hesitated. Her evidence was far from overwhelming.

"Will you promise to keep what I tell you between us?"

"All right, but I'm only agreeing because I need to know if there is any possibility that our students might be affected."

"I'm taking Joshua's writing class. We're supposed to submit something we're working on. Each week, he's going to read our submissions, then the class critiques the work."

"Yes?" Casey asked impatiently.

"He read a very disturbing piece at the first class. It was in the first person. It was about a serial killer and it went into detail about the rape and dismemberment of a girl Ashley's age and her parents. It was horrible and very graphic."

"I can see how that would be disturbing but. . . ."

"Anyone who could write something like that has to be sick."

"Joshua is a novelist, Terri. There's a book featuring a serial killer on every bestseller list. Do you think those authors are murderers?"

"You don't understand. Maxfield knew things that happened in my house when Ashley was attacked that the police never released to the public."

Casey's look was halfway between shock and amusement, as if she was unsure if she was the butt of a practical joke. Terri looked grim.

"You're serious?" the dean said.

Terri told Casey Van Meter about the snack. The dean paid close attention. When Terri was through, Casey shook her head.

"I'm not convinced. How do you know that Joshua was reading something he'd written?"

"I know it wasn't written by any of the other students. I talked to all of them. And he told me that he's working on a new book."

"Yes, but. . . ." Casey stopped. She shook her head. "I find this very hard to believe. I know Joshua. . . ."

"You think you know him. I've been reading about the pathology of serial killers. People assume that it would be easy to spot the type of person who could . . . could kill my husband and attack two helpless teenage girls but you can't tell just by looking at them. Ann Rule worked side by side with Ted Bundy on the rape hotline in Seattle while she had a contract to write about the murders he was committing as soon as the case was solved. She never suspected that she was a friend of the man who would become the subject of her first bestseller. And think about the usual reaction of neighbors when they learn they've been living next door to someone like John Wayne Gacy. They can't believe that the nice guy they've chatted with about mundane things like their lawn or a favorite TV show could be a monster."

"That may be true, but I'm sure you're wrong about Joshua."

"There was the incident with the female student at Eton College."

"He didn't murder her, Terri. He made an indecent proposition. That's very different from serial murder."

"Then how did he know about the snack?"

Casey remembered what Maxfield had said when she asked him if he really knew how to plant a bomb in a car.

"He's a writer of fiction. He's very creative. He earns his living by making up scenes that we could never conceive because we don't have his imagination."

"No, I don't buy it. That would be too much of a coincidence."

Casey paused. She looked upset. "Why did you come to me, Terri? Let's assume that you're right, that Joshua is a killer. What do you expect me to do?"

"You have access to Maxfield's personnel file. There have been other murders in New England, the Midwest, Montana, and Idaho. Maybe there's something in his file."

Casey looked concerned. "You're so emotionally involved that I don't think you've thought this through clearly. Have you told your suspicions to the police?"

"No."

Casey took a deep breath. "Thank goodness. Think of the harm you'd do to this school's reputation if one of our teachers was wrongly accused of any kind of crime, let alone being a serial killer who preys on children the same age as our students."

"I don't intend to talk to anyone about my suspicions until I'm certain I'm right. That's why I've come to you. Let me take a look at Maxfield's file. . . ."

"Certainly not."

"Then you review it. Now that you know what I'm looking for, something you thought was unimportant may look totally different."

Casey hesitated for a moment, then made a decision.

"All right. I can see how concerned you are about this. I'll take another look at his file. If I find something I'll tell you. But you have to promise me that you won't go any further with this unless you have hard evidence. The damage to the Academy and Joshua would be irreparable."

"I don't want to hurt Joshua if he's innocent but I'll do everything I can to put him in prison if he killed my husband."

Waves of doubt assailed Terri during the drive home. Was she jumping to conclusions because of a work of fiction? Was she right to break her promise to Larry Birch? Would there be consequences to the police investigation because she had revealed the information about the snack to Casey Van Meter? Should she take Ashley out of school immediately? If Joshua Maxfield was a serial killer, her daughter was in grave peril.

Terri heard the phone a moment after she opened the front door to her house. She rushed into the kitchen and picked up on the fifth ring.

"Terri, thank God I caught you," Casey Van Meter said. She sounded short of breath and very tense.

"What's wrong?"

"I've got to talk to you. I went through Joshua's file. There's something in it."

"What?"

"I can't talk now. Can you come to the school, tonight?"

"Of course."

"I don't want to meet in my office. Do you know how to get to the boathouse by the service road?"

"No."

"Go a quarter of a mile past the main entrance.

There's a gravel road that follows the river and ends at the boathouse. Meet me at eight."

Terri started to ask another question but the dean said she couldn't talk and hung up. Terri sat down at the kitchen table. Energy coursed through her. If Casey Van Meter had discovered something solid, she could take it to Larry Birch. There was no way that Maxfield's arrest could bring Norman back, but Ashley would be safe if his killer was behind bars. Terri looked at her watch. It was almost six. In two hours she would know if she was closer to putting her husband's killer in prison.

CHAPTER EIGHT

Ashley had been serious about soccer since she was in elementary school, and she always put in the extra effort it took to be the best. In addition to the daily workouts at the soccer clinic, she ran every night around eight. Sally Castle ran with her on most evenings, but her roommate had an upset stomach tonight and had begged off.

Ashley liked running along the shaded paths that twisted through the forest on the school grounds, because the thick canopy kept the route cool even on warm days. Tonight there was an extra spring in Ashley's step. After the morning session, the Academy coach had pulled her aside and told her that there was an excellent chance that she would be the starting center forward in the fall. Ashley knew that she was better than the other Academy girls who played that position but it was nice to hear the coach say that it was hers if she worked for it.

Just when her spirits were highest, Ashley remembered that her father wouldn't see her play this year. Ashley had started to climb out of her depression after visiting the Oregon Academy. As soon as she moved to the dorm and began working as a counselor there were large parts of the day when she was actually happy. But there were dark periods, too; moments when she would remember Tanya's muffled screams or recall her father's death. On occasion, these moments would be more than memories. Ashley would re-experience the events as if they were happening now. Her heart rate would accelerate; she would break into a sweat and grow dizzy. Only force of will kept her from being paralyzed by sorrow.

As soon as she thought about Norman Spencer, Ashley's energy slackened and tears pooled in her eyes. She didn't want this to happen. She told herself that her father would be happy if he learned that she was going to start on a nationally ranked team. She had vowed to dedicate her senior year to his memory.

Norman had tried to be at every one of her games, but he had missed a few. Ashley was in second grade the first time that happened. She had been very upset until Terri told her that her father's spirit was always with her, even when he wasn't rooting for her on the sidelines. Ashley had felt him inside her during the game, urging her to do her best, and she had scored three goals. Now she conjured up Norman's spirit. She took deep breaths as the good feeling filled her. When she smiled, the anxiety dissipated and she knew Norman was still with her.

Ashley ran through the quadrangle and down the road to the large parking lot where one of the trails started. Shadows dappled the forest floor, and a light breeze caressed her arms. The air smelled of pine and wildflowers. Within minutes, Ashley settled into a rhythm that moved her forward with a loose and practiced stride.

After a while the path turned parallel to the river, and she could see the water rolling by through breaks in the trees. The air was still, and there was a blanket of silence broken occasionally by the songs of birds. Something moved in her peripheral vision. Ashley turned her head and saw Joshua Maxfield walking in the direction of the boathouse. Then the trees thickened and she lost sight of him. She was not surprised to see Mr. Maxfield. All the girls knew that he lived in a cottage near the river. Many of them had a crush on the handsome novelist. There were stories about girls he was rumored to have seduced, though Ashley doubted they were true.

Ashley remembered the way her mother had acted around the writing teacher on the day they toured the campus. Terri's reaction had surprised and upset her. Ashley didn't like her mother showing an interest in a man so soon after her father's death, but sometimes people acted silly around celebrities, and Mr. Maxfield was a famous writer.

A high-pitched scream tore through the silence. Ashley froze in mid-stride. A second scream forced her backward off the trail. The screams were like the light in the second before sunset—riveting and scarlet for one second and gone without a trace the next. Silence blanketed the forest again. The screams had come from behind Ashley, in the direction of the boathouse. She strained to hear anything that would give her a clue to what had just happened. She battled with herself as she waited, terrified by the screams but compelled by her conscience to find the person who had made them.

Ashley forced herself to jog toward the boathouse. She moved cautiously, alert for the slightest sound or movement. When she caught sight of the rectangular wooden building between breaks in the trees she left the path and crept through the forest. There was a narrow gravel road that followed the river and stopped on the east side of the building. The south side abutted the river and the forest came up to the west wall. A pale light bled out of one of the windows on the north side.

Ashley heard a high-pitched shout that was muffled by the boathouse walls. She kept low and darted to the closest window before rising just high enough to see inside. The windowpane was coated with dust and the interior was dark. A flashlight rolled back and forth on the floor next to one of the boat slips. Its beam cast a pale glow that illuminated the legs and torso of a woman who was slumped against one of the thick oak beams that supported the roof. She was not moving. Standing over her was Joshua Maxfield.

Ashley gasped involuntarily. Maxfield swiveled toward the window. He was holding a hunting knife with a serrated blade that was soaked with blood. Maxfield's eyes bored through the glass and into Ashley. She stood up. Maxfield took a step forward. A motorboat bobbed at anchor in its slip.

Next to the boat was a second body.

Ashley tore through the woods. She heard the boathouse door smack against the wall as it was flung open. Maxfield was fast, but so was Ashley. She had to be in better shape. She worked out hard all the time.

Twigs snapped and branches broke as Maxfield crashed through the trees. Ashley decided that her only hope was to reach the dorm. There was a security guard and other people there. The light was starting to fail. In moments it would be dark. Ashley strained to see the path that led to the main campus. She spotted it and broke out of the woods. Adrenaline fueled her headlong plunge down the trail. It curved, and Ashley saw the parking lot. She gritted her teeth. The dorm was so close. Her running shoes pounded the asphalt. She slashed across the quadrangle searching for another human being, but the school was deserted except for the counselors and the students in the soccer clinic.

Ashley rounded the side of the science building. The dorm was at the other end of a narrow parking lot. Moments later, she was through the door and screaming for help. The guard jumped up from his post and ran to her.

"He's behind me. He's got a knife."

The guard gripped Ashley's arms and stared over her shoulder.

"Who's behind you?" he asked.

Ashley turned. There was no one there.

As soon as she realized that she had escaped from Maxfield, Ashley broke down. The guard summoned Laura Rice, a graduate student who was the summer dorm proctor. Sally Castle and some of the other summer residents were drawn to the lobby by Ashley's cries. The proctor shooed them away but Sally insisted on staying with her roommate. Rice saw the wisdom in letting Ashley have a friend for company and she led the two girls to her office.

"Tell me what happened," Rice said as soon as Ashley calmed down.

Ashley told her about the screams and what she'd seen through the boathouse window.

"You're certain that the man who chased you was Joshua Maxfield?" Rice asked, fighting to hide her incredulity from her terrified charge.

"He looked right at me through the window."

"But it was dark," Rice argued, still finding it hard to picture the charming teacher as a murderer.

"Miss Rice, Joshua Maxfield killed those women."

"All right, I'm not saying you didn't see him but. . . ."

"I saw him walking to the boathouse and seconds later I heard the screams. He was holding a knife. There was blood on it. He chased me."

Ashley was starting to get hysterical again. Rice held up her hand.

"It's okay. I believe you. Could you see who the women were?"

"No. It was very dark in the boathouse. I only saw them for a second. The flashlight beam stopped halfway up one woman's body so I couldn't make out anything above the bottom of her blouse. The other woman was curled on her side and she was facing away from me. She was in the shadows. I could just make out her body."

"Give me your home number, Ashley."

Rice turned toward the security guard.

"Arthur, call the police. I'll call Dean Van Meter and Ashley's mother."

Rice dialed the dean, but there was no answer. The proctor left a message on her machine before calling Terri Spencer. She didn't answer, either. Ashley heard Rice leave a message on her mother's machine. If her mother wasn't home, where was she? Probably working, Ashley told herself.

"I'm going to the lobby to wait for the police unless you want me to stay with you," Rice said.

"No, that's okay. Sally's here."

The door closed. There was an awkward silence for a moment. Sally felt it was her duty to stay with her friend, but she'd seen TV reports about the murders at the Spencer house, and they frightened her. She stared out into the night through the office window.

The first squad car arrived a few minutes later. A uniformed officer talked with Ashley long enough to understand what was going on. A short time later, Larry Birch checked on Ashley before heading to the boathouse.

The girls waited in the dorm proctor's office while the police collected evidence from the boathouse and searched the grounds for Joshua Maxfield. Half an hour after Birch's visit the door to the office opened. Ashley looked up expectantly, hoping it would be her mother. Instead, Detective Birch entered and pulled up a chair next to Ashley. He seemed to be under a terrible strain.

"I have a question I need to ask you," the detective said.

"Okay."

"Your mother came to see me yesterday. She was very agitated. Do you know why she came?"

"No. I didn't even know she talked to you."

"Okay." Birch took a deep breath. "I'm afraid I've got bad news for you."

"Has Mr. Maxfield escaped?" Ashley asked, not wanting to think about another possibility that she'd considered and quickly rejected in order to preserve her sanity.

"We haven't found him on the grounds and his car is missing. We have an all-points bulletin out for him. He won't get far."

"That's good."

Birch took hold of Ashley's hands and looked into her eyes. Ashley tried to stop all of her thoughts.

"We know who was in the boathouse with Joshua Maxfield." Ashley tensed. "One of the women was Casey Van Meter."

"Is . . . is she . . . ?"

"No, she's alive but she's not conscious. She's been taken to the hospital."

"Who was the other woman?" Ashley asked.

Her voice sounded far away to her, as if someone in another room had asked the question.

"She's dead, Ashley."

Ashley could not understand a word Birch was saying. The room spun around and Ashley passed out.

Birch had foreseen the possibility that Ashley would collapse and had made sure that a doctor was available. Everyone waited outside the office while the doctor saw to Ashley. After she came to, she couldn't stop crying. The doctor gave her a sedative and helped her to her room. Birch followed Ashley upstairs. He waited until she was under the covers. The poor kid, he thought. No one should have to go through what she'd experienced.

Birch left Ashley with the doctor as soon as a guard was posted outside the door. Terri Spencer had been stabbed to death, and so had the victims at the Spencer home. Birch was not a big believer in coincidence. If Maxfield was the man who invaded Ashley's home, he'd succeeded in killing everyone in the Spencer family except Ashley. Birch had no idea why he would do such a terrible thing—there might not be a rational explanation—but the guard was in the hall in case Maxfield made another attempt on her life.

A policeman was waiting in the lobby with a summons from Tony Marx, Birch's partner. He escorted the detective along a path that led down to the river. The klieg lights that had been set up around the boathouse turned the night into day. Birch had been in the boathouse earlier. It had been a grim scene. Ashley's mother had been the victim of a savage attack. Birch would have to wait for the autopsy report to find out how many times Terri Spencer had been stabbed. There had been too many wounds for him to count.

Casey Van Meter had not been stabbed at all. Birch believed that Ashley had saved her life. She had been struck forcefully on the jaw. The blow had driven the back of her head against the roof support, and she would have been unconscious when Ashley distracted Maxfield and forced him to flee. Attempts to revive Casey had been unsuccessful, and she'd been rushed to the hospital.

Birch's escort led the detective past the boathouse. A minute later they arrived at a stone cottage. The path was close to the river, and Birch could see a narrow deck in the back. The setting was idyllic. The detective imagined himself sitting peacefully on the deck at dusk with a glass of scotch, watching the sunset. Maxfield wouldn't be doing much of that anymore after they caught him.

The inside of the cottage looked lived-in but tidy. There was no television in the front room, but there were many books lying about. Birch glanced at some of the titles. He recognized a few from his college literature courses. There were also several books about creative writing. A shout distracted Birch.

Tony Marx was a chubby African-American with salt-and-pepper hair, ten years older than Birch. Marx had seen it all during his career, so Birch was surprised by how excited his partner seemed.

"Larry, you've got to see this," Marx said as he grabbed his partner's arm and dragged him into a room that opened off a narrow hall. It was obvious that this was where Maxfield wrote. A comfortable armchair was stuck in a corner of the room. A lamp stood behind the chair, next to an end table. On the table was a pen, some Post-its, a steno pad, and a stack of paper that looked like a manuscript.

A window looked out at the river. In front of the window was a desk dominated by a computer monitor. Beside the monitor was another stack of paper covered in type. Marx smiled when he saw where Birch was looking. He handed his partner a pair of latex gloves like the ones he was wearing. Birch picked up the top page and started to read.

"I smiled when Martha screamed. Her pain was a symphony more beautiful than any Beethoven had ever composed. I held her ear by the edge and began to slice slowly to prolong her agony. . . ."

Birch looked up. "What is this, Tony?"

Marx's smile widened. "A novel Maxfield was writing. He was kind enough to put his name at the top of each page so we wouldn't think that another psycho killer wrote it. He's only about one hundred and seventy pages in but there's enough there to hang him." Marx threw a thumb over his shoulder that pointed at the manuscript on the table by the armchair. "That's more of the same. Probably an earlier draft, because it doesn't have his name on it. But I spotted several similar scenes."

"Didn't you say that this is a novel?"

"Yeah."

"The DA can't use this. Maxfield's lawyer will argue it's make-believe."

Marx grinned. He looked like a child who had just been given a really great toy for Christmas.

"I didn't give you the good part. Take a gander at this scene."

Birch took the new pages. At first he didn't get it. The scene was pretty gruesome but it was still only a scene in a novel. When the murderer tied up the parents and the teenage daughter with duct tape, Birch got a funny feeling in his gut. Then he reached the part where the serial killer went to the kitchen. When the killer selected a piece of pie and a glass of milk to ease his hunger, Birch stopped reading.

"We've got him," Birch said. Involuntarily, his lips began to mimic his partner's triumphant smile. Then he remembered Ashley Spencer and the smile faded, and his features hardened into a look of grim determination.

CHAPTER NINE

Ashley was awake but lightly medicated when the door to her room opened. Detective Birch stepped aside and an old man limped to Ashley's bed with the aid of a stout walking stick. He was over six feet tall, with thick, stooped shoulders. Behind him was a male version of Casey Van Meter, dressed in a rumpled suit with his tie askew.

"Ashley," the detective said, "this is Henry Van Meter, Dean Van Meter's father."

Henry Van Meter was rarely seen anymore except at official functions or on occasional walks around the Academy grounds when the weather was warm. He had been a vigorous man until he suffered a stroke that almost killed him. Ashley had seen him a few times from a distance, strolling slowly through the campus, leaning heavily on his walking stick.

Van Meter's sad blue eyes peered at her through the thick lenses in a pair of old-fashioned, wire-rimmed glasses. His hair was snowy white. His skin was sallow and sagged at the jowls. He wore brown corduroy pants and a bulky wool sweater, even though the outside temperature was in the mid-eighties.

"And this," the detective said, pointing to the younger man, "is Miles Van Meter, Dean Van Meter's brother. He's just arrived from New York."

Miles nodded. He looked terrible.

"They came here directly from the hospital after visiting the dean," Birch said. "They insisted on seeing you."

There was no reaction from Ashley. Birch felt awful. The doctor told him that she had been talking about wanting to die. He prayed that she would put those thoughts behind her, and he was furious that a sweet kid like Ashley would ever have to feel that way.

"We want you to know how sorry we are about your tragedy," Henry Van Meter said. His speech was slurred because of his stroke.

Ashley turned her head away so they wouldn't see her cry.

"My sister means the world to me, just like your folks meant the world to you. Casey isn't dead but she might as well be." Miles's voice sounded hoarse and on the edge of a sob. "The doctors say that she may never come out of her coma. So we've both lost people dear to us in the same insane act."

Miles stopped, unable to go on.

"We will do everything we can for you," Henry said. "You must tell us if there is something you want, something that will help you survive this terrible ordeal."

"Thank you," Ashley mumbled. She knew they meant well but she wanted these people out of her room.

Birch saw Ashley's distress and touched Henry Van Meter on the arm.

"The doctor said we shouldn't exhaust Ashley."

"Yes," Henry agreed. "We'll leave you. But we are very sincere. We want to help you."

"God bless you," Miles said as he followed his father into the corridor.

Birch waited until the door closed before pulling a chair next to Ashley's bed.

"Doctor Boston told me that you were talking about killing yourself."

Ashley looked away but she didn't answer.

"I'm a homicide detective, Ashley. Do you want to know the worst part of my job?" Birch waited a heartbeat to see if Ashley would answer. "It's not the bodies or the bad guys, it's dealing with the people who are left behind. So many of them feel like you do, like there's no reason to go on anymore. I've never felt that way but I've talked to so many people who have that I think I have some understanding of the way you feel. They tell me it's like being a living dead person—you're walking around but there's no feeling inside. They say they feel like they're empty and they'll never get filled up again." Ashley turned her head toward him. "Before the murder they had all these good feelings. They loved and they were loved. And then the person who loved them disappears and it's like those feelings are sucked out of them and they can't get the person or the feelings back. If you give into that kind of despair you're rewarding Maxfield. He lives to make people suffer, he feeds on suffering."

"I don't care about Joshua Maxfield," Ashley whispered.

"You have to, Ashley. You have to hate him for what he did. You have to make yourself feel something, anything. You can't give in to the sadness. You're too good a person. You're the kind of person who makes a difference. Look at how much you've done already. There are your soccer accomplishments and your grades in school."

"That doesn't mean anything now."

Ashley started to cry. Her body shook. Birch touched her on the shoulder.

"You are special, Ashley. You are unique. Your parents were so proud of you. Don't do this to them. Don't let them down."

Birch watched her cry. He didn't know what else to do. He'd wanted to bring her back and he'd failed. He stood up, utterly defeated.

"We'll catch Maxfield," Birch whispered. "I will bring him to justice."

Ashley turned her tearstained face toward the detective. "What good will that do? My parents are dead. Catching him won't bring them back."

Larry Birch felt horrible when he left Ashley. He had a daughter. She was much younger than Ashley Spencer but he could imagine how she would feel if her parents were taken from her in such a horrible way, one after the other. Birch killed the sick feeling inside him by smothering it with anger. He knew that it was unprofessional to take a case personally but he hated Maxfield and wanted him dead. The detective liked Ashley. She was so decent, so innocent. Maxfield had murdered her too, just as surely as he'd murdered Norman and Terri Spencer. Maxfield had cut out Ashley's heart and trampled her spirit to dust, and Birch swore that he'd make Maxfield pay for that.

But why had he murdered Tanya Jones and the Spencers, and beaten Casey Van Meter into a coma? Birch's partner, Tony Marx, opted for the simplest explanation. He believed that there was no rational explanation for Maxfield's crimes. He saw Maxfield as a psychopath whose motives made sense only in the killer's twisted mind.

At first, Birch thought that Marx was probably right. Then, shortly after returning to the Justice Center, he received a call that led him to believe there was a rational motive for the crimes Maxfield had committed in the boathouse.

"This is Detective Birch."

"Are you the detective who's investigating the attacks on Dean Van Meter and Terri Spencer?" a woman asked.

"Yes, ma'am."

"I'm Cora Young, Dean Van Meter's secretary."

"What can I do for you?"

"I only found out about what happened at the

school this morning. I would have called sooner but it was such a shock. I wasn't thinking clearly."

"Do you have some information that will aid the investigation?"

"I'm not sure, but yesterday afternoon, around four, Mrs. Spencer met with the dean at the school."

"Do you know why?"

"No, but she seemed tense when she was waiting for the dean. I thought you should know."

"Thank you. It might be important."

"There's something else. Joshua Maxfield had permission to use one of our classrooms for a writing group he was teaching. The class had nothing to do with the school. It was for adults. Terri Spencer was one of his students. They had their first meeting the night before Mrs. Spencer met with the dean."

"Bingo!" Birch thought. The secretary had provided a connection between Maxfield and Terri Spencer, and Spencer and the dean.

"Am I speaking to Lori Ryan?" Birch asked after dialing the first name on the list of the writing students Cora Young had given him.

"Yes?"

"I'm Larry Birch, a detective with the Portland Police Bureau. I'd like to talk to you about Terri Spencer."

"I'm so glad you called. Actually, I was going to call you. I read about the murder in the morning paper. Do you think Joshua Maxfield killed Terri?"

"He's a suspect."

"Did he really run away?"

"Yes, ma'am."

"It's . . . well, unbelievable. I knew both of them. We were together in the same room, just the other day."

"That's why I'm calling. I wanted to learn a little about Joshua Maxfield's writing class. What exactly was the class for?"

"To help unpublished writers with their work."

"I understand that there were six students?"

"Yes. We all had books we were writing. Mindy Krauss and I took the class together because we're working on a murder mystery. I don't know what Terri's book was about."

"And Maxfield helped you with your books?"

"Yes. We gave him our manuscripts and he read parts of them to the class. Then we critiqued what he read. That's why I was going to call you. I thought that you should know about something that happened during the first class that upset some of the students, including Terri."

Ryan told Birch about the chapter that Maxfield had read at the first meeting. He recognized it as one of the chapters in Maxfield's manuscript that he had read at the cottage.

"I was sitting across from Terri when Maxfield read the part where the killer tortures those people. She looked terrible. I thought she might pass out. After I read the paper this morning it all made sense. The scene was so similar to what happened at her house.

"Terri was looking at Mr. Maxfield in a very peculiar way all the time he was reading. After the class, she questioned Mindy and me to find out if we'd written the chapter, and I think she asked one of the men in the class about it, too. I'm sure she suspected Maxfield of writing the piece and was eliminating the rest of us. I think she suspected Maxfield of writing about something he'd done."

Birch talked to Lori Ryan a little longer before phoning the next person on the list. He got through to two of the other members of the writing class. They didn't add anything to what Lori

Ryan had told him but they confirmed her observation that Maxfield's reading had disturbed Terri Spencer.

Birch was certain that he knew what had happened between the class and the attacks in the boathouse. Maxfield's story raised a red flag for Terri. She'd come to see him to find out if the information about the snack had been released to the public. Once she discovered that it had not, she would have continued investigating Maxfield. Terri was a trained reporter. Talking to Maxfield's employer would be a natural step. Casey Van Meter's phone records revealed a call from the dean to Mrs. Spencer after their meeting. That's when they would have arranged to meet at the boathouse. Maxfield must have discovered why they were meeting and attacked Spencer and Van Meter to keep them from telling the police about Terri Spencer's suspicions.

"Larry." Birch looked up and saw Tony Marx standing in the entrance to his cubicle.

Marx sat down. "I spent all morning reading Maxfield's book and making notes on the different murders he describes. Then I called the FBI and read the descriptions of the murders in Maxfield's novel. Remember how the killing in the novel is different from the killing in the

Spencer house but there's the snack and the duct tape?"

"Go on."

"Well, the murders in the book don't match any of the real murders that the Feds have linked to this guy, but they do contain details from the real murders, like the snack, that were never released to the public."

Marx leaned forward. Birch could see the excitement in his eyes. "He can claim that the details are a coincidence, that he made them up. Maybe his lawyer would get away with that if there were only one, but we've got three gems, Larry. We're gonna nail him. Joshua Maxfield is going to go down."

CHAPTER TEN

Three days after her mother's murder, sunlight streamed through the window in the Academy dormitory and woke up Ashley. She lay still, listening. Something was different. There was no noise—no early-morning hustle and bustle as there had been during the soccer clinic. Everyone connected with the clinic had gone home. Ashley was still in the dorm because no one could figure out where she should stay. Her house was out, because Joshua Maxfield was still at large. She didn't want to stay there anyway. It would be a terrible place to be by herself. Too many ghosts, too many empty rooms.

Detective Birch had asked about relatives who might take her in but Terri and Norman were only children whose parents had passed away. Detective Birch had mentioned a foster home.

That had made Ashley hysterical. Then Henry Van Meter stepped in. He said Ashley could stay in the dorm or move to his mansion. Either way, she was to consider the Academy her home until she decided what she wanted to do.

Ashley sat up and rubbed the sleep from her eyes. Straight ahead, taped to the wall, was Sally's poster of Brandi Chastain ripping off her shirt after scoring the winning goal against China in the World Cup. Sally had left that poster and another of Mia Hamm, Ashley's favorite soccer player. Sally wanted to stay with Ashley in the dorm, but her parents had taken her away. Sally called every day, but it wasn't the same as having her friend with her.

Ashley studied the poster of Brandi Chastain. Chastain looked so powerful, so invincible. Ashley had felt like that on occasion. She remembered last year's game against Wilson for the Portland Interscholastic League championship. It had been tied up with a minute to go when she had raced downfield with the ball, ready to set up the winning goal. Everything had been perfect until she slipped. When she saw her go down, the Wilson goalie stopped dead and straightened up, thinking that the threat was over.

When Ashley felt her legs go out from under her

she'd kicked the ball into the air. Her back had slammed into the ground but she'd tucked her chin. Her eyes had stared forward and she watched the ball fall. To this day Ashley had no idea how she'd had the presence of mind to turn on her hip and kick the awkward shot that had skipped past Wilson's stunned goalie. In her room in the Academy dormitory, she re-experienced that feeling of pure joy and she smiled—her first smile since her mother's death. A second later, she sobered, but something had changed inside her. She was still sad but she knew she didn't want to die. She was tired of feeling sorry for herself, and there were things she had to do, like taking care of her mother's funeral. The thought made her tear up. She knew she could break down if she didn't fight, so she took a deep breath and inhaled the rancid odor of days-old sweat.

Ashley's nose wrinkled. Her body odor hadn't bothered her before. She had not had the energy or will to bathe anyway. But this morning the smell repelled her. Ashley stared at herself in the mirror over her dresser. She looked awful. Her hair was tangled and unkempt, she'd lost weight, there were dark shadows under her eyes.

The shower was in a communal women's bathroom near the stairs. Ashley remembered the police guard. She put on her sweats, grabbed her toiletries, said hello to the guard, and shuffled down the hall.

The hot shower helped. It was short because she did not feel right luxuriating in it with her mother and father dead. Guilt would keep her from enjoying a lot of things for a while. But she could not avoid the pleasant feeling of being clean and having smooth, untangled hair.

Ashley returned to her room. She had just dressed in a fresh Eisenhower High T-shirt and shorts when the police guard knocked on her door. The knock was tentative. Everyone was still walking on eggs around her.

"Miss Spencer?"

"Yes?"

The door opened a crack and the policeman stuck his head in. "There's a Mr. Philips here to see you. He says he's your lawyer."

Ashley didn't know anyone named Philips and she was certain that she did not have a lawyer, but she welcomed the novelty of a visitor. The policeman stepped back and a young man slipped past him. He was about Ashley's height and slender, with pale blue eyes and shaggy light brown hair.

The lawyer was wearing a business suit, white shirt, and tie, but Ashley thought he could still pass for someone in high school.

"Miss Spencer, I'm Jerry Philips. I'm an attorney."

Philips held out a business card. Ashley hesitated before crossing the room to take it. The lawyer gestured toward a chair. "May I?"

"Sure, okay."

Ashley sat on the bed and examined the business card. Jerry Philips sat down and balanced his briefcase on his knees.

"I want you to know how sorry I am about your folks." The young lawyer looked down and Ashley saw him swallow. "My mother died a few years ago and my father died shortly before your father . . . passed away. So I have an idea of what you're going through."

Now it was Ashley's turn to feel uncomfortable. "I'm sorry," she mumbled.

Philips smiled sadly. "That seems to be the opening line for a lot of people I've met since Dad passed away. I'm sure you've heard it a lot, too." He laughed self-consciously. "I just said 'I'm sorry,' didn't I?"

Ashley was growing impatient. The lawyer seemed like a nice person but she didn't want to discuss the death of her parents or hear about his tragedy.

"Mr. Philips, why are you here?"

"Right. I should come to the point. Did your mother or father ever mention my father, Ken Philips?"

"I don't think so."

"He was a lawyer, too. He was partially retired and living in Boulder Creek in central Oregon. Your mother and father were two of the clients he was still handling. Dad wrote their wills."

"Oh."

"I thought you'd like to know how you stand financially."

Ashley suddenly realized that she had no idea how she would feed herself or whether she could afford a place to stay once she left the Academy. While her parents were alive, Ashley had the luxury of going to school, playing soccer, and having a good time without worrying how to pay for anything. All that had changed.

"Another thing." Philips looked uncomfortable again. "I talked to Detective Birch. He said you could bury your mother now." Philips didn't tell Ashley that there had been an autopsy. He didn't want her thinking about her mother lying on cold steel as a stranger made incisions in her flesh and unemotionally dictated findings about cause of death. "I can arrange the funeral, if you want me to."

"Yes, if you could," Ashley answered, relieved that someone would take the burden of organizing the funeral from her shoulders.

"Okay." Philips took out a yellow pad and made a note. Then he took out some papers.

"We don't have to get into details today. We can do that at your convenience. I can tell you that you're going to be okay financially if you watch yourself. You'll inherit some money and both of your parents had good life insurance policies. The money will probably last a while if you're careful. I can suggest a financial adviser when we get together."

Ashley wanted to know how much money she would inherit but she could not bring herself to ask. She didn't want Philips to think that she was greedy, and it felt wrong to think that she had profited from her parents' deaths.

"You should also think about selling your house," Philips continued.

Ashley took an involuntary breath.

"It's hard, I know. I sold my dad's place and it broke my heart. It's where I grew up."

"I know I'll have to let it go."

"The market is good now. With the life insurance, what you'll get for the house, and the other money, you should be fine."

Ashley wiped a tear from her eye. Philips stood up and handed her a handkerchief. He spotted a glass on her night table.

"Do you want some water?"

"I'll be okay. It's just so hard to. . . ."

Ashley bit her lip. Philips looked down. "Anyway," he continued self-consciously, "I'll take care of the funeral arrangements. Do you want to set a time to meet so we can go over all of the financial stuff?"

"Anytime is okay," Ashley said sadly. "I don't have anything else except the funeral."

"Do you have any questions?" Philips asked.

"Not now. I'll call you about the meeting. And thank you for coming to see me."

"It's my job," Philips answered with a kind smile. He stood. "See ya."

"See ya," she answered.

As soon as Jerry Philips left, Ashley realized that she was famished. She had barely eaten anything in the past few days. Someone had brought meals to her room while the school cafeteria was open for the soccer clinic but she only picked at them, leaving most of the food. Laura Rice's duties as dorm proctor had ended with the soccer clinic. After she packed, Laura visited Ashley to say good-bye and to deliver a message from Henry Van Meter, who had invited Ashley to take her meals in the Van Meter mansion.

Ashley pulled on a pair of sneakers and cut across the campus toward the mansion. Her bodyguard followed her at a discreet distance. The morning was spectacular. The sky was bright blue and decorated by fluffy white clouds, the air was fresh with the smell of pine and roses and birdsong filled the air. The very perfection of the morning was pure torture for Ashley. Every bird that sang, every heavenly scent, and every multi-colored flower garden made her remember what she had lost.

Ashley heard the hum of a lawnmower, and the mansion came into view. A crew of gardeners was mowing the grass, edging the bushes, and tending the flower gardens. To get to the kitchen Ashley walked between a pool and a large flagstone patio furnished with lounge chairs and glass-topped tables shaded by sturdy umbrellas. Ashley caught a glimpse of the main dining room through a leaded-glass window. It was paneled in dark woods, and a crystal chandelier hung over a polished oak table that looked as if it could seat her soccer team.

Ashley knocked on the kitchen door, and a woman dressed in a short-sleeved check shirt, khaki slacks, and an apron let her in. The woman was in her forties and her brown hair was starting to streak with gray.

"I'm Mandy O'Connor. I cook for Mr. Van Meter. You must be Ashley. Come in."

"Thank you."

The kitchen was huge and dominated by a cooking island over which hung racks of copper pots and pans and cooking utensils. To one side was a table already set for two.

"Sit down while I fix you something. I can whip up oatmeal, a batch of pancakes, or bacon and eggs with some toast. What would you like?"

Ashley was ravenous and just the mention of the food made her mouth water.

"Bacon, scrambled eggs, and toast sounds great."

"Milk, coffee, orange juice, tea?"

"Orange juice and milk, please."

Ashley sat at the table, where she found a copy of the morning paper. The headline was about a crisis in the Middle East, but there was a story about the manhunt for Joshua Maxfield below the fold. Ashley turned over the paper so she couldn't see that story and searched for sports. In the back was an article about a summer league soccer playoff. Ashley had been on the winning team last year. She could only read part of it before she had to stop.

The door connecting the kitchen to the interior of the house opened and Henry Van Meter shuffled in. He was not using his cane, and each step looked tortured. He spotted Ashley and smiled.

"Miss Spencer, welcome," he said, his speech slurring slightly. "You are joining me for breakfast?"

Ashley stood. "This is very kind of you, Mr. Van Meter. Thank you for thinking of me."

"You have been in my thoughts constantly for the past few days."

It seemed to take an eternity for Henry to reach the table. Ashley pulled out his chair and he sat down slowly, with a great effort.

"My usual, Mandy," Van Meter said. Then he looked at the page in the sports section that Ashley had been reading.

"You would be playing today, no?"

Ashley was surprised that he knew that. She nodded. He patted the back of her hand. His touch was cold.

"You will play again. You are young, so this tragedy consumes you, you believe that you will be as sad for the rest of your life as you are now, but time will make your pain fade. Trust me. I have suffered tragedies and outlived the pain. Nietzsche said, that which does not kill us makes us strong. I have lived the truth of that philosophy. The strong survive and you are strong."

"How can you know that?" she asked.

"There is one unalterable fact. Life goes on whether we wish it or not. I was wounded in the war, in my leg. Badly wounded. The doctors amputated it."

Ashley's lips parted, her eyes widened. Henry laughed.

"You are shocked. It's the right leg below the knee. They do wonderful things with prosthetics nowadays. But back then. . . ." Henry shook his head.

"Can you imagine, twenty-two years old and looking at life as a young man with one leg? What girl would have me? I would be a cripple, the subject of pity. But I woke up one morning and accepted the fact that I was a man with one leg. Some people had bad eyesight, others were uncoordinated or stupid—I had one leg. So be it. I never let my grief overwhelm me again. I rejected self-pity. When I returned home I courted and married the most beautiful and talented woman in Portland society, I improved the business that my father started, I traveled to far-off places instead of sitting in the dark, brooding." Henry tapped his temple. "It is force of will. You must make your will like iron. It is the only way to conquer life, which can be unremittingly cruel at times."

Henry's words stirred Ashley. She remembered how different she'd felt this morning when she made her decision to get out of the bed in which she had been hiding and do something as simple as taking a shower.

Mrs. O'Connor laid a plate of crisp bacon, steaming eggs, and hot, buttered toast in front of her. The smell banished all thoughts except those connected with food. Henry ate a bowl of oatmeal. Ashley took a drink of orange juice and dug in. Henry watched her eat. He smiled.

"Have you thought about what you will do with your life?" Henry asked.

"I was planning on college, if I can afford it," Ashley answered. She was still uncertain about her financial situation despite Jerry Philips's assurances.

"Ach, college. That is something you will not

have to worry about. I have seen your grades, young lady. I know about your athletic scholarship possibilities."

Ashley looked surprised.

"This is my school. My daughter is the dean," he said, as if Casey were still in her office, hard at work, "but I know everything that goes on here. So you have no worries where college is concerned. I am talking about after college. What will you do with your life?"

Ashley's tragedy had made it hard to think beyond the day. The rest of her life seemed as far away as the jungles of Africa.

"I don't know. I was interested in medicine, I'd like to travel," she answered vaguely.

"Travel! That is important. To see things, to have experiences. My trips gave me some of my best memories."

Ashley had visions of Saharan pyramids and snow-covered Himalayan peaks.

"Where did you go?"

Henry began his answer but a knock on the kitchen door interrupted him. Detective Birch walked in with a determined look on his face.

"Mr. Van Meter, Ashley, I have good news. We caught him."

"Joshua Maxfield?" Van Meter asked.

Birch nodded. "They ran a piece on the case on the national news. The Omaha police got a citizen tip and picked him up in a motel. Maxfield has a court appearance in Nebraska, tomorrow. If he waives extradition he'll be in custody in Oregon by the end of the week."

Ashley had been badly frightened while Joshua Maxfield was at large. She felt relieved now, knowing he was in custody. But she didn't feel joy. Her mother and father were still dead and nothing the state did to Joshua Maxfield would bring them back.

CHAPTER ELEVEN

Before Barry Weller entered the jail reception area, he went to the men's room in the Justice Center to calm his nerves. As he washed his hands, Barry studied himself in the mirror. His reddish-brown hair had been cut two days before and was neat and crisp, and his suit hung just right from his lanky frame. Behind his contacts his eyes were a piercing and decisive green. When he left the restroom Barry believed that he was the very picture of a successful and dynamic attorney.

Weller had barely been able to contain his excitement during the crosstown walk from his law office to the jail at the Justice Center, a sixteen-story concrete-and-glass building a block from the Multnomah County Courthouse. The jail took up the fourth through tenth floors of the building, but the Justice Center was also the home of the central precinct of the Portland Police Bureau, a branch of the Multnomah County district attorney's office, several courtrooms and, currently, Joshua Maxfield, the country's most notorious serial killer.

Two years ago, Weller had left the public defender's office after five distinguished years to go into private practice. It had been rough sledding the first year, but business had finally started to pick up. Weller had been in court yesterday with one of his clients when Maxfield was arraigned. He was certain that the famous defendant would hire one of Portland's big-name criminal attorneys. When his secretary told him that Joshua Maxfield was calling from the jail, visions of Mercedes began dancing in Weller's head.

Barry showed his bar card to the corrections officer who was manning the reception desk in the jail, then passed through the metal detector. The jail elevator let him off in a concrete corridor painted pastel-yellow. He rang for the guard and waited nervously in front of a thick steel door. The guard let Weller into another narrow corridor and opened the door to one of the contact visiting rooms in which attorneys met their incarcerated clients.

"Ring when you want out," the guard said, pointing to a black button affixed to an intercom that was built into the wall. Then he locked the door behind him.

Weller sat on one of two plastic chairs that were separated by a small circular table secured to the floor by metal bolts. He was arranging his notepad and composing his thoughts when the steel door to the corridor that led to the cells opened. A moment later, Joshua Maxfield entered the contact room.

Maxfield was about Weller's size. He was dressed in an orange jumpsuit and his hands were manacled, but he didn't seem to mind. The corrections officer unlocked Maxfield's chains and motioned Joshua onto the empty chair.

"Thank you for coming, Mr. Weller," Maxfield said as soon as the door closed behind the guard.

"Call me Barry," Weller responded with a smile.

Maxfield smiled back. "Barry, then. I must tell you that I was flattered when you took my call. Everyone in the jail speaks so highly of you that I assumed you'd be too busy."

Weller tried to conceal his surprise and pleasure. He'd had some modest successes but he had no idea that his reputation had grown so fast.

"I'm never too busy to take calls from the jail. I

know how isolated a person feels when they're locked up."

"That's true. I've never been in a situation like this. It's very unnerving to be totally at the mercy of other people."

Weller thought Maxfield looked anything but unnerved. In fact, he seemed remarkably composed for a man who was almost certain to face the death penalty.

"Are they mistreating you?"

"I'm fine. Actually," Maxfield said with a smile, "I watch a lot of crime movies and I was a bit disappointed when no one brought out a rubber hose."

Weller laughed. Good, he thought. A client with a sense of humor.

"What about when you were arrested?"

"The police were all holding guns and yelling but they calmed down when I told them I wouldn't resist. Since then, everyone has been a perfect gentleman."

"Have you been questioned by the police?"

"A little."

Weller had lost count of the clients who had convicted themselves by talking too freely to the police. He hoped the damage wasn't irreparable.

"Where was this?" the lawyer asked.

"In Nebraska, after my arrest."

"Who interrogated you?"

"The two detectives who flew me back to Portland."

"What did you tell them?"

"Not much. They wanted to know what happened in the boathouse. I told them I didn't do it."

"How long did this conversation with the detectives go on?"

"Not long. We just talked for a bit. Then I got suspicious that they were trying to get me to say something incriminating, so I asked for a lawyer and they stopped questioning me."

"From now on, you don't discuss your case with anyone, understand?"

"Of course. I'm not stupid."

"You don't have to be stupid to say something that can hang you. Even the most innocent statements can be misinterpreted."

"That couldn't possibly happen to my statements, Barry. I'm completely innocent."

Weller smiled but the smile was forced. Before coming to the jail, Barry had demanded discovery from the DA who was handling Maxfield's case.

What he'd read was not good. But before he discussed the facts of the case there was an important matter that Weller had to get out of the way.

"I want to get to the nuts and bolts of your case, Mr. Maxfield. . . ."

"If I'm going to call you Barry, you should call me Joshua."

"Joshua it is. If we're going to work together it's good to be on a first-name basis. But before we decide whether you want me to represent you, you need to know how much my representation is going to cost."

"Ah, business. Let's get it over with."

"I always get the money part out of the way first, so I can concentrate on your case and not get distracted."

"Terrific."

"Let me be frank with you. The state is going to go for the death penalty. And we're talking about more than one murder charge and possibly more than one set of murders."

Maxfield looked puzzled. "When I was in court the other day all the judge talked about was the murder of Terri Spencer and an assault on Casey Van Meter. What else could there be?"

"The DA has a theory that you're a serial killer."

"That's preposterous."

"It's based on a confession they found in your bungalow."

"What confession?"

This was the first time that Maxfield had displayed any emotion since the interview started. The sudden outburst convinced Weller that the thread that was holding Maxfield together was very thin.

"We're getting ahead of ourselves here, Joshua," the attorney said. "We need to agree on a fee first. Then we can discuss the DA's case and our strategy."

Maxfield seemed anxious to ask more about the confession but he regained his composure.

"What is your fee?" he asked.

"Investigating a capital murder case is not like investigating any other kind of criminal case. A death case is divided into two trials. Every other murder case only has one, the trial to decide guilt or innocence. In a death case, there is a second trial to decide the penalty if the defendant is found guilty of a type of murder that has death as a possible sentence. This second phase starts right after a guilty verdict, so I can't wait until you're convicted to prepare for the penalty phase. I have to start that investigation immediately even if we have a strong defense. So we're really talking about two complex investigations instead of one and, in this case, I may have to investigate a number of murder allegations in Oregon and in other states."

"Let's cut to the chase, Barry. What is this going to cost me?"

Weller's stomach churned as he prepared to state a fee that was far greater than all the fees he'd collected in his two years of private practice.

"I'll need an immediate retainer of $250,000, but the final amount could be much higher."

"That shouldn't be a problem."

"That's great," Weller said, hiding his surprise.

"In fact," Maxfield said, "you can count on collecting far more than a quarter of a million dollars."

Weller looked puzzled. Maxfield grinned. "I'm thinking you'll end up with at least a million dollars, win or lose. But you'll have to do a little extra work to earn it."

"I'm not following you."

"I've heard that top criminal lawyers have a knack for cutting good deals with prosecutors. Are you a good negotiator?"

"I'd say so."

"Excellent. You're going to need your skills as a negotiator to maximize your fee."

"You want to plead guilty?"

"Definitely not." Maxfield folded his hands on the table and leaned forward. He looked intense. "What do I do for a living, Barry?"

"You're a writer."

"A **best-selling** writer. How much money do you think my publisher will pay for a firsthand account of the trial of the century written by a best-selling author accused of serial murder?"

"You're going to write a book about your case?"

"I heard that you were quick," Maxfield said with a big smile. "Let me tell you how a writer is paid. When you ink a contract with a publisher you receive a chunk of money called an advance. Getting a quarter million for my story will be easy. If you're a good negotiator, you might get a publisher up to a million or more.

"But that's not all. The advance is technically an advance against royalties. My contract will guarantee me a certain percentage of the cover price on every book that sells. Let's say that the royalties are ten percent, the book goes for twenty-five dollars and it sells one million copies. Do the math, Barry."

"That's two million, five hundred thousand dollars."

"On the hardcover. There's also a paperback edition and foreign sales and movie rights and books on tape, and you will be collecting half of everything I receive if you take my case whether you win or you lose. How does that sound?"

Barry was having trouble breathing. "You'll split everything down the middle?" he managed.

"What choice do I have? I need your help and this is the only way I can get the money to hire you. Is it a deal?"

"I'll have to give it some thought," Weller said, regaining some of his senses. "I've never done business like this."

"That makes two of us. Before you leave I'll tell you how to structure the contract and the name of my editor. He's in New York. With all this publicity he might even call you when he learns you're representing me.

"Now, do you feel comfortable telling me what you found out about my case even though you haven't formally accepted my offer?"

"Sure. Most of what I'm going to tell you was in the papers, anyway. The indictment focuses on the murder of Terri Spencer and the assault on

Casey Van Meter. As best I can make out, Ashley Spencer, Terri's daughter, is the key to the state's case. She says that she was jogging in the woods at the Oregon Academy when she saw you walking toward the boathouse. Shortly after she saw you she heard two screams from the direction of the boathouse. She looked in the window and saw you standing over Casey Van Meter, who was stretched out on the floor with her head against a wooden beam. You were holding a knife and the blade was covered with blood. She also saw her mother lying on the floor. Spencer says that you saw her and chased her."

"Poor kid." Maxfield shook his head. "She's telling the truth."

"You killed Spencer's mother?" Weller asked, surprised.

"No. I didn't hurt anyone," Maxfield said. "I was in the boathouse but Terri was dead and Casey was unconscious when I got there. I'm innocent. But I can see why Ashley thought I killed Terri and attacked the dean."

"Tell me what happened."

"I often take a walk around the grounds in the evening. That's why I was near the boathouse. It's on the way to my cottage. I heard the same screams that frightened Ashley. Like I said, the women had already been attacked when I got there."

"What about the knife?"

"It was lying on the ground near Terri. I picked it up because I thought that the killer might be hiding in the boathouse and I was in fear of my life. Ashley looked in the window a second after I got it. At first, I thought she was the murderer. I probably made an aggressive move toward her because she startled me. Then I recognized her. She must have been as scared as I was and she rushed off. I chased her to explain that I hadn't hurt anyone but she was too fast for me and I never caught up. Then I realized how everything looked and I panicked and ran."

Weller made some notes. Maxfield waited patiently.

"Tell me about the confession," Maxfield said, when Weller looked up.

"It's not exactly a confession but the police are viewing it as if it was. It's your novel about the serial killer. You read a section of it to your writing class."

"So?"

"There have been murders in different parts of the country that the police believe were committed by a serial killer. In several cases the police held back evidence from the public. Your book contains scenes that have this evidence in them. For instance, when Ashley Spencer's father was murdered and her friend was killed, the murderer went into the Spencer kitchen and ate a piece of chocolate cake. At another murder the killer ate a piece of pie. In the scene you read to your writing class your killer eats dessert before raping and killing a victim."

Maxfield looked incredulous. Then he laughed. "You're not serious?"

"The DA is very serious."

"It's a novel. I made up everything."

"The state's position is that the details about eating the food are too grotesque to be a coincidence."

"They're wrong. Life imitates art all the time. Jules Verne predicted submarines, Tom Clancy had terrorists crash a plane into the White House."

"That's true, but in those cases the fictional incident preceded the real one."

"What does that matter?" Maxfield was very upset now. "They can't hang me because I have a good imagination."

"They're going to claim that you weren't imagining anything, that you were writing what you know. Isn't that what they tell you in writing classes?"

Maxfield looked like he was ready to explode. Then, as suddenly as he'd become unhinged, he calmed down.

"Write what you know," he repeated. Then he laughed. "Write what you know. Wouldn't it be hysterical if that old cliché put me on death row?"

The author stared into space for a moment. Then he smiled at Barry.

"You certainly have your work cut out for you. Are you up to it?"

"Definitely," Weller answered.

"The money should motivate you to do your best. Let me tell you the ABCs of negotiating my book contract."

Barry had planned to ask about something in the police reports that bothered him, but he forgot about the case as Maxfield taught him how to become a literary agent. One million dollars, two million dollars, three million dollars. Thinking about the money made it tough to concentrate on something as mundane as murder.

CHAPTER TWELVE

Deputy District Attorney Delilah Wallace had grown up in the poorest neighborhood in Portland and cleaned houses to pay her way through school. She couldn't help gawking at the Van Meter mansion's entry hall, which looked as big as the house she'd grown up in. The hall was paneled in dark wood and decorated with shields, maces, swords, battleaxes, and a massive tapestry portraying unicorns and the ladies of a medieval court cavorting in a copse of trees. Suspended from the ceiling was a gigantic iron chandelier originally designed to hold candles but wired for electricity. A suit of armor stood on either side of a grand stairway that swept upward to the second floor.

As the Van Meters' houseman led the way down a drafty corridor toward the library where Miles and Henry Van Meter waited, Delilah turned to

Jack Stamm, the Multnomah County district attorney.

"This place looks like the Oregon branch of Buckingham Palace," she whispered.

Stamm laughed because he'd had the same reaction the first time he set foot in the Van Meter home.

"The Van Meters started as dirt-poor loggers and built a timber empire," Stamm whispered back. "I guess they felt they earned the right to live like emperors."

The Multnomah County DA was a rail-thin bachelor with thinning brown hair and blue eyes. His deputy was a big-boned, ample-breasted, African-American woman with arms as wide around as a steel worker's. Delilah dwarfed her boss and Dr. Ralph Karpinski, a dapper dresser in his early sixties, who brought up the rear. As they walked toward the library, Delilah took in the artwork and museum-quality antiques that decorated the hallway. The library was what she expected, another massive space with a huge stone fireplace, more wood-paneled walls, and floor-to-ceiling bookshelves. Henry Van Meter was sitting in a high-backed armchair next to the fireplace, which had a fire roaring in it despite the summer weather. Miles Van Meter walked over as soon as they entered the room. He was wearing a navy blue pinstripe suit, a maroon tie, and a white silk shirt with French cuffs secured by gold cufflinks. Miles shook Stamm's hand.

"Thank you for coming, Jack," he said.

The Van Meters had always been big contributors to Jack Stamm's political campaigns and there was never any question that he would respond to Miles's request for a personal update on the Maxfield case.

"It's no trouble, Miles. I can only imagine how hard this has been on both of you." Stamm turned toward his companions. "This is Dr. Ralph Karpinski, an expert on comas. We've been consulting with him about how to proceed with our indictment. And this is Delilah Wallace. She'll be prosecuting Joshua Maxfield."

"Do you have any experience with murder cases?" Henry Van Meter asked, eying the black woman suspiciously. The question was really a challenge, but Delilah simply smiled.

"Yes, sir, I do. My brother was killed in a drive-by when I was in high school, so I take my murder cases personally. They're my specialty and I haven't lost one yet. And I'm definitely not what you'd call soft on crime. I've tried five death cases and there are five men sitting on death row today because I asked the jury to put them there. I intend to make Mr. Maxfield number six."

"Delilah won't let you down, Henry," Stamm assured him. "She's the best I've got and she's already putting in long hours on the case."

Everyone sat down and Stamm continued the conversation. "I wanted Dr. Karpinski to update you on Casey's condition so you'll understand why we're going ahead with her case now as an assault instead of waiting to see if she passes away so we can try Maxfield for murder. Then Delilah has some questions she wants to ask."

Karpinski had a head of white hair and a patrician air. He dressed as elegantly as Miles Van Meter. The doctor straightened his cuffs as he began to speak.

"Mr. Van Meter, your daughter is in a coma. That means that she is alive but unaware of herself and her surroundings. To be blunt, a coma is a type of living death."

Henry took a deep breath and closed his eyes for a moment.

"So you can better understand what's wrong with Casey, let me explain why a coma occurs. The cerebral cortex is the part of the brain that is ultimately responsible for processing all sensory input, motor output, and integrative functions of the nervous system. The reticular activating system, or RAS, is the core of neurons in the center of the brainstem that projects into the cerebral cortex and wakes up the cortex so it can process the information it's getting and do something about it. To put it another way, the RAS is like an alarm clock. If it doesn't go off, the cerebral cortex stays asleep and doesn't do its job, so you stay unconscious."

"Will Casey come out of her coma?" Miles asked.

"That's hard to say. There is a slim chance that she will. More likely, she will probably stay asleep for years. She may never regain consciousness."

"But there is a chance that she'll come back to us?" Henry asked.

"That's not something you can count on. Let me explain. There are three types of coma. In the first category, widespread areas of the cortex are damaged by causes such as severe trauma, absence of blood flow for more than seven to ten minutes, or advanced meningitis. In the second category, processes like prolonged seizure activity, intoxication and alcohol withdrawal, or liver and renal failure alter the ability of the brain tissue to function normally. In the third category, things like tumors, strokes, or compression of the brainstem damage the RAS.

"When a coma falls into the first two categories, meaningful neurologic recovery isn't possible. With the first type, even if the patient regains consciousness, they're severely incapacitated because of the widespread brain damage. In the second, say where there's liver failure or prolonged seizures, the patient dies if the metabolic cause of the coma isn't corrected quickly.

"Fortunately, Casey became comatose because of trauma damage to the brainstem RAS that occurred when she struck her head with a lot of force against one of the timbers that support the roof of the Academy's boathouse. Traumatic damage was done to the lower posterior portion of the skull just above the top of the neck. This covers the brainstem and cerebellum. The area that was damaged was the locus ceruleus, a section of the RAS. What's good about this is that people in a prolonged comatose state caused by damage to the RAS can spontaneously recover consciousness. In theory, recovery can also be induced pharmaceutically, though no one has done it yet."

"Are you saying that a drug exists that can wake up my sister?" Miles asked.

"No, but scientists are working to develop one. Theoretically, yohimbine, which has been around for years, should do the trick. The problem is that it causes extreme elevations of blood pressure even at relatively small doses. There have been attempts to develop a drug that will block the peripheral effect of yohimbine on the heart and blood vessels. That would allow us to administer high doses to the locus ceruleus and reverse the coma. The greatest success has been achieved by using a drug that is similar to carbidopa, which is used to treat Parkinson's disease, but the pharmaceutical companies are far from the point where the FDA will approve such a drug for use on living patients."

Miles struggled to maintain his composure.

"If I understand you correctly, Dr. Karpinski, Casey will wake up spontaneously, or a miracle drug, which does not currently exist, will bring her out of her coma. Otherwise she will stay a vegetable for the rest of her life. There is no other alternative."

Karpinski nodded. "Unfortunately, under the present state of our knowledge, those are the alternatives."

"That's why we're going after Maxfield for assault, Miles," Stamm said. "But we're also prosecuting him for Terri Spencer's murder, so he will receive the severest punishment the law allows."

Miles's hands curled into fists. He glared at Jack

Stamm. "I want that bastard dead, Jack. I want him dead."

"We're going to convict him, Miles. We're going to send him down," Stamm assured him.

"Mr. Van Meter," Delilah asked Miles in a calm voice that sought to defuse his hatred, "can you help us with any information about Joshua Maxfield or your sister that could help my prosecution?"

Miles took a deep breath and regained his self control.

"I don't think so. The night Casey was attacked, I was in New York City with two other members of my firm negotiating a deal for a client."

"How well did you know Joshua Maxfield?"

"Not well at all. I'm an attorney with Brucher, Platt and Heinecken. I don't have much to do with the Academy. I did meet Maxfield briefly at a fund-raiser for the school, and I had dinner with him when he was hired. Casey wanted me to meet him. She thought we might get along, but we really had little in common."

Delilah turned to Henry Van Meter. "Sir, did you have any contact with Joshua Maxfield?"

Henry looked very tired. He shook his head wearily.

"Almost none. Like my son, I met him at a few functions but we never talked much. I have not been well these past few years. My daughter handled the day-to-day operations of the school."

"I'm not going to take up any more of your time today," Delilah said, "but I may need one or both of you to testify at Maxfield's trial about Casey. The jury needs to see her as a human being, and family members—loved ones—can do that better than anyone. Would it be okay if I came back to talk to you about Casey?"

"Certainly," Miles said. He handed Delilah his business card. "You can call me at my office anytime. If you don't have anything more for my father, I'll walk you out."

As soon as they were far enough away from the library so Henry Van Meter could not hear, Miles turned to Jack Stamm and Dr. Karpinski.

"Thank you for coming to the house. I know how inconvenient it is to travel out here, but my father really isn't well."

"Glad to do it, Miles," Stamm said. "I only wish we could be more encouraging about your sister's chances."

"That's up to God and science, Jack. All Father and I can do is pray."

Miles turned to Delilah. "You have my card, Ms. Wallace. If there is anything I can do to put Maxfield on death row, just ask."

CHAPTER THIRTEEN

The preliminary hearing in **State of Oregon v. Joshua Maxfield** was scheduled for one in the afternoon, but Delilah Wallace had been working on her preparation since seven in the morning. She'd let herself into the district attorney's office with her key, first in as usual, turning on the lights as she walked past the empty offices.

Delilah was always first at everything she did; she'd been first in her high school class, first in her college class, and first in her law school class. Delilah was smart but she also worked as hard as she was able on everything she did; she didn't know any other way. She could hardly remember a time when she wasn't working. Her father had walked out on the family when she was born, and her mother had supported her and her brother with minimum-wage jobs because she had no education and no skills except the ability to push herself to exhaustion and beyond. That meant that Delilah worked, too, from the time she could work, to help pay the rent and put food on the table. She had been an adult long before she was one legally.

Religion and music had been Delilah's salvation. The church choir had given her purpose and pride in an ability to sing that was unique. Her voice had kept her in high school while her friends dropped out. Her solos put her in a spotlight that she came to cherish, and had pointed her toward trial work where she could continue to be the center of attention. There was no bigger spotlight than the one the press and public shone on a trial lawyer who was seeking the death penalty.

At eight A.M., someone knocked on Delilah's doorjamb. She looked up from a stack of police reports to find Tony Marx standing in her doorway with a smile plastered on his face and a small notebook in his hand.

"What is the reason for your shit-eating grin, detective?"

"My excellent detection skills. You have some time to hear what I've discovered about Joshua Maxfield?"

Delilah glanced at her watch. "I'm not prepping

Ashley Spencer until eleven, so I can spare a few minutes. What have you got?"

Marx took a chair in front of Wallace's desk, which was completely covered with law books, police reports, crumpled scraps of paper, and legal pads.

"How the hell do you ever find anything?" Marx asked as he opened his notebook.

Delilah tapped her temple. "It's all up here. Come on now, what have you got?"

"Our boy is definitely not what he seems. First, Maxfield isn't the name he was born with. That's Joshua Peltz. Mr. and Mrs. Peltz belonged to some fringe Christian sect in Massachusetts that subscribed to a spare-the-rod-and-spoil-the-child philosophy. When Joshua was eleven, he was truant from school for a week. A caseworker found him chained in a closet. He was emaciated, dehydrated, and covered with cigarette burns. My guess is that he was subjected to some really sick shit. The state must have thought so, too, because it terminated the Peltzs' parental rights and put our client in foster care."

"I just read Maxfield's first book, **A Tourist in Babylon,**" Delilah said. "Now I know how he can write so realistically about a classic abused childhood."

"He's also pretty knowledgeable about crime," Marx said. "Our boy developed quite a juvenile record. He set fire to his first foster home and spent time in juvenile detention for arson; there are several assaults in elementary and middle school, quite a few expulsions, too. The only consistent thing in his life was judo. One of his foster parents thought the discipline would do him good, but he only used his skills to bully kids. He was expelled from high school when he was a senior for breaking a boy's arm. After that, he bummed around for a year, then went back to school."

"When did Peltz become Maxfield?" Weller asked.

"His last foster family was named Maxfield. He had his name changed legally when he went to college at the University of Massachusetts. I guess Maxfield does sound classier than Peltz. He used to tell people that he was from a wealthy family in California."

"He wrote his big bestseller in college, didn't he?"

"Yeah, he started it in community college and finished it his senior year at U. Mass." Marx looked up from his notes. "I got a lot of his writing history from book reviews and interviews he gave when **Tourist** hit the big time. The story is that he wrote an essay about his childhood in an English class, and the professor suggested he expand it. There was a big-bucks advance, literary prizes, bestseller lists, the whole nine yards. Maxfield was on top of the world, a genuine boy wonder. The problem was that he used up all the material he'd accumulated from his miserable life in his first novel and couldn't write a decent follow-up. His second book tanked, and he hasn't written another one since."

"Unless you count his serial-killer opus."

"A point well taken." Marx paused. "You don't think he killed to get material for the book, do you?"

"Now that's an idea." Delilah stared into space for a moment. "I'm gonna think on that." She refocused on the detective. "You have anything more for me, Tony?"

Marx told Wallace what he'd found out about Maxfield's reasons for leaving Eton College.

"Can we get the name of the woman he hit on?" Delilah asked.

"I'm working on it."

"Any luck tying Maxfield to any of the out-of-state murders?"

"The FBI is working that angle and I haven't heard from them yet."

"Okay, good job. Now let me get back to work so I don't mess up this afternoon."

Ashley's nightmares were less intense after Joshua Maxfield's arrest. Boredom replaced fear as her preeminent emotion. She started exercising again, because it gave her something to do. One afternoon, Ashley kicked a ball around the soccer field and tried a few shots on goal. The next day, she practiced again. It felt good to be back on the pitch where her only problem was getting the ball in the net. On Saturday, Sally Castle drove Ashley to the mall where they saw a movie and ate pizza. Leaving the Academy campus made Ashley feel like a prisoner freed from solitary confinement.

Ashley looked forward to her meals with Henry Van Meter. She enjoyed Henry's stories about his travels, Oregon history, and interesting things he'd accomplished. By contrast, her life seemed dull. The only time she'd traveled was when her parents took her on vacations to Mexico and Aruba, but they had stayed at resorts with other Americans, and the places hadn't seemed as foreign as she expected.

Sometimes Miles joined Ashley and his father for a meal. He was as kind to her as his father, and she felt comfortable in their company. The Van Meters encouraged Ashley to think about her future. She resisted at first, but they assured her that she could attend the Academy for free in the fall and they mentioned the soccer team from time to time. There was a plan to send the girls on several trips out of state where they would test themselves against other nationally ranked powers.

Ashley's recovery took a step backward on the morning of the preliminary hearing. She woke up frightened and nauseated, passing on a morning run because nerves and fear sapped her energy. She had gone to the mansion for breakfast but she could only eat toast and tea. As usual, Henry Van Meter tried to distract her from her troubles with tales of far-off places, but she only half-heard him. None of his stories could stop her from imagining what it would be like to face Joshua Maxfield later in the day.

Detective Birch picked up Ashley from the Academy dormitory at nine and drove her to the courthouse. He asked her how she was feeling and she told him that she was nervous, but she couldn't bring herself to tell him how truly frightened she was at the thought of being in the same room with the man who had killed her parents and come within moments of murdering her.

Birch said that it was natural to be nervous, and he assured her that Delilah Wallace was a nice woman who would make sure that her ordeal was as painless as possible. Ashley pulled into herself after that, and there was very little conversation during the rest of the ride.

Jerry Philips was sitting in the reception area with his nose in a book when Ashley entered the DA's office. He smiled and stood up when she came in. Birch placed himself between Ashley and the attorney.

"Do you know this gentleman?" the detective asked Ashley without taking his eyes off of Philips.

"Yes. He was my parents' lawyer." She looked at Jerry. "What are you doing here?"

"I'm your lawyer, too, Ashley. I'm here because I thought you might need some moral support. I've already spoken to Ms. Wallace. She seems very nice, and she'd prefer to talk to you alone, but I'll go with you if you'd feel more comfortable with me sitting in. She has no objection."

"That's okay. I'll go by myself."

"Okay. I'll be out here when you're done."

Ashley was very tense at the start of the interview, but Delilah calmed her down in less than five minutes. Delilah told Ashley that she would not keep her on the stand for long. She was only going to ask questions about what Ashley had seen in the boathouse. Maxfield's lawyer would have a chance to cross-examine, but Delilah did not expect him to ask her anything that would embarrass her. And Delilah assured her that she would be right there in the courtroom to object if Maxfield's attorney got out of hand.

"Will I have to see Mr. Maxfield?" Ashley asked.

"You'll be in my office until I call you, so you won't see him until you testify. When you're in court he'll be sitting across from you at the defense table, but there's going to be extra security, so you don't have to worry. I picked my meanest officers to guard you. They'll beat Maxfield to a pulp if he so much as breathes in your direction," Delilah said sternly. Then she broke into a smile. "And I'll sit on that weasel when they're through, and really put the fear of God in him."

The thought of this massive woman crushing Maxfield under her tremendous weight made Ashley laugh. She covered her mouth, embarrassed, but Delilah broke out laughing, too, and, for a moment, they were girls together, giggling over a private joke.

Delilah spent the rest of their time together going over the questions she was going to ask Ashley and listening to her answers. Every once in a while, the prosecutor would comment on an answer and suggest different phrasing, but she never tried to make Ashley say anything that wasn't true. Finally, Delilah subjected Ashley to a mock cross-examination. She told Ashley that the best way to handle cross was to tell the truth. She advised her not to rush, to listen to each question before answering and to make her answer to the point and as short as possible.

"Admit you don't know an answer if that's true and don't be afraid to say that you aren't sure," Delilah instructed her.

After the mock cross, Delilah told her that she had held up pretty well. By the time the interview was over, Ashley was less frightened and she was convinced that she would get through her ordeal.

When Delilah escorted Ashley back to the reception area, Ashley's lawyer was still waiting for her.

"Mr. Philips," the deputy DA said, "Ashley will be my second witness so I'd like her at the courthouse, ready to go, at one-thirty."

"Not a problem. I'll get her some lunch and have her there on time."

"Thank you." Delilah turned to Ashley and put a hand on her shoulder. "You feed yourself, girlfriend. You ain't got enough meat on your bones."

Ashley smiled. She felt safe around Delilah. The DA smiled back, turned and walked down the hallway to her office.

"Are you hungry? Shall we get something to eat?" Philips asked.

Ashley hadn't eaten much for breakfast and she was famished, but she'd seen lawyer shows, so she felt she had to ask Philips something.

"Are you going to be with me this afternoon?"

"Would you like me to be?"

"Yes, but I know that lawyers charge a lot and I can't pay you. I don't have any money."

"Actually, you do. Remember I told you about the insurance, and there's been an offer on the house. We'll discuss that at lunch. But you don't have to worry about my fees for today. It's on the house."

"Why are you being so nice to me?"

"We're both in the same boat, remember? I know how alone I felt when Dad died, so I have some idea how you're feeling. I just don't want you to go through this alone."

CHAPTER FOURTEEN

A guard let Barry Weller into the visiting room in the courthouse jail, a cramped, broom closet–sized cubicle divided in two by a grille through which attorney and client talked. Weller wanted Maxfield to wear a business suit for the preliminary hearing. The jail commander had refused because no jury was present, so Joshua was wearing an orange jail jumpsuit. Weller expected his client to complain. Most clients wanted to be dressed nicely if their hearing was going to be in open court and TV cameras and photographers were going to be present. Maxfield didn't seem to care how he was dressed. The only thing he'd insisted on was a haircut, which Weller had been able to arrange. Maxfield had cut his hair short. It dawned on Weller that he and his client looked vaguely similar.

"Ready for the prelim, Joshua?"

"As ready as I'll ever be. What do I do?"

"Nothing. Most of the time only the state puts on witnesses at a prelim."

"Why is that?"

"The arraignment is the court appearance where the judge tells you your charges. It's held in district court, where misdemeanors—the less serious crimes—are prosecuted. Murder is a felony. Felonies can only be tried in circuit court. A preliminary hearing gives the DA an opportunity to convince a judge that there's enough of a case to warrant a trial in Circuit Court."

"And when will the trial take place?"

"In a couple of months."

"Why don't you try to win the case today? Then we wouldn't have to go to trial."

"It doesn't work that way. At the preliminary hearing the prosecution doesn't have to convince a judge that you're guilty beyond a reasonable doubt, like she does at a trial. Delilah just has to show that a reasonable person would conclude from the evidence that the crime of murder had been committed and that there is a reasonable possibility that you committed the murder. That's not much of a burden. It's not even fifty percent.

"What's great about a prelim is that we get a

chance to cross-exam the state's witnesses under oath before trial. We could put on witnesses if we wanted to, but that wouldn't make sense because it would give the DA a chance to do the same thing."

"So we'll probably lose," Maxfield said, "and I'll have to sit in jail for months waiting for the trial?"

"Yes."

Weller expected Maxfield to ask about bail, but he didn't. Instead, his client asked about Weller's progress with the book deal.

"Howard Martin called me yesterday," Weller answered excitedly, naming the man who had edited Maxfield's two novels. "He's not with your old publishing house anymore. He's editor in chief at Scribe."

"I thought I read something about that in **Publishers Weekly.**"

"He really wants the book. We've only had a preliminary discussion but he's talking seven figures already."

Maxfield smiled. "I guess this is how the outlaws in the Old West felt when they read a Wanted poster and saw that there was a big reward for them."

Weller laughed. "Big isn't the half of it. I've gotten calls from movie producers, and several television news shows are clamoring for interviews."

"Good job, Barry. I knew you'd come through for me."

Weller was about to go on when the guard told them that it was time for Maxfield to go to court. Weller waited in the jail near the elevator while the guards brought out his client. Weller, Maxfield, and two guards rode down to the third floor in silence. As soon as the elevator door opened, they were bathed in the glare of the TV lights. Weller shielded his eyes and rushed to keep up as the guards hustled Maxfield through a barrage of questions and flashbulb explosions. The noise didn't stop until the courtroom doors closed behind them. Weller followed Maxfield and his guards through the packed courtroom to his counsel table. Henry and Miles Van Meter were sitting in the front row of the spectator section. Weller couldn't tell what Henry was thinking, but Miles Van Meter's hatred of his client was obvious.

Delilah Wallace was already going over her notes at the prosecution's table. Delilah took no notice of the commotion caused by the entrance of Weller or his infamous client.

"Morning, Delilah," Weller said.

Delilah looked up with a welcoming smile. "Barry Weller! As I live and breathe. What are you doing here?"

Barry laughed. He got a kick out of Delilah. "I was going to have my client cop a plea but you looked so busy I've decided to wait."

Delilah burst out with a belly laugh that made her huge body rock.

"I always enjoy locking horns with you, Barry. You were one of the few public defenders with a sense of humor."

Weller took his seat next to Joshua. The bailiff rapped for order, and the Honorable Nancy Stillman limped into the courtroom with the aid of a cane. Stillman was a plump, gray-haired, motherly-looking woman who had been appointed to the bench two years before, after spending twenty years as a litigator with an insurance defense firm.

"This is the time set for the preliminary hearing in State of Oregon versus Joshua Maxfield," the bailiff intoned.

"Is counsel ready?" Judge Stillman asked.

Delilah struggled to her feet like a mountain forming. "As always, Your Honor, the people of Oregon are ready to proceed."

Stillman couldn't help smiling. "Mr. Weller?" the judge asked.

Weller stood. "Ready for Mr. Maxfield."

"Call your first witness, Ms. Wallace."

"Before I do that, Your Honor, I want to inform the court that for purposes of this hearing only, Mr. Weller and I have agreed to stipulate that the medical examiner's report can be submitted in lieu of her testimony with regards to the cause of Terri Spencer's death."

"Is Ms. Wallace correct, Mr. Weller?" Judge Stillman asked.

"Yes, Your Honor."

"We're also stipulating, again for purposes of this hearing only, that Mrs. Spencer was stabbed to death by a hunting knife with a blade similar to Exhibit 3, which was discovered on the grounds of the Oregon Academy and that, if called to testify, a forensic expert would tell the court that blood on the blade of Exhibit 3 is identical to Terri Spencer's blood."

"You're agreeable to that as well, Mr. Weller?" the judge asked.

"Yes, Your Honor."

"Finally, Judge," Delilah continued, "and also for purposes of this hearing only, the parties have agreed to stipulate that, if called to testify, Dr. Ralph Karpinski would tell the court that Casey Van Meter is in a coma due to a brain injury that occurred when the back of her head struck a roof support in the boathouse on the Oregon Academy grounds, and that bruises on the victim's face are consistent with a blow to the face."

Weller agreed to the stipulation, and the judge made several notes on a yellow pad. When she was done, Judge Stillman nodded at Delilah and told her to call her first witness.

"The State calls Lawrence Birch."

An hour later, Delilah's secretary entered her boss's office and told Ashley that it was time to testify. Ashley turned pale. Jerry Philips squeezed her hand.

"Hey, you've had more pressure on you than this. You're a big-time athlete," he said, trying to loosen Ashley up with a smile, but she was paralyzed by the thought of being in the same room with Joshua Maxfield. She remembered the heat of his body and the way he smelled when he'd pressed down on her and rubbed his sex against her buttocks. She thought she might throw up.

Jerry put a hand under her arm and helped her stand. Her legs trembled. Her breath caught in her chest. She felt dizzy.

"I don't know if I can do this," Ashley whispered, on the edge of tears.

Philips turned her toward him. He gripped her shoulders and made her stare into his eyes.

"You must do this, Ashley. This is for your mom and dad. Maxfield is a terrible person."

Now Ashley was crying. Philips held her. The secretary looked on, almost in tears herself.

"Can you get Miss Spencer a glass of water?" Jerry asked. The secretary walked away. When she returned, Ashley was still shaky but calmer. Jerry stood back and held out a handkerchief. He waited while Ashley wiped her eyes and drank some water. She knew Jerry Philips was right. She had to do this for Terri and Norman. She was the only one who could stop Joshua Maxfield, and she was going to stop him.

"Let's get this over with," Ashley said.

Philips squeezed her shoulder and they started down to Judge Stillman's courtroom.

The walk from the courtroom door to the witness box seemed to take a lifetime. Ashley looked straight ahead and did not see Jerry Philips slip into a seat in the last row. She kept herself rigid and turned her head away from the defense table so she could see Delilah Wallace but not Joshua Maxfield. There was a low wooden barrier that separated the spectator section from the front of the courtroom. Delilah smiled warmly and pointed toward the gate that opened into the bar of the court. Just before Ashley pushed through the gate she saw Henry Van Meter. He smiled at her and the smile helped to steel her for her ordeal.

Ashley's legs felt heavy as she walked past Barry Weller. She kept her back to the defense table when she took the oath, but there was no way that she could stop herself from casting a quick glance at Joshua Maxfield once she was in the witness box. The most difficult thing for Ashley to accept was that Maxfield had not changed into a monster. He still looked like the friendly instructor of creative writing who had chatted on the Academy quadrangle with the young girl he had tried to rape and murder and the woman he would soon stab to death. At the moment their eyes met, Maxfield smiled. His smile was as warm as Delilah's. How could evil be so undetectable?

"Miss Spencer," Delilah said, "for purposes of this hearing I am going to confine most of my questions to the events that took place on the evening of June 24 of this year. But I will ask you a few other questions, so Judge Stillman can put those events in context."

Ashley was glad that the questioning had

started so she had an excuse for staring at the DA and away from Joshua Maxfield.

"You are between your junior and senior years in high school, are you not?"

"Yes," Ashley answered, remembering Delilah's instructions to keep her answers short.

"And you've spent your high school years at Eisenhower?"

"Yes."

"Have you played any sports at Eisenhower?"

"Soccer."

"Do you also play on an elite club team when the high school season is over?"

"Yes."

"Have you done well in your sport?"

"Yes."

"Tell the judge a few of the honors you've won as a soccer player."

Ashley started with her honorable-mention all-state designation as a freshman and went on to list her other achievements.

"Is the Oregon Academy a private school?"

"Yes."

"Does it have a nationally ranked women's soccer team?"

"Yes."

"Were you offered a full scholarship to the Academy for your senior year in high school?"

"Yes."

"Were you planning to accept that offer?"

"Yes. I had told them that I would go in the fall."

"Now, Ashley, please tell the judge what you were doing on the Academy campus on June 24."

"The Academy runs a summer soccer clinic. Kids come from all over the country. Some of the instructors are members of the Olympic team and some are top collegians. I was hired as a counselor."

"Where did you live during those two weeks?"

"In the dorm with the kids and the other counselors."

"So you were on campus on the evening of June 24?"

"Yes."

"Tell the judge what happened after dinner."

Ashley had trouble answering the question. She had blocked all thoughts of her mother until now, but she could put them away no longer. She took a sip of water to stall for time so she could gather herself. Judge Stillman knew what had happened to Ashley, her father, and Tanya Jones, because of

Larry Birch's testimony. She gave Ashley a smile of encouragement.

"I like to run in the evening," Ashley said. "My roommate, Sally Castle, usually ran with me but she wasn't feeling well that night so I went alone."

"Where did you run that evening?" Delilah asked.

"There's a lot of woods on the Academy grounds with trails through them. I ran on the trails."

"Does a river run alongside the Academy land?"

"Yes."

"Is there a boathouse on the river?"

"Yes."

"Did your route take you near the boathouse?"

"Yes it did."

"How was the light when you started out?"

"Good."

"When your route took you near the river and the boathouse, did you see anyone you knew?"

Ashley hesitated. She took a breath. "I saw Mr. Maxfield."

"Ashley, I know that this is hard for you. . . ."

"Objection," Weller said. "That's not a question."

"Sustained," Judge Stillman said. "Just ask your question without preamble, Ms. Wallace."

"Yes, Judge. Ashley, please face the defendant."

Delilah had told Ashley that this moment would come, but she was still not prepared. As her head turned toward Maxfield, she clasped her hands in her lap, squeezing hard enough to cause pain.

"Is that the man you saw in the woods near the river and the boathouse on the evening of June 24?"

Ashley's eyes locked on Maxfield's. His smile was gentle and not threatening. He seemed to be making her task easier. Ashley nodded and looked away.

"We need a verbal response, Miss Spencer," the judge said.

Ashley took a deep breath and let it out. Delilah had told her how important it was that she make a positive identification without hesitation. If Maxfield was going to be punished for what he'd done to her, her family, and her friend, she would have to tell the judge that he was the man she saw at the boathouse.

"I saw Joshua Maxfield that night." She pointed at Maxfield. "He is the man sitting in the court-room with his lawyer."

"Let the record reflect that Miss Spencer has identified the defendant, Joshua Maxfield," Judge Stillman ordered.

"What was the defendant doing when you saw him that night for the first time?" Delilah asked.

"He was walking along the river toward the boathouse."

Delilah paused and consulted her notes. Ashley wished they could stop now but she knew that they couldn't.

"Ashley," the prosecutor asked, "did anything unusual happen shortly after you saw the defendant walking toward the boathouse?"

"Yes."

"Tell the court what happened and what you did."

"I heard a scream. Actually, there was more than one."

"How many screams did you hear?"

"Two."

"Was there time between the screams?"

"Yes, but not much."

"Could you tell who was screaming?"

"A woman. It was a woman's scream."

"What did you do when you heard the scream?"

Ashley looked down. Her voice dropped when she answered.

"I got scared. I froze. I thought about hiding."

"Did you hide?"

"No."

Ashley choked up. She reached again for her glass of water.

"What did you do after the second scream?"

"I went through the woods toward the boat-house."

"Why the boathouse?"

"It sounded like they came from there."

"Did you hear or see anything else before you arrived at the boathouse?" Delilah asked.

"No."

"How close did you get to the boathouse?"

"I was right next to it. I went to one of the side windows and looked in."

"Did you hear anything from your position?"

"Just before I looked in the window I heard a woman shout."

"What did she say?"

"I couldn't tell."

"Why do you think a woman, not a man, shouted?"

"It was high-pitched."

"How soon before you looked in the window did you hear the woman shout?"

"A few seconds."

"What did you see when you looked in the window?"

Memories came flooding back: the body on the floor sprawled against the timber that supported the roof, the body curled into a fetal position on the floorboards. She wobbled in her seat and squeezed her eyes shut.

"Do you want to take a break?" Delilah Wallace asked, alarmed by Ashley's pallor.

"No," Ashley answered in a voice bereft of strength. "I want to get this over with."

"You're certain, Miss Spencer?" the judge asked. "We can recess."

"No," she answered more forcefully. "I can answer the question."

Ashley turned to face Maxfield. She pointed at him.

"He was standing over Dean Van Meter. He was holding a knife. There was blood on the knife. I must have made some sound because he turned toward the window and stared right at me. Then he moved and I saw . . . I saw my . . . my mother."

"Now, let me clarify this point. Did you know the identity of the two women then?"

"No. I couldn't see their faces. It was dark in the boathouse."

"But you could see the defendant?"

Ashley felt stronger now. She glared at Maxfield. "Definitely. It was him. He was very close to the window, holding the knife. There was blood all over it."

"What happened next?"

"I ran and he chased me. I got to the dorm and told the security guard. He called the police."

Delilah checked her notes. She had covered everything she wanted to bring out from Ashley for purposes of the preliminary hearing. The medical examiner's report and the stipulations established that Terri Spencer had been murdered and that Casey Van Meter was in a coma because of an assault. Ashley had placed Joshua Maxfield at the scene of the murder and the assault moments after Ashley had heard two screams. She had also established that a woman had shouted something inside the boathouse seconds before Ashley had seen the defendant holding the bloody knife that had been used to murder Terri Spencer.

"No further questions," Delilah said, regretting that Ashley would now be at the mercy of Maxfield's attorney. She had seen how hard even the friendly questions had been for her witness. Barry Weller was a decent sort. Delilah hoped that he would not be too rough on Ashley.

"Any cross, Mr. Weller?" Judge Stillman asked.

Weller started to say something, but Joshua Maxfield touched him on the arm and whispered in his ear.

"May I have a moment to consult with my client, Your Honor?"

"Of course," Stillman said.

Weller leaned toward Maxfield.

"We need to talk," Maxfield said.

"I'll ask for a recess after I cross."

"No, now. We have to talk right now," Maxfield insisted.

"Look, Joshua, Spencer is rattled. I don't want to give her time to get her legs back under her."

"Cross won't be necessary, Barry. I want to change my plea to guilty."

"What!" Weller said in a tone loud enough to attract attention. He looked around briefly. Everyone in the courtroom was staring at him. Barry lowered his voice.

"Are you serious?"

"Very."

"If you plead, it doesn't mean you'll avoid a death sentence. You understand that the DA can demand a sentencing hearing if she still wants to go for death?"

Maxfield looked over his shoulder at the spectators. Miles Van Meter caught his eye for a moment and Maxfield looked away.

"People are listening to us," he said nervously. "Can we go someplace where we'll have some privacy?" He pointed at the door to the jury room. "Is that a place we can talk?"

"Let me ask the judge."

Weller stood. "May I approach the bench, Your Honor?"

The judge summoned the attorneys to the dais. As soon as Delilah joined him, Weller leaned toward the judge.

"Your Honor, my client and I need to discuss an important matter in private. Could we take a brief recess? Perhaps we could use the jury room."

"This young woman is barely holding on, Barry," the judge said. "I want to get her out of here as soon as possible."

"Without revealing any confidences, Judge, I can tell you that the outcome of our conversation might benefit Miss Spencer."

Judge Stillman looked puzzled.

"I have no objection, Your Honor," Delilah said. She thought Ashley could use a break.

"Very well. You can use the jury room."

The judge called over the court guards and told

them that she was going to let Weller confer with his client during the break. Two guards escorted Weller and Maxfield to the jury room while another corrections officer left the courtroom to watch the door that opened into the hallway.

Judge Stillman ordered a recess and left the bench. The spectators filed into the hall or stood chatting at their seats. Delilah walked over to the witness box.

"How you feeling?" she asked Ashley.

"I wish it was over."

"Me too, but you were good up there and you'll handle Weller's cross just fine if you remember my simple rules."

"Think before I answer, always tell the truth, don't be afraid to say that I don't know an answer, and always ask Mr. Weller to explain his question if I don't understand it."

Delilah beamed. "A-plus, young lady. You're ready for law school right now. Come on down out of that chair and stretch your legs for a while."

Ashley and Delilah walked over to the counsel table. Larry Birch, Tony Marx, and Jerry Philips joined them. The Van Meters asked the DA how she thought the proceedings were going. Delilah said that she had no doubt that Maxfield would be bound over for trial. She complimented Ashley again for doing so well during her direct examination.

"What are they doing in the jury room?" Ashley asked Delilah.

"I don't know."

Wallace did have a hunch but she didn't want to get Ashley's hopes up. The DA suspected that Ashley's testimony had convinced Maxfield that he would lose at trial. She hoped that he was asking his lawyer to negotiate a deal.

"Do you think . . . ?" Before Philips could finish his question, a man in an orange jumpsuit staggered out of the jury room. The guard stepped back, startled, before grabbing him. Delilah stared at the prisoner's face.

"That's Weller, the lawyer," she shouted at the guard as she crossed the courtroom. "Where's Maxfield?"

The guard looked confused.

Delilah pointed at Weller. "This is the lawyer. Your prisoner changed clothes with him. He's escaping."

The guard took one more look at the man he was holding and finally figured out what was going on.

"Watch Ashley," Larry Birch told his partner as

he rushed toward the jury room. Delilah was already inside. A conference table that seated twelve dominated the long, narrow room. The guard who had been posted in the hallway was sprawled on the floor between the table and the corridor door. Larry Birch raced past Delilah and checked the guard for a pulse. He was breathing.

"Get a doctor up here," he told Delilah as he pulled his gun and entered the corridor outside Judge Stillman's courtroom. Two women gasped and moved against the wall. A muscular construction worker had the opposite reaction—he looked ready to take on the armed detective. Birch held up his badge.

"I'm a police detective," Birch said. "Did you see a man in a suit leave this room?"

The man shook his head without ever taking his eyes off Birch's gun. The detective ran down the hall toward the wide marble stairway that led to the courthouse lobby. He held his gun at his side to avoid a panic. Most people rode the elevators. The detective guessed that Maxfield would take the stairs where there was little traffic. The few people he passed were concerned about their cases, or courthouse business, and paid no attention to him. They wouldn't have paid attention to Maxfield, either.

Metal detectors had been set up in the lobby at the front of the courthouse. A number of security guards were screening the lawyers, employees, and litigants who were entering the building. No one was paying any attention to the people who were leaving. Birch walked outside into a crisp, cool afternoon. A summer rain had fallen a short time before, but the sun was shining now and the air was heavy with ozone. He looked up and down the street and across Fourth to the park. There was no sign of Joshua Maxfield.

When Larry Birch returned to the courtroom, Barry Weller was seated at the defense table, surrounded by Judge Stillman, the Van Meters, Delilah Wallace, Tony Marx, Jerry Philips, and Ashley Spencer.

"I walked into the jury room and put my brief-case on the table," Weller was saying. "Maxfield was behind me. Before I could turn, he put on a chokehold. It was so tight I couldn't shout or breathe. He wrestled me to the floor and wrapped his legs around me. It was some kind of wrestling hold. I struggled for a few seconds and passed out. When I came to, I was dressed in Maxfield's jumpsuit and my clothes and briefcase were gone."

"Do you have any idea where he went?" Tony Marx asked.

"No. He never said anything that made me think he'd try something like this. He was planning on writing a book about the case. He seemed resigned to going through a trial."

Marx spotted his partner. "Any luck?"

Birch shook his head. "Did you put out an alert?"

"Yeah. It sounds like Maxfield's been planning this for a while. Weller thinks he was hired because he looks a lot like Maxfield."

Birch studied the lawyer for a moment. "Damn. That never occurred to me."

"Or me," Weller said sheepishly.

A doctor came out of the jury room followed by the guard who had been attacked. The guard looked shaky but he was walking on his own. The doctor spotted Weller and walked over to him.

"Let me take a look at you to make sure you don't need to go to the hospital."

Everyone moved away to let the doctor work. Delilah noticed how pale Ashley looked.

"It's okay," Delilah assured her terrified witness. "We'll protect you."

Ashley sank onto a chair. Her breathing was shallow.

"He's going to run, Ashley," the DA said. "The first time he was captured he was in Nebraska. Maxfield doesn't want to be anywhere near you. He wants to get as far away from Oregon as he can."

Ashley looked like someone who had seen her own death. "Maybe he'll run now," she said in a voice devoid of energy, "but he'll come back for me. He's killed everyone I love and he's tried to kill me. I don't know why he wants me dead but he does and he won't stop."

CHAPTER FIFTEEN

Larry Birch stopped at McDonald's to get Ashley dinner before driving her to the dorm. By the time they arrived, a policeman was sitting outside her room. Birch told her that another officer was patrolling the grounds.

Ashley did not like being the only person in the dorm. After Maxfield's arrest, she was lonely and bored. With Maxfield on the loose, the empty building felt threatening. It was old and musty, with dark wood paneling and little natural light. Without the noise made by the students, Ashley could hear the eerie whine the wind made when it slipped through cracks in the wall. The building creaked, and Ashley was certain that she'd heard scuttling sounds in the walls.

Before she went to bed, Ashley turned out the

lights in her room and stared out the window. The dormitory was next to the science building, and the front faced the quadrangle. Ashley's room was at the rear of the building and faced the woods. Streetlights illuminated a lot of the campus, but there were no lights in the dense forest. When the dorm was full, ambient light from the rooms cast a glow over the trees. The rooms were deserted now, and the only light came from the dim glow of a quarter moon.

Ashley watched the trees sway in the wind. She looked up at the stars. Where were her mother and father? She hoped that there was a heaven or some kind of afterlife where they were together and happy. She wanted to believe that they weren't simply decomposing; that there was something more than rotting flesh and naked bone to mark their time on Earth. A friend of hers was into New Age stuff. She spoke of auras and spiritual energy left behind by the dead. Ashley remembered how she used to feel her father's spirit inside her when she was little and he could not make it to her soccer game, but the brutal murders that had taken her parents from her had also murdered her belief in magic. Ashley had searched for some trace of her parents—their spirit, a soul that lived on when the body was gone—but all she felt was an absence; a cold, hollow feeling that was the opposite of life.

Ashley closed her shades and got into bed. She cried silently as she pulled up the covers. She used to say a prayer at bedtime, but she had not been able to since her father died. Now she just hoped that she would sleep without dreams.

The bedside clock read 2:58 when Ashley woke up. She had finished off a large Coke at McDonald's and had to go to the bathroom. It was hot, and she'd slept in panties and a T-shirt. She remembered the guard and pulled on sweatpants.

The policeman who was guarding her room stood up when he heard the knob turn. He was in his mid-twenties and wore his blond hair in a crewcut. He looked strong. He had been reading **Sports Illustrated,** and Ashley caught him trying to hide it.

"I'm just going to the bathroom," she said, a little embarrassed about having to discuss her toilet habits.

"Okay," he said. Then he smiled. "I'll be here all night."

Ashley closed the door behind her. Low-wattage bulbs created a pattern of shadows and dimly lit spaces on the floor as she shuffled groggily down the hall. The bathroom was just beyond the stairs. Still half asleep, Ashley went into one of the stalls and peed. She was wiping when she heard a noise. It was so quiet in the dorm that she could hear sounds from any place on the floor. She had no idea where this one had come from, but it unnerved her because it sounded like a gasp of pain.

Ashley told herself that she was being paranoid but that wasn't true. She had a lot of justification for her fear. She decided to wait before flushing. If someone was out there she didn't want him to know where she was. She opened the bathroom door wide enough to let her peek into the hallway. Ashley could see the hall outside her room. The guard was still in his chair but he was slumped sideways at an odd angle as if he was sleeping, which made no sense. She had just talked to him. He knew that she was only going to be gone for a few minutes.

Ashley was attracted by a red glow to the left of the police officer. It took a moment to figure out that she was seeing the digital clock on her nightstand. That meant that the door to her room was open. She was certain she had shut it. The digital glow disappeared then reappeared. A shape had passed in front of the clock. Ashley's heart raced.

Joshua Maxfield had killed the guard and he was in her room.

Ashley had to fight to keep from racing down the stairs. She forced herself to move quietly. Halfway to the second-floor landing she heard the sound of her closet door slamming against the wall. She moved faster. Moments later, footsteps pounded along the third-floor landing toward the bathroom.

Ashley stopped in the shadows in the entry hall. Maxfield was going to figure out that she wasn't on the third floor and come looking for her. She could try to hide in the deserted dormitory but it would be easier for Maxfield to trap her in a confined space. There were many more places to hide outside. And there was the officer who was patrolling the grounds! She'd find him and he would radio for help.

Footsteps thudded down the stairs from the third floor. Ashley ran into the night and around the side of the dormitory. Her feet came out from under her and she sprawled on the ground. When she rolled over to stand up she found herself staring into the dead eyes of the other patrolman. His head lolled to one side. The material in the front of his shirt was ripped open where the officer had been stabbed repeatedly. There was also a red gash that started at one side of his neck and ended on the other side.

Ashley fought the urge to throw up and struggled to her feet. Maxfield would be coming fast. She had to run. Ashley raced toward the woods, which were dark and offered many places to hide. When her guards didn't check in someone was bound to come to find out why. Maxfield would not hunt for her all night and risk being discovered. If she stayed concealed until morning she would be safe.

A path led into the woods. Ashley did not take it. She ran along the edge of the forest for several steps then disappeared between two trees. She was just in time. A figure darted across the front lawn of the dormitory and stopped on the quadrangle. He passed under two streetlights and Ashley got a good look at him. He was wearing a ski mask and gloves. Ashley couldn't see his face but he had the height and build of Joshua Maxfield and he looked identical to the man who had killed her father.

The man turned slowly in a circle. He stopped when he faced the woods. He seemed to be staring right at her. Ashley held her breath. She prayed that he would not come searching for her. Her prayers were answered. As Ashley watched, the intruder disappeared into the night.

Ashley suddenly remembered Henry Van Meter and the other people in the mansion. She had to warn them about Maxfield. Ashley was barefoot, and the forest floor had done some damage to the soles of her feet. Fortunately, the Academy was a field of green with lawn everywhere. She hugged the buildings and crept along the side of the dormitory until she reached the dead policeman.

Ashley gagged, squeezed her eyes shut, and took a deep breath. She could not afford to panic. She knelt down and searched for the officer's radio. It was missing. If she was going to warn Henry Van Meter she would have to go to the mansion.

Ashley was hidden by the shadows at the side of the dorm but she would be in the glow of the streetlights if she took even a few steps. She couldn't risk crossing the quadrangle, so she ran behind the dormitory and followed the backs of the school buildings to the end of the quadrangle. She peeked around the corner of the building closest to Administration. She didn't see Maxfield anywhere.

Ashley took a deep breath and sprinted across the open ground to the rear of the Administration building. Now she was on the same side of the quadrangle as the gym, and there was another building to shield her. If Maxfield hadn't seen her sprint to the Administration building, she would be safe.

Ashley reached the rear of the gym when she heard a sound. There was a hill at the back of the building that led down to the soccer field. Ashley dove over the edge and pressed herself against the cold grass. Sneakers scraped against the cement path that circled the gym. Ashley peered over the edge of the hill. A man opened the door to the gym and slipped inside.

Ashley was about to make a run for the mansion when headlights illuminated the street in front of the gym and a police car moved into view. Ashley leaped from her hiding place and raced to the car. She waved and screamed. The car stopped.

"Maxfield's here," she yelled. "He killed my guards. They're both dead."

A muscular black patrolman got out of the car, gun drawn, after telling his partner to radio for backup.

"He's in the gym. I just saw him go in. He has a knife. He cut their throats."

The driver stared at the gym and hesitated. The second officer, a stocky Latino, came around the car after finishing his call for backup.

"She says he's in the gym, Bob."

Bob nodded toward Ashley. "What do we do about her?"

"Don't go in alone," Ashley said. "He already killed two policemen tonight."

"How many exits are there to the gym?"

Ashley was about to answer when they heard sirens. The two officers relaxed. A second police car raced onto the Academy grounds seconds later. Several other patrol cars were close behind.

"You have to send someone to the mansion," Ashley said. "Mr. Van Meter is there."

The officers left her at the car and conferred with the other policemen. Moments later, Ashley was driven to the mansion. She looked out the back window of the car as she drove away and saw several armed men walking around the side of the gym.

Henry Van Meter was standing in the entryway of his home when Ashley arrived. He had heard the sirens and had just finished dressing. After Ashley explained what had happened at the dormitory, Henry told her to wait in the den while he talked with the authorities, and had ordered Mrs. O'Connor to bring Ashley a pot of tea and something to eat.

An hour after she entered the den, Larry Birch

told her that Joshua Maxfield had not been found in the gym or anywhere else. That was all she needed to know to come to a decision. As soon as Birch left, Ashley walked over to the phone. Jerry Philips had given Ashley his home phone number and she'd called him there last week to discuss the sale of her house. Philips sounded groggy when he answered the phone.

"Ashley, what time is it?"

"Five twenty-eight."

"Has something happened?"

"Maxfield tried to kill me tonight."

"Are you okay?"

"Yes, but I have to talk to you."

"Where are you?"

"At Mr. Van Meter's house at the Academy."

"I'll be there in half an hour."

Ashley hung up. She sat in the armchair near the fireplace and closed her eyes. She knew she had drifted off, because Jerry Philips was sitting across from her when she opened her eyes.

"How long have you been here?" Ashley asked.

He smiled. "About an hour."

"Why didn't you wake me up?"

"We all thought that you could use the sleep," Philips said. "Do you want something to eat, some coffee?"

Ashley shook her head. She remembered why she'd summoned Philips, and she was suddenly scared to death.

"You're my lawyer, right?"

"Sure."

"On TV what a client tells the lawyer is private. . . ."

"Confidential."

"Confidential. What does that really mean?"

"The law protects conversations between an attorney and his client so the client can talk freely about her problems without being afraid that someone else will learn what she's said. It encourages full disclosure by the client, so the attorney will have all the facts and be able to give his client good advice."

"So anything I tell you is protected?"

Philips nodded. "Now what is this about?" he asked.

"How much money do I have?"

"I don't have the exact figures, but with the sale of the house, the insurance. . . . I'd guess around five hundred thousand dollars."

"Could you set up an account for me that I could draw from if I wasn't in the United States?"

"Yes."

"Could it be in another name?"

"Ashley, what are you thinking of doing?"

Ashley sat up. Her back was straight and her hands were folded in her lap.

"I'm going away."

"Where?"

"Out of the country."

"Where out of the country?"

"I don't want you to know where. I don't want anyone to know."

"I'll keep anything you tell me confidential. That doesn't mean I can't give you advice. That's why you have a lawyer. Now, where are you planning to go?"

Ashley looked down but did not answer.

"Do you know anyone where you're going?"

"No."

"Do you speak any foreign language?"

"Spanish. I have three years of Spanish."

"What are you going to do when you get where you're going?"

"I don't know." She looked down at her lap. "I just know that I can't stay here. They can't protect me and I can't live like this, locked up, surrounded by guards."

Ashley looked up. "Maxfield won't look for me where I'm going because I don't even know where I'm going. I'll change my name. I'll live cheaply. I'll contact you by email. If they catch him I'll come back."

"This is crazy. I can understand why you're afraid. Your life has been hell. But you're not making sense. Let me see if I can get you in the witness protection program. Maxfield has killed in different states. Maybe I can get the Feds to help you."

"I don't trust them."

"You're frightened now. I can't imagine what you went through tonight and those other times. But you're not thinking straight."

Ashley's hands tightened on each other. "This is what I want to do. If you won't help me I'll find another lawyer."

"Ashley. . . ."

"No, my mind is made up. I have a passport. I'll book a flight over the Internet. All I need is for you to set up an account for me so I can get money to live on."

"This is crazy."

"My life is crazy. Maxfield wants to kill me. He's murdered my family. If I stay here I'll never be able to live a normal life. It will be like I'm the criminal. I'll be locked up, surrounded by guards. I won't be able to go to school. I won't have friends. And I'll be afraid every minute. Don't you see? I have to get away from him."

CHAPTER SIXTEEN

"Ashley Spencer has disappeared," Larry Birch said as soon as he walked into Delilah Wallace's office.

"She what?!"

"She's been living at the Van Meter mansion. Henry Van Meter moved her over from the dorm and hired a team of private guards. This morning, after breakfast, she slipped out. No one has seen her since. Mr. Van Meter called me as soon as he was certain that she was really gone."

"Did Maxfield . . . ?"

"I don't think so. Van Meter has the estate looking like an armed camp. I doubt Maxfield would try to take her from there again."

"So you think she's running away?"

"That's my guess. She definitely took steps to evade the guards. But none of her clothes are missing, and her toothbrush, hairbrush, stuff like that, are still in her room."

Delilah sat back in her chair and shook her head slowly. She looked sad.

"That poor, lonely kid. How frightened she must be. I can't imagine."

Delilah's intercom buzzed. "There's a Jerry Philips at the front desk," the receptionist said. "He wants to talk to you about Ashley Spencer."

"Send him back."

Two minutes later, Jerry Philips was shown into Delilah's office. He looked embarrassed and could not meet the DA's eye.

"Where is she, Mr. Philips?" Delilah demanded. Jerry noticed that she was not calling him by his first name as she usually did.

"I can't tell you."

"Listen, Jerry," the homicide detective said, "Ashley is a material witness in a murder investigation and she's in great danger. . . ."

"You don't understand," Philips interrupted. "I can't tell you because I don't know. Believe me, I tried to find out, but she wouldn't tell me where she was going."

"Then why are you here?" Delilah asked.

"Ashley instructed me to come. She didn't want

you to worry that Maxfield had her. She wanted you to know that she's safe."

"Did you help her get away?"

Jerry looked down at his shoes. "My conversations with Ashley are covered by the attorney-client privilege. I can't tell you what we talked about."

Larry Birch had rarely seen Delilah angry, but she was angry now. She levered her two-hundred-fifty-plus-pound bulk up from her chair and stared at Ashley's lawyer. He avoided her eyes.

"We are talking about a frightened young girl, Mr. Philips. She is a child and she has no business being out in the world on her own."

"I really can't tell you," Jerry mumbled. "You know I'm forbidden by law to reveal client confidences."

"Don't you care about her?" Delilah asked.

Philips looked miserable. "Of course I do. Don't you think I tried to talk her out of this? But she's terrified." He gathered his courage and looked first at the DA then at the detective. "And you couldn't protect her." Now it was Birch and Delilah's turn to look uncomfortable. "That's why she ran. She doesn't think you can stop

Maxfield. She's convinced that he will kill her if she stays in Oregon."

Delilah sat down. "Do you know how to get in touch with her?"

"I can't discuss that."

Delilah started to get angry again but she checked herself.

"If she does contact you, will you ask her to call me or write me? We need to get her back, Jerry. She may think she can hide, but Maxfield will find her if he wants to."

Ashley looked out the window of the plane and felt as if she was floating among the clouds that surrounded her. She was free for the first time since the night Maxfield invaded her home. The feeling was exhilarating and left her giddy with relief. Each mile the plane traveled put another mile between her and her former life. Her fear was fading and hope was building. Before her stretched a future filled with adventure and exotic sights, sounds, and experiences, a future free of terror and despair.

Jerry Philips had tried to get her to change her mind from the moment he met her on the service road that led to the boathouse until he dropped her off at the airport. He hadn't given up until he'd handed her the dufflebag full of clothes and toiletries she'd told him to buy, and five thousand dollars. Ashley's plane ticket was electronic, and she already had her passport.

Ashley's plane would land in Frankfurt, Germany. Then she would take a train to a destination she would decide on in the airport lounge. By operating with spur-of-the-moment choices she hoped to avoid leaving a trail based on her past. She had no favorite places anyway. Everywhere she went would be new and exciting. And every place she went would be free of Joshua Maxfield.

BOOK TOUR

The Present

Miles Van Meter closed the copy of **Sleeping Beauty** from which he had been reading. While the audience applauded, he drank from the bottle of water that Jill Lane had left on the podium.

"Joshua Maxfield's home invasion devastated Ashley," Miles said when the applause died down, "but the loss of her mother, several months later, was a killing blow. Then Maxfield made his spectacular escape from the courtroom and returned to the Oregon Academy that very night to try to murder Ashley.

"The authorities claimed that they would protect Ashley, but she had no faith in them after Maxfield's near miss at the Academy. She fled to Europe and stayed there until the totally unforeseen events that compelled her return to Oregon.

"In the years between his escape and recapture,

Joshua Maxfield went underground. The best efforts of the FBI and international police organizations were of no avail. When interest in the manhunt began to wane, I wrote **Sleeping Beauty** to keep my sister's plight and the memory of her killer in the public eye. I had no idea how successful my tribute to Casey would be.

"Meanwhile, Ashley was living under assumed names and leading the life of a vagabond; staying for short periods in small towns throughout Europe, working odd jobs when she could get them, and drawing money from her account when she had to. But, of course, I didn't know that when I wrote **Sleeping Beauty,** and the original book ended with Maxfield's escape, Ashley's disappearance, and a brief account of the efforts of the authorities to track one of history's most diabolical serial killers.

"And now I'd be pleased to answer your questions."

In the back of the room, a well-built young man dressed in khaki pants and a plaid shirt raised his hand. Miles pointed at him.

"I'm thinking of writing a true-crime book about a real murder case that my cousin was involved in, but I don't know how to get started. There were some things in the case that happened in other states. Can you tell me how you did your research on the other murders that Maxfield committed around the country?"

"Sure. Researching **Sleeping Beauty** wasn't that different from preparing a case for trial. When I'm litigating, I have to interview witnesses, read documents, and learn all of the facts in the case. I approached my book as if I was preparing for Maxfield's trial.

"By the time I started writing **Sleeping Beauty,** the FBI had already done a pretty good job of matching up the fictional murders in Maxfield's novel with real crimes in Connecticut, Montana, and other states. Larry Birch and Delilah Wallace were very helpful. They gave me access to the reports of the Oregon police and the FBI. I also read stories about these crimes in local newspapers. After that it was simply a question of contacting the person in charge of each case in each state. Detective Birch called these people to vouch for me. That helped me get my foot in the door.

"When I traveled to a state, I would contact the detective in charge, read the reports, then interview witnesses. I also visited the crime scenes and read autopsy reports and viewed the crime scene photographs. Some jurisdictions videotaped the crime scene, which really helped me write accurately about what went on."

"Weren't you working as a lawyer during all this?" an older man in a sweatshirt and jeans asked.

"Yes, but my firm was very supportive. On the few occasions I needed it, they gave me time off for my investigation. But I was fortunate, because a few of Maxfield's crimes were committed in cities like Boston, where I traveled frequently on business."

A young man wearing jeans and a T-shirt from a local college raised his hand.

"Mr. Van Meter, I just finished reading **Sleeping Beauty.** I thought it was great. One thing bothered me, though. Everyone always assumed that Joshua Maxfield murdered Ashley's parents, but in light of what happened when Ashley returned to Portland I wonder if Randy Coleman was ever a suspect. Ashley never saw the face of the man who killed her father and tried to kill her after Maxfield escaped. Coleman fit the description of the man who invaded her home and hunted her at the Academy."

"That's right," Miles agreed, "but you're forgetting one thing: Coleman had no motive to murder Ashley until everyone discovered who she really was."

PART TWO
SLEEPING BEAUTY

Two Years Earlier

CHAPTER SEVENTEEN

Ashley chose San Giorgio for her meeting with Jerry Philips because tourists rarely visited the little Tuscan hill town. The narrow, dusty streets were anything but picturesque, and none of the local shops sold goods that would be of interest to vacationers from Wisconsin or Osaka. Its only possible tourist attraction, a thirteenth-century castle, was in disrepair because there wasn't money to maintain it. Weeds had conquered battlements that had kept out human invaders for hundreds of years.

Chestnut trees shaded the piazza. There was a stone church with no famous frescos or relics at one end, and a restaurant at the other. In the center of the piazza stood an uninteresting fountain that was bone-dry at the moment. Ashley arrived an hour early and watched the square from the upper story of the church to make sure that her attorney had not been followed.

Jerry Philips had sent an email requesting an emergency meeting several weeks ago, but Ashley had not checked her messages until two days before, when she'd dropped into a cybercafé in Siena. Lawyer and client had exchanged several frantic messages. Ashley asked why Jerry needed to see her in person. Jerry swore that he should be with her when he explained a matter of the utmost importance. Time was of the essence, he had insisted, and he'd proved it by flying out of Portland the day Ashley agreed to the meeting.

Shortly after the churchbells rang in six o'clock, Philips appeared at the end of one of the cobblestone streets that emptied into the town square. He paused in the shade of a chestnut tree to catch his breath. The sun was still blazing in a clear blue Italian sky and the temperature was in the nineties. Jerry was sweating heavily. He'd had to park in a lot at the base of the hill, because the twisting streets were too narrow for ordinary traffic. The only vehicles he'd seen were small trucks delivering to the shops of the town. When one passed him on the way out of San Giorgio he'd been forced to press himself against a wall to avoid being hit.

Ashley watched Jerry drag himself across the piazza to the restaurant. She'd always liked her lawyer. She remembered how young she thought he was when they first met. Maybe that was it. He'd never seemed that much older than she was, even though he was an adult. She studied him as he scanned the piazza. He was dressing better than he had when they'd first met; he'd switched to contacts, and his hair was shorter. He looked handsome. Ashley smiled. Despite her reservations about meeting anyone who could lead Joshua Maxfield to her, it felt good to see a familiar face.

At the restaurant, two old men dressed in worn brown suits and open-necked white shirts were sipping espresso at a table on the piazza and debating the fortunes of a local football team. Another man, covered in dust—a laborer, a mason perhaps—was eating a sandwich and reading a newspaper. Jerry sat apart from them at a small table that was shaded by an umbrella. He angled his chair so he was completely in its shadow. Ashley saw him check his watch. After a minute he took off his suit jacket and loosened his tie. Ashley left the church.

The trek from the lot had made Jerry thirsty but there was no waiter in sight. He craned his neck toward the door of the restaurant. When he turned back, a woman with short, jet-black hair was sitting down at his table. She was dressed in a powder-blue shirt and tan slacks. Sunglasses hid her eyes. Jerry's face split into a grin.

"I didn't recognize you for a moment," he said. "You look great. The dark hair suits you."

Ashley touched her hair self-consciously. "Blond stands out like neon here."

As she spoke, Ashley checked for signs of danger.

"I'm pretty sure I wasn't followed," Jerry said to allay her fears. "When we hung up I phoned for tickets and I left for the airport two hours later. No one would even know that I was meeting you. I drove straight here as soon as I landed in Florence."

A waiter appeared in the doorway of the café.

"How well do you know this place?" Jerry asked.

"Why?" Ashley asked, quickly looking over her shoulder.

Jerry laughed. "Will you relax? I asked because I'm famished. I've been traveling for twenty hours and all I've eaten is the crap food on the plane. What's good here? This is Italy. They must serve pasta."

The tension drained out of Ashley's shoulders and she laughed, too.

"Sorry. It's just. . . ."

"You don't have to explain. You just have to get me something to eat and drink."

Ashley smiled. "This place is decent if you'll settle for something simple."

"I'll settle for anything that's food."

Ashley waved over the waiter and chatted with him in Italian.

"You sound like a native," Jerry said as soon as the waiter left.

Ashley shrugged. "If you know Spanish, Italian isn't that tough to pick up."

Jerry sat back and studied her. He could not get over how much Ashley had changed. It wasn't just the new hair color. It was the new maturity he saw in her body and face. It suddenly dawned on him that the last time he'd seen Ashley she was a teenage girl. The Ashley sitting opposite him was a woman.

"I've really worried about you," Jerry said. "How are you holding up?"

"I'm okay. I love Italy. I love the quiet." She shrugged again. "I feel safe."

Jerry sighed. He sat back. "You have to come home."

Ashley looked frightened. "I can't."

"You have to. Something's happened. Something that changes everything."

"What?"

"Henry Van Meter is dead. He passed away a week ago."

"I'm sorry," Ashley said. She looked sad. "I liked him. He was very kind. But what does his death have to do with me?"

"He's the one who hired me to come here and explain everything."

"Explain what?"

Jerry paused, trying to find the right words.

"Casey is still in a coma."

Ashley nodded. She wished that Jerry would stop dancing around the reason for his visit.

"While Henry was alive, he and Miles argued about what to do with Casey. Henry wanted to keep her alive and hope for a miracle. Miles wants to take her off life support. Henry was afraid that Miles would be appointed Casey's guardian when he died, and he's trying to do just that. Miles has filed papers with the court asking to be appointed Casey's guardian. The hearing is set for next week."

Ashley looked confused. "What does this have to do with me?"

"Everything." Jerry paused. He looked very uncomfortable. "When you hear what I have to say you'll understand why I felt you needed to be with someone when you learned why I'm here."

"Jerry, please. What is going on?"

Philips reached across the table and took Ashley's hands in his. He looked her in the eye.

"You have to come back to Portland and ask the court to make you Casey's guardian."

"Why would I want to do that? Why would the court even consider me?"

He tightened his grip on her hands. "Casey is your mother."

Ashley's mouth gaped open but she couldn't speak. She pulled her hands away and stared at Jerry as if he was insane.

"I know that this is hard for you to take. . . ."

"My mother?" Ashley laughed harshly. "My mother is dead, Jerry. Joshua Maxfield killed her."

"No, your mother is not dead. Casey Van Meter is your biological mother. I've seen the proof."

Ashley shook her head stubbornly. "Terri Spencer is my mother. I hardly knew Casey Van Meter."

Jerry let out a puff of air. "I knew this wouldn't be easy. Let me explain everything, okay? Then you can make up your mind. Remember I told you that my father died shortly before your father was killed?"

Ashley nodded.

"What I didn't tell you is that he was murdered."

"Oh, Jerry."

"A burglar broke into his house in Boulder Creek and. . . . He beat him to death. Now do you understand why I've tried so hard to help you? Both our fathers died horrible deaths within weeks of each other. I knew exactly what you were going through."

Ashley didn't know what to say.

"The burglar set a fire to cover up his crime. The fire destroyed all of the files that my father took to Boulder Creek with him. I thought that your father's files burned up. That's why I didn't know what was in them when I started representing you.

"A few weeks ago, Henry Van Meter asked me to come to his house. He showed me documents relating to your birth and adoption that he kept in his safe. They prove that Norman Spencer adopted you when you were born."

"Are you saying that Norman wasn't my real father?"

"No, he's your biological father." Jerry paused.

"Look, it's complicated. It took Henry a while to explain everything to me."

"How do you know that he didn't lie to you?"

"I know that he was telling the truth because I found your father's files. Dad must have brought them back to Portland when he met with your mother. They were in a filing cabinet but they'd been misfiled."

"I still don't believe this. It can't be true."

She sounded lost. Jerry reached out and touched her hand again.

"It is true, Ashley. You'll believe me when I explain everything I know. Let me tell you what happened from the beginning."

CHAPTER EIGHTEEN

1

Norman Spencer's father had worked in a lumber mill until a back injury put him on disability. His mother was a checkout clerk in a supermarket. Norman wanted to quit high school to help out, but his parents knew that education was the only way out of hard times for their only child. School was never easy, but Norm struggled to a B-plus average. Sports were easier, and earned him a wrestling scholarship to the state university, where he continued to struggle with the books and found that there were a lot of boys who were better than he was on the mats. Still, by his sophomore year, he was getting A's and B's and was an unspectacular, but sound, member of the varsity.

During the season Norm kept his hair short, because the coach insisted his team wear crewcuts. As soon as the wrestling season ended in his sophomore year, Norm decided to let his hair grow long. Norm's hair was down to his shoulders by the time school ended and he started back to work at Vernon Hock's Texaco in Portland. Even with financial aid and a scholarship for wrestling, his family could not afford to send Norm to school, so he was always working. He'd pumped gas at Uncle Vernon's gas station for the past two summers.

Vernon Hock, who had fought in Korea and was a one hundred percent, true-blue American, gave Norm some shit about his fag hair. But his uncle was also a pretty laid-back guy, so he didn't give him much shit. While he worked, Norm tied his hair in a ponytail and kept it tucked up under his hat so as not to upset his uncle's customers. That helped keep the grease out of it, anyway.

"I got a tow for you," Vernon said one Thursday night. Norm was under the hood of a Buick, working on the carburetor. He pulled his head out and wiped his hands on a rag. "Some broad's stuck out near the turnoff to Slocum Creek Road. She's calling from a house." Vernon gave him the address. "You can pick her up there and she'll take you to the car."

Norm was glad to get out of the garage. The weather was balmy but the garage was stuffy and smelled of gasoline fumes. He took the tow truck and headed out of town with the radio blasting and the window rolled down.

Slocum Creek Road crossed Blair Road a few miles past the new mall in what was still mostly farmland. Streetlights illuminated the area around the mall, but after a mile Blair Road turned pitch-black. Norm had to put on his brights and squint hard to find the address on the mailbox. The house was at the end of a dirt driveway. Norm parked the truck and knocked. A man dressed in chinos and a work shirt opened the screen door. When he saw Norm's grease-stained coveralls, he called out, "It's the tow guy." Then he asked Norm to step inside.

"Thank you, sir," he said, "but I'll wait out here. Don't want to track dirt in."

The man nodded before turning his head to look at a tall, blond girl around Norman's age. The girl was wearing a green Izod shirt and white cotton pants. Her straight blond hair was pulled back in a ponytail, and she was very tan.

"I'm from Hock's Texaco. I hear you've got a problem."

"My car is about a half mile down the road. It won't start."

The girl sounded put out, as if she found it inconceivable that something she owned would betray her.

Norm held open the passenger door of the tow truck. He threw a half-eaten bag of potato chips in the back and brushed at the seat.

"Hop in and we'll have a look."

The girl didn't hesitate. Norm liked that.

They drove to the car in silence, and Norm drew some conclusions about the girl. He figured that she was athletic, smart, self-assured, and way out of his league. Her car was a red Thunderbird convertible, a classic, and it was sitting on a grass strip on the side of the road. Norm added "rich" to his guesses about his passenger. He parked in front of the car and went around to the passenger side to let the girl out. She was already slamming the door shut when he reached the front of the truck.

"Nice car," Norm said. Then he noticed the Stanford sticker.

"You a Cardinal?" he asked.

The girl looked confused for a moment. Then she got it.

"Yes."

"What year?"

"I'm going into my junior year."

"Me, too. I'm at the U of O."

The girl gave him an indulgent smile and the temperature cooled by ten degrees. Norm figured he'd better go about his business and leave the sweet talk to someone from the girl's country club set.

"Can you crack the hood for me."

The girl leaned into the car and sprang the hood release.

"Thanks."

Norm got to work and surfaced a minute later.

"I've got bad news for you, Miss. . . ."

"Van Meter. What's the problem?"

"Your fan belt. It won't take long to fix, but we'll have to do it at the garage. That means a tow."

"Damn."

"Why don't I hook her up and take her in. There's a good chance we've got a belt for the car in the shop. If we do, I'll have her running within a half hour."

The girl waited in the cab while Norm hooked up the Thunderbird to the tow truck. After they'd been driving in silence for a while, a thought occurred to him.

"You said your name's Van Meter, didn't you?"

"Yes."

"Do you have a brother named Miles?"

She nodded.

"He wrestles for Stanford," Norm said, smiling. "We've tangled a few times."

The girl was suddenly interested. "How did you do?"

Norm laughed. "I lost both times, but I made it interesting."

"You don't seem to mind that you lost."

"It's only wrestling. You win some, you lose some."

"That's certainly not Miles's philosophy."

Norm shrugged. "It's just a sport. Something to help you blow off steam. Not real important in the grand scheme. . . . Say, I don't know your first name."

"Casey."

"I'm Norm."

They drove in silence for a while, with Norman stealing glances at his passenger. Being this close made him antsy. Her skin was so tan and smooth. He wondered what it would be like to touch it.

And there were her breasts, which pushed against the golf shirt.

"So," he asked, when he worked up the nerve, "what were you doing in the middle of nowhere, tonight?"

"I was headed home."

"You live out here?"

"At Glen Oaks."

"Isn't that where the Oregon Academy is?" asked Norm, who'd wrestled there once in a tournament sponsored by the school.

She nodded. Norm couldn't think of anything more to say, so they rode in silence for a little more until he decided to go for broke.

"Coming back from a date?" Norm asked, trying his hardest to sound casual.

Casey studied him closely for a moment. "Why would you want to know that, Norman?"

He turned his head and grinned. "I'm fishing to see if you've got a boyfriend."

"And if I don't?"

"Then I might get up the courage to ask you out."

Casey smiled. "You've got balls. I'll say that for you."

Norm was surprised when Casey swore but he liked the fact that she wasn't prissy.

"What if I told your boss that you're propositioning his customers?"

"My uncle owns the gas station. He thinks I should date more. So, what do you say? I've got Thursdays off. I promise I'll scrub off the grease and look presentable."

2

The couple made plans to meet at eight in front of the Fox, a grand old Art Deco movie house on Broadway, but they never saw the movie. Casey cruised by in the Thunderbird at a quarter to eight. She pulled to the curb and flipped Norman the keys.

"You drive," she said.

"I thought we were seeing the show."

"I'm not in the mood."

Norman gladly slipped behind the wheel. He was dying to see how this baby ran and he hadn't been that interested in the movie, anyway. It had just been a vehicle for getting close to Casey.

"Where to, madam?" Norm asked in a phony British accent.

Casey closed her eyes and rested her head against the back of the seat.

"Take the Banfield to Eighty-second."

Norm was tempted to ask where they were going but decided to just play along. The Banfield was the eastbound interstate, and he might get a chance to open up the car if traffic was light.

When they took the exit, Casey gave him some more directions.

"There," she said a few minutes later.

Norm looked in the direction she was pointing and saw the gaudy neon sign of the Caravan Motel. A knot formed in his stomach, but he drove into the lot.

"Park over there," Casey said, indicating a spot fifty feet from the office. As soon as they were parked, she held out a twenty-dollar bill. Norm hesitated. A mischievous grin formed on Casey's lips.

"Don't tell me this is your first time, Norman."

"No," he answered, trying not to sound defensive.

"Too proud to take money from a woman?"

Norm grabbed the twenty.

"Good boy," Casey said with a grin. "Register as Mr. and Mrs. John Smith, a classic. I don't think the clerk will ask why you don't have a ring if you pay cash."

Norm took the money and started to get out of the car. He hesitated.

"I don't have any rubbers."

"Not to worry."

Norm colored when Casey pulled several foil-wrapped condoms out of her purse. She laughed.

"Didn't expect to get laid on the first date, did you? Now get us a room fast, Norman. I'm wet already."

Before Norm could turn on the lights, Casey was stroking his crotch and unbuttoning his shirt. Moments later, they were naked and rolling on top of the bedspread. Casey pushed him down and sucked until he thought he'd explode. Her mouth disappeared just when he was going to come. When he opened his eyes, Casey had turned her body so her crotch was over him and she was commanding him to use his tongue to make her come. In his limited experience, Norm had never gone down on a woman but he was so eager to be touched again that he did as she said. Whenever his efforts slackened, she stroked him for encouragement, but stopped before he was satisfied.

Bringing her off proved easy. He tried to get inside Casey, but she made him bring her to orgasm a second time before she'd touch him again.

When she finally let him inside her he was so excited that he came instantly and collapsed beside her.

"Jesus," he gasped. Casey didn't say anything. After a few seconds she stood up, grabbed her purse and walked to the bathroom. A yellow glow framed her for a moment when she turned on the light. Her back was to him. Norman took in her perfect form, the long, tanned legs, the symmetry of her back, the line of her spine, and her long, golden hair. Then she shut the door and left him in the dark. Norm was covered with sweat. He felt like he'd run a marathon. This was the best sex he'd ever had by miles.

The toilet flushed and Casey came out of the bathroom. In the few seconds that she was standing in the light, Norm thought he saw a trace of white powder on her upper lip. Then the lights went out and she was on him again.

3

For Norm, the next two months were a blur of heavy sex and heavier longings. He and Casey spent every Thursday and Sunday night together, and Norm spent the other days fantasizing about the next time they would be together. The couple made love in motels, forest glens, the alley behind a bar, the back seat of Norm's car, and any other place where the urge overcame them. In all that time, Casey never asked him to Glen Oaks or let him pick her up there. She would not let him call her at home, either. She wouldn't even give him the Van Meters' unlisted number. Casey always called him at the garage to set up their trysts. Norm guessed that she didn't want her folks to know that she was slumming. He was insulted when he thought about it, but mostly he thought about Casey naked and sweating in bed with him.

Then the phone calls stopped. A Thursday and a Sunday went by without seeing Casey. Norm was wound so tight that he almost took off two fingers with a power tool and dropped a mug of hot coffee. Vernon noticed that his nephew was on the prowl but said nothing. He knew Norm was in love, and people in love acted the way Norm was acting.

Norm tried to get the number for the mansion, but the best he could do was the Academy office. Twice, the receptionist promised to give Casey a message asking her to phone. The third time the receptionist told him that Miss Van Meter did not wish to speak to him. Desperate, Norm drove to Glen Oaks. The houseman left him standing outside while his request to speak to Casey was delivered. Moments later, the houseman returned. Casey had instructed him to tell Norm that he was forbidden to try to contact her again and that the police would be informed of any further harassment.

Norm had always known that he was in over his head, but he'd convinced himself that the affair would go on forever. He even had fantasies in which he and Casey married and moved to her estate where he drove the Thunderbird every day and lived in luxury. The threat of police action convinced him that his dreams of marital bliss would not come true. It was a bitter pill. Withdrawal from sex with someone like Casey was as difficult as swearing off heroin. Norm wrote one pain-filled letter, which was never answered, before resigning himself to the fact that he would probably never see Casey again.

Norm's desperate letter contained his return address. The Wednesday after he sent it, Vern told him that he had a phone call. Norm's heart pounded. He wiped his damp hands on a rag as he rushed to the gas-station office.

"Norman Spencer?" a man asked.

"Yeah."

"If you want to find out why Casey dumped you

come alone to the parking lot at Tryon Creek State Park tonight at ten."

"Who . . . ?" Norm started, but the line had gone dead.

Norm walked back to the garage in a trance. The man had not sounded friendly, but there was no question that he was going to the park.

Tryon Creek State Park abutted the campus of Lewis and Clark College's Northwestern School of Law in Southwest Portland. Hiking trails crisscrossed the wooded acres. During the daylight hours the park was a popular spot for lovers to stroll and joggers to run. At ten, the park was dark, and the lot was empty except for a beat-up pickup truck that was parked in a space near the entrance to one of the nature trails.

Norm parked a few spaces down from the truck and walked over to take a look. The night was warm, and he was dressed in a T-shirt and jeans. He bent down and peered through the cab window just long enough to satisfy himself that the truck was empty.

"Spencer," a voice called from the trailhead. When Norm turned, he saw a man standing in the shadows several feet in on the trail. He walked forward, and the man faded into the darkness.

Norm grew wary, but his need to find out what had happened with Casey overrode his common sense. He headed down the trail but the man had disappeared. He stopped and looked around. The voice called out again from farther down the trail.

Norm peered into the night. "I'm getting tired of playing hide-and-seek. If you've got something to say, come out and say it."

There was no answer. Norm was angry. He knew that he should get in his car and drive away, but he did not want his tormentor to know that he was scared, so he rushed up the trail hoping to catch the man off guard. A baseball bat slammed into his shin, taking him off his feet. The pain was excruciating. He came down hard on his head and lay in the dirt, dazed. The second blow crashed across his shoulders.

Norm tried to stand but more blows drove him down. He could see his attackers through a red-tinted haze. There were three of them, and two of them hefted bats. The third reared back and delivered a brutal kick to Norm's ribs. He heard something crack. An electric jolt of pain seared him, and he passed out for a second. When the world came back in focus, Miles Van Meter was squatting next to him, holding a handful of

Norm's hair. He used the hair to lift Norm's head off of the ground. Rage distorted Miles's features.

"You knocked up my sister, you fuck, but you will never see her or your little bastard. If you ever try to contact her again you'll think this beating is the best thing that ever happened to you."

Miles smashed his fist into Norm's nose, crushing it. Then he stood up and nodded. The other two men beat Norm until he passed out.

4

Norm forced himself to drive to the nearest hospital where he was told that he had two cracked ribs, a fractured shin, and a concussion. When he was ready to be released, Norm's parents took him home. His nose was broken, his leg was in a cast, his ribs were wrapped tight, his face was purple and yellow, and he had a splitting headache.

During the next week, Norm was confined to bed and had a lot of time to think. He felt terrible about Casey's pregnancy. They had taken precautions most of the time, but there had been an occasion or two when they'd done without in the heat of the moment. Now she would have to pay for their mistake with her youth. His initial impulse was to do the right thing and marry Casey. He soon realized that marriage was not an option. How could he propose when she wouldn't even speak to him? Norm wanted to believe that her family was keeping them apart, but it was more likely that he'd only been a summer fling for Casey. She'd never really shown any signs of affection. Now that he thought about it, they didn't really have much in common other than screwing. He'd tried to tell her he loved her a few times, but she'd laughed him off. And she had never said she loved him.

Norm was reading **The Oregonian** the first time he thought about the baby as anything more than an abstraction. He was looking for the comics when the name "Casey Van Meter" brought him up short. An item in the society column mentioned that she was going to spend her fall semester in Europe. Norm's first thought was that she was going to have an abortion. He felt cold and sad. It suddenly occurred to him that their baby would look a little like him. Norm was young and never one for long-range thinking, but the concept of immortality came to mind. A child was your immortality. Your child carried your genes after you were dead. If Casey aborted, part of Norm would die.

After further consideration, Norm decided that Henry Van Meter, a strict Catholic, would never countenance an abortion. On the other hand, he had a hard time picturing Casey giving up her dreams and desires to raise a child, knowing what he did about her. The most likely possibility was that Casey would give birth in Europe so no one would know she was having a baby. Then the baby would be put up for adoption. That did not seem right to Norm. He did not want his child to be raised by strangers. He wanted a say in what happened to his child.

If you went by appearances, Ken Philips was the last lawyer you would hire. Nothing about the short, balding man with the potbelly, mangy, gray-specked beard, and mismatched clothes hinted at his brilliance or his success. Philips's office was small and furnished with the secondhand furniture he had purchased when he opened for business fourteen years before. There were no clippings on the wall advertising his courtroom victories. Instead of his diplomas he had framed his children's first kindergarten art and a set of his wife's photographs of the Oregon coast.

Unpopular causes were Philips's passion. As soon as he was awarded his law degree, he had gone to the Deep South in the darkest days of the civil rights movement to represent blacks in violence-plagued voter registration drives. During the Vietnam War, he was the war protesters' first line of legal defense. When he wasn't involved in politics, Ken Philips earned a good living as a personal-injury lawyer.

"How does the other guy look?" Philips asked as soon as his secretary left them alone.

"Much better than me."

When Philips laughed, his body jiggled like Santa Claus.

"So, do you want me to sue the bastards?"

"I just want to ask you some questions, if that's okay. But I don't have much money."

"We can talk about the money later. Let me hear the questions."

Norm looked down at his shoes. He had not thought about what he would say if he gained an audience with Ken Philips. It had taken all of his courage to go to the lawyer's office.

"Are you in some trouble with the law?" Ken prodded.

"No. I don't think so. It's more like a personal thing with a girl." He took a deep breath. "Mr. Philips, let's say a girl gets pregnant and she wants to give the baby away. What about the guy, the father?"

"I don't follow you."

"There's this girl. We slept together. Had sex. I think she wants to give our baby away. I don't think it's an abortion. Her dad is Catholic. He sent her to Europe to have the baby and I want to know my rights."

"How long have you known this girl?"

"Just for the summer. I work at a gas station and my uncle sent me out to tow her car. We got to talking and I asked her out."

"You work at the gas station full-time?"

"In the summer. I'm at Oregon. I'll be a junior."

"How old is the girl?"

"Nineteen. She goes to Stanford."

Philips leaned back and tented his fingers on his ample stomach. "So we've got a summer romance here that got out of control?"

Norm colored. "We really tried to be careful. But a couple of times. . . ." He swallowed.

"How do you know she's pregnant?"

Norm pointed to his face. "Her brother and some of his friends did this after he found out. And she stopped seeing me. She won't take my calls. I went over to her house but she wouldn't see me. She said she'd call the cops if I tried to talk to her."

"Did you tell the cops about the beating? That the brother did it?"

Norm shook his head. "It didn't seem right. If it was my sister and some guy did that. . . ." He looked down. "I guess I felt I had it coming."

Philips nodded to show that he understood. "Why have you come to see me?"

"Like I said, Casey's folks sent her to Europe. If it's an abortion I guess I'm too late. But if she's having the baby and is going to give it away I don't want that."

"Do you want to marry the girl?"

"If she wanted me to I would, but I don't think she wants to marry me. Her dad probably wouldn't let her, anyway."

"Why is that?"

"She's really rich. Besides, I don't think she loves me."

"Do you love her?"

"I like her. We get along but . . . I don't know."

"If you don't want to marry her and she doesn't want to marry you and the child is probably going to be put up for adoption, I don't understand what you want from me."

Norman looked across the desk at Ken Philips.

His hands twisted around each other and he hunched forward.

"Mr. Philips, can a man raise a baby? Do I have any rights to my kid?"

"You want to raise the child?"

"I've thought about this. It's my kid, too, isn't it? I don't want a stranger taking care of my baby. It doesn't seem right."

"How old are you?"

"Nineteen. I'll be twenty in a few months."

"Do you have any idea how hard it is to raise a child? It's a full-time job. How would you go to college? How could you support the baby and take care of it?"

"I can work. I'd get a job and go nights to finish school. I can go to Portland State."

"Who would watch the baby while you were working and going to school?"

Norm hadn't thought about that. "My father is on disability. He's home all day."

"And he's willing to take care of an infant? Have you talked to him, or your mother, about this?"

"No, but they've always stood by me," Norm answered stubbornly.

"How do you know that this girl won't want the baby?"

"I don't for sure. Like I said, she won't talk to

me, so I can't ask her anything. But I know Casey. She's not the type to keep a baby. She likes to party, she's ambitious."

"You could be wrong about her. Maybe she does want the baby."

"Then why is she in Europe? And, even if she does want it, wouldn't I still have rights? I'm the father."

Philips was quiet for a few minutes while he thought about the case. He liked this earnest young man. There weren't many teenage boys who would be willing to give up everything to raise a child.

"Who is Casey's father? Maybe I could talk to them on your behalf."

"Henry Van Meter."

Ken Philips blinked. "The Van Meters of Van Meter Industries?"

Norm nodded. "Does that make a difference?"

Philips laughed. "Of course it does. Henry Van Meter is one of the most powerful men in this state and a totally ruthless bastard. If Henry doesn't want you to have custody, there will be a no-holds-barred battle and you will be on his shit list forever."

Norm's face dropped. He looked pathetic. "So you won't do it?"

Philips shook his head slowly. "I didn't say that."

He leaned back and rested his chin on his hands. Norm waited, shifting nervously in his chair. Finally, Philips sat up. He had an idea but he didn't want to discuss it with his young client just yet.

"I need to meet with your parents," Philips said. "I'm not going any further until I've talked with them."

Norm had been afraid of this, but he guessed there was no way to avoid it.

"What about the money? Can you tell me what this will cost?"

"Don't worry about my fee right now. You're a minor, and we're not going to do a thing if your folks won't support you."

"I guess you have to talk to them."

"You guess right. And there's something else I have to do. Sit tight while I get my camera."

5

Anton Brucher clothed his lean, storklike frame in hand-tailored silk suits. His sunken cheeks and the dark circles under his eyes were a testament to the hours he put in on behalf of his clients. Brucher was a hard and humorless advisor with a finely honed intellect and no perceptible morals. He viewed lawyers like Ken Philips, who worked for Communists, Negroes, and the like, with distaste, but he did not underestimate Philips's intelligence.

Henry Van Meter studied Ken Philips with disdain from the end of the conference room. Van Meter's jet-black hair was swept back from his high forehead. His violent eyes and craggy nose warned of a rock-hard temperament and a philosophy that had no room in it for mercy. Henry had fumed at the idea of meeting with Philips, and consented only when Brucher warned him that the lawyer had ruined the lives of several powerful men who had chosen to ignore him.

Brucher, Platt and Heinecken occupied the top two floors in an office building in the heart of Portland. They were meeting in a small conference room located on the second of these floors, in the rear, to lessen the risk of Henry being seen with Philips. When Brucher introduced Norman's lawyer, Van Meter did not extend his hand.

"What is it you want?" Henry asked without preamble.

"A peaceful solution to a difficult problem."

"I know of no problem that involves me and your client. I'm only here because Anton insisted that I listen to you."

Philips smiled. "I'm glad there isn't any problem between you and Norman Spencer. He's a fine young man who's only interested in doing what is right. If we can agree to resolve this matter amicably, Norman and your family will benefit."

"You're being obtuse, Mr. Philips. Please come to the point."

Philips's head bobbed. "You're right, Mr. Van Meter. Forgive me. I'll be blunt. Norman and your daughter, Casey, had a summer romance. Your daughter became pregnant. Now she's somewhere in Europe, supposedly for a semester abroad, but I'm guessing it has something to do with her pregnancy.

"You're Catholic, so abortion is probably not on the agenda. I think she'll carry the baby to term and put it up for adoption. If that's the case, Norman wants to raise the baby. He wants to adopt. That's why I'm here, to work things out."

Van Meter's features tightened as Philips spoke. He was livid by the time the lawyer finished.

"Your client is lucky that I'm not suing him for

slander, which I will if you breathe one word of this scandalous accusation outside this room."

"Your daughter isn't pregnant?"

"The private life of Mr. Van Meter's daughter is none of your business," Brucher said.

"I beg to differ with you, Anton," Philips answered calmly. "If she's carrying my client's child it is definitely my business. It will become the business of the courts if you and Mr. Van Meter persist in insulting my intelligence and threatening my client."

Philips turned to Henry Van Meter. "If we sue for custody, your daughter will be fodder for every gossipmonger in the state. Is that what you want?"

"How much?" Brucher asked.

Philips shook his head in disgust. "Now that is insulting. But I'll let it pass. Norman isn't after Mr. Van Meter's money. He is a very moral young man who wants to do what is right."

"Your client has been misinformed," Henry said. "My daughter is studying abroad. I'm not convinced that she even knows this person. She never mentioned him to me."

Philips took several photographs of Norm's battered face and laid them on the conference table.

"If Casey doesn't know Norman, and she isn't pregnant, what was your son's motive in beating my client to a pulp?"

"Miles did not do this," Henry said after casting a brief glance at the pictures.

"He'll have a chance to prove that at his trial," Philips said.

"Now you're threatening my son?" Van Meter asked, outraged.

"I'm not threatening anyone. I'm just making certain that you understand that many people will be hurt and embarrassed if you continue to deny the truth. I would think that you'd be happy to have this problem off your hands. You might even have a personal interest in the child's welfare, Mr. Van Meter. The baby will be your grandchild."

Philips paused for a moment to let what he'd said sink in.

"Would you step outside for a moment so I can confer with my client?" Brucher asked.

"Sure."

Ken Philips smoked a cigarette in the hall while Brucher and Van Meter conferred. They called him back twenty minutes later.

"We don't concede that there is any merit to your claim, Ken," Brucher said, "but, hypothetically, if Casey is pregnant and agreed to let Mr. Spencer adopt her baby, would Mr. Spencer be willing to refrain from any future contact with the Van Meters and to agree to keep the identity of the child's mother secret?"

"Let me talk to my client."

CHAPTER NINETEEN

"Your father agreed to Henry Van Meter's terms," Jerry Philips explained to Ashley. "His parents helped him raise you. Norman worked during the day and went to Portland State at night to get a degree. That's where he met Terri. They fell in love and Norman told her about you. Getting a ready-made family wasn't something Terri had bargained for, but she loved Norman and she fell in love with you."

"How do you know all this stuff about my parents' private life?" Ashley asked.

"My father had notes of interviews with your father in his files, and Henry told me a lot. My dad's point about you being his grandchild hit home. Henry was a bastard, but he was a bastard who wanted his line to continue. He assumed that Miles or Casey would have other children some-

where down the line, but you were his first grandchild, and he had an investigator from Brucher's
law firm keep track of you and Norman."

"He spied on us?"

Jerry shrugged. "I don't know if he thought of it
that way. At some point he realized that neither of
his children was going to give him another grandchild anytime soon, maybe ever. Then he became
ill. Once he decided that you were the last of his
line, he watched you more closely."

Ashley sat back. Her life had been an illusion
orchestrated by her father, Henry Van Meter, and
men she'd never met. How could her father and
Terri have lied to her all these years?

"Does Miles know about this?"

"Only Henry, Anton Brucher, my father, Norman, his parents, and Terri knew until Henry told
me."

"So Dean Van Meter never knew I was her
daughter?"

"As far as I know, Casey never learned who
adopted her child."

"Then how did I get the scholarship to the
Academy? After what you've told me, I don't believe it was chance."

"Henry arranged for the scholarship after your
father was murdered. He also talked to someone

at Brucher, Platt about putting you in his will shortly before your father was murdered, but he had his stroke and Casey was hurt and he never got around to it. He asked me about drafting a new will for him when he hired me to find you. Then he died."

"Why would he care about me all of a sudden? He'd never done anything for me before."

"He changed after the stroke almost killed him. He became very religious and he developed a social conscience. When he was younger, Henry had no sympathy for or interest in the poor. He believed in a class system run by men like his father who had started with nothing and became rich. The Academy started as an elite boys' school and he didn't let in girls until Casey was old enough to attend. In recent years, he started giving scholarships to deserving minority students and children of the poor."

"That was big of him," Ashley said bitterly. "And now he's trying to manipulate me from the grave to get me to rescue a selfish bitch who thought nothing of giving me away so I wouldn't interfere with her fucking and partying."

"Like it or not, Casey Van Meter is your mother. If she comes out of her coma who knows what might happen between you."

"Why should I care if anything happens? She never gave a damn about me."

"Ashley, I know this has hit you hard. It's overwhelming. Don't make any decisions now. Give yourself some time to think it through. The hearing is next week. We've got some time."

"If I go back, Joshua Maxfield will know where I am. Why should I risk that? What's the chance that she'll come out of her coma, anyway?"

"Henry invested a lot in a biotech company that's working on a drug that offers some hope. It's being administered to Casey as part of a trial."

Ashley's face was tight with anger.

"She gave me away, Jerry. I was nothing to her. Did she ever even try to find out what happened to me? Has she ever shown any interest in me at all?"

"I don't know," Jerry answered softly. "Look, you're right. Casey was selfish. . . ."

"**Is** selfish. Being unconscious doesn't change her. She's a self-centered bitch. I'm not going to risk my life to save her. I don't care if she dies."

Jerry could think of no argument to persuade her, so he said nothing.

"And my father, Terri. . . . They lied to me my whole life. How could they do that?"

"They did it because they loved you. Don't let

your anger poison you. Your father was coura-
geous. Think about it. He could have forgotten
about you. It would have been easy. I bet you
ninety-nine out of a hundred guys in his situation
would have breathed a big sigh of relief when they
found out that Henry Van Meter was tidying up
their mistake and it wasn't going to cost them a
penny.

"He was poor, Ashley. To finish school he had to
work all day and go nights. He gave up his scholarship, his normal life. He did it all for you. And
Terri came through for you, too. How many
young women would have run as soon as Norman told them that he had a kid? But she didn't.
She took you in, she made you her daughter."

As Jerry talked about her family, Ashley's anger
faded. When he finished, she looked exhausted.

"It's been so hard, Jerry, hiding all the time, living from moment to moment. Now this."

"I know. I can't imagine what you've been going through."

The waiter walked out with their dinner, and
they stopped talking. As soon as the waiter left,
Jerry dove into his food. He was famished and he
wanted to give Ashley time to think. Ashley
picked at her dinner, as she tried to grasp what
Jerry had just told her.

"This was good," Jerry said when he was finished.

Ashley snapped out of her trance and looked at Jerry's plate. There wasn't a strand of pasta left.

"I guess you were hungry," she said.

Jerry smiled sheepishly. "I told you I was starving." He wiped his mouth with his napkin and drank some more wine. "I need a place to stay. Is there a hotel you can recommend?"

"I have an apartment just north of Siena. It's not far away. You could stay with me. There's a guest room."

"I don't want to impose."

"I'd really like it if you stayed. I don't want to be alone tonight."

"That settles it then."

"You're very kind, do you know that?"

Jerry blushed. "I'm just doing this so I can up my billable hours. I've got to pay the rent, you know."

Now it was Ashley's turn to reach across the table and lay her hand on top of Jerry's.

"Thank you," she said.

It was dark by the time they arrived at Ashley's apartment. It was above a butcher shop, and the butcher was her landlord. She gave Jerry a tour. There was a small front room, a smaller kitchen, a bathroom with a narrow shower, a bedroom, and another room with a pullout sofa and a small dresser.

The apartment was sparsely furnished. There were no pictures or posters on the walls, or knick-knacks on the shelves. It had the feel of temporary occupancy, a place that could be vacated on the spur of the moment.

Ashley kept a few pictures on her nightstand. Jerry thought he might have seen them in Ashley's dorm room at the Academy. In one photograph, Terri and Norman Spencer smiled at the camera from the front lawn of the house in which Norman was murdered. In another, Terri and Norman flanked Ashley, their arms over her shoulders, large smiles plastered on the face of each member of the family. The last photograph had been taken after the district soccer finals. It showed the Eisenhower team with Ashley front and center holding the championship trophy. The pictures made Jerry sad. He tried to imagine what life must have been like for Ashley since she fled to Europe. Lonely was the first word that came to mind. Ashley had not known Italian, she had no friends, and she could not confide in anyone or get too comfortable in one place. Yet she had survived. She was tough.

Ashley found a pillowcase and some sheets and led Jerry into the room with the pullout sofa.

"You're in here," she told him. "I'm going to wash up while you settle in."

Jerry put his clothes in the dresser and set up his bed. When he was done, he joined Ashley at the kitchen table. She had changed into a T-shirt and shorts and was sipping some wine.

"Want some? It's a good local chianti."

"No thanks. I'm exhausted. One drink would put me out."

"I'm strong. I'd get you into bed."

Jerry laughed. "How long have you been living here?" he asked.

"Five months. It's the longest I've stayed in one place."

"Made any friends?"

"A few. There's a women's football club. I've been playing for them. They don't know my real name or anything about me. They think I'm taking a year off from college."

"That's good, that you have friends."

"It's made me feel like I belong, but it's hard living a lie. I have to be careful to keep my fictitious life straight. I've made my story simple but I always have to be on guard."

"Where do you play?"

"There's a men's pro team in town. We use their stadium. There's a league. We play games on the weekends. Our crowds are small, but they're enthusiastic. It's fun."

"Do you still have your old stuff?"

"I'm rusty but I'm holding my own."

During the next hour, Ashley filled him in on what she'd done since fleeing the States. At some point, Jerry started to yawn. A few times, his eyes closed.

"It's time for you to go to sleep," Ashley said.

"Good thinking. I'm so exhausted I'm afraid I'll pass out."

Jerry stood up.

"It's good seeing a familiar face again," Ashley said.

"It's good seeing you again, too."

They were standing close together. They both felt awkward. Jerry wanted to kiss her goodnight but was afraid she would misinterpret his action. Suddenly he remembered something that gave him an excuse to break the tension.

"I brought you something."

"What?"

"Wait here."

He went into the guest room and rummaged around in his suitcase. When he returned he was holding a folded sheet of paper.

"You know how I told you I found the file my father kept on your father's case?"

Ashley nodded.

"I found this in it. My dad wrote it to your dad after he graduated from college. I thought you might want it."

Ashley took the letter.

"Well, that's it for me," Jerry said. "See you to-morrow."

Jerry left the kitchen, and Ashley put the wine-glasses in the sink with some plates that were left from lunch. As she washed the dishes she thought about Jerry. The first time they'd met he was in his mid-twenties and she was a teenager. They seemed ages apart. Now he didn't seem that much older.

She could hear Jerry moving around in his room, settling into bed. It was odd having some-one else in her apartment, especially a man. She had not let herself get involved with anyone since running from Portland. Not that she would ever get involved with Jerry. He was her lawyer. Their emails had mostly been about business, although he always asked how she was doing and offered her encouragement. She didn't know much about him, anyway. He didn't wear a wedding ring but that didn't mean he didn't have a girlfriend. And he was educated. She didn't even have a high school diploma.

Ashley shook off her thoughts and went to her room. She wanted to read the letter but waited until she was in bed. There were two holes in the top of the paper. They'd been made so it could fit on the metal prongs in a file. The copy had been made with carbon paper and the letter had been typed on a typewriter, not a word processor. Some of the words were smeared.

Dear Norman:
I wanted to drop you a note to thank you for inviting me to your graduation ceremony at Portland State. I was very moved when you carried Ashley on stage to accept your diploma. I know that this must have been a terrific moment for you, but it was also a terrific moment for me. Law is a tough profession. There are a lot more downs than ups. But seeing you, your daughter, and Terri, and you holding

that diploma, made up for a lot of disappointments. As you know, I have a son, Jerry. Some parents want their son to grow up to be the president of the United States or the quarterback of a pro football team. I want my son to grow up like you. You have been an inspiration to me. Good luck with your teaching job next year. Congratulations again,
Ken

Ashley's throat constricted as she read the letter and she fought to keep from crying. There was a picture in one of her folks' albums of Norman Spencer carrying her onto the stage at Portland State when he accepted his diploma. She had seen it a few times but never appreciated the sacrifice that her father and Terri had to make to bring about that moment. Then her father had made the ultimate sacrifice when he rescued her from Joshua Maxfield.

Ashley closed her eyes. She thought about the last moments she'd shared with her father, something she had tried to block out since the night he died. He had been in pain; he had been on the verge of death, yet he had smiled, because he knew that she would be safe. If she stayed here she would be safe, but her father had not sacrificed his life so she could grow old hiding in a small, dark apartment.

Ashley got out of bed and walked into the hall. The door to the guest room was closed. She knocked on it.

"Yeah?" Jerry said. He sounded half asleep.

"Can I come in for a second?"

"Sure."

Ashley opened the door. Jerry was under the covers. She stood in the doorway.

"This isn't a life, Jerry. I have to lie all the time, I'm always looking over my shoulder. I can't have any real friends. Sometimes I wonder if Joshua Maxfield is interested in me anymore. What if he doesn't care and I'm holed up here, scared to death of someone who doesn't even think about me anymore?

"And there's Casey. That's very . . . confusing. I've gotten used to having no one, but now I find out I have a mother." She looked down. "I want to go home."

"Then I'll take you. We can leave whenever you want to go."

"I want to go as quickly as possible."

"We will. I'll take you home."

CHAPTER TWENTY

"Look at this," Jerry said as they walked toward their gate in the airport in Florence.

They were in front of an airport shop that sold magazines and books. One shelf had paperbacks in English. Jerry walked over to it and took down a copy of **Sleeping Beauty.** A black-and-white photograph of a smiling Casey Van Meter graced the cover.

"Have you read it?" Jerry asked.

"No."

"Miles did a good job. It's very accurate. Do you want me to get it for you for the trip home?"

"Thanks, Jerry, but I really don't want to read it. I don't want to bring back bad memories. I know what happened to my parents and Casey."

Ashley paused. If Jerry was right, Casey was also her parent. It was strange thinking about the dean in that way. She still had trouble getting her head around the idea that the icy, elegant blonde she'd met on her first visit to the Oregon Academy had carried her inside her body for nine months and had given birth to her.

Last night, Ashley had looked in the mirror and tried to see something that reminded her of Casey Van Meter. They both had blond hair but Casey was tall and willowy while Ashley was stockier and more muscular. Their complexions were similar. After several years in Italy Ashley's skin was as tan as she remembered Casey's.

The dean had been strong and self-possessed. Ashley remembered the way she'd dealt with Randy Coleman when her husband had accosted her at the Academy pool. Was she like that? She was a leader on the soccer field. In high school, the girls always looked to her to show them the way. Even though she was a foreigner and new in town, the women on her team in the village saw her as their leader.

Jerry put back the book and they sat down at their gate. Ashley looked around at her fellow passengers. Some seemed excited. Many seemed tired or bored. Five years before, when she'd gone to the airport in Portland, Ashley had felt that she was on the brink of a great adventure, that she

was flying to freedom. Today, Ashley was frightened. She hoped that Joshua Maxfield was not interested in her anymore, she hoped that Casey
Van Meter would come out of her coma filled
with love for her long-lost daughter, but she knew
that both of these dreams could become nightmares.

A town car met Jerry and Ashley at the airport
and drove to an apartment that he had rented under his name. Jerry told the driver to wait while he
helped Ashley carry her bags up to the apartment. He had called ahead and had his secretary
stock the refrigerator. She probably thought that
he had a mistress. Jerry smiled at the thought. His
love life had been pretty dull since he'd ended a
two-year relationship with an ambitious stockbro-
ker. She had dropped into a deep depression after being laid off when the market tanked, and
had finally moved to New York when a new job
opened up. In retrospect, Jerry believed it was for
the best. He hadn't been interested in any of his
infrequent dates since she'd left.

"Is this okay?" Jerry asked after Ashley made a
brief inspection.

"Yeah, it's fine."

"It's only rented for the month, so you can
move out if it doesn't suit you."

"No, I like it."

"I paid for cable," Jerry said, pointing to the TV. "You can catch up on all the bad television you missed while you were away."

Ashley walked over and kissed her attorney on the cheek. "You've been so great, Jerry. I couldn't have gotten through this without you."

"Hey," Jerry said, embarrassed by Ashley's show of affection, "we're a full-service law firm."

They stood inches apart in awkward silence for a few seconds. Then Jerry took a step back.

"The hearing is at ten. I'll pick you up at nine-thirty."

"I'll be ready."

"See you then."

"Okay."

"Sleep tight."

Ashley walked to the front window and watched Jerry get in the car. She stayed at the window until the taillights disappeared. Jerry had been fantastic. He was so steady. He made her feel safe. But the feeling would not last. Tomorrow, everyone would know that she was back.

CHAPTER
TWENTY-ONE

The Multnomah County Courthouse, a massive concrete building that took up a city block, looked as grim and ominous as it had on the day five years ago when Ashley testified at Joshua Maxfield's preliminary hearing. There was a short line at the metal detectors in the lobby when Ashley and Jerry Philips arrived. Her attorney was dressed in a gray suit, white shirt, and pale-yellow tie. She was wearing a black suit they had purchased in Florence before they left.

As soon as they cleared security, Jerry led Ashley up the stairs to the third floor, four marble hallways built around a central airshaft. The Honorable Paula Gish was hearing cases in a modern courtroom in the back corridor. Judge Gish was a heavyset woman in her early forties with short brown hair and thick glasses. When Ashley and Jerry walked in, Gish was thumbing through a set of pleadings while a white-haired attorney droned on about an order for attorney fees.

After Ashley and her lawyer took seats in the last row, she looked at the spectators. There weren't many of them, so she had no trouble spotting Miles Van Meter. He was sitting in the front row next to a balding, overweight African-American who dressed as elegantly as Miles.

Ashley was surprised to see Randy Coleman seated a few rows down on the other side of the aisle. He was wearing a shabby suit very different from the stylish getup he had worn when he accosted Casey at the pool. Ashley guessed that the intervening years had not been kind to Coleman. Sitting next to Casey's husband was a short, athletically built man with receding sleek, black hair. He was clutching an attaché case, and Ashley assumed he was Coleman's lawyer.

An attractive young woman with a steno pad was seated in the back of the courtroom. Given the notoriety that **Sleeping Beauty** and the case that inspired it had achieved, Ashley was not surprised to discover a reporter covering the guardianship proceedings. She was surprised to see Larry Birch seated in the back of the room.

The detective looked at Ashley for a second then looked away. She guessed that her black hair and dark glasses had fooled him.

Judge Gish ruled on the attorney fee request and the clerk called **In the Matter of Casey Van Meter: Petition for Appointment of Successor Guardian and Conservator.** Miles and the black man stood up and walked to counsel table.

"If it please the court, I am Monte Jefferson and I'm representing Miles Van Meter, Casey Van Meter's brother and the son of Henry Van Meter, who was Casey's guardian and conservator until his recent death."

He was about to continue when Randy Coleman's attorney led his client to the other counsel table.

"Anthony Botteri, Your Honor, appearing on behalf of my client, Randy Coleman, Casey Van Meter's husband. Mr. Coleman is also seeking to be appointed as his wife's guardian and conservator."

"Your Honor should not consider Mr. Coleman's petition," Jefferson said calmly. "When Ms. Van Meter was attacked, she was divorcing Mr. Coleman because he beat her up and was cheating on her. The court ruled against a similar request by Mr. Coleman soon after Ms. Van Meter went into her coma. He's a gambler and a small-time crook who's only interested in Ms. Van Meter's money."

Coleman started to say something but Botteri laid a firm hand on his client's forearm.

"It's unfortunate that an attorney of Mr. Jefferson's lofty stature has to stoop so low," Botteri said. "My client is a Las Vegas businessman. Living in that city does not make him a gambler or a criminal."

"Mr. Botteri has a point about your accusations, Mr. Jefferson," the judge said. "Let's try to keep this hearing civilized."

"My apologies, Judge, but I believe the record of this case supports my assertions."

Judge Gish addressed Coleman's attorney. "Mr. Botteri, I am new to this case, but I did review the file and there is a ruling by the court choosing Henry Van Meter, Ms. Van Meter's father, over your client. It does mention an assault on Ms. Van Meter and a police record."

"From many years ago, Judge," Botteri said. "And there are changed circumstances. Mr. Van Meter has left a very important piece of information out of his petition."

"What is that, Mr. Botteri?"

"To put it as bluntly as I can, Your Honor, Miles Van Meter needs your ruling appointing him Casey Van Meter's guardian so he has legal authority to kill his sister."

"That's outrageous," Miles shouted.

"Are you telling the court that you don't want to pull the plug on your sister's life-support machines?" Botteri challenged Miles.

"Your client never loved my sister. He's only after Casey's money."

"Gentlemen," Judge Gish said as she rapped her gavel for order.

"I have support for our position," Botteri said. He took several sheets of paper out of his attaché, handed one to Monte Jefferson, and walked to the dais.

"This is an affidavit from Dr. Stanley Linscott, Casey Van Meter's treating physician. It recounts a conversation in which Mr. Van Meter asked about the steps he would have to go through if he wished to have my client's wife taken off life support."

"May I see a copy of that affidavit?" Jerry Philips asked. While Miles and Botteri were arguing, he and Ashley had passed through the bar of the court. Miles turned and saw Ashley. He stared at her for a moment. Then his jaw opened in surprise.

"Who are you?" Judge Gish asked.

"Jerry Philips, Your Honor. I represent Ashley Spencer, who also wishes to be appointed Ms. Van Meter's guardian and conservator."

"What is the basis of your client's request, Mr. Philips?" the judge asked.

"Ashley Spencer is the daughter of Casey Van Meter, her only child."

Miles gaped at Ashley, then engaged in a frantic whispered conversation with his lawyer. Shock also registered on Randy Coleman's face.

Jerry Philips handed several documents to opposing counsel and the judge. "This is Miss Spencer's petition asking to be appointed as her mother's guardian. Attached to it is a signed affidavit from Henry Van Meter outlining the facts that support Ashley Spencer's claim that she is Ms. Van Meter's daughter. I have attached other documents supporting the claim."

Coleman and his lawyer engaged in a heated conversation as they read through the documents Jerry had given to them. When they finished, Botteri addressed Judge Gish.

"My client tells me that his wife never had a child. This woman's mother is Terri Spencer. She was murdered at the same time Casey Van Meter was beaten into her coma."

"Terri Spencer did raise Ashley as her daughter," Philips said, "but Casey Van Meter is Ashley's biological mother."

"Mr. Jefferson, what do you have to say?" the judge asked.

"This is the first time that my client has heard Ms. Spencer's claim."

"But it's not the first time that someone in your firm has been aware of the fact that Miss Spencer is Casey Van Meter's daughter." Jerry handed copies of a motion for discovery to the judge, Jefferson, and Botteri. "You and Miles Van Meter are both in the Brucher firm, aren't you?"

"Yes," Jefferson answered as he scanned the document. "The firm has always handled the Van Meters' business and personal affairs."

"Norman Spencer, Ashley's father, had a summer love affair with Casey Van Meter when they were in college. Ms. Van Meter became pregnant but she kept this fact from Norman. Henry Van Meter arranged for Ashley to be adopted. Norman found out and hired my father, Ken Philips, to fight for Ashley. After negotiations with Henry and his attorney, Norman Spencer was permitted to adopt Ashley in secret. Anton Brucher and your firm handled the matter. I want the court to see the files. They should prove that Ashley Spencer is Casey's daughter."

"These files would be so old that they might not exist anymore," Jefferson said. "And even if they do exist, I can't agree to turn them over. They're protected by attorney-client privilege."

"Where would your firm keep them, if they do exist?" the judge asked.

"There is a company that specializes in storing business files. They own a warehouse. Our closed files are stored there."

"I want you to look for the files and tell the court if they exist," Judge Gish said. "If they do, and your client doesn't want to turn them over, make your legal arguments and we'll go from there."

"Good enough, Judge."

"Now, I want everyone to sit down while I read the papers Mr. Philips and Mr. Botteri have handed me, and I don't want to be interrupted."

The parties waited while Judge Gish read the documents. When she was done, she removed her glasses and massaged her closed eyelids.

"And I thought that I was going to have an uneventful day."

The judge replaced her glasses and looked at the litigants.

"This is much too complicated to decide this morning."

"I've been thinking, Judge," Botteri said. "A DNA test would settle the question of Ms. Spencer's relationship to Casey Van Meter."

The judge turned to Ashley's lawyer. "Mr. Philips, would your client be willing to have her DNA tested to clear up any questions of maternity?"

Jerry and Ashley conferred for a moment. Then Philips addressed the court.

"Miss Spencer has no problem with the test, Your Honor."

"All right. I am going to adjourn to give Mr. Jefferson time to find the files and Miss Spencer a chance to take a DNA test. I want the parties to agree on the procedure and what lab will do the testing. When the parties are ready, notify me and we'll set a new date for the hearing."

As soon as court was adjourned, Randy Coleman and his attorney left the courtroom followed by Monte Jefferson, but Miles stayed behind.

"Jerry," he said, nodding to Philips. Then he smiled warmly at Ashley.

"It's so good to see you."

"I heard about your father," Ashley said. "I'm sorry he passed away. He was very kind to me."

"He was very fond of you, Ashley. He really worried when you disappeared. We both did."

"I didn't mean to upset you. I didn't want to worry anyone. I . . . I just had to go."

"I understand. Where have you been?"

"Overseas," Ashley answered evasively, still unwilling to trust anyone with any information about her hiding place in case she had to return to it.

Miles looked her over and smiled. "Well, the five years haven't hurt. You look great. I like the hair."

Ashley smiled. "Thanks."

Miles glanced at his watch. "I have to go back to my office for a meeting." He paused, as if he'd just gotten an idea. "Would you like to have dinner tonight? I'd like to catch up on what you've been doing."

"I don't think that's a good idea," Jerry said.

"Why?" Ashley asked.

"You shouldn't be socializing. You're adversaries in this lawsuit."

"We may also be relatives," Miles said to Jerry. "This claim of yours has been a total shock to me, but I couldn't be happier if it's true."

"I would like to talk to Miles," Ashley told Philips. "It's just dinner. I'll be okay."

Miles handed Ashley and Jerry business cards. "You two talk this over. I don't want to do anything improper. If you want to have dinner with me tonight, give me a call."

Miles headed up the aisle. Jerry watched him until he was out of earshot. They both cast nervous looks at the reporter and Larry Birch, who were walking in their direction.

"If you talk to Miles, remember that you're on opposite sides in this case."

"Don't worry. Miles has always been nice to me. I don't think he'd try to take advantage."

"You have no idea what he'll do now that you're adversaries."

"I'll be on guard, okay?"

Jerry blushed. "Sorry, it's the lawyer in me."

"I'm glad you're looking out for my interests."

The reporter appeared at their shoulder and cleared her throat.

"Ashley, my name is Rebecca Tilman," she said. "May I ask you a few questions?"

"Miss Spencer is not going to grant an interview now," Jerry said. "If she decides to, we'll contact you."

"But this is an important story," the reporter insisted.

"That may be true, but Miss Spencer will not agree to be interviewed now."

The reporter started to say something, then decided to leave with her scoop. She turned and headed for the door.

"Hello, detective," Ashley said.

"Long time no see," Birch answered. It sounded like a joke but Birch looked dead serious.

"I'm sorry I left the way I did."

"We were sorry, too. But you're okay, and that's what counts."

"Have there been any new developments with Joshua Maxfield?"

"He's still wanted, and there are at least two new homicides in other states that might be his work."

"Where were they?"

"Ohio and Iowa."

"So he's left Oregon?"

"Apparently, but that may change now that you're back"

"We're worried about that ourselves, detective," Jerry said. "We were going to get in touch with you about protection for Ashley."

"That may be a little hard to arrange after the stunt she pulled."

"She was running for her life after your people failed to protect her," Jerry said.

"Two good men died trying," Birch answered angrily.

"I'm sorry," Jerry apologized, "but you can see why Ashley ran."

Birch took a deep breath and calmed down.

"I felt very badly about what happened at the Academy, but you still shouldn't have run. I'll talk to my captain and see what we can do to keep you safe."

"Do you want me to drive you back to your apartment?" Jerry asked when Birch left.

"No. I'll walk. I'm used to that from Italy. And I want to look around the city. I might even shop a little."

"Okay. I'll be at the office if you need me. And think twice before you accept Miles's dinner invitation."

"Jerry. You've been great. But you don't have to baby-sit me. I'm twenty-two and I've been taking care of myself for a while."

Jerry's neck flushed. "Point taken. I just want what's best for you."

CHAPTER
TWENTY-TWO

Miles had chosen an upscale restaurant loaded with glass and chrome and he was waiting in a quiet corner booth when Ashley arrived. He wore a tan suit, an Oxford blue shirt, and a striped tie. Ashley wore the suit she'd worn to court, because it was the only nice outfit she owned.

Miles stood when the maitre d' showed her to the booth.

"I'm so glad you agreed to have dinner," he said as she sat down. "Do you want a cocktail or some wine? They have a very good cellar here."

"Wine is okay."

Miles told the waiter what he wanted while Ashley busied herself with the menu. As soon as the waiter left, Miles stared at her. The examination made Ashley uncomfortable. Miles noticed. He smiled.

"Sorry, but I can't help myself. This idea that you might be my niece is very strange."

"No stranger than the idea that Casey might be my mother."

"I was so relieved to see you in court today and to know that you were safe. There were times on my book tour when I would be giving a reading and I'd look around the audience, hoping you'd be somewhere in the back. I really worried about you."

Ashley felt guilty because she had thought very little about Miles over the years.

"Congratulations on your book."

"Have you read it?" Miles asked expectantly.

"No."

Miles's smile sagged for a moment.

"It would have been too painful," Ashley said, hoping that this explanation would ease his disappointment.

"I understand. It was very hard for me to write **Sleeping Beauty**, but I felt that it had to be done."

The waiter came for their orders.

"Were you always interested in writing?" Ashley asked as soon as the waiter left.

"I dabbled a bit in college, but I never actually tried to write a book before I started **Sleeping Beauty.**"

"Then what made you do it?"

"After Maxfield escaped, my father and I were inundated with calls from movie producers, television shows, and literary agents who wanted to cash in on our tragedy. I got rid of most of them, but Andrea Winsenberg and I hit it off. She gave me the idea of writing a book that would preserve Casey's memory. She wanted one of the writers she represents to ghostwrite it for me." Miles smiled. "Andrea thought I was nuts to try it myself."

"It's certainly been a huge success."

"I'd trade the money and the fame for Casey's recovery."

"Is there any possibility that will happen?"

"No." Miles looked grim. "Look, I don't want to talk about Casey's situation. I'd much rather hear about your adventures. But we do have to get this out of the way. I don't know if you're really Casey's daughter. . . ."

"But you knew that Casey became pregnant the summer my father dated her," Ashley interrupted.

"Yes," Miles answered cautiously.

"I know you and two men beat my father because you were angry that he made Casey pregnant."

Miles's eyes dropped to the tablecloth. "We all do things that we're not proud of. I was very young when I attacked Norman. I've always regretted what I did." He looked up at Ashley. "But I did it for Casey. I love her, Ashley. If you really want to help her, you'll let her go."

"You mean, I'll bow out and let you take her off life support?"

"Yes. I understand why you'd want to keep Casey alive. My God, you thought you'd lost your mother. Now you have this bomb dropped on you. But keeping Casey alive is wrong. You'd know that if you saw her."

Miles paused. He took a deep breath. "Casey and I are very close. I love her very much, but I've come to accept the fact that she died in the boathouse along with Terri." He shook his head. "What you'll see if you visit the nursing home isn't Casey. It's a corpse, a shell that was once a vibrant woman. Her spirit has left her, Ashley. Everything that made her human is gone."

"Your father didn't give up hope."

"My father never let anything go. He was never

around when Casey and I were growing up but he tried to control every aspect of our lives."

"You sound bitter."

"I am bitter. You have no idea what it was like for us."

"Didn't your mother . . . ?"

"Our mother was a drunk. If she showed the slightest gumption Henry beat it out of her. She was lucky to die young."

Ashley could not hide her shock. Miles noticed.

"You only knew Henry after he found God, the benevolent version. The man Casey and I knew was like the wrathful God of the Old Testament. He was never wrong and he always believed he could get what he wanted through sheer willpower. Henry fooled himself into believing that Casey would wake up from her coma like Sleeping Beauty. But the children's fable and his dream are both fairy tales."

Miles paused again. "It kills me to see her wasting away, Ashley. I want her to die with some dignity. I want Casey to be able to rest in peace."

"I can see how painful this is for you, Miles, but I thought I lost my family. Then, a few days ago, Jerry Philips showed up and told me that my real mother is still alive. I can't just condemn her to death. What about the new drug? Isn't Casey in a clinical trial?"

"That drug is never going to work. Even if it wakes her up, there's no guarantee that she'll be in possession of her mental faculties. She'd probably be a vegetable."

Miles took a deep breath. "I didn't want to bring this up, but I feel I must. You won't want to hear this but it's the truth. Casey doesn't deserve your loyalty. She never wanted you. Do you know how I found out she was pregnant?"

"No."

"She wanted an abortion and she knew that one of my fraternity brothers had arranged one for his girlfriend. Then Henry found out. I think a servant may have said something. We had a family meeting. Casey was evasive until Henry threatened to disinherit her. That's when she told us that Norman was the father."

Miles took a drink of his wine. Then he looked across the table at Ashley.

"She wanted Henry's money but she never wanted you. That's the truth. You don't owe her a thing."

Ashley found it hard to speak. "How . . . how did she feel about my father?"

"She was slumming. When she got tired of him

she dumped him without a second thought. Look, Ashley, I love my sister—we're blood—but Casey has never been a nice person. She was always self-centered and self-destructive. She would have made a terrible mother. You know about her marriage to Coleman?"

Ashley nodded.

"That's typical of the way she's lived her life. After Father made her the dean of the Academy she was more careful, until that fiasco. She was always promiscuous and emotionally unstable. She used drugs. She even tried suicide once."

"No."

"She was irresponsible, Ashley. She bounced from project to project. She'd get wrapped up in something, pour herself into it, then drop it as soon as she got bored. That's what she did with your father."

"She seemed to do a good job at the school," Ashley said, wanting to defend Casey but suddenly realizing that she was totally devoid of any facts to muster on her behalf. Casey may have given birth to her, but she knew almost nothing about the dean.

"This is typical. Father gave her the position at the school in a last-ditch attempt to help her make something of herself, and I have to admit that she did a great job at first. She was always very bright and she was well educated, but I really doubted that she'd be able to stick with it. But she did. She liked the challenge and the responsibility. The Academy was very important to Henry and she knew that he was placing a lot of trust in her. He didn't do that often.

"Then she went to a convention in Las Vegas and married that piece of trash on a whim." Miles looked down and shook his head in wonder. "Do you have any idea the harm that can be suffered by a school like the Academy if there's even a whiff of scandal? Her marriage to that cheap crook had the potential to be a disaster."

It must have occurred to Miles that he was getting angrier as he spoke, because he checked himself and took a deep breath.

"There's nothing to be gained by keeping Casey alive," Miles said. "She didn't care about you, she didn't care about anyone except herself and me. She did love me. Now I've got to pay back that love by ending her living death."

Ashley shook her head. "I can't give up on the possibility that she might come back. I'm sorry."

Miles's features softened. "Look, Ashley, you shouldn't be burdened with the added worries you'd have if you had to care for Casey. These past few years must have been tough. I imagine you haven't been able to work much, and you don't even have a high school diploma, do you?"

"No."

"You should be trying to get your life back together. You should be in school. I could help you. Maybe find you a job with Van Meter Industries while you get your GED. Then I could help you with college tuition. We are family. We shouldn't be adversaries. We should be helping each other."

Ashley wasn't certain what to make of Miles's offer. She hoped that it wasn't an attempt to buy her off.

"Would you help me even if I continued to oppose you?" Ashley asked.

Miles looked sad. "This isn't a bribe, Ashley. I'm trying to get you to realize that Casey is not coming back. I want what's best for both of you, and you should be making up for the time you've lost."

"Thank you, Miles. Let me think about what you've said. I'll visit Casey tomorrow. Maybe seeing her will help me decide what to do."

Miles saw the waiter arriving with their meals. "Fair enough," he said. "I promise not to mention the guardianship again."

Over dinner, Miles told her a series of fascinating stories about his book tour. Ashley drank a little too much wine and found herself laughing hysterically when Miles recounted a bizarre negotiation with a pair of unscrupulous movie producers who claimed to have Tom Cruise and Jennifer Lopez lined up to play Joshua Maxfield and Casey.

Miles asked her about her years abroad. Ashley told him about her travels but was sober enough to keep any important details from him. By the end of the meal, she'd forgotten the serious way the evening started.

Miles waited outside with Ashley while the valet got their cars. When she was about to leave, he gave her a hug and a brotherly kiss on her cheek. A light rain was falling, with more and heavier rain forecast for the next day. Ashley switched on her wipers and concentrated on the road. Occasionally, she glanced in her rearview mirror. A pair of headlights shone in it. She paid no attention to them, because the things that Miles had said about Casey over dinner distracted her.

Was Casey Van Meter really as cold, calculating, and insensitive as Miles claimed? Had Norman meant so little to her? Had getting rid of her own child meant so little to her? If she was this uncaring, how would she react to Ashley if she did survive her coma?

Ashley knew that Terri had loved her unconditionally. There had never been a moment when she doubted that love. So who was really her mother? Did giving birth make you a mother in any but the technical sense? Was Terri, who raised her, loved her, and cared for her any less her mother simply because she had not borne Ashley?

Ashley turned onto a side street and noticed that the headlights in her mirror were still behind her. Alarm chased away her thoughts about Casey. She decided to make a few random turns to see if the car stayed with her. It did. She tried to convince herself that no one was following her, but it was too much of a coincidence that the other car was driving a random route that mirrored hers. She made a sudden U-turn. Her tires squealed on the wet pavement. As she drove past the other car, she stared at the driver's window, but the rain streaks and the darkness obscured the driver's face.

Ashley drove fast until she was certain that she'd lost her tail. Then she headed to her apartment as quickly as she could. Her heart was racing, and it didn't slow down until she was inside, behind locked doors. She rushed to her window before turning on the lights and studied the street below for any sign that someone was watching her apartment. There was no one standing in the rain, and there were no suspicious cars.

As Ashley got ready for bed, she tried to remember everything she could about the ride home. By the time she fell asleep, she half-believed that the tail had been a figment of her imagination.

CHAPTER
TWENTY-THREE

It was raining when Ashley woke up. She dressed in sweats, dark glasses, and a hooded windbreaker, and walked two blocks to a local coffee shop for breakfast. After breakfast, she planned to go to Sunny Rest and visit Casey Van Meter.

The coffee shop sold **The Oregonian.** She picked up a copy and slid into a booth. The waitress took her order, and she opened the paper. Her face stared back at her from the front page. It was an old photo, taken when she was in high school. She glanced around to see if anyone was staring at her, but no one in the restaurant seemed to have made the connection between the blond athlete in the newspaper and the dark-haired woman in the rear booth.

MISSING WITNESS RETURNS TO BATTLE FOR

SLEEPING BEAUTY'S $40,000,000 FORTUNE, the headline screamed. Ashley blinked and reread the figure. The byline of the article belonged to the woman who had tried to interview her at the courthouse. According to the story, which summarized the hearing, rehashed the murder case, and recapped Miles's rise to literary fame, the person who was appointed Casey's guardian would control a fortune estimated at forty million dollars. Jerry Philips had never mentioned that little bit of trivia. Forty million! Ashley couldn't imagine that much money. She'd been living in low-rent apartments and getting by on baguettes, cheese, and cheap wine. Forty million dollars was caviar, penthouses, and yachts.

Ashley gulped down her breakfast and went back to her apartment. As she showered and changed, she wondered what she would be allowed to do with Casey's money if the court appointed her as the dean's conservator and guardian. Jerry had told her that she could use Casey's money to pay for her care at the nursing home, but he hadn't told her anything else about a guardian's powers. Would she have to decide how to invest Casey's money? Would she be able to use the money for her own needs? Ashley decided that she needed to know the answers to these questions. And she needed to know one other answer. If she was Casey's daughter, and Casey died, would she inherit some of Casey's fortune? If she was an heir to millions, how could she put herself in a position to decide whether Casey lived or died?

Ashley drove through suburban Portland in the pouring rain to the Sunny Rest retirement community. The complex was surrounded by housing developments and shopping centers. It was large, and a road ran through it. On one side of the road were independent-living apartments for retirees who could still take care of themselves. The sprawling one-story complex across from the apartments was for assisted living.

Ashley found a spot in the last row of Sunny Rest's large parking lot. She dashed through the rain and was drenched by the time she made it through the front door. Water ran off her windbreaker onto the tile floor, and her pants were spotted and stained by the rain. When she finally paid attention to her surroundings, she felt queasy. The hospital smell had something to do with it, but most of her discomfort was caused by the stares of the elderly people in the lobby. Some of them pushed walkers in front of them, others sat in wheelchairs. They were all frail; their veins were blue streaks under waxy, parchment-thin skin, their hair was white and sparse. Some of the residents stared at her with great intensity. Ashley had the eerie impression that their lives were so uneventful that her visit was seen as a major event. Several of the residents seemed lost in their own worlds, heads bobbing to a voice only they heard, or talking incoherently to someone only they could see.

Ashley was halfway to the reception desk when a woman wheeled over and smiled radiantly.

"Hello," the woman said excitedly. "Are you Carmen? Have you come to visit me?"

A nurse hurried over and took hold of the wheelchair. She smiled apologetically at Ashley.

"Betty, this young lady isn't Carmen. Carmen visits on Saturday."

The nurse turned the wheelchair so Betty could not see Ashley. She kept up a steady patter as she wheeled her charge away. The receptionist gave Ashley directions to the wing where Casey was staying. To get there, Ashley had to walk by Betty again. The old woman looked up and smiled.

"Are you Carmen? Have you come to visit me?"

Ashley suppressed a shudder as she walked down a corridor lined with other chairs occupied by more elderly residents. The smell of disinfectant was strong, and the odd behavior of some of the residents unsettling. Ashley knew that she would be old someday, and she hoped that she would not end up in a place like this.

A young nurse was at a station at the end of the corridor. Ashley introduced herself and asked to speak to Stanley Linscott, Casey Van Meter's treating physician.

"Dr. Linscott isn't in today," the nurse told her.

"Is there someone else I can talk to about Ms. Van Meter?"

The nurse suddenly looked wary. "You'll need to talk to Ann Rostow. She's the administrator. I'll call her."

Ashley took a seat at the nurse's station. A few minutes later, a slender woman with short gray hair and glasses appeared at the end of the corridor. She was wearing a tan pants suit and a beige blouse. Her walk was energetic and she looked crisp and efficient.

Ashley stood up. The woman stopped in front of her.

"I'm Ann Rostow. I understand that you have some questions about Casey Van Meter."

"Yes. I wanted to see her and I'd like an update about her condition."

"Why?"

"I may be her daughter."

"Is your name Ashley Spencer?"

"Yes."

"I thought you might come here."

Ashley's brow furrowed.

"I read the story in the paper this morning," Rostow explained. "It said that you were claiming to be Ms. Van Meter's daughter. Can I see some identification?"

Ashley handed Rostow her driver's license. The administrator examined it, then handed it back.

"We have to be careful with Ms. Van Meter," Rostow said. "Reporters are always trying to get information about her. We had some calling this morning. When she first came here, a television crew from one of those tabloid shows tried to sneak in through the kitchen."

"Ms. Rostow, can I see her? I'll only stay a minute. If she is my mother. . . . I only knew her for a while, five years ago. I just. . . ."

"This must be very hard for you."

"It is. It's very confusing. There's going to be a DNA test to settle the maternity issue but, from what I've learned, she probably is my mother. I just want to see her."

"You just want to look in?"

"Yes. It would mean a lot to me."

"All right. Follow me."

Rostow led Ashley through a set of swinging metal doors and halfway down the next corridor. She stopped in front of one of the rooms and opened the door. Ashley hesitated on the threshold before stepping inside. The walls were painted a sterile tan and there were no pictures on them. A sink was affixed to one wall. Over it was a mirror. Facing the sink was a hospital bed with the side rails up. Ashley forced herself to look at the woman who was lying in it. An IV drip was taped to her forearm. At the far side of the bed a gastric tube disappeared under the blankets. The tube was connected to a pump, which was turned on when Casey was fed.

Ashley expected to see a wasted, shrunken, corpse-like creature that no longer resembled a human being. What she saw was less horrifying but much sadder. Casey had only lost ten pounds during her years of unconsciousness, because she was fed and hydrated regularly. If Ashley had walked into the room by mistake, she might have thought the dean was just sleeping. On closer inspection, Ashley saw why Miles had given up hope. She remembered the animated, dynamic woman who'd shown her and her mother around the Academy campus. That woman had been so energetic, so full of life. Casey Van Meter's body was a shell devoid of life, a cruel façade. Her face was pale, and her skin looked unhealthy, her muscle tone was gone, and her arms were flabby. She had aged badly, and her lustrous, blond hair had gone gray. There was no light in her eyes.

Ashley fought the impulse to bolt from the room and forced herself to walk closer to the bed. She stared down, heartbroken. She had no urge to touch her mother. Casey Van Meter elicited no feelings of love. She just made Ashley feel uncomfortable.

When she thought she'd been in the room a decent amount of time, Ashley turned to Ann Rostow.

"Thank you. I think I'll go now."

"The first time you see someone in her condition, it can be very unsettling, especially if it's someone you're close to."

"We weren't close. She gave me away without a second thought when I was born. I knew her as the dean at the school I attended and nothing more."

"But she may still be your mother," Rostow said softly.

Ashley nodded.

"Then you can come back and visit anytime."

"Thank you. I mentioned a DNA test. If we need a sample of Casey's blood. . . ."

"I'll need a court order, but it shouldn't be a problem."

"One more thing, Ms. Rostow. Do the doctors think she'll get better?"

"I've sat in on meetings when Mr. Van Meter asked that very question. Dr. Linscott always answered that the odds on a full recovery for Ms. Van Meter were very long."

Ann Rostow walked Ashley back to the lobby. Outside, the rain was cascading down in heavy sheets and bouncing off the asphalt. Ashley pulled up the hood on her windbreaker, ducked her head, and ran across the street, keeping her eyes on the pavement, preoccupied by thoughts of her brief visit with the dean. Now she understood what Miles had been trying to tell her. Casey was not the strong, determined woman who had stood up to Randy Coleman at the Academy pool. She was one of the living dead. If some miracle of God or science did bring her back to this world, there was no assurance that she would not end up as pathetic and helpless as the ghost people who moved through the halls of

Sunny Rest. Logic told Ashley that she should back off and let Casey rest in peace, but something inside her clung to the hope that Casey was still fighting, that she could save her mother.

Ashley spotted her rental car. She fished out her keys and made a dash for it. Rain was dancing on the roof and the windshield. She leaned down to unlock the door and saw the reflection of a man. Rain poured down from the roof across the driver's window distorting his features, and a hood partially hid his face, but there was no mistaking the knife he was holding.

Ashley swiveled and lashed out with her foot as if she was powering a shot on goal. The man was turned sideways and she struck his thigh. He grunted, stumbled back a few steps and his knees buckled. Ashley ran. Feet pounded the pavement behind her. Out of the corner of her eye, Ashley saw a dark blur shoot out from between two cars. Then she heard the sound of bodies crashing to the asphalt. Before she could look back, a shape materialized in front of her. She threw a punch at a hooded, black rain slicker and connected. The apparition staggered. She swung again and strong arms grabbed her.

"I'm a cop, Miss Spencer," a male voice shouted. "We've got him."

Ashley froze and looked at the man who was holding her. She could see part of a uniform under the rain gear. Behind her, over the rain, she heard shouts of "Freeze, police."

"Let's go back," the officer said. She hesitated. "It's okay. You're safe. He's down. I can see a crowd a few rows back, and they're our men."

The officer led Ashley through the rows of cars toward several policemen in plain clothes. They were surrounding two men in dark clothes who were sprawled on the pavement face down, with their hands clasped behind their necks. A knife lay between them on the waterlogged ground. When Ashley arrived, a detective holding a see-through evidence bag was stooping for it.

Larry Birch walked over to Ashley. Rain was cascading down his face but he was smiling.

"It's a good thing we had you under surveillance," he said.

Ashley was shivering, and it wasn't from the rain. "Who are they?" Ashley asked, her eyes riveted on the prisoners.

"We'll soon find out."

Birch signaled to one of the officers. "Cuff them then get them on their feet."

Several officers kept guns trained on the captives while other officers snapped on handcuffs and helped the men to their feet. Ashley stared at the two prisoners. Their hoods had fallen back to reveal their faces.

"Ashley," Randy Coleman shouted. "Tell these cops to get these cuffs off of me. I just saved your life."

The other man said nothing. He just stared at Ashley. She stared back until it dawned on her that she knew him. Then she looked away quickly and took a step back.

Rain cascaded off his shaved head and ran down the length of his thick, jet-black beard. His eye color was different, too. Probably contacts. But there was no doubt that the police had captured Joshua Maxfield.

CHAPTER
TWENTY-FOUR

Larry Birch brought Ashley to Ann Rostow's office where she was given a mug of hot tea and a towel to dry her hair.

"Tell me what happened in the lot," Larry Birch said when she was ready to discuss the attack.

"I was bending down to unlock my door when I saw someone's reflection in the window."

"Maxfield?"

"I can't tell you. The rainclouds blocked most of the sunlight. You know how heavy the rain is. And the window was streaked with water. It distorted everything. And he was wearing a hood."

"So you can't say if Maxfield or Coleman assaulted you?"

Ashley stared at the detective. She saw that his question was serious.

"It had to be Maxfield," Ashley said. "You don't think Coleman attacked me?"

"I have to keep an open mind."

"What does he say?"

"Coleman is screaming bloody murder. He's taking credit for saving your life and capturing Maxfield. He says that he came to visit his wife and just happened to be in the right place at the right time."

"That makes sense."

"Our problem is that his car pulled into the lot after you parked, but he never went inside the nursing home."

"What does he say about that?"

"He says that he hasn't seen Ms. Van Meter since she went into the coma and he felt that he should find out about her condition first-hand."

"I bet his lawyer told him to go so he'd look good in court."

Birch shrugged. "I don't know anything about that."

"Why didn't he go in?"

"He claims he had a change of heart after he parked, because he wasn't sure he could handle seeing Ms. Van Meter so helpless. According to

Coleman, he was working out his feelings when he saw you leave. He says that he was coming over to talk to you when Maxfield attacked and he came to the rescue."

"Is that what your surveillance team saw?"

"Unfortunately, we didn't have a clear view. You were between the cars and the attacker came from the middle of the lot. We didn't even see that you were in trouble until you ran. Then someone rushed out from between two cars, but our view was obstructed by the other cars and our angle, and they were dressed similarly."

"Is Maxfield saying he rescued me from Coleman?"

"Maxfield isn't talking."

"He's tried to kill me before."

"Yeah, he has. And I suspect that we'll be charging him with another attempt."

The door opened and an officer stuck his head in. "There's a Jerry Philips out here. He says he's Miss Spencer's attorney and that you called him."

"Let him in," Birch said.

Jerry went to Ashley as soon as he walked in the door.

"Are you okay?"

Ashley nodded.

"What happened?" Philips asked Ashley and the detective.

"Joshua Maxfield tried to kill me," Ashley answered.

"He's in custody," Birch added.

"Thank God," Philips said.

"Randy Coleman saved me."

"Coleman? What was he doing here?"

"He says that he was going to visit his wife when he saw Maxfield try to kill Miss Spencer," Birch said. "She was running for help when Coleman tackled him."

"Are you hurt?"

"No, I'm fine."

"She didn't panic," Birch said. "She fought him off. She was very brave."

Jerry turned to Ashley. "You must have been scared to death."

"I was, but I'm better now."

Jerry looked at Birch. "Are you finished? Can I take Ashley home?"

"Yeah. I'll need a statement but we can do that tomorrow. Can you drive Miss Spencer? We have to go over her car for evidence and we can't turn it back to her today."

"That's fine. It's a rental. You can give it back to the agency when you're through."

"This is great," Jerry said as soon as they were underway. "Maxfield is going to prison. You don't have to be afraid of him anymore."

"They arrested him before and he escaped," Ashley said.

"That won't happen this time. He'll be watched like a hawk."

Ashley didn't reply. She shut her eyes and laid her head against the back of the seat. Jerry must have thought that she was asleep, because he didn't speak for the rest of the trip.

"We're here," he said as soon as he parked in front of her building.

Ashley got out of the car without saying a word. Jerry followed her inside. There was a clock in the living room. The time shocked her. It was only a little after one in the afternoon. Ashley felt as if she'd been up for days.

"Are you hungry?" Jerry asked. "Do you want me to fix something for you?"

"Okay?"

"Let me rummage around in the fridge."

Ashley slumped down at the kitchen table.

"Feel like telling me what's bothering you?" Jerry asked while he made them ham-and-cheese sandwiches.

"Do you think it's possible that it was Randy Coleman who attacked me?"

The question took Philips by surprise. "I thought he saved you."

"He probably did. But the attack seemed—I don't know—clumsy. I saw Maxfield in action once. It was at the pool at the Academy. Coleman was bothering the dean and he got violent. Maxfield was there. He handled Coleman very easily. It was like in the movies, almost choreographed it was so smooth, bang, bang, and it was over. Maxfield didn't break a sweat."

Ashley lost color for a moment. She looked down and swallowed.

"What is it?" Jerry asked, concerned.

"I was remembering when . . . when I was attacked. In my house. I was overpowered easily, too. Maxfield was so efficient. The man who attacked me in the lot. . . ." She shook her head.

"You reacted quickly. You knocked him off balance. He probably wasn't expecting that."

"I guess."

Jerry carried the sandwiches and two glasses of soda to the table and sat down.

"Do you have any reason to doubt that Joshua Maxfield murdered your parents and attacked you in the Academy dorm?"

Ashley thought before answering.

"I never saw his face in my house or in the dorm, but I definitely saw him in the boathouse. And he wrote that novel where the killer eats before he murders the teenage daughter. How could he possibly know that happened at my house?"

"So, there you are. If he tried to kill you several times before, why would he suddenly save your life today?"

Ashley was about to take a bite out of her sandwich when an idea occurred to her.

"Would Coleman benefit if I died?" she asked.

Jerry thought about that. "With you out of the picture there would be one less person trying to be appointed Casey's guardian and conservator."

"Miles would still be opposing him."

"Yes, but he and Miles want the same thing, even if Randy claims otherwise."

"What's that?"

"They both want to take Casey off life support."

"But Randy's attorney said. . . ."

"I know what he said but I don't believe it. Casey doesn't have a will and she has a large estate. If she dies intestate Coleman will get a lot of it because they're still married. He may say he wants to keep her alive but I bet he'd change his tune in a minute if he's appointed her guardian. You're the only one who's dedicated to keeping Casey alive."

Ashley stared across the table at Jerry. She felt frightened.

"You just said that Coleman would get 'a lot of' Casey's estate. Does that mean he doesn't get it all, even though she doesn't have a will?"

Jerry colored. "He wouldn't be the only heir."

"Would I get any of Casey's money if she died?"

Ashley watched Jerry carefully as she asked the question. He hesitated. She thought he looked uncomfortable.

"Am I an heir, Jerry?"

"You're her only surviving issue and Coleman isn't your father. Under the statutes, you'd be entitled to one half of her estate."

Ashley stared at Jerry. "That's twenty million dollars."

"Somewhere in there."

"And Coleman gets it all if I'm dead?"

"Yes."

"Oh, my God." Ashley stood up. "Why didn't you tell me?"

"I don't know," he answered nervously. "I guess the point was to keep Casey alive—that's why Henry hired me—so I didn't think about telling you what would happen if she died."

"You shouldn't have kept this from me. It changes everything. Everyone will think I'm after her money. That's what the newspaper said, that I was battling for the forty million dollars."

"You're battling to keep your mother alive."

"It's too much responsibility. I can't do this."

Jerry walked around the table until they were standing inches apart. He put his hands on her shoulders.

"You have to, Ashley. Miles and Coleman will do everything in their power to take Casey off life support."

Suddenly, Ashley was angry. "What makes you think I don't want her dead, now that I know how much I'll inherit? Is that why you didn't tell me about the money?"

Jerry looked directly into Ashley's eyes while he answered.

"I believe that you are a good, moral person. If I thought that you would let Casey Van Meter die so you could inherit her money I wouldn't have agreed to find you."

Ashley looked down. She was embarrassed. "I'm sorry," she said. "I shouldn't have said that. You've always been so good to me."

"You've been through hell. You deserve to be treated with respect."

Ashley looked at Jerry and he held her gaze. He was so decent. He'd been a rock for her. Before Jerry could say anything, she kissed him. He tensed. Then he tried to say something.

"No," she said and she kissed him again, holding him tight, like a survivor clinging to a life raft. Jerry took her in his arms and held her just as tight.

"This isn't right," he said, though everything he'd just done contradicted his words. "I'm your attorney. You're vulnerable."

"I'm twenty-two, Jerry. I'm a virgin." The admission embarrassed Philips but Ashley's voice was strong. "I've been so afraid all these years that I haven't let myself get close to anyone. Now I want to start being human again."

"I'm the wrong person, Ashley. You've come to depend on me. That's not love."

"Are you telling me that you don't want me?"

He looked down and swallowed. "It doesn't matter how I feel. I'm your attorney."

"The way you feel matters to me. You tell me you don't care about me and we'll stop now."

"I do care for you. You're strong and smart, you're a good person, and you're beautiful. But that doesn't matter. There are ethics rules that prohibit a lawyer from . . . from taking advantage of. . . ."

"You're not taking advantage of me, and if the ethics rules are worrying you, I have a simple solution. You're fired."

Jerry looked at her wide-eyed. "What?"

"You heard me."

Jerry laughed and shook his head. "You're something."

"What's it going to be?"

"I've been fired before, but never because my client wanted to sleep with me."

"I don't want you to sleep with me. I want you to make love to me."

Jerry was gentle and tender, but it was still painful when he entered her the first time. The second time she was tense, because she expected more pain, and she was relieved when all she felt was pleasure. The third time was wonderful. After they climaxed, they held each other for a while.

Then Jerry kissed her forehead and lay beside her, breathing deeply.

Ashley was slick with sweat and exhausted, but she felt completely at peace. Jerry laced his fingers with hers. She turned her head and watched his chest rise and fall in the pale light that filtered through the bedroom blinds. It was smooth—not fat but not muscular, either. Not at all like the male model bodies in the fashion magazines. She decided that having muscles wasn't all that important when you were making love.

Cool air touched her skin, reminding her that she was nude, lying next to a naked man. She wasn't uncomfortable or embarrassed. She felt free, unburdened. She smiled. So this was what sex felt like. She wondered if it would be different with someone she didn't love.

The word stopped her dead. Love was a big word, a very serious word. Did she really love Jerry or was she just a vulnerable girl who'd latched on to a man who had been nice to her? No, that wasn't right. Jerry had been more than nice to her. He cared for her. She could tell when they kissed the first time. The kisses of Todd Franklin, her high school boyfriend, had been greedy and hungry. He said he loved her because he hoped that she would sleep with him. Ashley knew in her heart that Jerry would have been satisfied just to hold her, and that the sex was not as important as being together.

She was so happy, and she hadn't been happy in a long time. Maybe Jerry was right. Maybe her nightmare was over. Maybe Joshua Maxfield would never bother her again.

Thinking about Joshua Maxfield brought unwanted memories of the attack in the parking lot. Ashley stopped smiling. Jerry must have sensed something because he turned toward her.

"Are you okay?"

She squeezed his hand. "I'm great, Jerry. Thank you."

"My pleasure. And I mean that."

"Was I okay?" Ashley asked, nervous that the sex had not been as good for him as it had been for her.

"You are definitely a hot piece of ass."

"And you are a pig," Ashley answered, slapping him playfully.

"A pig who has to pee real bad."

Jerry pecked her on the cheek and got out of bed. She watched him walk to the bathroom. The door closed. Against her will, she started thinking about the attack in the parking lot. The only logical conclusion a rational person could draw was that Joshua Maxfield had tried to kill her, and Randy Coleman had saved her life, but something was still nagging at her.

Coleman was supposed to be a small-time crook who had married Casey Van Meter for her money. Would someone like that risk his life to save her from an attacker? But he must have. No other explanation made sense. If Coleman attacked her, then Maxfield had rescued her. Coleman had a twenty-million-dollar motive to kill her, but what possible motive could Joshua Maxfield have to save her?

An absurd thought occurred to Ashley. What if Maxfield wasn't the man who killed her parents and tried to murder her in the dorm? What if Coleman was the killer? No, that made no sense. The attacks on her and the murders of her mother and father had to be linked, which meant that the killer had a motive to murder everyone in her family. Coleman didn't know that she was Casey's daughter and heir until the hearing, five years after her parents were murdered.

And there was the boathouse. There was no guesswork there. She had heard the screams. She had seen the bodies. It wasn't Coleman standing in the dark holding that knife, it was Joshua Maxfield.

Jerry stepped out of the bathroom and walked over to the bed.

"I'm going to my apartment to shower and change. Then I am taking you to the restaurant of your choice to celebrate Joshua Maxfield's arrest and the loss of your virginity. How does that sound?"

Ashley rolled on her side and touched his thigh. "Are you sure you want to leave?"

Jerry laughed. "God, you're a pervert. Is sex all you think about?"

Ashley was about to answer when the phone rang. She was going to ignore it until she remembered that very few people had her number. One of them was Larry Birch and she worried that he was calling to tell her that Maxfield had escaped. She rolled to the other side of the bed and picked up the receiver.

"Ashley?" a woman asked.

"Yes."

"I'm so glad I got you. This is Ann Rostow from Sunny Rest."

"Yes?"

"How are you feeling?"

Ashley thought about the last two hours and couldn't help smiling. "Thanks for asking. I'm fully recovered."

"I'm glad to hear that. Do you think you'd have a problem coming to Sunny Rest tomorrow morning?"

"No, why?"

"There's been a development here."

"What happened?"

"Casey has regained consciousness."

"What?"

"She woke up."

"Oh, my God!"

Ashley sat up and Jerry mouthed, "What's going on?" Ashley held up a hand to silence him.

"Dr. Linscott wants to meet with the interested parties tomorrow morning at nine o'clock," Rostow said. "Can you make it?"

"Of course. Can you tell me how she is? Can she talk, is she . . . ?"

"I'd rather have the doctor explain her condition. I'll see you tomorrow."

Ashley hung up and stared into space.

"Who was that?" Jerry asked.

"The woman from Sunny Rest. Casey Van Meter has come out of her coma."

Jerry sat on the edge of the bed. "That changes everything," he said.

CHAPTER
TWENTY-FIVE

When Jerry and Ashley arrived at Sunny Rest in the morning, Miles Van Meter was waiting with Monte Jefferson, his attorney, in the reception area outside Ann Rostow's office. Larry Birch, Tony Marx, and Deputy District Attorney Delilah Wallace also wanted to hear what Dr. Linscott had to say. Randy Coleman and his attorney, Anthony Botteri, were sitting as far as possible from everyone else. Coleman did not look happy. Now that his wife was awake, their divorce could proceed, and his chance of securing any part of the Van Meter fortune was disappearing.

As soon as Ashley walked in, Delilah Wallace levered herself off the couch. She had a big grin on her face.

"How you doin', girl? You had me worried something fierce."

"I'm sorry I. . . ."

"No apologies. I'm just glad you're safe." She spread her arms. "Let me give you a hug."

Delilah engulfed Ashley, crushed her to her bosom, then let her go.

"No more running, promise?"

"I'm staying put."

"Just like Mr. Maxfield. The only place he's going is death row. That's a promise. He's gonna be under guard twenty-four hours a day and chained up anytime he's out of his cell. No more freedom for Mr. Maxfield, ever."

Miles had watched the exchange without expression, but he smiled as soon as Ashley turned toward him.

"You must be very happy," she said.

"I should have had more faith."

"No one could have predicted this."

The door to the right of the receptionist's desk opened and Ann Rostow walked out, followed by a short, bespectacled man in a brown sports jacket and gray slacks. The man's red complexion extended across a bald pate over which he had combed his few remaining strands of hair. He looked uncomfortable facing a group.

"I'm glad you could all make it," Rostow said. "This is Dr. Stanley Linscott, who has been treating Ms. Van Meter. Let's go into the conference room so he can bring you up to date on her condition and answer your questions. Then we can go to her room."

A long table dominated the conference room. Everyone assembled around it except Larry Birch and Tony Marx. The detectives stood against the wall. Ann Rostow and Dr. Linscott sat at the end of the table near the door.

"Go ahead, Doctor," Ann Rostow said.

"Yes, well, I can tell you that I was quite surprised yesterday when the duty nurse phoned me. She said that she was in Ms. Van Meter's room dealing with her feeding tube when the patient's eyelids fluttered and she muttered something, which the nurse could not discern. Then Ms. Van Meter opened her eyes and looked around her room. She was confused and did not know where she was, but she did know her name. The nurse did not want to startle Ms. Van Meter, so she told her that she'd had an accident and was in a hospital. Then she phoned me. I came to Sunny Rest immediately and examined her."

"Doctor, how lucid is Ms. Van Meter?" Delilah Wallace asked.

"She is aware of her identity and she is able to carry on a short conversation. She tires easily."

"Does she know how long she's been unconscious?" Miles asked.

"Yes. I told her this morning. That has been very disconcerting for her, but I would have been surprised if she wasn't upset."

"How much does she remember about being attacked?" Delilah asked.

"I haven't discussed the incident in the boathouse with her. It might be too traumatic at this stage of her recovery."

"Has she said anything about it?" Miles asked.

"No."

"How long will it be before we can talk to her about what happened in the boathouse?" Detective Birch asked.

"I can't answer that today. It will depend on her rate of recovery."

"Is there a chance that waking up is only temporary?" Randy Coleman asked.

"Could she suffer a relapse?" Miles asked anxiously.

"Those are questions I can't answer. As you know, Ms. Van Meter was part of a trial of a new drug that was developed specifically for this purpose. It seems to have worked, but I have no idea of the side effects that might be tied to the drug or how permanent her recovery will be. We can only pray that she'll stay with us."

"If there's any possibility of a relapse, she should be questioned as soon as possible," Delilah said. "She's the only living witness who knows everything that happened in the boat-house."

"I understand your concerns," Dr. Linscott said, "but my concern is for my patient. I'm not going to subject her to any situation, like reliving her assault, that might trigger a relapse."

"Which brings us to the ground rules for this morning," Ann Rostow interjected. "Dr. Linscott and I have decided that we will only allow Ms. Van Meter's husband, brother, and daughter in the room with her. You may stay fifteen minutes and you may not ask her any questions about the murder of Terri Spencer or the assault on her." She looked at Miles Van Meter, Ashley, and Randy Coleman. "Is that clear?"

"If you want to avoid trauma, you shouldn't let Coleman in," Miles said. "Casey was divorcing him because he beat her up."

"Listen, Van Meter . . . ," Coleman started.

"Enough!" Rostow said. "If there is any prob-lem I will cancel the visit."

"But . . . ," Miles started.

"Mr. Van Meter, I can understand your concern, but Mr. Coleman is legally married to Ms. Van Meter. He has a stronger legal claim to visit her than you do."

Miles clamped his jaw shut, but he was obviously unhappy.

"Mrs. Rostow," Ashley said, "do you think it's wise to let me in to see Dean Van Meter?" Ashley still could not bring herself to call Casey "mother." "She doesn't know that I'm her daughter. My presence might confuse her or make her remember my mother—Terri—and what happened to them in the boathouse."

"That's a good point," Rostow responded. "Dr. Linscott, as I understand it, Ms. Van Meter put Ashley up for adoption as soon as she gave birth to her and never learned who adopted her. When she went into her coma she did not know that Ashley was her daughter. Ashley only learned a short time ago who her biological mother was."

Linscott looked troubled. "Do you want to see your mother, Miss Spencer?"

"Yes, if it's possible. If she does have a relapse, this may be my only chance to talk to her. But I don't want to do anything to harm her."

"Why don't we do this," Dr. Linscott said. "I'll

let you go in with the others, but don't tell Ms. Van Meter that you're her daughter."

"What should I say if she asks who I am?"

"Tell her that you went to the Academy and that you're a friend of her brother."

"Why don't we go down to Ms. Van Meter's room," Rostow said as she opened the door to the conference room. They filed out of the room and Delilah moved next to Ashley as they walked toward Casey's room.

"This must be scary for you," the deputy DA said.

"A little. I'm more confused than frightened," Ashley answered.

"You think you and Ms. Van Meter are going to get along?"

"I don't know, but it's worth a try."

"Sort of like a second chance."

"Sort of."

"That's how I feel about getting Maxfield back. Unfinished business. I lost a lot of sleep after he flew the coop."

Dr. Linscott and Ann Rostow stopped at the nurse's station nearest Casey's door.

"I would like everyone except Mr. Coleman, Mr. Van Meter, and Miss Spencer to wait here."

The doctor opened the door to Casey's room.

She was sitting up in bed watching television. A nurse was sitting by the bed reading a magazine.

"Good morning, Ms. Van Meter," Dr. Linscott said.

Casey looked reluctant to turn away from the set and only gave Dr. Linscott a quick look before going back to her program. She did not look at anyone else.

"I've brought some visitors with me. Do you recognize anyone?"

Casey did not respond.

"She's been watching nonstop since it was connected," the nurse told Dr. Linscott. Linscott flicked his fingers toward the nurse and she turned off the set with her remote. Casey looked upset.

"There will be plenty of time for TV," the doctor said. "We won't be staying long."

Casey stared at the invaders. Her brow furrowed. Then she focused on her brother and her eyes widened slowly.

"Miles?"

Miles walked over to the bed. There were tears in his eyes. He looked like he wanted to hug his sister but he restrained himself.

"It's me, Casey. It's so good to have you back."

Casey fell back against her pillow. She seemed stunned.

"You look so different," she said.

"I'm five years older. You've been asleep a long time."

"Honey," Randy Coleman said, taking a step toward the bed.

Casey looked puzzled for a moment. Then she looked agitated. Dr. Linscott put a restraining hand on Coleman's arm. Coleman tensed but he stopped.

"This is Randy Coleman, Casey. Your husband," the doctor said.

Casey's hands opened and closed on her blanket. She pulled back toward the headboard.

"Why don't you step out, Mr. Coleman," the doctor said.

Coleman started to protest.

"Please," Linscott said firmly. Casey's husband scowled but left.

"I'll go, too," Ashley said.

Casey turned toward her and stared. "Who are you?"

"A friend of Mr. Van Meter," Ashley answered.

Casey put a hand to her forehead. "No, there's something. . . ."

She looked lost and sounded frightened. Her breathing became shallow. Dr. Linscott looked worried.

"Perhaps this is too much, too soon," he said. "I think everyone should leave."

"Good-bye, Casey," Miles said. "I'll come back as soon as the doctor says it's okay."

Ashley and Miles joined Randy Coleman in the hall outside the door to Casey's room. A few minutes later, Dr. Linscott came out.

"What happened?" Delilah asked.

"I may have acted hastily in letting her have visitors," Dr. Linscott replied.

"She's okay, isn't she?" the DA asked, concerned about losing her witness.

"Oh, yes. Just a little overwhelmed by her situation."

"When do you think I'll have another chance to talk to Casey?" Miles asked.

"It will depend on her rate of recovery and her mental state. It's a good sign that she recognized you, though."

They discussed Casey's condition a little longer. When the doctor and Ann Rostow excused themselves, Delilah turned to Ashley.

"I'm going back to my office to start working on

my case, but I'll be in touch soon. You okay about going through this again?"

"I wish I didn't have to, but I want Maxfield punished. I want him in prison."

"Good," Delilah said, flashing a big smile. "That makes two of us."

"Is he talking?" Jerry asked Delilah. "Has he admitted killing Terri Spencer?"

"Mr. Maxfield asked for a lawyer as soon as he was arrested and hasn't said a word since. He may be evil, but he's not dumb." Delilah took Ashley's hand in hers and patted it. "Not that it matters. I have you as a witness. Ms. Van Meter will just be icing on the cake."

They reached the reception area and the homicide detectives escorted Delilah out of the building.

"I've got to get back to work," Miles said to Monte Jefferson. "You coming?"

"I'll be right with you. I've got to talk to Jerry Philips for a second."

"Meet you at the car. So long, Ashley."

Miles left, and Jefferson turned to Jerry Philips. "Now that Ms. Van Meter is out of her coma, do you still need the files on Miss Spencer's adoption?"

"I'd better keep the motion alive. If she has a relapse, we'll be back in court."

Jefferson frowned.

"Is there a problem?" Jerry asked.

"Maybe. We keep our closed files at Elite Storage's warehouse. They have a record of the file but they can't find it. It may be misfiled."

"I don't want to drop the motion but you don't have to keep looking. If Ms. Van Meter stays awake, I'll dismiss the motion. The case will probably be dismissed anyway as soon as Dr. Linscott gives Ms. Van Meter a clean bill of health."

While Monte Jefferson was talking to Jerry, Ashley noticed Randy Coleman talking to his attorney in a corner of the room. He looked angry. The lawyer shrugged and held up his hands. Coleman swore and started to leave. Ashley intercepted him before he reached the door.

"Mr. Coleman, please."

Coleman whirled around and glared at her. "What do you want?"

"I didn't get a chance to thank you yesterday for saving my life."

Coleman relaxed and forced a smile. "Glad I was there for you."

"Me, too. I'd be dead if it wasn't for you. You were very brave."

Coleman shrugged. "I didn't really think about it. I saw you were in trouble and I just acted."

"I'm glad you did."

Coleman stepped back and examined Ashley. She felt uncomfortable.

"I don't see it," he said with a shake of his head.

"See what?"

"The resemblance. And you sure ain't alike personality-wise. You seem nice. Casey is a bitch on wheels."

Ashley flushed. Even if she didn't know her well, she didn't like to hear someone run down her mother.

"She was always nice to me," she said, feeling the need to defend Casey.

"Oh, she can be nice. She was real nice to me, at first. Then she got bored and she wasn't so nice."

"What do you mean?"

"You sure you want to know?"

"Yes," she answered, but she wasn't really certain that she wanted to know about her mother's dark side. Miles had been frank about his sister. Would her husband make her sound even worse?

"I don't know what being in that coma did do to her. Maybe you'll be lucky and she'll change.

But the Casey I knew was a self-centered, vicious bitch."

Coleman rolled up his sleeve. Ashley saw a series of faint, circular scars.

"Cigarette burns," he said, answering her unspoken question. "Know how I got them? We had an argument one night. I can't even remember what it was about. We'd been drinking and we probably both said some shit to each other. I passed out. When I came to I was naked and handcuffed to the bed." He pointed at the scars. "These aren't the only ones. I got them all over my body. They hurt like a son-of-a-bitch. Your mom said she did it to teach me manners. Know what she did after she got tired of hearing me scream?"

Ashley shook her head.

Coleman flashed a humorless smile. "She left the house with me still cuffed to the bed. At first, I was sure she'd come back and we'd make up. We'd fought before and that's the way it always ended up. But she left me to die."

Ashley's eyes widened. Coleman could see that she didn't believe him.

"I was chained up on that bed for a day and a half. No food, no water, lying in my own piss. The only reason I'm here is because a friend of mine dropped by to tell me my boss was mad that I missed work. He heard me screaming and got in through a window. Otherwise I'd be dead."

Ashley felt sick and scared. She hoped that Coleman was exaggerating. She couldn't believe that Casey could be that cruel. Ashley was also tempted to confront him and ask why he had followed Casey to Portland if she was that awful. Of course, she knew the answer to that one. He wanted Casey's money. And she didn't confront Coleman because she owed him her life.

"That sounds awful," was what she did say.

"It was the worst experience I ever had," Coleman said. He had a faraway look in his eyes and an odd tone to his voice that made Ashley think that he was telling the truth.

"Well, kid, I wish you luck. You're gonna need it with that bitch for a mother."

"That's one bitter man," Ashley said when Coleman was out of earshot.

"You'd be bitter too, if your shot at millions of dollars just went down the toilet," Jerry said.

"It has," Ashley answered, "and I'm not bitter at all."

Jerry threw his head back and laughed. "You are one amazing woman."

During the walk across the parking lot to his

car, Jerry seemed preoccupied. When they were ready to leave the lot he didn't start the engine right away.

"What's wrong?" Ashley asked.

"Nothing's wrong. I've just been thinking. You have to pay rent every month on that apartment, which is an okay apartment, but not that great. And I've got this house I'm living in that's really too big for one person."

Ashley stared at Jerry for a moment. Then she frowned. "Are you asking me to move in with you?"

"Yeah. That's what I was getting around to."

"For a lawyer, you can be pretty inarticulate at times."

"So?"

Ashley leaned across the seat and kissed her attorney. "I'd love to shack up with you, Jerry."

CHAPTER
TWENTY-SIX

Two guards led a heavily manacled Joshua Maxfield into the contact visiting room. The smaller of the two guards jammed his baton into the prisoner's ribs to prod him forward, even though it wasn't necessary. The other guard said nothing. Maxfield knew that it was no use protesting and maintained a stoic silence.

Eric Swoboda, Maxfield's new attorney, unreeled from the plastic chair on which he was sitting. He was basketball-player tall, with a weightlifter's neck and a defensive lineman's girth. His head was huge and his jaw jutted out like a granite shelf. They had already met when Maxfield was arraigned on escape-and-assault charges stemming from his attack on Barry Weller. In light of what he'd done to his last attorney, Maxfield suspected that his new attorney's physique had been the main reason that the presiding judge had appointed him. Joshua hoped that the behemoth's brainpower was commensurate with his size.

The guards left the visiting room, but another guard stood in the corridor and watched the attorney-client meeting through the window. Swoboda started to offer his hand but stopped when he realized that Maxfield's hands were chained in a way that made it impossible to extend them more than a few inches.

"Looks like they got you trussed up like a Thanksgiving turkey," the lawyer said.

"I would appreciate it if you could get the court to ease some of its restrictions," Maxfield answered in a reasonable tone.

"I'll try, but don't get your hopes up. Everyone gets real uptight when your name is mentioned."

Maxfield looked down, a shy smile on his face. "I guess I have no one to blame but myself."

"Say, before I forget," Swoboda said, "I read **A Tourist in Babylon.**" Maxfield looked up expectantly. "I don't read much fiction, but I liked it."

"Most people did," Maxfield said, smiling with relief.

"I heard that the book won a lot of awards."

"Yes, several," Maxfield said proudly. "It was a national bestseller, too."

"You wrote another book, didn't you?" Swoboda asked.

"The Wishing Well," Maxfield answered, his smile ebbing.

"I hear it didn't do as well as your first book."

The smile disappeared. "The critics were too stupid to understand it, so they panned it," Maxfield answered bitterly. "The pack always tries to bring down someone who has risen too high, too fast."

"How come you waited so long to write a new book?"

Maxfield colored. "Writing can't be rushed. I'm an author of serious fiction. I don't churn out potboilers. I'm not a hack."

"The DA included a copy of your new book with the discovery. I read a little of it. It doesn't sound that high-minded."

"You have to understand what I am trying to do. My book is an exploration of madness. How does the human mind really work? How can a man look normal, marry, have children, and appear to be just as sane as you or I, yet have a demon within him that compels him to commit unspeakable acts? That is what I am exploring, the depth of the human soul."

"Yes, well, Delilah Wallace thinks you're describing murders that you committed."

Maxfield's fists clenched. "I am an artist. Artists use their imagination to create on paper a world that is as real as that which exists around us. If she believes that what I've written is real, I have succeeded as an artist. But the crimes in my novel are the product of my imagination. If I actually killed those people it would be a betrayal of my art. My book would be no more creative than a reporter's account of a traffic accident. Don't you see, I could never do what she is suggesting? It would be a complete betrayal of my craft. I am innocent of these murders."

"I talked to Barry Weller. He says you claimed you were innocent right up until the minute you coldcocked him and stole his clothes."

Maxfield flushed. "How is Barry? Not still mad at me, I hope."

"You hope in vain. Every time I mentioned your name I had to listen to a string of swear words I didn't know you could hook together in one sentence."

"I'm sorry I hurt him, but I was certain I'd be convicted if I went to trial. I needed time to find the evidence that would clear me."

"And did you?"

"I know who murdered Terri Spencer and tried to kill Casey."

"Let me hear it," Swoboda said, trying hard to keep from sounding sarcastic.

"Randy Coleman. He's Casey's husband. If she dies before the divorce becomes final, Coleman inherits millions. That's why he tried to kill Ashley Spencer. As Casey's daughter, Ashley will inherit a substantial portion of Casey's estate. With her dead, Coleman gets all of it."

"Coleman says that he stopped you from killing Miss Spencer."

"He's lying. It's the other way around."

"Who do you think a jury will believe, Coleman or the man Ashley Spencer saw standing over Casey Van Meter holding a bloody knife?"

Maxfield started to answer the question, but he realized how lame any protest would sound. His shoulders slumped and he sagged on his chair.

"And why would you want Ashley alive?" Swoboda asked. "Her testimony can put you on death row."

"As long as Casey is in that coma I need Ashley alive."

"Why is that?"

"Miles wants to pull the plug on his sister and

Coleman needs her dead so he can inherit her money. Ashley is the only person who wants to keep her alive."

"Why is keeping Casey alive important to you?"

"She's the only one who knows what really happened in the boathouse. She's the only witness who can clear me. You'll see if she ever comes out of her coma."

Swoboda smiled. "She has. That's why I'm here."

Maxfield looked stunned.

"Casey Van Meter came out of her coma yesterday. Delilah Wallace called me with the news. She was at the nursing home this morning."

"Did she tell them I didn't do it?"

"Right now Ms. Van Meter isn't saying anything. I guess she's pretty groggy."

"When are they going to question her about the boathouse?"

"I don't know. I'll be notified when they do."

"That's great. She'll tell them I didn't kill Terri."

"I hope so for your sake. Because I don't see any other way of winning your case."

CHAPTER
TWENTY-SEVEN

Eric Swoboda was the only addition to the group that had met at Sunny Rest on the morning of Casey Van Meter's resurrection.

"I'm going to set some ground rules, just as I did the last time I permitted Ms. Van Meter to have visitors," Dr. Linscott told them. "Only a few people will be allowed to visit. I don't want my patient to be overwhelmed, especially when she's going to be asked about a very traumatic event. Miss Wallace represents the prosecution and Mr. Swoboda represents the defendant. Miss Wallace wants to have one of the investigating officers with her, so I'm going to let Detective Birch go in with her. That's it."

"Mr. Coleman is Ms. Van Meter's husband,"

Anthony Botteri said. "He should have a right to be with his wife in this stressful moment."

"We don't let relatives sit in when we question witnesses in homicide cases," Delilah told Coleman's lawyer.

"You've let Miles Van Meter visit and. . . ."

Dr. Linscott held up his hand. "Mr. Botteri, my patient asked to have her brother visit. She had a very negative reaction to your client the last time and has specifically asked that Mr. Coleman not be permitted in her room."

"She's confused, doctor," Randy Coleman said. "She just woke up from a five-year-long coma."

"And she's still not fully recovered from her ordeal. That's why I'm excluding everyone but the people I've named."

Dr. Linscott looked at the detective, the defense attorney, and the deputy DA. "At the slightest sign of a problem, I'll terminate the interview. Is that understood?"

Delilah, Eric Swoboda, and Larry Birch nodded their assent, and Dr. Linscott led them out of the conference room.

The television was on and Casey was still in bed, but she turned her head as soon as Dr. Linscott opened the door. Her color was better and she seemed to be more alert.

"Good morning, Casey," the doctor said.

"Good morning," she replied.

"I've brought some people who want to talk to you. Do you feel up to having visitors?"

Casey turned off the set. "I'm glad you brought them. I've been getting tired of having nothing to do but watch TV."

"This is Delilah Wallace, a deputy district attorney in Multnomah County," Dr. Linscott said. "This is Larry Birch. He's a detective who's helping Miss Wallace with a case. And this is Eric Swoboda. He's an attorney who's representing someone involved in the case."

"Is this about me, how I got here?" Casey asked.

Delilah was pleased at the speed with which Casey figured out the purpose of their visit. This woman was able to think fast and appeared to be in charge of her faculties. That was going to make it hard for Swoboda to argue that Casey's memory had been affected by her coma.

"You're right, Ms. Van Meter," Delilah answered. "I'm here because of the attack that put you in your coma. Do you feel up to answering some questions about it?"

Suddenly Casey looked drained. She closed her eyes and rested her head against the pillow.

"Ms. Van Meter?" Delilah asked, concerned by the rapid change.

Casey's eyes opened. "Let's get it over with." She sounded resigned to having to discuss the incident in the boathouse.

"You're certain it's okay?" Delilah asked. "We don't want to do anything that might harm you."

Casey stared at Delilah. Her gaze was firm. "Ask your questions," she said, and the DA sensed an inner strength that boded well if Casey had to testify in court.

"I guess the best way to handle this is to just ask you what you remember about the night you were knocked out."

Casey started to say something, but she stopped dead, turned pale, and brought her hands to her face.

"Casey?" Dr. Linscott asked.

She shook her head, as if she was shaking off a terrible dream, and then took a deep breath.

"It's okay," Casey assured the doctor.

"Is Terri Spencer dead?" Casey asked Delilah.

"Yes, ma'am," Delilah answered as she suppressed her excitement. Van Meter was going to remember it all and they were going to nail Joshua Maxfield's coffin shut.

Casey took a deep breath. "I was hoping. . . . But I knew in my heart that she didn't survive. It's my fault. If I hadn't asked her to meet me she wouldn't be dead."

Delilah's heartbeat quickened. "Who killed Terri, Ms. Van Meter?"

Casey looked at her. She seemed puzzled. "Why Joshua Maxfield, of course. Didn't you know that?"

CHAPTER
TWENTY-EIGHT

Ashley experienced déjà vu as soon as she drove through the gates of the Oregon Academy. Little had changed in the intervening five years. Groups of garrulous students lounged on the grass and walked on the grounds, oblivious to the murder that had robbed Ashley of the woman she still thought of as her mother. Their innocence made her sad. She had been a child once, but Joshua Maxfield had forced her to grow up in the space of one horror-filled evening.

The mansion came into view. Ashley expected it to look different because it had been uninhabited since Henry Van Meter's death, but Henry had established a healthy endowment for the school before he died, part of which had gone to keep up the Van Meter home. Henry held out hope for

Casey's recovery to the last and he wanted his daughter to have a familiar place to live when she arose from her deathlike sleep. Last week, Dr. Linscott had decided that Casey was well enough to move back to her childhood home.

Ashley parked in the circular driveway that curved in front of the entrance to the mansion but she did not get out of the car. She felt light-headed. Her stomach was upset from worrying about her meeting with her mother. Would Casey reject her? Would she show any affection for the child she'd abandoned? Jerry had volunteered to come with her, but Ashley told him that this was something she had to do alone.

Ashley gathered herself and got out of the car. She was dressed in a conservative suit she had purchased for this meeting. Her palms were damp and her heart raced when she rang the doorbell. A stocky Korean woman with short black hair let her in.

"You must be Ashley."

"Yes."

"I'm Nan Kim, Ms. Van Meter's nurse."

"Did Dr. Linscott talk to my . . . Ms. Van Meter about . . . ?"

"They had a long talk about you. He explained everything, and she wants to see you. She's waiting for you in her room. She wanted me to ask if you want any refreshment."

"No, I'm fine, thank you." Ashley wouldn't have been able to hold anything down anyway.

"Let's go up then," the nurse said.

Casey was waiting for Ashley in a large, airy room with high ceilings. Her bed had been moved next to the window so she could look out at the garden and the pool. She was propped up on pillows and had regained some of her lost weight and a lot of her color. Her hair had been dyed blond to look as it had before her accident. A wheelchair and a walker stood in one corner. A comfortable armchair had been placed next to the bed.

"Thank you for seeing me," Ashley said as soon as she was seated and the nurse had left the room.

"I should be thanking you for visiting. I'm bored out of my mind. I stay in bed most of the day. The only time I get out is for physical therapy or when they help me downstairs for meals."

"How are you feeling?"

The question sounded awkward, and they both knew that Ashley was stalling so she would not have to start asking the hard questions that had brought her here.

"Coming back from the dead takes some getting used to. There are my missing years and my physical problems."

Casey paused. She studied her visitor. The close scrutiny made Ashley uncomfortable.

"There's also you." Casey smiled. "For instance, what shall we call each other? I don't know if 'mother' is appropriate."

Ashley looked down. "I don't want to offend you, but it would be hard for me to think of anyone but Terri as my mom."

"I can understand that, and it doesn't offend me in the least. You used to call me Dean, but I'm not anymore, and that's way too formal for our relationship. So why don't you call me Casey and I'll call you Ashley. How does that sound?"

"Okay."

"How did you find out about your father and me?"

"Your father told Jerry Philips, my attorney, about the adoption. He told me."

"And why did Henry reveal our relationship after so many years?"

Ashley decided not to tell Casey that Henry needed her to prevent Miles from taking his sister off life support, because she wasn't certain how much Casey knew.

"I guess he wanted me to know that I still had a family."

"Do you hate me for abandoning you?" Casey asked.

The directness of Casey's question caught Ashley off guard. Then it dawned on Ashley that Casey Van Meter was once again the dean. Casey was back in charge.

Ashley decided that she would be direct, too. "I did at first."

"How do you feel now?"

"Confused, but I don't hate you anymore. I tried to look at it from your point of view, to imagine how I would have felt if I was pregnant by a man I . . . I didn't love."

Ashley looked down.

"You're right, Ashley. I didn't love your father. Marriage would have been wrong for both of us. It would never have lasted. And I was too young to be a mother. When I gave you up for adoption it had nothing to do with you. It wasn't your fault. I never even saw you. They took you away the moment I delivered. I was sedated. I don't even have a clear memory of the birth. But it turned out for the best, didn't it? Norman was a good father?"

"The best."

"And you loved Terri?"

"Very much."

Ashley paused and gathered the courage to ask the next question. "Did you ever regret giving me up?"

"There have been moments when I wondered what became of you. I'm glad you had loving parents. I'm happy that you're a strong, self-confident woman, even if I can't take any credit for what you've become."

"Did you ever try to find me?"

"No, never."

"Why?"

"May I be brutally honest?"

"Please," Ashley said, steeling herself.

"You were never real to me. You were like a dream. I never held you, I never saw you. How could I love you or want you? And what good would it have done if I showed up out of the blue and destroyed your peace of mind? Look at the turmoil you've been through since you learned I was your mother."

Ashley swallowed, fighting the tightness in her throat and the fear that she would cry. She kept her next question overly formal to distance herself from the emotions that were raging inside her.

"What about now? Do you want to get to know me or would you prefer that we not contact each other?"

Casey cocked an eyebrow and flashed a wry smile. "What a silly question. Of course I want to get to know you. I liked you from the first day we met. Do you remember when I showed you the campus? I knew that you were a good person, immediately. I admired the way you dealt with the horror of your situation, your steel, your poise. Had we been the same age I would have wanted you as a friend. There's still the age difference, but that means less and less as we get older. So I propose that we start off as friends. We can see each other from time to time and try not to force anything. Let's see how it goes. Is that acceptable to you?"

"Okay."

"Good. Now, you know what I've been doing for the past five years. I think it's only fair that you bring me up to date on how you spent your time while I've been asleep."

Jerry had to work late, so Ashley agreed to meet him at Typhoon, a Thai restaurant on Broadway a few blocks from his office. The hostess showed

Ashley to a table in the crowded restaurant where Jerry was waiting.

"How did the meeting with Casey go?" Jerry asked as soon as she was seated.

"Better than I thought it would."

"You shouldn't be surprised. You liked Casey when you were at the Academy, didn't you?"

"Yes, but I only saw her a few times. Except for when she took Mom and me around, I never did more than say hi when we passed on campus. It was real superficial. And when I was at the Academy I didn't know that she abandoned me and I hadn't heard all of these bad things about her."

"Bad like what?"

"You told me how wild she was when she met Dad. Miles said pretty much the same thing. She's been in rehab. She was promiscuous. If you can believe Randy Coleman, she could also be violent and sadistic."

Ashley related what Coleman had said about Casey chaining him to their bed and burning him with cigarettes. Jerry was appalled.

"But being in the coma and coming out of it, maybe that changed her," Ashley said. "This afternoon we really clicked. I want to get to know her better."

Jerry reached out and took Ashley's hands. "This is good, Ashley. This can really help you. With Maxfield in prison and finding out that you get along with Casey, you can have a new start. You can get your life back."

"You left something out."

"What?"

Ashley squeezed Jerry's hands. "You, Jerry. If anyone has saved me, it's you."

BOOK TOUR

The Present

"Did Ashley and your sister become friends?" a young woman in the back row asked Miles Van Meter.

"Yes, Ashley started visiting Glen Oaks regularly. When Casey was able to walk, Ashley would keep her company on the trails at the Academy. They're still good friends."

A hand went up in the second row. Miles smiled at a middle-aged woman in a business suit.

"**Sleeping Beauty** reads like a murder mystery," she said. "Have you ever tried your hand at fiction?"

"I took a creative writing course in college. I did rather well in it. And, of course, there are all those lawyers who are writing legal thrillers. When that trend started I thought about trying my hand at one, but I practice business law and my cases were too dull for a good plot."

"Are you going to write another true crime book?"

"No. Writing about my sister's case was enough for me."

"What about a novel?"

Miles smiled shyly. "Well, I do have an idea for a thriller. I'm working up a proposal. If my agent thinks it's any good I'll probably take a stab at it."

A heavyset man in the front row raised his hand and Miles acknowledged him.

"Whose idea was it to write a new edition of **Sleeping Beauty**?"

"Actually, my editor got the idea after Maxfield's arrest. He asked me if I had any interest in writing additional chapters that would include the trial for a new edition of the book. I agreed. I thought that the book needed these final chapters to bring the events in it to an end. It also gave me closure."

A woman who was standing between the bookcases in the back of the room raised her hand. Miles pointed at her.

"Has your sister read **Sleeping Beauty** and, if she has, what does she think of it?"

"Casey has read it. I think it was tough for her, but she's one tough lady."

The audience applauded.

"To answer the second part of your question, Casey said she liked it, but I don't think she'd be honest with me if she hated it. After all, we love each other. That, by the way, is one reason to never ask your mother to critique your work."

Miles waited for the laughter to die down before calling on a scholarly-looking gentleman with gray hair and wire-rimmed glasses who was wearing a tweed sports coat with leather patches on the sleeves.

"Was it hard for you to sit through Joshua Maxfield's trial?"

"Yes and no. I didn't like to hear about the terrible things he'd done, but I felt great relief that he was finally facing justice. I think it was much harder for Ashley."

PART THREE

STATE V. JOSHUA MAXFIELD

One Year Earlier

CHAPTER
TWENTY-NINE

The bailiff rapped his gavel to start the fourth day of Joshua Maxfield's trial. Delilah Wallace smiled in anticipation of the day's events. She was delighted with the jury that had been empaneled during the first two days. They were a group of tough, no-nonsense people. She was certain that they would see through any defense tricks and have no qualms about finding death to be the appropriate sentence after they convicted the defendant of aggravated murder.

Delilah was also pleased with the way opening statements had gone. Hers had been detailed and impassioned. She had laid out the evidence the jury would hear in chronologic order and had named the witnesses who would establish each piece of evidence. By the time she was through with her presentation she noticed more than one juror nodding unconsciously when she made a point. They also smiled when she brought a little levity to the proceedings. It was easy for Delilah to make friends, and she felt that she had twelve new ones by the time she sat down.

In Delilah's opinion, Eric Swoboda's opening statement had been boring and uninformative. He had talked about the concept of reasonable doubt but he had not mentioned a single reason why the jury was going to have one when the trial was over. He had been vague about how the defense would counter the state's arguments. He had talked theory but had presented no facts. Delilah knew why. The defense had no arguments to counter hers. It had no evidence that would create any kind of doubt, much less a reasonable doubt. Joshua Maxfield was guilty, guilty, guilty, and Delilah was satisfied that she had the means to bring him to justice.

The Honorable Andrew Shimazu had been assigned to hear Joshua Maxfield's case. Shimazu was a short, chubby, congenial Japanese-American with a full head of straight, black hair. After graduating from the University of Hawaii with an engineering degree, Shimazu had attended the Northwestern School of Law of Lewis and Clark

College in Portland and stayed on. After he spent several years with a large firm and two terms in the state legislature, the governor had appointed him to the Multnomah County Circuit Court. This was his sixth year on the bench. His intelligence and judicial temperament had made him one of the most popular judges in the courthouse.

"Call your first witness, Miss Wallace," Judge Shimazu ordered.

Delilah had decided to begin her case with her most appealing and deadliest witness. The prosecutor wanted the jury to be convinced of Maxfield's guilt from the get-go. Once they had formed their opinion, it would be very difficult for Eric Swoboda to change it.

"The State calls Ashley Spencer," Delilah said.

As Ashley walked down the aisle to the witness box she remembered how terrified she had been when she testified at Joshua Maxfield's preliminary hearing. Today, she was focused and angry. When she passed the defense table, Ashley glared at Maxfield. She noticed with great satisfaction that he could not meet her steady gaze. Ashley looked away and walked to the front of the witness box where she stood with her head held high as the bailiff administered the oath.

Ashley took her seat and waited for Delilah Wallace to begin her direct examination. Jerry was seated behind the prosecutor in the first row of the spectator section. He flashed her a smile of encouragement when their eyes met. Ashley knew better than to smile back. Delilah had instructed her to be serious from the moment she took the stand to the moment she finished testifying.

Seated next to Jerry was Miles Van Meter. Delilah had not included him on her witness list. He was in court to lend moral support to his sister when she testified and because he was writing an updated edition of his book.

Delilah started her direct examination gently, by walking her witness through her relationship with her parents and her high school soccer career. In her opening statement, Delilah had outlined the testimony that she expected Ashley to give, and the jurors listened sympathetically to what Ashley had to say.

After laying her groundwork, Delilah led Ashley to the night that Tanya Jones and her father were murdered. Ashley told the jury how she and Tanya had been attacked and bound, and how she had watched helplessly as the man who invaded her home dragged Tanya into the guest room. Ashley's poise broke momentarily when she recounted Tanya's rape and murder, and she had to pause and drink some water before she could go on.

"Do you want to continue, Miss Spencer?" Judge Shimazu asked. "We can take a recess."

Ashley took a deep breath and looked across at Joshua Maxfield. Once again, Maxfield refused to meet her eyes. That gave her strength.

"I'd like to go on, Your Honor. I'm okay."

"Very well. Miss Wallace."

"Thank you, Your Honor. Now, Ashley, you said that you heard Tanya Jones's muffled screams. What was the first sound you heard from the man who attacked Tanya after he took her into the guest room?"

"I . . . I heard a gasp."

"What did you believe that signified?"

"Objection, Your Honor," Eric Swoboda said. "Speculation."

"Your Honor, there will be testimony that Miss Jones was a virgin and that there was evidence of rape. Miss Spencer's observation will be amply corroborated by this other evidence."

"Mr. Swoboda, I'm going to let Miss Spencer testify."

"Ashley?" Delilah said.

"It sounded like he was . . . like it was sex." Ashley reddened. "That he'd had an orgasm."

"What did you hear after that?"

"Tanya was whimpering. Then I heard a. . . . It was like an animal. It didn't sound human. Then there were these grunts and Tanya stopped screaming."

"Did the grunts stop when Tanya stopped screaming?"

"No. They went on and on. Then the door to the guest room slammed open."

"What did you think was going to happen next?"

"I . . . I thought he was going to rape me and kill me, like Tanya. The same thing."

"What happened instead?"

"He stopped in the doorway and looked at me. That seemed to go on forever. But he didn't come in. He went downstairs."

"Did you hear anything downstairs?"

"I heard the refrigerator door open."

"We'll get back to what happened in the kitchen in a bit, but I want you to tell the jury how you escaped."

Ashley sat up straight and turned to the jurors. In that moment, she felt as she had in the second grade when she'd played soccer with her father's spirit inside her. Norman was there once again and he made her strong. He filled her with power and lifted her up.

"My father saved my life," she told the jurors. "My father sacrificed his life for mine. I would not be alive today if it was not for my father, Norman Spencer."

Delilah had Ashley detail her escape from her home and her subsequent decision to attend the Oregon Academy. Ashley told the jury about her contacts with Joshua Maxfield and her mother's involvement with his writing seminar. Then Ashley testified about the incident at the boathouse.

"Ashley," Delilah asked, "you were real serious about your soccer, weren't you?"

"Yes."

"In addition to your team workouts, did you have your own conditioning program?"

"Well, I did extra workouts."

"Did you like to run in the woods on the Academy grounds in the evening to build up your wind and your legs?"

"Yes."

"Did you take a run on the evening that Terri Spencer was murdered?"

Ashley paled. She looked down and said, "Yes," so softly that the court reporter had to ask her to repeat her answer.

"During your run, did you see anyone?"

"Yes."

"Who did you see?"

Ashley looked across the room and pointed at Joshua Maxfield.

"I saw him, the defendant."

"What was he doing?"

"He was walking by the river."

"Was there anything unusual about the way he was walking?"

"No. I really didn't think anything of it because he lived near the boathouse."

"Was he walking toward or away from the boathouse?"

"Toward it."

"Did anything unusual happen shortly after you saw the defendant?"

"Yes, I heard a woman scream. Then I heard another scream."

"How close together were the screams?"

"Pretty close. I can't say exactly."

"Where did the screams come from?"

"The direction of the boathouse."

"What did you do after you heard the screams?"

"I was scared. I froze after the first one. Then I thought someone might be hurt so I cut through the woods and ended up on the side of the boathouse."

"Did you see anyone else on your way to the boathouse?"

"No."

"What happened next?"

"I heard a woman say something."

"What did she say?"

"I don't know. I just heard the sound. It was muffled by the walls."

"How do you know it was a woman?"

"It was high-pitched."

"What did you do after you heard the sound?"

"I looked in the window of the boathouse."

"What did you see?"

Ashley pointed at Maxfield. "I saw him and there were two women lying on the floor. And he was holding a knife. There was blood on it." Ashley was finding it hard to breathe, but she forced herself to finish her testimony. "He saw me and he tried to kill me. He killed my mother and he ran after me and tried to kill me."

"Who killed your mother, Ashley?" Delilah asked. "Who tried to kill you?"

"Him. Joshua Maxfield. He tried to kill me. He killed my mother."

Ashley began to sob.

After a recess, Delilah had Ashley recount her recovery on the Academy grounds and the attack in the dormitory that followed Maxfield's escape. Eric Swoboda's cross-examination was mercifully short, and her testimony ended just before five o'clock. Judge Shimazu adjourned court for the day. Delilah, Jerry Philips, Larry Birch, and Tony Marx formed a protective circle around Ashley and helped her get through the crowd outside the courtroom. Delilah stopped in front of the elevators and faced the cameras and microphones. Her body shielded Ashley from the glare of the lights and the questions shouted at her by the reporters.

"Miss Spencer will not answer any questions. She is exhausted. These past five years have been a terrible ordeal for her and I ask you to respect her privacy. She has been very brave today. Let her have some peace."

Several reporters shouted questions at Delilah. She answered them while Jerry and the detectives hustled Ashley into the elevator.

"You were fantastic," Jerry said when the elevator doors closed.

"I don't feel fantastic," Ashley said.

"Well it's over now and Swoboda didn't lay a glove on you."

"I didn't see it as a boxing match, Jerry."

"No, no. I meant that your testimony was basically unchallenged. It was everything Delilah could have hoped for. You're going to be a major reason that Maxfield will be convicted. He couldn't even look you in the eye. The jury saw that."

Ashley felt no elation, only exhaustion, although there was also a feeling of peace because her part in the trial was over.

The elevator stopped and Jerry and the detectives brought Ashley to Delilah's office. A few minutes later, Delilah joined them. There was a huge smile on her face.

"Come here, girlfriend," she said as she wrapped Ashley in a warm embrace. After a moment, she stood back and held her witness at arm's length.

"You can be mighty proud of yourself, young lady. You have single-handedly brought a terrible murderer to justice. I know we have a way to go but I was watching the faces of those twelve jurors and they are converted. It would take the intervention of the Almighty to work an acquittal for

Joshua Maxfield, and he only has Eric Swoboda and Satan on his side."

Ashley blushed at Delilah's effusive praise.

"How you feelin'?" Delilah asked. "You feelin' relieved?"

Ashley nodded.

"You'll sleep good tonight, child, because you done good. You avenged your parents. You did them proud."

"I'm so glad I don't have to come to court anymore."

Delilah's smile disappeared. "I know you want to stay away and put this behind you, but I need you in court every day until the trial ends."

Ashley looked stricken. Delilah looked right at her. When she spoke her tone was firm.

"Your parents need you in court to face down their killer. You represent Norman and Terri Spencer and Tanya Jones. It's important that the jury see you every day. They have to know that you're watching them and holding them to account."

"All right."

Delilah gave Ashley's shoulders a gentle squeeze. "Your day of rest will come soon, but you have to play your part to make sure that Joshua Maxfield never has another peaceful day."

CHAPTER THIRTY

Jerry couldn't go to court with Ashley the next day because he had an appearance in Washington County in a divorce case. He offered to try to set over the case, but Ashley wouldn't hear of it. When she walked into the courtroom, Miles Van Meter was already in his front-row seat.

"I didn't get a chance to talk to you yesterday," Miles said. "Your testimony was excellent. I was watching the jurors. They hung on every word. I hope Casey holds up as well as you did."

"I'm sure she will. She's a very strong woman."

"I appreciate the time you're spending with her. It's helped her recovery tremendously."

"She is my mother," Ashley responded. Thinking of Casey as her mother was getting easier.

"The way she treated you, you don't owe her

anything. That's what makes what you're doing so great."

"Getting to know Casey has helped me, too. It's like I'm starting to build a family again."

Miles was about to respond when the bailiff rapped the gavel and called the courtroom to order.

Delilah began the day by calling three members of Joshua Maxfield's writing seminar. They told the jurors how upset Terri Spencer was during Maxfield's reading of the excerpt from his serial-killer novel. Delilah's next witness was Dean Van Meter's secretary, who established that Terri had met with the dean on the day of her death. After the secretary, Delilah called a representative of the phone company to prove that the dean had phoned Ashley's mother within an hour of the meeting at the Academy.

During the testimony, Ashley would glance at Joshua Maxfield when a witness made an important point. He never looked back. His shoulders were hunched and he stared at the tabletop. It appeared to Ashley that he had given up.

Delilah's next witness was Dr. Sally Grace, the medical examiner. It took a good part of the morning for her to explain the cause of death for Tanya Jones and Ashley's father and mother. Dr.

Grace's explanation was accompanied by graphic photos, which were passed to the members of the jury. Fortunately for Ashley, the spectators could not see the autopsy and crime-scene photographs. The testimony about her parents' and her friend's injuries was gruesome enough. Even though Delilah had warned her about what she would hear, it took all of Ashley's self-control to stay in the courtroom.

After the lunch break, Delilah used Tony Marx to introduce evidence that had been gathered at the boathouse and Joshua Maxfield's cabin. Then she called Detective Birch, who introduced the evidence that had been discovered at the Spencer home crime scene. After an hour of this, Delilah asked a question about another subject.

"At some point in your investigation did you develop a theory that the man who committed these murders had committed murders in other states?"

"Yes," Birch answered.

"What steps did you take to find out if you were right?"

"We sent information about the case to the FBI."

"Why did you do that?"

"There is a division of the bureau that tracks serial killings from around the country."

Delilah addressed Judge Shimazu. "I have no further questions of Detective Birch at this time. But I plan to recall him, Your Honor."

"You may cross-examine, Mr. Swoboda."

"May I reserve my cross until Detective Birch has completed all of his testimony?"

"Any objection to that, Miss Wallace?"

"No, Your Honor."

"Call your next witness, Miss Wallace."

"The State calls Bridget Booth, Your Honor."

A moment later, a woman with short gray hair and a pale complexion walked down the aisle. Her bearing was military and she wore a gray business suit, white blouse, and practical shoes.

"What is your occupation, Mrs. Booth?" Delilah asked as soon as her witness had been sworn.

"I'm a special agent with the Federal Bureau of Investigation."

"Where are you headquartered?"

"Quantico, Virginia."

"Would you please tell the jury your educational background?"

"I received a bachelor's degree in psychology

and a master's degree in behavioral science from the University of Missouri."

"Where did you work after obtaining your degrees?"

"I was a policewoman and a homicide detective in St. Louis, Missouri, for seven years. Actually, I obtained my master's while I was on the force. During my seventh year in St. Louis, I applied to the FBI and was accepted. I completed basic training at Quantico, Virginia, and served four years as a special agent assigned to the Seattle office. Then I applied for VICAP and I've been there for thirteen years."

"What is VICAP?"

"It's an acronym for the FBI's Violent Criminal Apprehension Program. The program originated from an idea developed in the 1950s by the late Pierce Brooks, a detective with the Los Angeles Police Department. Detective Brooks was investigating the murders of two Los Angeles women who were found bound by rope in the desert. They had both answered an ad for photographic models. Detective Brooks was convinced that this was the work of a killer who had murdered before and would strike again, so he used his off-duty hours to read out-of-town newspapers in hopes of finding an account of another similar murder. He did find such a case and it led to an arrest and conviction.

"Detective Brooks became convinced that putting information about open homicide cases on a computer would enable law enforcement officers from around the country to solve cases with similar modus operandi. In 1983, the National Center for the Analysis of Violent Crime was created and placed under the direction and control of the FBI training center at Quantico. VICAP is a part of the center. Its goal is to collect, collate, and analyze all aspects of the investigation of similar-pattern multiple murders on a nationwide basis."

"Approximately five years ago, did you receive a call from Detective Larry Birch of the Portland Police Bureau concerning some homicides that had occurred in Oregon?" Delilah asked.

"Yes."

"Why did Detective Birch contact you?"

"The crimes were unusual, and he wondered if we were aware of other crimes with similar modus operandi. He was also in possession of an unpublished novel....."

"Objection, Your Honor," Swoboda said. "We object to any evidence about that book. It's irrelevant. It's made-up fiction."

"I've ruled on this pretrial, Mr. Swoboda," Judge Shimazu said. "I have decided that evidence concerning the book can be introduced for certain limited purposes. So I will overrule your objection and you can have a continuing objection. You may proceed, Miss Wallace."

"Thank you, Your Honor."

Delilah turned back to the witness. "Agent Booth, let's leave the novel aside for the time being. Did you find other murders that were similar to the murders Detective Birch was investigating?"

Booth turned toward the jurors. "We have identified murders in Iowa, Connecticut, Massachusetts, Rhode Island, Ohio, Michigan, Arizona, Montana, and Idaho that have been committed over a period of several years that may be the work of the same serial killer."

"What led you to that conclusion?"

"In each instance, the killer broke into a home in the early-morning hours. In each household there were parents and a teenage daughter. The killer bound the victims with duct tape and tortured the parents by cutting them to death slowly." Several members of the jury blanched. "He then raped the daughter before stabbing her to death."

"Did these murders have other things in common?"

"Yes. In more than one, there was evidence that the killer ate a snack at the home. For instance, the murderer ate a piece of pie at the home in Connecticut. A candy bar was consumed in the Montana case. During the Spencer and Jones murders—this case—the killer ate a piece of cake and drank some milk.

"Another thing they had in common was that the duct tape used in every case was manufactured by the same company. Furthermore, the tape used in the Michigan and Arizona cases came from the same roll."

"Has the FBI constructed a profile of the person who is responsible for these crimes?" Delilah asked.

"Objection," Swoboda said. "This would be sheer speculation."

"I'm inclined to agree, Miss Wallace," Judge Shimazu said. "The police can use certain tools in an investigation, like a lie detector, that are not sufficiently reliable to use as evidence in court. Unless you can lay a foundation for the scientific reliability of profiling, I'm going to sustain Mr. Swoboda's objection."

"Very well, Your Honor. Agent Booth, have you

had an opportunity to read two drafts of a novel that the defendant was writing at the time of his arrest?"

"Yes I have."

"Was this novel about a fictional serial killer?"

"Yes."

"Were there any similarities between the details of the crimes committed in the novel by the fictitious serial killer and evidence found at the real-life crime scenes created by the real serial killer you were profiling?"

"Yes."

"Did the similarities between the novel and real life involve evidence in the real cases that the police had not revealed to the public?"

"Yes."

"Will you outline the similarities for the jury?"

"In the novel, the killer breaks into a home in the early-morning hours and murders the parents of a teenage girl. He plans to rape and murder the girl, but before following through he eats a dessert in the kitchen of the crime scene. As I've testified previously, all of the real murders occurred in the early-morning hours and involved families with two parents and a teenage daughter. Furthermore, the murderer in Montana and Connecticut ate a snack at the crime scene, and the person who murdered Tanya Jones and Norman Spencer ate a piece of cake and drank some milk in the kitchen of the Spencer home."

"Did the police organizations in Montana, Connecticut, and Oregon release information about these snacks to the public?"

"No."

"Why did they keep these details secret?"

"Investigators keep unusual details of crimes secret to guard against false confessions. They want to be sure that they have arrested the right person for the crime. A person who knew a detail of a crime that was not made public is probably the perpetrator."

"Your Honor, I move to introduce Exhibit 75, pages from the defendant's novel, which contain the scene with the snack that Agent Booth just discussed."

"Objection," Swoboda said.

"Is this objection on new grounds, Mr. Swoboda?" the judge asked.

"No, Your Honor."

"Overruled. You're deemed to have a continuing objection to all similar exhibits. You don't have to object every time the novel is mentioned. Go on, Miss Wallace."

When Agent Booth was finished testifying

about other scenes in Joshua Maxfield's book that were similar to the real crimes, Delilah turned her over to Eric Swoboda.

"Agent Booth, you testified that the police organizations that investigated the crimes in places like Montana, Oregon, and Connecticut kept certain information secret."

"Yes."

"These are big organizations, are they not?"

"Yes."

"Have you ever heard of information that was supposed to be secret leaking from big police organizations?"

"Yes."

"There would be many people at a crime scene who would learn about a killer eating a snack during the commission of his crime, would there not?"

"There could be."

"Any one of these people could make this secret information public?"

"Yes."

"Agent Booth, are the crimes about which you've just testified the only ones of which you are aware in which the perpetrator used duct tape to bind a victim?"

"No."

"Isn't the use of duct tape common in crimes where a victim is tied up?"

"Duct tape is used by criminals."

"As part of your duties with VICAP or out of a personal preference, do you read fictional books about make-believe serial killers?"

"Yes."

"Have you ever read a novel that had a plot that mirrored aspects of a real case?"

"Yes."

"And there are many true-crime books about real serial killers, aren't there?"

"Yes."

"And these true-crime books describe in great detail how serial killers operate?"

"Yes."

"Novelists use their imagination to make a living, don't they?"

"Yes."

"And they do research? They read about real serial killers to make their characters come alive?"

"I suppose so."

"And novelists who write about serial killers would naturally develop ideas about how to kill someone or how a killer might act that might be very close to the way a real murderer might act?"

"I suppose so."

"Are you aware of novels involving serial killers where the killer uses duct tape to bind his fictional victims?"

"Yes."

"Agent Booth, you admitted that novelists frequently research real cases to make their fictional stories more believable, didn't you?"

"Yes."

"Has any author ever contacted VICAP to get background for a made-up story about a serial killer?"

"Yes."

"Do you know if Mr. Maxfield ever spoke with someone at VICAP or an FBI agent in another division or a police officer or a detective about serial killers for background?"

"He never spoke to me."

"That's not what I asked."

"I have no knowledge one way or the other about the defendant talking to someone at the FBI or other law enforcement officers about his book."

"Now, I believe that you testified that the duct tape in all of the cases came from the same manufacturer."

"Yes."

"How many rolls of this duct tape does the manufacturer make every year?"

"I don't have the exact figures with me."

"Is it safe to say that the company manufactures a lot of duct tape every year?"

"Yes."

"Thousands of rolls?"

"Probably."

"And these rolls are distributed nationally?"

"Yes."

"So it's quite possible that a murderer in Michigan and another totally unconnected murderer in Arizona could have purchased rolls from the same company?"

Agent Booth glanced toward Delilah before answering, and received a brief smile. Booth looked back at Swoboda.

"That is correct."

"When you began your testimony you stated that the FBI had identified murders in several states that—and I quote—'**may** be the work of the same serial killer'—unquote. That's correct, isn't it?"

"I believe so."

"Why did you say '**may** be the work'? Why weren't you more positive?"

"The evidence points to the same person committing the murders, but we can't say that this is a fact with one hundred percent certainty until the person confesses."

"Are there dissimilarities between some of the murders?"

Agent Booth glanced at Delilah, who kept her face blank.

"Did you understand my question, Agent Booth?"

"There were indications in the Connecticut and Montana cases that more than one person may have been in the home when the murders occurred."

"There were two killers?" Swoboda asked, trying unsuccessfully to hide his surprise.

"The perpetrator of these two crimes may have had an accomplice, but we could never be certain. In all other respects, the modus operandi in all of the crimes I mentioned was consistent with a single murderer having committed all of the murders."

"But if there were two killers involved in two of the crimes and only one killer in the other crimes, we might be dealing with unrelated homicides, right?"

"That is one possibility."

"If that's true then we'd have a situation where one person independently committed a crime that was almost identical to a crime committed by two other people, right?"

"Yes."

"And that would make it less amazing if a third person—a writer, say—also thought up a make-believe plot with a similar crime, wouldn't it?"

"I guess so," Agent Booth answered reluctantly.

"Thank you, Agent Booth," Swoboda said with a triumphant smile. "I have no further questions."

"Any redirect, Miss Wallace?" the judge asked.

"Yes, Your Honor. Agent Booth, Mr. Swoboda brought up the possibility that a killer in Arizona and a different killer in Michigan purchased separate rolls of duct tape made by the same manufacturer before committing their crimes, creating the false appearance that the crimes were related."

"Yes."

"Did the FBI ever establish a link between the duct tape used in Arizona and the duct tape used in Michigan that eliminated the possibility of coincidence?"

"Yes. The same exact roll of duct tape was used by the killer in Arizona and the killer in Michigan."

"How do you know that?"

"Our lab examined the ends of the duct tape used in every case and they found that one piece that was used to bind the hands of one of the Arizona victims fit a piece from the Michigan case like pieces of a jigsaw puzzle. It was a one hundred percent physical match."

CHAPTER THIRTY-ONE

The next morning, Ashley and Jerry Philips watched Randy Coleman swagger down the aisle, looking right and left, like a boxer entering the ring in an important fight. Coleman was wearing a new suit and he'd shaved and gotten a haircut. Ashley guessed that Coleman had not had many high points in his life and he was making the best of his fifteen minutes of fame.

"Mr. Coleman, are you the husband of Casey Van Meter, one of the victims in this case?" Delilah asked her witness.

"Yes, ma'am."

"When did you get married?"

"Six years ago."

"After two months of marriage, did Ms. Van Meter file for divorce?"

"Yes, but we were working that out when Maxfield tried to kill her."

"Objection. Not responsive to the question," Swoboda said. "Move to strike."

"Sustained. Jurors, you will disregard all of the witness's answer, except his affirmation that he and his wife were in the midst of a divorce."

"Mr. Coleman," Delilah said, "can you tell the jury about an encounter you had with the defendant at the Oregon Academy pool?"

Delilah had gone over the questions that she was going to ask on direct with Coleman. She had told him that there was nothing wrong with admitting that he and Casey Van Meter had been arguing, but Coleman had been very defensive and she prayed that he wouldn't mess up her case.

"Yeah, sure. I came to the school to talk to Casey. I knew she really didn't want to split up with me and I was sure we could work things out if we talked about our problems. She liked to swim in the pool and I found her doing laps. We'd just started talking when Maxfield attacked me from behind. I didn't have a chance. If he hadn't sneak-attacked me, I. . . ."

"Mr. Coleman," Delilah cut in, "during this altercation did the defendant make any threats to you?"

"Yeah. He threatened to kill me. He said he'd rig explosives to my car or my apartment."

"Moving to another subject, were you present at the Sunny Rest nursing home when the defendant was rearrested?"

"Yes, ma'am." Coleman's chest puffed up and he smiled at the jurors. "I captured him and saved Ashley Spencer's life."

"Please tell the jury what happened."

"Casey had been in this coma for years. At first, I was really bummed out. I tried to convince myself that she'd wake up someday soon. I didn't think visiting her would do any good. Her doctor told me she couldn't hear me or say anything, and I was afraid I'd be too upset if I saw her like a vegetable. Plus her father was real hostile to me. I think he was the one who talked Casey into filing for divorce. He was very domineering."

"Objection," Swoboda said. "The witness isn't answering the question."

"Yes, Mr. Coleman," the judge said, "you are getting pretty far afield."

"Sorry, Judge."

"Why don't you tell the jury what happened during your visit to the Sunny Rest nursing home on the day of the defendant's arrest?" Delilah said, praying that Coleman would stay on track.

"Okay. I was in town for the guardianship hearing and I decided to visit Casey. It was raining real heavy. I parked my car but I didn't get out. At first I really wanted to visit Casey, but then I worried about what she'd look like. I mean she'd been knocked out for five years. So I was sitting in my car, wondering what to do, when I saw Ashley Spencer leaving the nursing home. I figured that she'd just come from visiting Casey and I'd ask her what it was like."

Ashley looked over at Maxfield. He was sitting up and his eyes were drilling into Coleman. It was the first time in a while that he'd shown any signs of life.

"Lucky for her I decided I wanted to talk," Coleman went on. "By the time I got out of my car, she was running toward hers. I ducked my head because of the rain and followed her. When I looked up, a guy was coming at her with a knife."

"Could you see the assailant's face?" Delilah asked.

"No. He was wearing a hood."

"What happened next?"

"Ashley kicked him and ran. He went after her.

I knew the guy had a knife, but I wasn't gonna let that stop me. So I tackled him and wrestled him to the ground. Then, the cops arrived."

"Did you finally get to see the face of the man who tried to murder Ashley Spencer?"

"Yes, I did."

"And who was it?"

Coleman paused for effect before pointing at Joshua Maxfield. Maxfield glared at Coleman.

"The man who tried to stab Ashley Spencer to death is Joshua Maxfield, the defendant," Coleman said, raising his voice dramatically.

"No further questions."

Eric Swoboda crossed the room and stood a few inches from the witness.

"Mr. Coleman, I noticed that the prosecutor didn't ask you what you do for a living. Is that because she doesn't want the jury to know that you work for the Las Vegas mob?"

"That's a lie. I'm a businessman. Just because I work in Las Vegas doesn't make me a gangster."

"What is the name of your company?"

"American Investments."

"Hasn't American Investments been the target of a federal grand jury looking into money laundering?"

"That was a mistake. Nothing came of that."

"Is that because Myron Lemke, the government's star witness, was murdered before he could testify?"

"Objection," Delilah said. "Hearsay, irrelevant, and it violates the evidentiary rules on prior bad acts admissibility."

"I'm going to sustain the objection. Move on, Mr. Swoboda."

"Have you ever been convicted of a crime?"

"Yeah, years ago."

"What was the crime?"

"Assault."

"Were you ever convicted of theft?"

"That was a mistake. I thought I had money in my checking account and. . . ."

"The jury didn't agree with your defense, did it?" Swoboda asked.

"No," Coleman answered reluctantly.

"Mr. Coleman, you testified that Mr. Maxfield attacked you at the Oregon Academy swimming pool?"

"Yeah, from behind."

"At the time that he confronted you, were you holding Casey Van Meter's wrist and calling her a bitch?"

"I don't remember that."

"You don't remember attacking Ms. Van Meter?"

"No. We were talking."

Delilah sighed inwardly but showed the jury none of what she was feeling. She'd needed Coleman to prove that Maxfield tried to knife Ashley at Sunny Rest and that point had been made. Fortunately, the jurors didn't have to like Coleman to believe him.

"You're saying that Mr. Maxfield attacked you from behind for no reason in front of scores of witnesses?"

"The guy's a psycho. He didn't need a reason."

"Mr. Coleman, your wife is going to testify later in this case. Do you still contend that you were not assaulting her when Mr. Maxfield came to her rescue?"

"She's had a serious head injury. I don't think her memory is too good."

"We are prepared to call several former students who were in the pool that day. Do you still want to maintain this fiction?"

"Call anyone you want. I don't know what they'll say. We may have been arguing. Casey could get upset over nothing."

"What were you arguing about?"

"The divorce. I was trying to make her see reason."

"That's because Ms. Van Meter was rich and you couldn't get your hands on her money if she divorced you?"

"No. I didn't care about the money. I love her."

"That's why you didn't go see her at any time while she was wasting away at the nursing home?"

"I already told you about that. It was too much for me to see her like that."

"Yes, we can all see how sensitive you are," Swoboda said.

"Objection," Delilah said.

"Sustained," Judge Shimazu answered.

Swoboda turned his back on Coleman and took a few steps down the jury box.

"So it was love, not Ms. Van Meter's money, that caused you to seek an appointment as the guardian of her forty million dollars?"

Several jurors reacted when they heard the sum. Coleman didn't answer. Swoboda turned back toward him.

"How long did you know Ms. Van Meter before you married?"

"Three days," Coleman mumbled.

"I didn't hear that, Mr. Coleman," Swoboda said.

"Three days."

"Gee, it must have been love at first sight."

"Yeah."

"And where did you meet?"

"The casino at the Mirage."

"And in what church were you married?"

"It wasn't a church."

"Oh. Then where did you get hitched?"

"The, uh, Chapel of True Love."

"I see. What time of day or night were the nuptials?"

"Four in the morning, I think."

"Mr. Coleman, if Casey Van Meter died before coming out of her coma, you would have inherited millions of dollars, wouldn't you?"

"I don't know the exact amount."

"In fact, since no one knew that Ashley Spencer was Ms. Van Meter's daughter until recently, you would have inherited everything that Ms. Van Meter had, because she had no will and you were her husband."

"What's your question?" Coleman asked.

"My question? Okay, I'll ask one. You had a good reason to want Casey Van Meter dead, didn't you?"

"No. I love her."

"More than forty million dollars?"

"Asked and answered," Delilah cut in.

"Overruled," the judge said. "Do you understand the question, Mr. Coleman?"

"No."

"Miles Van Meter was trying to be appointed as Ms. Van Meter's guardian, wasn't he?" Swoboda asked.

"Yes."

"He had made it clear that he wanted to end his sister's suffering, had he not?"

"I heard something about that."

"That would have let you inherit her money, right?"

"I guess."

"You knew that Ashley Spencer was trying to be appointed Ms. Van Meter's guardian, didn't you?"

"Yes."

"She wanted to keep her mother alive, didn't she?"

"Yes."

"Which would mean that you wouldn't get any money."

"So?"

"With Ashley dead, either you or Miles Van Meter would have been appointed as guardian, right?"

"Yes."

"Either way, Ms. Van Meter would have been taken off life support and you would have inherited Ms. Van Meter's millions. Only Ashley stood in your way. That gave you a pretty good motive to stab her to death in the nursing-home parking lot, didn't it?"

"I told you, he tried to kill her," Coleman said, pointing at Maxfield.

"Your Honor, I'd like to put a diagram of the Sunny Rest nursing home on the easel."

"Go ahead, Mr. Swoboda."

Maxfield's attorney placed a large piece of poster board on an easel that sat next to the witness box. The off-white rectangle had been filled in with a diagram of the Sunny Rest parking lot. The main building was at the top. Below it were two parallel lines that designated the road that separated the building from the parking lot. Each parking space was designated by a blue square. At the bottom were two more parallel lines that represented another road. Swoboda held a red Magic Marker over a square in the second row from the building that was two in from the left side of the lot.

"This is where you were parked, isn't it?" the lawyer asked.

"Looks right," Coleman answered.

Swoboda wrote COLEMAN in the parking space. Then he moved the marker down two rows and over to the second square from the right to a box that was three rows from the bottom of the diagram.

"And this is where Miss Spencer parked?"

"Yeah."

Swoboda wrote SPENCER in the box.

"You testified that you saw Miss Spencer come out of Sunny Rest and walk to her car?"

"It was more like running."

"Okay. Where was she when you got out of your car?"

"About a row from hers."

"What route did you take to get to Miss Spencer?"

"Uh, I went straight up to her row and across."

"So you were moving from left to right when you reached her row?"

"Yeah."

"Were there cars on either side of Miss Spencer's car?"

"I'm not certain."

Swoboda went back to counsel table and picked up a photograph. He handed it to Coleman.

"This was taken by the police shortly after Miss Spencer was attacked. It shows her car?"

"Yeah."

"And there is a van closest to you on one side and another car on the other side of Miss Spencer's car?"

"Yes."

"I move to admit Defense Exhibit 79, Your Honor," Swoboda said.

"No objection," Delilah said.

"Mr. Coleman, you testified that your head was down as you ran because of the heavy rain. Then you looked up and saw a man attacking Miss Spencer."

"Right."

"You were in the row between the cars with Miss Spencer's car to your right?"

"Yeah."

"How far were you from Miss Spencer's car?"

"A few down."

"So the assailant is in front of you and Miss Spencer is between the cars in front of her assailant?"

"Yeah."

Swoboda drew X's for Coleman, the attacker,

and Ashley. Then he stood back so the jury could see the diagram clearly.

"How was it possible for you to see Miss Spencer kick her attacker, Mr. Coleman? A kick is delivered from the waist down. From three cars away, your view would be blocked by the van that was next to Miss Spencer's car and the attacker's back."

"I . . . I saw it," Coleman insisted.

"Yes you did, because you're the one she kicked when you attacked Ashley Spencer in the parking lot. It was my client who rescued her."

"Bullshit!"

Judge Shimazu rapped his gavel. "This is a courtroom, Mr. Coleman. Watch your language."

"Sorry, Judge," Coleman said. "But this guy is lying."

"No more swearing, Mr. Coleman," Judge Shimazu admonished the witness. "You'll restrict yourself to answering Mr. Swoboda's questions and you will not swear."

"Okay."

"Mr. Swoboda," the judge said, "you may continue."

"You had a forty-million-dollar reason to want Casey Van Meter dead, didn't you?"

"That's . . . not true."

"Isn't it? Did you learn that Casey Van Meter was a rich woman before you married her?"

"Yeah. So what?"

"Then she sobered up, wised up, and decided to dump you?"

"I told you, we had problems with our relationship. We just needed some counseling."

"When you thought about all that money flying away it made you angry, didn't it?"

"No," Coleman answered, his voice rising.

"So you weren't angry when you grabbed Casey Van Meter's wrist at the pool and called her a bitch?"

"I might have been a little angry," Coleman conceded grudgingly. "But I never tried to kill her."

"And I suppose that you're also going to deny murdering Terri Spencer in the boathouse at the Oregon Academy."

"What!" Coleman said, half standing.

"Isn't it a fact that you followed Casey Van Meter to the boathouse on the night she was attacked?"

"No."

"Isn't it true that you found her with a witness, Terri Spencer, and murdered Mrs. Spencer because she could identify you?"

"No!"

"Then you attacked Ms. Van Meter, but had to flee when you heard Joshua Maxfield approaching?"

Delilah wanted to object but she didn't, because an objection would just give more credence to Swoboda's outrageous accusations.

"You had forty million reasons to want Casey Van Meter dead before your divorce went through, and you had a motive to kill Ashley Spencer before Ms. Van Meter came out of her coma."

"Do I have to sit here and take this?" Coleman asked the judge.

"No further questions," Swoboda said, as he left Coleman half standing and twisted in the witness box.

"That was something," Jerry said to Miles Van Meter as soon as court recessed and Randy Coleman had stormed out of the room.

"Very bizarre," Miles answered. "I hope it was also ineffective."

Ashley was worried. Delilah was standing in front of her, gathering up the documents she'd used during Coleman's examination. Ashley leaned across the railing and tapped the deputy DA on the arm. Delilah turned.

"You don't think any of the jurors bought that, do you?" Ashley asked, trying to conceal her nervousness. She did not know what she'd do if Joshua Maxfield was acquitted.

"Don't worry yourself about Mr. Swoboda's Perry Mason act," Delilah assured her. "He's probably got the jurors thinking, but Casey will set them straight on who attacked her in the boathouse."

CHAPTER
THIRTY-TWO

As soon as court reconvened, Delilah Wallace had Dr. Ralph Karpinski educate the jury about comas. He also gave the opinion that Casey's coma occurred when the back of her head collided with one of the timbered supports in the boathouse after she was struck in the face. Next, Dr. Stanley Linscott testified about Casey Van Meter's current physical and mental state.

When Dr. Linscott was excused, the prosecutor called Casey Van Meter to the stand. Every eye in the courtroom followed "Sleeping Beauty" as she limped down the aisle, leaning on her cane. Casey looked wraithlike because she had not put back all of her lost weight, but her pale beauty was electrifying. Her dress was black, and a strand of pearls graced her neck. She reminded Ashley of

Lauren Bacall in an old movie she'd watched with Terri.

"Ms. Van Meter, what was your position at the Oregon Academy when the tragedy at the boathouse occurred?" Delilah asked after a series of introductory questions.

"I was the dean of the school."

"In your capacity as the dean, were you involved in hiring the defendant?"

"Yes."

"Tell the jury about the hiring decision."

"It was a hard decision for the school. On the one hand, we had the opportunity to expose the students to a world-renowned author. But Mr. Maxfield had been forced out of his last college-teaching position because he'd made inappropriate advances to a student. We were also aware that Mr. Maxfield had a drinking problem while at the college. In the end, we were persuaded to take a risk by Mr. Maxfield's most recent employer—a high school in Idaho—and by his forthright attitude during his interviews."

"How did the defendant perform his teaching duties?"

"He was an excellent teacher."

"At some point after the defendant was hired did you become lovers?"

Casey colored and looked down at her lap. "Yes."

Ashley was stunned. She had not been allowed in the courtroom until she testified, so she had missed Delilah's opening statement in which this fact had been revealed. Ashley looked at Maxfield for confirmation but he was focused on the dean and she could not see his face.

"When did this happen?"

"A few months before he attacked me."

"Objection," Swoboda shouted. "That's not responsive to the question. Ask that the answer be stricken."

Delilah started to speak, but the judge silenced her by holding up his hand, palm toward her. "Overruled."

"What were the circumstances that prompted the relationship?"

"I had married a few months before it started."

"This was to Randy Coleman?"

"Yes."

"Go on."

"Very shortly after my marriage I learned that my husband was a criminal. He was also physically and verbally abusive. I filed for divorce and also hired an attorney to see if I could have the marriage annulled. It was a very trying time for me. The marriage was a huge mistake and I was under tremendous stress because of my situation. Mr. Maxfield was very understanding." She shrugged. "One thing led to another."

"Let's move to the day of Terri Spencer's murder and the assault on you. When was the first time you saw Terri Spencer on that day?"

"She visited my office late in the afternoon."

"What was the purpose of her visit?"

"She told me that she was investigating the possibility that Joshua Maxfield had murdered her husband. She asked me to check his personnel file to see if there was any information that would help her prove it."

"Did you find anything in the file that bore on her concerns?"

"Yes."

"What did you find?"

"Terri told me that the person who murdered her husband might be a serial killer who had committed murders in other states. There was information in Joshua's personnel file about a New England state where he taught college. One of the murders occurred there. And he taught high school in Idaho, another state she'd mentioned."

"What did you do after you made this discovery?"

"I called Terri and I asked her to meet me at the boathouse."

"Tell us what happened in the boathouse," Delilah said.

Casey took a deep breath. "I was talking to Terri when he came in. He had a knife. He . . . he stabbed her." Casey closed her eyes but kept talking. "She screamed. He kept stabbing her." She put her hands over her face. "I don't remember anything after that."

"Who was the man who stabbed Terri Spencer?"

"Joshua Maxfield."

Delilah waited for a few seconds to let the jurors digest Casey's testimony before asking her next question.

"Did you see your husband, Randy Coleman, at the boathouse that evening?"

Casey looked puzzled. "No."

"You're certain that Randy Coleman did not stab Terri Spencer to death?"

"Yes." She pointed at Joshua Maxfield. "He did it."

"The State rests," Delilah said when Eric Swoboda finished a short and ineffective cross-examination of Casey Van Meter.

"Very well," Judge Shimazu said. "We'll be in recess until one o'clock. If you have any motions, Mr. Swoboda, you can make them then."

The bailiff banged the gavel. Casey left the witness stand and Ashley intercepted her when she pushed through the gate in the low fence that separated the spectators from the area where the court conducted business.

"Are you okay?" Ashley asked.

The question seemed to puzzle Casey. Then she smiled. The emotion Casey had shown on the stand was nowhere to be seen.

"Of course I'm okay," Casey answered. "Why wouldn't I be? My testimony should be enough to destroy any hope Joshua has for an acquittal. We've both done our part to avenge Terri."

Ashley felt odd when she should have been happy. Casey was right. The two of them had sealed Maxfield's fate, but she didn't feel triumphant.

"He'll probably die," Ashley said.

Casey's eyes narrowed and her mouth tightened. "That bastard deserves to die. He put me in a coma. I lost years of my life. I'm just sorry he'll be getting a lethal injection instead of a more painful death."

Ashley was shocked. "I know Maxfield is a terrible person." She remembered her terror as he lay on top of her and her despair when Norman and Terri died. "It's just . . . I don't know. He deserves what he gets, but I don't feel good."

Ashley paused. She wanted to tell someone about the emotions that were twisting her up inside, and Casey would have the best chance of understanding the way she felt.

"Do you have some time? I'd like to talk to you about the trial. Do you want to go for lunch?"

"Sorry, dear," Casey said. "I'd love to but I have a Portland Symphony meeting. But call me. We'll get together soon."

Casey hurried off and Ashley looked after her, shocked by the way she'd been treated. Terri would never have put Ashley off under these circumstances. Terri had always put her daughter first.

Ashley wanted to cry but she wouldn't let it happen. She had tried to form some kind of bond to her mother, but it wasn't working. The dean still treated her like a potential student she was trying to woo to the Academy. Try as she might, she had been unable to establish an emotional link with the woman who had given birth to her.

CHAPTER
THIRTY-THREE

As soon as Eric Swoboda finished his cross-examination of Casey Van Meter, Joshua Max-field demanded that they talk. Fifteen minutes after court recessed, Swoboda was seated in the narrow interview space in the courthouse jail and his client was on the other side of the iron mesh partition.

"I want to testify," Joshua said.

"We've been over this before. If you take the stand, you're fair game for Delilah."

Maxfield smirked.

"Don't underestimate her," Swoboda said. "I know you're smart but she cross-examines people for a living, and she's very good at it. And we made a lot of headway when I crossed Coleman. I can argue. . . ."

"Casey said she didn't see Coleman in the boathouse. She said she saw me. So did Ashley. I have to explain what happened."

"What can you say?"

"Don't worry about that. Just call me as a witness."

"You don't understand what you're letting yourself in for. Delilah will crucify you."

"How?"

Swoboda thought for a moment. "The novel, Joshua. Delilah will ask you about the novel. She'll ask you how you were able to give such an accurate account of murders you claim you know nothing about."

Joshua squeezed his eyes shut and pressed his fingertips to his temples. He looked like he was trying to keep his head from exploding.

"That fucking book," he muttered. He opened his eyes and glared at Swoboda. "I'll say I didn't write it, that it was someone else's book. I'll say I copied someone else's ideas."

Swoboda shook his head slowly as he tried to figure out how to be tactful with a client who was going over the edge.

"No one will believe you. You printed your name on the top of each page. Don't you see, you'll be committing suicide if you testify."

"No," Joshua said as he swung his head from side to side, "it's my only chance. They'll see I'm telling the truth. They have to believe me."

"I still think. . . ."

Maxfield looked directly at his lawyer. There was steel in his voice when he spoke.

"I don't care what you think," Maxfield said. "You're my lawyer and you'll do as I tell you."

"The defense calls Joshua Maxfield," Eric Swoboda said as soon as court reconvened. Delilah could barely conceal her surprise and delight. She salivated like a guest at Thanksgiving dinner when the big, juicy turkey is carried out of the kitchen.

Joshua straightened his suit jacket and strode confidently to the front of the courtroom to take the oath.

"Mr. Maxfield," Swoboda began when his client was seated in the witness box, "what is your occupation?"

"I am a novelist," Maxfield declared proudly.

"Have you had a successful career?"

"I would say so."

"Tell the jury about some of your accomplishments."

"Certainly. My first novel, **A Tourist in Baby-**

lon, was published to international acclaim soon after my graduation from university. It won or was nominated for several literary prizes not only in the United States, but also in Europe. The critics loved it, and the reading public made it an international bestseller."

"Did you publish another novel?"

"Yes, **The Wishing Well.**"

"Was **The Wishing Well** another bestseller?"

"Yes."

"In addition to writing fiction, have you taught fiction-writing?"

"Yes, at Eton College in Massachusetts and in high school. My last job was at the Oregon Academy."

"Would you please tell the jurors how you develop the idea for a novel?"

Maxfield smiled at the jurors. He was charming and, despite the charges they were considering, several of the jurors smiled back.

"Ideas come from everywhere, and they come when you least expect them. The idea for the novel I was working on at the Academy was born when I was teaching in Massachusetts and read about a home invasion that resulted in the death of a young girl and her parents. I wondered what sort of person could commit a crime like that.

"Quite by chance, a year later, I learned of another, similar murder. I became fascinated with the concepts of good and evil, much as Robert Louis Stevenson was when he wrote **Dr. Jekyll and Mr. Hyde.** I decided that I would write a book from the viewpoint of a truly twisted mind. I went to the library and read newspaper accounts of the two real cases. I read books about serial murderers and the psychology of sociopathic individuals to learn how these people think and act, so my book would have the ring of authenticity."

"The prosecutor says that you must be guilty because you wrote about a murder that has certain similarities to the murders in the Spencer home."

"That's what's most frustrating for me. I find it impossible to believe that I am being condemned for having a fruitful imagination."

"What about the snack? How do you explain the fact that a real killer ate a dessert while committing murder in Montana, Connecticut, and the Spencer home, and your fictional murderer eats a dessert in between murders in your novel?"

"A writer tries to engage his reader and he also tries to create characters that feel alive. I wanted my readers to be appalled by my narrator. But a cardinal rule of good writing is that you show instead of tell. Rather than write, 'My villain is a terrible person,' I tried to think up an action that my villain would take that would illustrate his depravity. I toyed with several ideas, like having my character murder a pet or a baby, but I concluded that those acts were so repulsive that they would alienate my readers. I wanted to illustrate a point, not make my readers ill. So I wrote a scene in which my murderer eats a snack in between the commission of several ghastly murders. I wanted the reader to conclude that my narrator was heartless and totally devoid of feeling, and I thought that this would be a wonderful way to do that. It is understated, non-violent, and yet truly horrible.

"Now, am I surprised that my art imitated real life? No, I am not. Anyone who could commit those terrible murders in Montana, Connecticut, and here would be just like my fictional killer—cruel and uncaring. I'm not shocked that he did something so grotesque. And, think about it. Would I include that scene in my novel if I had committed the murders? Would I read Terri Spencer a scene that was identical to something that had happened in her house? It would be insane. The first thing I would expect her to do is go to the police. Why would I commit suicide?"

"Let's move to the murder and assault in the Oregon Academy boathouse. Tell the jury what happened there," Swoboda said.

"I lived on the Academy grounds in a cottage that the school provided as part of my terms of employment. The grounds of the Academy are beautiful, and I often took walks through the woods in the early-evening hours. That night I was strolling through the grounds, thinking about a problem I was having with my book, when I heard a scream coming from the direction of the boathouse. A second later, I heard another scream. As I ran toward the boathouse I saw a man running away."

"Could you identify him?"

"No, other than to say that he seemed of average or athletic build. He wasn't obese or short."

"Could the man have been Randy Coleman?"

"It's possible. I can't swear to that, though."

"What happened next?"

"I went into the boathouse to see if anyone was hurt. It was dark except for some light from a flashlight that was on the floor. It took a moment for my eyes to adjust. That's when I saw the two women and the knife. Casey Van Meter was on the floor, up against a timber that supported the roof. Terri Spencer was covered with blood. I panicked and picked up the knife for protection. Then I saw Ashley at the window. She ran off and I went after her to explain that I hadn't done anything wrong, but she was too fast for me."

"Why didn't you follow her to the dormitory and wait for the police?"

Joshua's head dropped. "I should have. But I'd never seen anything so terrible. There was blood everywhere, and poor Terri. . . ."

Maxfield closed his eyes for a moment and took a deep breath. When he spoke, he seemed shaken and he cast his eyes down.

"I'm ashamed of the way I acted, but I was terrified and I wasn't thinking straight. So I ran."

Maxfield raised his head and made eye contact with several of the jurors.

"I don't blame Ashley Spencer one bit for what she said about me. She's a very nice young lady who testified to what she saw. I did have the knife. I was there. But I did not hurt anyone."

"After you were arrested, why did you escape?" Swoboda asked.

"My lawyer told me that the police were going to use my novel as a confession; Ashley was going to testify that I'd killed her mother and beat Casey unconscious. I didn't see any way of avoiding conviction, so I decided to escape so I could find the evidence that would prove that I was innocent."

"Have you succeeded?"

"I believe so. I suspected Randy Coleman from the beginning. The man who ran from the boathouse was too far away for me to identify, but he could have been Coleman. I knew he had a multimillion-dollar motive for murder and I learned later that he'd been convicted of assault. I knew from personal experience that he was capable of violence. I'd seen Mr. Coleman attack Casey Van Meter at the pool."

"What did you conclude happened in the boathouse?"

"I believe that Casey was his target and Terri was in the wrong place at the wrong time."

"Did something happen that made you certain that Randy Coleman murdered Terri Spencer and assaulted his wife?"

"Yes. Henry Van Meter died and a new guardian had to be appointed for Casey. Miles Van Meter applied to be appointed. I learned that he wanted to take Casey off her life-support system for humanitarian reasons. Coleman also ap-plied. I believe that he too would have asked to have Casey's life support disconnected. In either case, Casey would die. Since she had no will, and Coleman was still her husband, Coleman would inherit all of Casey's estate.

"Then Ashley Spencer returned to Portland and applied to be Casey's guardian. If Ashley had been appointed Casey's guardian, she would have kept Casey alive. That meant that Coleman would inherit nothing. It also became general knowledge that Ashley was Casey's daughter. Un-der the probate laws, if Casey died Ashley would inherit half of her estate. Whether Casey lived or died, Randy Coleman would lose millions.

"I became convinced that Coleman would try to kill Ashley to keep her from being appointed guardian and to make sure that he would inherit everything. I started following Ashley to protect her and to try to catch Coleman attempting to commit murder."

"What happened at the Sunny Rest Home on the day you were arrested?"

"I followed Ashley and noticed another car that was following her. I parked on a side street several blocks from the home. Then I concealed myself in the parking lot. It was raining so hard that I didn't notice the police surveillance, but they didn't see me either.

"The car that was following Ashley pulled into the lot shortly after she did. Randy Coleman was the driver. He waited for her to come out. Then he tried to kill her. Ashley got away. I tackled Coleman. When the police came, we were wrestling on the ground, neither one of us had possession of the knife. The police couldn't tell which of us had tried to kill Ashley. Naturally, they suspected me."

"Mr. Maxfield, did you murder Terri and Norman Spencer and Tanya Jones?"

"No."

"Did you assault Casey Van Meter?"

"No. I saved her from Coleman at the pool."

"Did you attack Ashley Spencer in her home, at her dormitory, or in the parking lot of the Sunny Rest nursing home?"

"No, never."

"No further questions."

Delilah smiled at her prey. She was feeling good.

"I read your first novel, Mr. Maxfield. I liked it."

"Thank you."

"It was a real big success."

"Yes."

"But that second book, **The Wishing Well,** that book didn't do so well, did it?"

"It had decent sales," Maxfield answered defensively.

"Nowhere near what **Tourist** sold."

"No, but it was a **New York Times** bestseller."

"Yes, you testified to that. But let me ask you, wasn't **A Tourist in Babylon** on the list for twenty-two weeks?"

"Yes."

"Your second book was only a bestseller for two weeks because people didn't like it, right?"

"I don't know what **the people** like," Maxfield replied haughtily. "I don't write to please the average reader."

"Well, the critics didn't like it either, did they?"

"I had some good reviews."

"Really? I had my assistant get a complete collection off of the Internet. We can read them to the jury if you'd like. By my count, three reviewers thought your book was pretty good, and there were twenty-eight bad reviews, some of which were downright nasty. Seems those critics really went to town on you."

Maxfield colored as Delilah spoke. "The critics

were jealous of my success. They're just failed writers who couldn't stand the idea of someone in his early twenties accomplishing something they could only dream of."

"So the reviews were the product of some conspiracy?"

"I didn't say that," Maxfield snapped.

"Do you think these reviewers are part of a plot to frame you for all these murders?"

"Objection," Swoboda said.

"Sustained," Judge Shimazu ruled.

"Mr. Maxfield," Delilah said, "you haven't written a book in ten years, have you?"

"No."

"Were you teaching at Eton College because you couldn't earn a living writing anymore?"

"No, that is not correct. You don't just manufacture literature like you do toasters. I enjoy teaching creative writing, and the job gave me time to write."

"Didn't your publisher give you an advance for a new book and demand it back because you couldn't deliver?"

"We had creative differences."

"I see. Is that why your publisher was threatening you with a lawsuit?"

"Objection," Swoboda said.

"Sustained."

"After so much early success, being a failed writer must be hard on you."

"I am not a failed writer."

"Weren't you having trouble thinking up a plot for a new book?"

"I had several ideas. I was looking for the right one."

"Doing research?"

"Yes."

"Wanting to have all the little details right to make your scenes real for your readers?"

"Yes."

"Committing horrible murders so you could paint an authentic torture scene for your readers?"

"No. I did not kill anyone."

"Let's talk about the boathouse, Mr. Maxfield. Is that okay with you?"

"Yes."

"I want to make sure I have this right. You were out for a stroll in the forest when you heard a scream?"

"Yes."

"Then you heard another scream?"

"Yes."

"So you decided to investigate?"

"Yes."

"And that's when you saw a man running away?"

"Yes."

"That would be pretty important, wouldn't it, this man running from the scene of the crime?"

"Yes."

"I would imagine you'd want the police to know about that, especially when they were accusing you of murder and mayhem?"

Maxfield didn't answer.

"Well, you did think it was important, didn't you?"

"Yes."

"The first time you came in contact with the police after you went on the lam was in Nebraska when you were arrested, right?"

"Yes."

"Did you tell the arresting officers about this man you saw running from the boathouse?"

"No. I was terrified. They had guns drawn, they were shouting at me."

"What about when you calmed down?"

"They didn't ask me any questions. They just put me in a cell."

"You know Detectives Birch and Marx, right? They were the detectives who testified in court."

Maxfield looked worried. "Yes."

"Did Detectives Marx and Birch escort you back to Oregon from Nebraska after you waived extradition?"

"Yes."

"But first they interviewed you in jail in Nebraska, didn't they?"

"Yes."

"You testified that you had a lot of time to think about what had happened after your arrest?"

"Yes."

"Do you remember what you told the detectives about what happened at the boathouse?"

"Not word for word."

A boom box was sitting on the floor next to counsel table. Delilah picked it up. She stood.

"Your Honor, may I have permission to play the short interview that the defendant gave Detectives Birch and Marx, to refresh Mr. Maxfield's memory?"

"Objection, Your Honor. No foundation has been laid for this," Swoboda said, anxious to keep the tape out of evidence. He knew what was on it and had tried to warn Maxfield, but his client wouldn't listen to him.

"I agree with Mr. Swoboda, Your Honor," Delilah said. "May I recall Detective Birch?"

The judge told Joshua Maxfield to retake his

seat at the defense table and Larry Birch went into the witness box.

"Detective Birch, you're already under oath," the judge said. "Miss Wallace, you may proceed."

"Detective Birch, after the defendant was arrested in Nebraska, did he waive extradition?"

"Yes."

"How did he get back here?"

"My partner, Tony Marx, and I flew to Nebraska, and the authorities turned over the defendant to us. Detective Marx and I then flew back with the prisoner."

"Prior to returning to Oregon, did you interview the defendant?"

"Yes."

"Where did the interview take place?"

"In an interview room at the jail where the defendant was being held."

"What was the defendant's condition?"

"He looked rested. We asked if he wanted something to eat or drink. He asked for a sandwich and soft drink and we provided them to him."

"Did you read the defendant his **Miranda** rights before questioning him?"

"Yes."

"Was the interview recorded?"

"Yes."

Delilah stood up. She was holding a plastic evidence bag. Inside it was a cassette.

"Detective Birch, have you reviewed the interview on this tape?"

"Yes."

"Is it the interview of the defendant that you conducted in Nebraska?"

"Yes."

"Your Honor," Delilah said, "I move to introduce this cassette tape of Detective Birch's interview into evidence."

"Mr. Swoboda?" Judge Shimazu asked.

Maxfield's lawyer could not think of a way to keep the tape from being played. When he did not object, Judge Shimazu gave Delilah permission to play the tape. She put the cassette in the boom box and pressed the PLAY button. The jurors heard Birch introduce himself and Tony Marx and read Maxfield the **Miranda** rights. There was some discussion about food and drink. Then Birch asked Maxfield if he minded if their conversation was recorded.

"What does it matter what I want? You're going to do what you want. That's what I learned in here. I'm the prisoner. I have no rights."

"Hey, Josh. . . ."

"Joshua."

"I stand corrected. You have rights. This is America. Didn't I just read you a card listing several constitutional rights?"

"That's just to get me to talk."

"Well, that's true. But you don't have to talk to me if you don't want to, and I won't record this conversation unless you say it's okay. I'm taping this for your benefit. This way, if I misrepresent what you say, you've got this tape to prove me wrong."

"Okay. Keep taping."

"You've had some wild days, Joshua."

No reply.

"What made you choose Nebraska as a hideout?"

No reply.

"You've got to answer for the tape. We can't hear a shrug on the tape."

"I just drove."

"Well, you led us on a merry chase. I'll give you that. But I should have expected that from someone with your imagination. I've read your book."

"You have?"

"Hey, not all cops are dumb. I read A Tourist in Babylon as soon as it came out. Everybody was reading that book. I thought it was great. My wife did, too. We were both disappointed that you're in this mess."

"I am not in a mess. I didn't hurt those women."

"We have a witness who says you did."

"Ashley Spencer, right? Poor kid. She must be devastated. First, her father. Now, her mother."

"She says that you killed her mother and assaulted Casey Van Meter."

"I'm sure she believes what she's told you, but it's not true."

"If you didn't attack those women, who did?"

"I don't know."

"You see our problem? Ashley says she saw you holding a bloody knife."

"Yes, but I didn't kill anyone with it. I picked it up to protect myself. When I came into the boathouse the women had already been attacked. I thought that the killer might still be in the boathouse. I saw the knife and picked it up in self-defense. What possible reason would I have to hurt Casey or Terri?"

"There are rumors that you and Ms. Van Meter were close. That you were sleeping with her."

"She was going through a rough patch. Just married. Then she finds out her husband is a petty crook. He was beating her. She turned to me for comfort. It just happened. You know how that is."

"We heard about your rescue at the pool. That was very brave, considering that you thought he was a mobster."

"I guess I didn't think about that. All I knew was that Casey was in trouble. That's what makes this whole thing ridiculous. Why would I rescue Casey, then turn around and kill her?"

"Maybe you two had a falling out."

"No. She stayed at my place the night before she died. We were still friends. It makes no sense that I'd kill her."

"It does if you read your novel. I thought it was really well written, by the way."

"What does A Tourist in Babylon have to do with what happened in the boathouse?"

"Not Tourist, your new novel."

"My . . . ?"

"The book you read to Terri and the rest of your writing seminar."

"I don't understand."

"Look, Joshua, you've been pretty forthcoming so far. That's going to go a long way with a judge. So. . . ."

"What are you talking about?"

"I've read the novel, Joshua. That scene you read in the writing seminar sounds a lot like what happened in the Spencer home on the night Ashley's father and her teenage girlfriend were murdered. The scene was so real that we think Terri went to Dean Van Meter and told her that she suspected you of killing her husband. How did you find out she'd made the connection?"

"That was made up. I'm a writer. The scenes in my books are the product of my imagination."

"You're a pretty clever guy, Joshua. You

have Tony and me stumped. We can't figure out how you found out that Terri and Casey were investigating you. Did Casey let it slip?"

"I didn't know. I. . . ."

"Yes?"

"I want an attorney. This is crazy. My God, how did this happen? How could . . . ? Oh, no."

"What did you want to say, Joshua?"

"I want a lawyer. I'm not saying another word."

Delilah turned off the boom box.

"Is that the end of the tape, Detective?"

"Yes."

"Thank you. I have no further questions for Detective Birch."

"Mr. Swoboda?" Judge Shimazu asked.

"No."

"Mr. Maxfield, please retake the stand," the judge said.

"Mr. Maxfield," Delilah said, "what happened to the man who ran away, the real killer? How come you didn't tell Detectives Birch and Marx about him?"

"I don't know. I was upset. I was in jail. I wasn't thinking straight."

"I see. Well let me ask you something else. You came in the door of the boathouse, saw the women, both of them were unconscious or dead, you picked up the knife, then saw Ashley in the window?"

"Yes."

"Just a few seconds inside the boathouse before you saw Ashley?"

"Yes."

"And both of those women were just lying there?"

"I told you that already."

Delilah made a note on her legal pad. She was smiling when she looked at the witness.

"Who cried out, Mr. Maxfield?"

"What?"

"You were in court when Ashley Spencer testified, weren't you?"

"Yes."

"You heard her say that she heard two screams and went through the woods to the boathouse?"

"Yes."

"Then you also heard her say that she heard a woman say something right before she looked in the window and saw you standing over Casey Van Meter with a bloody knife in your hand?"

Maxfield was frozen.

"If Terri Spencer was dead and Casey Van Meter was unconscious all the time you were in the boathouse, how did one of them say something?"

"I. . . ."

"Or maybe it happened differently? Maybe the women were alive when you entered the boathouse."

"No."

"You stabbed Terri and she screamed twice. Then you attacked Casey Van Meter and she called out."

"No," Maxfield said, but the answer sounded false and his face told the jurors that he was lying.

Delilah had no more questions for Joshua Maxfield, and Eric Swoboda had no idea how to repair the damage her cross-examination had created. Swoboda called a few more witnesses before resting. Delilah did not feel that she needed to call any witnesses in rebuttal. As far as she was concerned, Joshua Maxfield's conviction was a foregone conclusion.

Judge Shimazu told the parties to be ready to

argue in the morning and recessed court. As soon as the jurors filed out and Joshua Maxfield had been led out of the room, Delilah swiveled her chair so she was facing Ashley.

"You got him. Your testimony buried Mr. Maxfield."

"I didn't. . . ."

Delilah laughed. "Don't be modest, girl. You heard a woman call out seconds before you saw Maxfield with that knife. One of the women had to be conscious when he walked into the boathouse. When he said that they were both out I knew he was lying, and you're the one who proved it."

Ashley didn't look as happy as Delilah expected her to be.

"What's the matter?" the DA asked. "You seem troubled."

"It's just. . . ." She shook her head.

"No, what? Tell me."

"I don't feel like I won anything. Even if Maxfield is executed, Tanya and my parents are still dead."

Delilah looked solemn. "I hear you," she said. "I was wrong to be so happy. Sometimes I get so wrapped up in the fight I forget that a courtroom victory doesn't end the suffering. But you have to think about this, Ashley. A conviction won't bring back your folks and Tanya Jones, but your testimony saved lives. We don't know who they are, but we can be certain that there are people alive today who would have been dead if Joshua Maxfield was on the loose."

"What's going to happen now?" Ashley asked.

"We argue in the morning. Then the judge will instruct the jury on the law. After that, the jury deliberates and brings in a verdict. My guess is that we'll have a verdict by tomorrow night. If Maxfield is convicted of aggravated murder, the jury comes back and we have another trial to decide his sentence."

Ashley reached out and touched the prosecutor. "Thank you for caring so much, Delilah. Thank you for everything you've done."

Delilah's face split into a mile-wide grin. "You just gave me the bonus that makes this all worthwhile."

BOOK TOUR

The Present

Miles Van Meter had been speaking for thirty-five minutes when the door of Murder for Fun opened and closed. Claire Rolvag, Miles's escort, looked toward the front of the store. Bookshelves blocked her view, but she was certain that she knew who had just entered. She turned her attention back to the author, who was answering a question about his writing habits.

"I was working full-time as a lawyer while I was writing **Sleeping Beauty,** so I had to sneak in the writing when I could. Sometimes I'd get an hour or two in during the week by setting my alarm for four-thirty. On the weekend, I'd try to get in at least four hours on Saturday and four on Sunday. That's eight hours, which amounts to a full eight-hour workday. You'd be surprised how much you can write each week if you're disciplined about it."

A mousy-looking woman with thick glasses and a T-shirt from a mystery fans' convention raised her hand. Miles pointed at her. She sounded nervous when she spoke, and Miles smiled warmly to encourage her.

"Mr. Van Meter, I've read the old edition and the special edition of **Sleeping Beauty** and I think that your book is the best true-crime book I have ever read."

"Thank you. I appreciate your kind words. Did you have a question?"

"Yes I did. Your book is so realistic, especially when you write from Ashley's point of view, but I've heard that you never interviewed her. Is that true? And, if it is, how did you make those chapters so real?"

"I knew Ashley, of course, and we spoke several times before I started the book. She was staying at the Academy for a while. However, I never discussed the case with her before she left for Europe. It would have been insensitive. While she was rooming at the Academy, my father and I were trying to take her mind off her tragedy.

"Obviously, I never had a chance to interview Ashley when I was writing the first edition of

Sleeping Beauty, because she was hiding in Europe. I did have access to the transcript of the preliminary hearing and the police reports with the interviews of Ashley that Larry Birch conducted. I also interviewed her friends, her teachers, and people like her attorney, Jerry Philips. My father was a big help. He and Ashley spent a lot of time together when she was staying at the Academy."

"What about after she returned to the States? Did you interview her for the new edition?"

"No. By the time I decided to write an updated edition of the book I had heard her testimony at Maxfield's trial and didn't feel it was necessary."

"So chapter one, where you tell what happened in the Spencer house, and the chapter where you describe the attack at the Academy after Maxfield's escape, that all came from research and not from talking to Ashley?"

"Yes."

"That's amazing, because it feels so real."

Miles blushed. "Thank you for that. It's always music to a writer's ears to hear that he has been successful in making his subject live. Of course, re-creating Ashley's personality was easy, since I did get to know her. And you have a good chance of guessing how a person will react in a situation if you know what type of person they are. Ashley is a good woman with a lot of inner strength."

An overweight man with a heavy beard raised his hand, and Miles pointed at him.

"Mr. Van Meter, have you ever thought of volunteering your time to the FBI to help catch serial killers? With your imagination and insights, you'd be a natural."

"No, for several reasons. First, the FBI has trained professionals to do that work. I couldn't begin to approach their qualifications. Second, and most important, as far as I'm concerned, one close encounter with a serial killer is one too many. You have no idea how emotionally draining it's been to have Joshua Maxfield in my life. I have no desire to place myself in a position where I would experience the suffering of other families. Quite frankly, I don't know how the police and the FBI handle the emotional strain of dealing with such horror, day in and day out."

A young woman in a business suit raised her hand. "Will you be glad when Joshua Maxfield is executed?" she asked.

Miles looked thoughtful. He took a moment to frame his answer.

"Society will be better off with Maxfield gone. I firmly believe that he cannot be rehabilitated. I'm also certain that he would kill again if he were released. But glad . . . I don't think you can ever rejoice at the death of a human being."

"So you think he is human?" the woman asked.

"Well, there's certainly a good argument against that position, but I'll leave that question to theologians and philosophers. I'm just happy I have my sister back."

Several people raised their hands. While Miles called on one of them, Claire Rolvag looked toward the front of the store again. Standing at the end of the bookshelf that held the novels featuring classic detectives like Sherlock Holmes and Hercule Poirot was a woman flanked by two men. As Claire turned back toward the speaker, she put her hand under her jacket and touched the butt of her Glock 40-caliber pistol.

PART FOUR
SPECIAL EDITION

Three and a Half Weeks Earlier

CHAPTER
THIRTY-FOUR

Jerry Philips pulled up at the VALET PARKING sign, and a college kid in a white shirt and black slacks swapped a claim check for his car. Jerry took Ashley's hand and they walked up the driveway to the mansion that Casey Van Meter had inherited from her father. Miles Van Meter's publisher had decided to kick off the book tour for the special edition of **Sleeping Beauty** exactly one year after Joshua Maxfield had been sentenced to death, and Casey had opened up Glen Oaks for the publication party.

All of the lights in the house were on, and the couple could hear music and laughter coming from the backyard where a band had been set up near the pool. People were chatting on the front lawn, waiters were offering hors d'oeuvres on silver trays, and Jerry had to shoulder his way through the boisterous crowd in the entry hall to get to the bar. Ashley was checking out the fashion statements and the jewelry while she waited for her drink when someone shouted her name. She turned and was swept up by Delilah Wallace, who embraced her ex–star witness, then held her at arm's length.

"You're looking a lot better than you looked when I saw you last," said Delilah, who had not seen Ashley since Joshua Maxfield's sentencing.

"You're looking good, too, Delilah."

"Nah. I'm as fat as ever, but I sure am happy, because I came here hoping to find you and here you are. So tell me what you've been up to."

"I'm engaged," Ashley said as she showed the prosecutor her ring.

Delilah grabbed Ashley's hand and inspected the stone. "That's lovely. Do I know the lucky man?"

"Merlot, madam," Jerry Philips said as he handed Ashley a glass of red wine. "Hi, Delilah."

"I was just congratulating Ashley. When's the wedding?"

"Probably not until Ashley graduates," Jerry said. "We're both too busy for a honeymoon right now."

"I'm going to Portland State," Ashley explained. "I'm premed and that really keeps me hopping."

"Did you have any trouble getting back in the swing of school after being away so long?" Delilah asked.

"It was tough at first. I was pretty nervous."

"She's getting straight A's," Jerry said proudly.

Ashley blushed. "What have you been up to?"

"The same old, same old. Murder and mayhem."

Ashley was about to tell Delilah that she'd been reading about the DA's most recent trial when Casey Van Meter walked into the entry hall and spotted Ashley. The mistress of Glen Oaks looked radiant. Except for a barely noticeable limp, all evidence that she had been one of the living dead had been erased during the past year, as had the presence of Randy Coleman, whom she had finally divorced. Casey had not resumed her duties as dean, leaving in place the capable woman Henry had hired while she was in her coma. But she had become active in civic affairs and was much sought after to sit on boards and committees because of her wealth and intelligence.

Casey said hello to Delilah Wallace. Jerry

saluted Casey with his glass. Ashley had seen less of her mother since she started college. Her heavy premed load left little time for socializing. When she did have free time, she spent it with Jerry. Jerry wasn't sorry that Ashley had cut down on her visits to her mother. Her relationship with Casey had helped her get through the Maxfield trial and had given her a new family, but Jerry thought that there was something cold and artificial about Casey Van Meter. Of course, he'd never said anything about his feelings to Ashley.

"Miles has been asking for you," Casey said. "He's signing books in the living room. Come on. Let's visit."

Ashley promised to talk to Delilah later. Jerry followed as Casey took Ashley's arm and led her through the crowd. Heads turned and people whispered when they saw the two women. Miles and the media had made them celebrities. Ashley had never welcomed her fame and she was glad when the attentions of the press waned after the trial. She had not been thrilled when the publicity blitz for the special edition of **Sleeping Beauty** had raised her public profile again.

Miles was sitting with his back to a massive

stone fireplace at a table piled high with his books.

"I've brought you someone," Casey said. Miles had his head down and was inscribing a book for a couple. He looked up and broke into a grin.

"Ashley," he said as he rose. "I'm so glad you came. Hi Jerry."

Miles turned to a short, gray-haired man who had been watching the signing.

"Jack, this is Ashley Spencer and her fiancé, Jerry Philips. This is Jack Dunlop, my editor."

Dunlop smiled and held out his hand to Ashley. "I'm so glad to finally meet you. After editing **Sleeping Beauty** and spending another couple of months with the new edition I feel like I know you."

Ashley forced a smile and prayed that Dunlop would not ask her what she thought of the book, which she had never read. Ashley wanted to place the horrors perpetrated by Joshua Maxfield behind her. Every time she saw a copy of Miles's book she felt old wounds opening.

"I have something for you," Miles said, as he picked up a copy of **Sleeping Beauty** that was not part of the stacks of books that stood in front of him. He opened the cover and showed Ashley what he had written on the title page.

For Ashley Spencer, A special person whose courage has been an inspiration to me.
Miles Van Meter

"Thank you, Miles," Ashley said.

"I'm sincere about that." He turned to Jack Dunlop. "This is the bravest lady I've ever met."

The party was still going strong around midnight when Jerry and Ashley left. She'd enjoyed talking to Delilah, but the attention bestowed on her by the guests had made Ashley very uncomfortable, and the couple begged off as soon as they could do so politely. Jerry drove them back to the blue, two-story Victorian on the east side of the river that they'd been sharing since the end of the Maxfield trial. A high hedge enclosed a small backyard and a covered porch fronted the street. There was a television, CD and DVD players, and a state-of-the-art sound system in the living room, but most of the furnishings were antiques, in keeping with the age of the house.

When Jerry went into the kitchen for a glass of water, Ashley carried Miles's gift into the living room and put it on the bookshelf. Jerry came up behind her and laid a hand on her shoulder.

"Are you ever going to read that book?" he asked.

She reached back and covered his hand. "Maybe someday when I'm certain it won't hurt too much."

Jerry leaned down and kissed her neck. "Let's get to bed."

Ashley turned out the lights and they climbed the stairs.

CHAPTER
THIRTY-FIVE

Two weekends after Miles's party, Stan Getz was playing low on the stereo and Ashley was curled up on the couch in the living room finishing her organic chemistry homework. She completed the last problem and closed the textbook. Organic chemistry made her brain hurt, but she got it and she was proud that she did. She stretched and walked over to the front window. A heavy rain was pounding the front yard. The white noise and the smooth jazz were making her sleepy.

Ashley went into the kitchen to fix a cup of instant coffee. While the water boiled she thought about her new beginning. She'd been nervous about going back to the classroom after being away for so long but she'd also been excited about living life like a normal person. Her years on the run had worn her down.

The water boiled and Ashley spooned some instant coffee into a mug. She took a sip then carried the mug back to the living room. Jerry was at the office for a few hours grinding out a brief. Thinking about him made Ashley smile. She had been so happy since she'd moved in with Jerry. His love, and the closure that Maxfield's conviction had brought, had enabled her to deal with all of the death and despair that had made her so unhappy since her parents were murdered. Jerry had given her back her life and had provided her with a future.

Jerry wouldn't be home for a while and she'd done the household chores during breaks from her homework. She didn't feel like watching TV. Ashley scanned the bookcase for something to read. One title jumped out at her. She hesitated before pulling the autographed copy of **Sleeping Beauty** off the shelf. Just touching the cover made her nervous. Ashley carried Miles Van Meter's book to the couch. She held it with both hands. The thought of opening the book frightened her. The murders of her mother and father were inside. So were Tanya Jones's muffled screams and her own brushes with death. She steeled herself and turned to the introduction.

Ashley had read an account of a near-death experience in which a clinically dead patient told of floating above his own body in an operating room while he watched his doctor bring him back from the brink. Reading about her life from someone else's viewpoint was a little like that. Some of the scenes made her shiver or sweat, but the printed words put distance between Ashley and the horror of the years that had started with the murder of her parents and ended with Maxfield's trial.

There were many things that had gone on in her case that Ashley knew nothing about. The manhunt for Joshua Maxfield after his escape from the county courthouse fascinated her. Miles had interviewed FBI and Interpol agents and had detailed the steps that had been taken to find the fugitive. And the escape itself was amazing. Ashley could not help admiring the planning and imagination that had enabled Maxfield to conceive and execute his plan. Joshua Maxfield was brilliant, and she suddenly realized how lucky she was to be alive.

There were also several chapters about Casey

and everything that had been done to help her while she was in her coma. Ashley was saddened by Miles's account of Henry's plight. Casey's father had put on a brave front during their meals together. He had never let Ashley see the depth of his sorrow. Ashley had no doubt that watching helplessly as his daughter wasted away had shortened Henry's life.

An hour after she started the book, Ashley reached the chapter detailing her escape from the Academy dormitory. Her eyes were tired from reading. Ashley closed the book. It was almost noon. She was hungry. She placed **Sleeping Beauty** on the end table and carried her mug into the kitchen for a refill. As she fixed a sandwich, Ashley tried to evaluate **Sleeping Beauty.** Miles had done an outstanding job of telling what had happened to her and her family, but he had failed to re-create the terror she had experienced. Ashley could not fault Miles for not succeeding here. Only someone who had lived through a rape or an attack knew what it was like. No one could imagine the despair, the disorientation and the stark terror, or the way your heart pounded.

Ashley was starting to put mustard on a slice of rye when she froze. Something was not right. She frowned and put down the knife. A moment later, she was in the living room thumbing through the bestseller until she found what she'd been looking for. She read the paragraph and lost her appetite.

"No," she said out loud. "This can't be right."

So much time had passed. Her memory had to be faulty. There was a logical explanation. She just wasn't seeing it. She read the paragraph again. When she finished, Ashley felt sick and confused. If she was right. . . . But she couldn't be. It didn't make sense. She had seen Maxfield in the boathouse holding the knife that had killed Terri.

Ashley read the paragraph a final time. The words had not changed and neither had the import of those words. What should she do? She could talk to Jerry, but she didn't want to worry him. And she didn't have enough facts yet. To be certain, she'd have to review the police reports and the trial transcripts. How would she get them? Delilah, of course. And who better to talk to about what was troubling her.

Delilah picked up after three rings.

"Hi, this is Ashley."

"What a nice surprise! You recovered from the Van Meter bash yet? I never saw so many VIPs in one place."

"Casey knows how to throw a party," Ashley

agreed. Then she paused, unsure of how to proceed.

"What's up?" Delilah prodded.

"There's something I wanted to talk to you about."

"So talk. I'm listening."

"Do you have the Maxfield file?"

"It's at the office."

"Does it have a transcript of the trial and the preliminary hearing and the police reports of my interviews?"

"Sure. Why?"

Ashley hesitated. The more she thought about it, the more certain she was that she was wrong.

"You still there, hon?" Delilah asked.

"I've been reading **Sleeping Beauty.** I never read it before."

"I thought you wanted to put all that bad stuff behind you."

"I did, but the book was there and I wasn't reading anything and. . . . Anyway, there were some things that Miles wrote about that I didn't know. It made me curious. I was wondering if I could look at the file today or tomorrow?"

"You want to make me come down to the office on my days of rest?"

"It's important."

"Important how?"

Ashley didn't answer. She was afraid of sounding foolish.

"What are you up to, Ashley? What's really going on here?"

"Something might be wrong."

"Wrong how?"

"I'd rather not say until I read the file. I'm probably way off base. I don't want to waste your time if that's the case."

"I'm not following you. What type of thing is wrong?"

"What if we're all mistaken about Joshua Maxfield?"

Delilah laughed. "Joshua Maxfield is a bad man, Ashley. Make no mistake about that. He's on death row because he deserves to be on death row."

"I know, but. . . ."

"Look, the man is going to be executed and you had a lot to do with that. Any normal person is going to feel bad about having some responsibility for a man's death even if that man is a monster. That's why you're not a serial killer, because you have empathy for people. But don't let those feelings blind you."

"Delilah, I've got to see the file. Please. I'm sure I've got this all wrong, but if I don't. . . ."

"Okay, sugar, spell it out for me. Let me hear what you've got to say. Be an advocate for your position. If you convince me, I'll take you to the office in an hour."

There were a few deputy DAs working in their cubicles when Delilah let Ashley into the district attorney's office, but most of the office was dark and deserted. Delilah put Ashley into an empty room with a large table and returned fifteen minutes later pushing a dolly loaded down with banker boxes. Ashley helped stack the boxes on the table, and the two women unpacked them. One box contained Delilah's files, including an indexed set of the police reports. Two large boxes held copies of the transcripts of Maxfield's trial, which was under review in the Oregon Supreme Court. Several boxes contained exhibits that had been introduced at trial. Another box held evidence that Delilah had not entered as exhibits. While Ashley was unpacking the last box, Delilah disappeared. She reappeared moments later with a mug and a thermos of coffee.

"Figured you could use this. You're in for a long

day. And don't worry, girl. This ain't the horrid office brew. It's Delilah's caffeine special, a secret blend I perfected during years of late nights and early mornings."

Delilah left and Ashley got down to business. She grabbed the transcript first. Since she knew what she was looking for she didn't have to read all of it. She skimmed the opening statements and closing arguments of both attorneys, her testimony, and the testimony of Larry Birch and Tony Marx. When she was done with the transcript, Ashley read through the police reports, concentrating on the interviews that Larry Birch had conducted with her but also reading any report that summarized the case. Two hours later, she had not found what she was looking for, and that scared her to death.

Even if she was right about this one thing, there were other unanswered questions. She pulled the draft of Maxfield's unfinished novel out of the court exhibits, hoping it would hold the answer to one of them. Delilah had not offered the whole manuscript into evidence. Only those pages that had scenes that corresponded to the evidence that had been withheld from the public had been marked as exhibits. **Joshua Maxfield** was printed on the top left corner of each page. She skimmed the one hundred and seventy-odd pages, but none of them contained an answer to her questions.

Ashley had read the police report that detailed the search of Maxfield's cabin. She knew that an earlier draft of the novel had been found on a table in the room where Maxfield did his writing. After a few minutes of searching she found it. The earlier draft did not have Maxfield's name on it and it was significantly different from the other draft. By the time Ashley was through reading it, she was certain she knew what had happened, but there was one more thing she had to do to be certain that she was right. She walked down the hall and knocked on the doorjamb of the prosecutor's office.

"Delilah," she said when the deputy DA looked up, "I have to talk to Joshua Maxfield."

CHAPTER THIRTY-SIX

The Oregon State Penitentiary is located near the I-5 freeway in Salem, Oregon's capital. At ten o'clock on Monday morning, Ashley parked in the visitor's lot. A tree-shaded sidewalk ran past a row of small white houses that served as offices for the prison staff. At the end of the walk, across a stretch of asphalt, was the prison with its egg yolk–yellow walls topped by razor wire and guarded by gun towers.

Ashley checked in at the visitors' desk, then took a seat in the reception area. While she was waiting for the guard to call her name, Ashley almost changed her mind about meeting Joshua Maxfield. She was that frightened of him. Delilah had arranged for the interview and had volunteered to go along. Jerry had also volunteered, after his attempts to talk her out of the meeting had failed. She'd turned them both down, because she believed that she had a better chance of getting the death-row inmate to talk if she was alone.

The guard summoned Ashley to the metal detector. After she walked through without setting off an alarm, he escorted her down a short ramp to an enclosed area sealed off by two sets of movable bars. Inside the enclosure, behind bulletproof glass, were several members of the prison staff. One of them hit a button. There was a loud buzz and the bars in front of Ashley slid back. She entered the holding area and pushed her driver's license through a slit in the glass while the bars slid back in place. As soon as her identity was verified, the guard pressed another button and a second set of bars slid back, admitting her to a narrow hallway that led to the interior of the prison. The walls of the hallway seemed to close in on her, and the clanging sound that the bars made when they slammed shut reminded Ashley that she was now locked in prison.

After a short walk her escort stopped in front of a thick metal door with a small window in its upper half. Ashley stood aside while he unlocked the door and admitted her to the visiting area. To the right was a large open room filled with prison-made couches and low wooden tables. A few

vending machines stood against the far wall. At
the end closest to Ashley a guard sat on a raised
platform that gave him a view of the room. Her
escort identified Ashley before returning to the
reception area.

Ashley looked around the visiting room nervously while the guard phoned death row and
asked to have Joshua Maxfield brought down.
She had never been in a prison before. She half
expected to see tattooed bodybuilders and greasy
Hell's Angels eyeing her coldly with rape on their
minds. Instead she found the room filled with
unspectacular-looking men dressed in jail-issue
jeans and blue workshirts, who were talking quietly to family members and friends. One middle-
aged man with a potbelly and a shaggy mustache
was sitting on the floor playing with a little girl
Ashley judged to be four. A shy young man in
his late twenties was holding hands with a tired-
looking young woman who was in the last stages
of pregnancy. At the far end of the room, a short,
skinny black man was laughing at something an
elderly black woman had said.

After a fifteen-minute wait, a new guard entered
the visiting room and spoke to the officer on the
platform. A few moments later, he took Ashley
across the hallway to another visiting section,

where the only furniture was the hard metal
bridge chairs that stood opposite windows of
thick glass. Behind these windows, in narrow concrete rooms sat prisoners deemed too dangerous
or too much of an escape risk to be allowed into
the main visiting area. The guard led Ashley to
two doors at the far end of the room. He opened
one of them and Ashley found herself in a tiny cubicle. The only furniture was a bridge chair that
faced a glass window. A small metal shelf pro-
truded from the bottom of the window. There was
a narrow slot at the bottom of the glass through
which sheets of paper could be passed. Above the
slit was an equally narrow metal grate that permitted people on either side of the glass to speak
to each other.

"They're bringing Maxfield down, now. He'll
sit in there," the guard said, pointing at an identical cubicle on the other side of the glass. "This is
the only place where visitors are permitted to talk
to the inmates on death row. When you're ready
to leave, go back to the desk and we'll have someone come down from reception and get you."

The guard left Ashley alone in the room. The air
was close and she started to feel claustrophobic.
Delilah had told her that it would be impossible
for Maxfield to get at her, but she had been afraid

of him for so long that she had to convince herself that he did not have supernatural powers that would enable him to break through the thick glass and concrete that separated them.

The door to the other cubicle snapped open with a metallic click, and a guard prodded Joshua Maxfield into the narrow space. His hair had turned partially gray and his skin was pasty from lack of exposure to the sun. Ashley remembered how fit he'd looked on the day they'd met outside the gym. Now his skin looked slack. The only thing that had not changed was his eyes, which never left her while the guard unlocked his hand and leg irons.

"What a pleasant surprise," Maxfield said as soon as the door closed behind the guard, but he did not look pleased.

"Thank you for seeing me, Mr. Maxfield."

"Credit my appearance to curiosity. Except for my lawyer, I haven't had a visitor since I was sentenced. And I would never have guessed that you would be my first."

"Are you being treated okay?" Ashley asked, trying hard to hide her anxiety. As soon as the words were out, she realized how inane the question sounded, but Maxfield took it seriously.

"Death row isn't quite the Ritz, but I suspect

I'm treated as well as one can be in my circumstances. The guards actually give me paper and pen and let me write. They probably assume that I'll be more docile if I'm occupied."

He smiled, but his face was tight. "You might be interested to know that I'm working on a novel about an innocent man who is unjustly sentenced to prison. I sent some sample chapters to my former editor in New York. He's very interested but he doesn't want to ink a contract if I'm going to be executed. The publishers are afraid that I won't be alive long enough to finish the book. But enough about me. Why are you here?"

"I wanted to ask you some questions. If you answer truthfully I may be able to help you."

"Help me what?"

"Get out of here."

Maxfield cocked his head to one side and studied Ashley with renewed interest. "Why would you of all people want to help me?" he asked.

"I . . . I have some doubts about the verdict."

"It's a little late for that, isn't it?" Maxfield laughed bitterly. "Thanks to you and Casey I'm a dead man."

"You left out someone else who bears part of the blame."

"Oh, and who is that?"

"You, Mr. Maxfield. You lied about key evidence. Your case might have turned out differently if you'd told the truth."

"What are you talking about?" he asked warily.

"You lied about what happened in the boathouse. That's the first thing. I don't know why you did that but you did. And you lied about your novel."

Maxfield colored and shifted uncomfortably in his seat. "My novel?" he repeated.

Ashley steeled herself and looked Maxfield in the eye. "You didn't write it. You plagiarized the serial killer novel."

"Who told you that?" Maxfield asked angrily.

"No one. I figured it out. One thing always nagged at me. You're smart. Everyone says so. You had to be, to write so well. My mother went on and on about your books. That's why she took your course. And I couldn't figure out how someone so smart would do something as dumb as read the part of your book where the killer eats the pie to one of the few people in the world who would understand its significance. But once I considered the possibility that you didn't write the scene it all made sense. You had no idea that the person who murdered my father ate that snack."

Ashley paused for Maxfield's reaction, but he held himself rigid and gave her none.

"I read the two drafts, Mr. Maxfield, and I've read your books. You wrote the manuscript with your name on it. That manuscript has the same style as **A Tourist in Babylon** and **The Wishing Well.** The man who killed my father and Tanya Jones wrote the other manuscript. The first draft is so different that it had to be the work of someone else."

Maxfield still said nothing, but he didn't stop her either.

"I was in court when Delilah Wallace played the tape of the interview Detective Birch conducted at the jail in Omaha. You sounded shocked when he told you that the scene you read to my mother was just like what happened in my house. You didn't know. You could have told Birch that the book wasn't yours then, but, as bizarre as it seems, I think you'd rather die than admit you can't write anymore."

"That's ridiculous."

"Is it? You failed at everything you tried until you wrote **Tourist.** Your whole identity was wrapped up in the success of that book. Instead of being a screwup, you were suddenly revered, respected, rich, and world-famous. Then **The**

Wishing Well flopped, and you came up empty when you tried to write another novel. You had your moment of fame and you wanted it back. You saw the serial killer novel as your way to return to the top. Who wrote the first draft, Mr. Maxfield?"

"You think I can't write anymore? You're accusing me of . . . of stealing someone else's work?"

"I know you did, and I think your pride kept you quiet. We all thought that you were this superintelligent genius writer, but I think you're really a one-book wonder who would rather die than admit you stole someone else's idea for a book because you couldn't think up an idea of your own."

Maxfield's eyes dropped. He looked utterly destroyed.

"The reviews, those first reviews. They said I was the new Hemingway, the new Salinger, the voice of my generation. Everyone said it. The money came so fast, everything came so fast." Maxfield's face fell. "And it went so quickly. When **The Wishing Well** flopped, my editor told me it was the sophomore jinx; that I'd tried too hard. He told me to take my time with the next book and that I'd be back on top in no time. Only there was no next book. I couldn't come up with a single idea. Every time I tried I came up dry. Then the money ran out and they sued me. After I was forced out of Eton College I couldn't get a respectable job. Everyone knew about my drinking and the falsified résumé and what happened with that student. I had to teach high school, for God's sake. My only way back was with a new book."

"Who sent you the serial killer novel?"

"I don't know. I was critiquing manuscripts for money. Even with my salary from the Academy I was barely getting by. This one came anonymously through the mail, with a cash payment. There was a post office box for the return address. I saw the potential immediately. The writing was crude but there was such power in it. Now I know why. It was real: the horror, the reactions of the victims and the killer, the writer had experienced them."

"The author was bound to read your novel. Didn't you think he would recognize it?"

"I didn't care. I was at rock bottom. And I figured I'd win any lawsuit. I was going to destroy his manuscript when I was done, and I was the famous writer. I thought I was dealing with a nobody."

"Why didn't you tell anybody that you didn't write the book after you were arrested?"

"I tried once. Right before I testified, I told my lawyer that I'd stolen the idea for the book. He told me that no one would believe me. He was right. The manuscript was next to my computer. My handwritten notes were all over it. My name was on every page of my manuscript."

"What happened in the boathouse?" Ashley asked quietly.

Maxfield kept staring at the floor. He said nothing.

"What does it matter now?" Ashley asked. "You're already sentenced to death. It can't get any worse."

"You've got a point there. You certainly do."

He ran a hand across his face. "I didn't kill your mother. Terri was dead when I walked into the boathouse."

"Go on."

"I was almost there when I heard the first scream. I froze. That scream was terrible. It paralyzed me."

Ashley knew exactly what he meant.

"When she screamed again I went to the boathouse."

"Did you see Randy Coleman running away?"

Maxfield shook his head. "I made that up."

Ashley looked shocked. "If the police believed you, Coleman could have been tried for murder."

Maxfield's features hardened. "He deserved to be. He tried to kill you in the parking lot at Sunny Rest. I didn't lie about that. And he murdered Terri when he was trying to kill his wife."

"But you didn't see him at the boathouse?"

"No. He was probably hiding inside and got away when I chased you."

"What really happened in there?"

"When I came in, Casey was kneeling over Terri. The knife was on the floor next to her. She grabbed it and jumped up. Then she screamed 'Murderer,' and ran at me. She looked terrified. She thought that I had killed Terri. She tried to stab me. It happened so fast that I didn't think. I hit her on the jaw. She flew back and cracked her head on that oak beam. The sound was sickening. I knew she was badly hurt as soon as I heard it. I was going to check on her when it dawned on me that Terri's killer might still be in the boathouse. There hadn't been that much time between hearing the second scream and my entering, and I hadn't seen anyone go out the front door. Casey dropped the knife when I hit her. I picked it up for protection. A second later, I saw you at the window. I wanted to tell you that I was innocent but you took off before I could get close enough to say anything." He looked away. "When it dawned on me that you'd tell the police that I killed Terri and attacked Casey I panicked and ran."

"Why didn't you tell anyone what happened, later?"

"Who would believe me after you told the police what you saw and I took off?"

Ashley smiled confidently. "I do, Mr. Maxfield, and I'm going to make other people believe you. I know who killed my parents."

CHAPTER
THIRTY-SEVEN

It takes forty-five minutes to drive from Salem to Portland, and Ashley was thinking all the way. Joshua Maxfield had filled in most of the blanks, but one question still nagged at her. By the time she left the freeway, she thought she knew how to answer it.

Jerry was waiting for her in a dark booth in the rear of Huber's, where they had arranged to meet for a late lunch.

"Well?" he asked as soon as she sat down.

"He didn't kill them," Ashley answered, "and I know who did."

Ashley spent the rest of their lunch explaining her theory to Jerry. He played devil's advocate, but she beat back all his arguments. When she had finished her presentation, Jerry sat back and thought. She watched him expectantly. Finally, he shook his head.

"My God, Ashley, I think you're right."

Ashley let out a pent-up breath. She had worried that Jerry would not agree with her or that he would find some flaw in her reasoning. It meant so much that he was on her side.

"One thing bothers me, though," Jerry continued. "If you're right, the murders in your house weren't random. How did he know that you're Casey's daughter? That didn't become common knowledge until the guardianship hearing."

The question seemed to bother Ashley.

"Remember when we were in court for the hearing, the week I came back to Portland?"

"Sure."

"You wanted to get the file on my adoption from the firm that represented Henry Van Meter. What happened?"

"Monte Jefferson couldn't find it."

"Why?"

"He thought it had been misfiled or thrown away by mistake. It's over twenty years old. It happens."

"What if the file wasn't lost? What if it was stolen?"

The import of her question suddenly struck Jerry and he turned pale as he realized why Ashley was so upset. Jerry's face crumpled.

"Once he found your file he had the names of everyone who knew that you were Casey's daughter, including my father's name."

Ashley reached across the table and held Jerry's hands. "He won't get away with it. We'll get him. He'll pay. But we need proof. So, tell me, where did they store my file?"

Elite Storage owned a 186,000-square-foot warehouse in an industrial park in North Portland. Wide, metal overhead doors opened onto loading docks at set intervals around the building. Jerry and Ashley drove past several moving trucks parked at the loading bays. The office was located in the northeast corner of the warehouse. A balding, middle-aged man in a plaid shirt and khakis was doing paperwork when Ashley and Jerry walked in. A sign on his desk identified him as Raymond Wehrman.

"Help you?" he asked.

"I'm Jerry Philips, Mr. Wehrman. My dad was Ken Philips. You store our old law office files."

"If you say so. We handle about seventy percent of the law offices in town."

"I'm not surprised that the name doesn't ring bells. My dad passed away and I'm a one-man outfit now. But you store Brucher, Platt and Heinecken's files, don't you?"

"Oh, yeah. That's a big firm. I recognize that name."

"This is Ashley Spencer. The Brucher firm handled her adoption twenty-four years ago. I've been representing her in a probate matter and we needed to see the file." Jerry handed the man the document Judge Gish had signed ordering Miles's attorney to hand over Ashley's file. After Wehrman read the order he looked up. "Why are you here? Doesn't the firm's lawyer have to give you the file?"

"Yes, but he told us that the file is missing."

"From our warehouse?"

"Yes. We were wondering if you could try to find it. It's very important."

"Even if it's there, I can't give it to you. I can only give it to a lawyer from the Brucher firm."

"That's okay," Ashley said. "We just want to know if it's here."

The man checked his watch then looked at the piles of paper that covered his desk. He stood up.

"Let's go see what I can find. I've been sitting behind this desk all day and I can use a break."

Wehrman led Jerry and Ashley down endless rows of twelve-foot-high shelves illuminated by overhead fluorescent lighting until they arrived at the shelves rented by the Brucher firm. Wehrman pulled over a ladder and climbed up to the shelf that should have held the file with the record of Ashley's adoption. After several minutes, he slid the ladder to another section. Finally, he gave up and climbed down.

"It's not here," Wehrman said.

"What does that mean?" Jerry asked.

He shrugged. "Any number of things. The file could still be at the law office. You know, they thought they sent it over but the problem happened at the firm. Or we could have misfiled it, which doesn't happen much, but does happen every so often. Or someone could have checked it out and forgotten to return it."

"If someone did take it out of the warehouse would there be a record?" Ashley asked.

"Yeah, we have everything on computer now, even the old stuff. Cost us a fortune."

Back in his office, Wehrman typed in **Brucher, Platt and Heinecken.** Then he typed in the title of the file.

"Says here we received the file seven years ago." He hit more keys. "That's funny."

"What is?" Ashley asked.

"The file was never checked out. It should still be here."

"If I gave you a year and a name, could you find out if the person checked out a file in that year?"

"Sure. I'll just run a search."

Ashley told Wehrman the year Ken Philips, her father, Terri, and Tanya Jones were murdered and gave him a name. A short time later, Wehrman had her answer.

"Miles Van Meter checked out a file that year but it wasn't yours."

"I didn't think it would be," Ashley said.

BOOK TOUR

The Present

Miles had been speaking for almost an hour when Jill Lane, the owner of Murder for Fun, came to the podium to rescue him.

"We have time for one or two more questions. Then Mr. Van Meter will sign your books."

A middle-aged man in the front row raised his hand. Miles pointed at him.

"Mr. Van Meter, I went online and found the itinerary for your first **Sleeping Beauty** book tour. Did you know that there were unsolved murders like the Maxfield murders in two of the cities on your tour, Cleveland, Ohio, and Ames, Iowa?"

"No, I didn't, but I spoke in twenty-six cities and it would be strange if there were no murders."

"These were pretty similar, though. Do you think you were stalked by a copy cat?"

"I hope not." Miles smiled and held up his hands in an attitude of prayer. "Please don't make me feel like Jessica Fletcher on the old **Murder, She Wrote** TV show. Did you ever notice how a murder occurred every place she went? I always wondered why the cops didn't suspect her of being a serial killer."

The audience laughed and Miles grinned.

"We'll take one more question," Jill Lane said.

A woman stepped out from behind a stack of books in the rear of the store and raised her hand.

"Miles," she said as she walked toward the speaker. Van Meter looked puzzled for a moment before breaking into a smile.

"I don't believe this," he told the audience. "We have a special guest, Ashley Spencer. Ashley, what in the world are you doing in Seattle?"

There had been a buzz in the audience when Ashley appeared. Some people recognized her from photographs in the book or from seeing her on television. As soon as Ashley's identity was confirmed the crowd broke into applause.

Ashley stopped several rows from Miles and held up his book. "I finally read the copy of **Sleeping Beauty** you signed for me. It was really good."

"That's high praise, coming from you."

"I did have a question," Ashley said.

"Ask away."

"You were very considerate of my feelings and never asked me what happened in my house on the evening my father and Tanya were killed."

"I knew it would have been tough for you to go over that."

"So you got all of your information about that night from the police reports and the court testimony?"

"Right. I think someone already asked me about that."

Ashley opened her copy of **Sleeping Beauty.** "Here's my question. In the first chapter, you wrote, **'Ashley lay on her bed waiting to die. Then the door to the guest bedroom closed and Maxfield, dressed in black and wearing a ski mask and gloves, was standing in Ashley's doorway. She believed that he had come to rape and murder her. Instead, after watching her for a few seconds, he whispered, "See you later," and went downstairs. Moments later, Ashley heard the refrigerator door open.'"**

Ashley closed the book and looked at Miles. "How did you know that the man who broke into my house said, 'See you later,' before he went downstairs?"

Miles shrugged. "I think it was in a police report or you might have testified about it."

Ashley had been smiling. Now the smile disappeared and was replaced by a look of cold hatred.

"No, Miles. I never told anyone that the man who killed my father spoke to me before he went to the kitchen. I was so traumatized by the attack that I blocked it out. In fact, I didn't remember that it had happened until I read your book for the first time, this week."

Miles kept smiling. "Well, you must have told someone."

"That's what I thought at first—that I told somebody but had forgotten—so I read every police report that mentioned me and I read the transcripts of my preliminary hearing and my trial testimony. Then I talked to Delilah Wallace and Larry Birch. Neither one remembers me telling them that the killer spoke to me."

Ashley paused and glared at Miles. "Only me and the man who broke into my house knew what was said in my bedroom."

A murmur began in the audience as Miles's fans turned to each other. Miles held up a hand.

"Whoa, Ashley, calm down. I don't know what's gotten into you, but Joshua Maxfield murdered your father and Tanya Jones. A jury determined that."

"Does the name Ken Philips ring a bell?"

Miles looked puzzled by the question. "No, should it?" he answered.

"He's the lawyer who arranged my adoption. He's also another of your victims. You killed him shortly before you broke into my house."

There were several gasps in the crowd.

"Why are you making these wild accusations?" Miles asked.

"Why did you go to the Elite Storage warehouse shortly before Ken Philips was murdered?"

Miles looked perplexed. "That was years ago, Ashley. How can I remember that? I'm not even sure I did go to Elite."

"The storage company records show that you checked out a file shortly after your father consulted an attorney at your firm about making me a beneficiary in his will. That was only a few weeks before Ken Philips's murder and the break-in at my house."

Miles flashed Ashley a patronizing grin. "If you say so," he said, "but I'm not following you, and I doubt anyone else is."

He turned toward the crowd for support but was greeted by confused and hostile stares.

"You learned that your father was changing his will," Ashley said. "I'm guessing that you looked in the file of the partner who was preparing the new will—probably after everyone had left for the day. You learned that 'Ashley Spencer' was going to get part of Henry's fortune. You had no idea who 'Ashley Spencer' was, so you went through all of Henry's personal files at the firm. When you couldn't find anything there you went to the storage company on the pretext of getting an old file.

"You knew that my father had made your sister pregnant and that she'd given birth in Europe, but you were never told what happened to her child. My adoption file was stored at the warehouse. You went there on the pretext of getting another file for a case. It must have come as a shock to learn that my father had adopted me and that I was living in Portland. But you also learned that my adoption was kept secret and that only a few people knew about it. Anton Brucher was dead, but my father, Terri, and Ken Philips were alive.

"Henry was cruel and dictatorial when he was younger, but his personality changed after his near-fatal stroke. You were afraid that he would go through with his plan to make me an heir or that I would try to assert a claim to his estate once I learned that I was Casey's daughter. Or maybe the hatred you bore my father for making love to your sister was rekindled. Whatever the reason, you decided to kill me and everyone who knew I was Henry's granddaughter. You tried to kill me at my house and in the Academy dorm after Maxfield escaped. You knew everyone would blame him."

"This is insane, Ashley. Why are you doing this?"

"Because you're a cold-blooded murderer."

"You're forgetting Joshua Maxfield's book. If I'm the man who broke into your house, how did he know that the killer ate some food in your kitchen after raping Tanya Jones?"

"That's an easy question to answer. **Sleeping Beauty** is your first published work but you've been writing for a while. You were proud of the murders you'd been committing. You wanted to brag about them but that would have sent you to death row, so you did the next best thing—you wrote a novel about your crimes and you sent it to Joshua Maxfield for editorial help. You didn't put your name on the manuscript for obvious reasons. There was a post office box as a return address. What you didn't know was that Maxfield had writer's block and was desperate for a story idea. He plagiarized your novel and planned to sell a rewritten version as his own."

"Ashley, I know you've been through a lot. I

hoped that Maxfield's conviction would bring closure to your tragedy. But this just shows that you still need professional help to work through your problems."

"You mean, you think I'm nuts?" Ashley asked.

Miles shook his head. He looked sad. "I know exactly what you're going through. Remember, I almost lost Casey. Experiencing that type of loss does funny things to a person."

"That's true, Miles, but does it make your fingerprints appear in odd places, like the first draft of Joshua Maxfield's book?" Miles froze. "The draft that Maxfield read to his writing seminar was a heavily rewritten version of a previous draft. Until recently, everyone thought that he wrote the draft, but once I figured out that you might have written it Delilah Wallace had the crime lab test each page for fingerprints." Ashley gestured toward the audience. "Would you like to explain to these people how your prints could have ended up on several pages of the manuscript?"

All eyes turned toward Miles, but Miles just stared at Ashley.

"The FBI got a search warrant for your house after they found the prints," she continued. "They found the critique Joshua wrote in the desk in your study. He was very discouraging. He wanted you to give up on the book so he could steal the idea without worrying that you would try to publish."

Miles turned quickly and took a step toward the backroom of the store but two men wearing blue windbreakers with "FBI" stenciled on the back were standing in the hall blocking his way.

"Freeze, Mr. Van Meter," Claire Rolvag said. The escort was standing inches from her author. "I'm an FBI agent and you are under arrest."

As Claire spoke, several members of the audience who had asked questions following the reading moved toward the front of the room and surrounded Van Meter. He gaped at them, then glared at Ashley.

"This is a setup. You set me up," Miles said incredulously as he was handcuffed.

Ashley walked up to Van Meter and glared at him. "Yes I did, you bastard."

Miles stared back. There was nothing behind his eyes. "I'm completely innocent, Ashley," he said in a flat, emotionless voice that was more threatening than a scream. "When I'm cleared, you and I will have to have a long, private talk about your error."

"You think you can scare me, don't you?"

Miles made the mistake of smirking. Ashley

took a step back and drove her foot into his crotch. Miles doubled over and retched and Ashley smashed her hardcover copy of **Sleeping Beauty** into his jaw. Claire pulled her away.

The audience gasped, then began talking excitedly.

"Not smart," Claire told Ashley as Miles was hustled toward the back of the store.

"Maybe not," Ashley answered, "but I'd do it again if I had the chance."

Jill Lane's mouth was open and her hand was on her heart.

"Oh, my God," she said finally. "I don't believe this."

"Sorry, but we couldn't tell you," Claire said. "We needed Miles to believe that this was just another speaking engagement so we could trap him into admitting that he hadn't learned about the 'See you later' statement from Ashley. Except for Barbara Bridger, no one knew what was going on."

"Don't apologize," Jill said. "This is the most excitement we've had around here since our grand opening. And our store will be on national television. We're going to be famous."

PART FIVE
SIBLING RIVALRY

Two Hours Later

CHAPTER
THIRTY-EIGHT

An FBI agent drove Ashley from Murder for Fun to Sea-Tac airport, and an FBI jet flew her home. Delilah Wallace and Larry Birch had a car waiting at Portland International. When they were on the road, Delilah told Ashley that Randy Coleman had been picked up for questioning in connection with the attack at Sunny Rest. Ashley had trouble concentrating on the details of the arrest and only heard half of what the prosecutor said. She felt drained after her confrontation with Miles Van Meter, emotionally spent and physically exhausted. Ashley wished that she could curl up next to Jerry in their big comfortable bed and sleep the night away, but there was still one thing she had to do first.

A little before midnight, Larry Birch parked his

unmarked car in front of the Van Meter mansion. Lights came on after the second ring. Moments later, a sleepy-eyed maid dressed in a nightgown and bathrobe opened the front door. Birch flashed his badge. The maid looked confused.

"We need to speak to Ms. Van Meter," Birch said.

"She's sleeping."

"Who is it, Angela?" Casey called from the top of the stairs. She was wearing a blue silk robe over her nightgown. Delilah pushed past the maid and stood next to one of the suits of armor at the bottom of the stairs.

"It's me, Delilah Wallace. Ashley is here, too."

"What's going on?" Casey asked. "It's midnight."

"I know, and I'm sorry to bother you, but something terrible has happened to Miles and we wanted to tell you in person. Is there someplace we can sit down and talk?"

"Please tell me what happened," Casey said when they were seated in the library, where Delilah had met with Miles and Henry Van Meter many years earlier. Casey had taken the sofa, and Ashley sat beside her. Delilah and Larry Birch were opposite the couch in their own deep armchairs.

"Let me, Delilah," Ashley said. "I should be the one to tell her. I'm her daughter. Miles is my uncle."

"Tell me what?" Casey said, as she looked back and forth between Ashley and Delilah. Ashley turned sideways so she was facing Casey. They were inches apart.

"Miles has been arrested," Ashley said. "Joshua Maxfield didn't kill my father or Tanya Jones. It was Miles."

Casey shook her head in disbelief. "That's ridiculous."

"I know this will be hard for you to believe," Delilah said, "but your brother is a serial killer."

Casey laughed. "I don't know who told you that but . . . it's insane. Miles isn't a killer."

"His vanity tripped him up," Ashley said. "Remember the book that Joshua Maxfield wrote?"

Casey nodded.

"There was a draft in Maxfield's cabin. It turns out that it was Miles who wrote it, not Joshua. If he could get it published, he could brag about his crimes without getting arrested, so he sent it to Maxfield for editing. But Joshua had writer's block and he was desperate for a story idea. He rewrote Miles's book. He plagiarized the draft."

Casey was rigid, her hands clasped in her lap, her back straight. "I don't believe any of this."

Ashley leaned forward and laid a hand on Casey's knee. "It's true. They found Miles's fingerprints all over the draft. They searched Miles's house. There was a letter in the den from Joshua trying to discourage Miles from looking for a publisher."

Ashley looked down. "They also found souvenirs that Miles took from his victims. They . . . Tanya Jones's panties were. . . ."

Ashley's breath caught and she couldn't go on. Casey's mouth gaped open. She shook her head again.

"How could it be possible? I would have known."

"Don't beat yourself up about this, Casey," Delilah said. "Miles had us all fooled."

"But he's my brother." Casey breathed deeply as she fought to control her emotions.

"We do have one problem, though," Larry Birch said. "We were hoping you could help clear it up."

Casey turned toward the detective.

"We know that Joshua Maxfield didn't kill Ashley's father and Tanya Jones," Delilah said. "And the only reason he would have had to kill Terri Spencer was to keep her from telling the police about his book, but he didn't write the book, so he didn't have a motive to kill Mrs. Spencer."

"We also know that Miles was three thousand miles away when you and Terri were attacked in the boathouse," Birch said. "We talked with the two attorneys from Brucher, Platt who were with him in New York. We are absolutely certain Miles could not have been in Oregon when Mrs. Spencer was killed."

"So, that's our problem," Delilah said. "If Miles and Joshua Maxfield didn't kill Mrs. Spencer, who did?"

Casey stiffened for a moment. Then she threw up her hands. "It had to be Joshua. He was standing there."

"But you never actually saw him stab Terri Spencer, did you?" Delilah asked gently.

Casey hesitated. She shook her head slowly. She seemed confused.

"No, I didn't. He was just there. I assumed. . . . Oh, my God. I feel terrible."

"Now that we know that Joshua Maxfield is innocent, we've arrested Randy Coleman for the attack on Ashley at Sunny Rest," Delilah said.

"Joshua testified that he saw a man who looked like Randy Coleman running from the boathouse. Do you think Coleman could have killed Terri Spencer? Maxfield thought he was after you and Terri was just in the wrong place at the wrong time. What do you think?"

Casey looked guilt-stricken. She wrung her hands.

"I've done something terrible," she whispered.

"What have you done, Mom?" Ashley asked.

Being called "mom" seemed to unsettle Casey. "You have to understand, I was certain that Joshua killed Terri and Ashley's father. I knew he'd attacked me. And Miles said. . . ."

"Said what, Casey?" Delilah prodded.

Casey swallowed. She looked awful. "You know that I asked Dr. Linscott to let Miles visit after I came out of my coma? He was my first visitor."

Delilah nodded.

"Miles told me what had happened while I was in the coma. He said that everyone knew Joshua killed Norman and that teenage girl at Ashley's house. He said that Joshua tried to kill Ashley twice more after he failed at her house. He said Joshua had killed Terri. I told him about Randy but he said I must have been mistaken, that I had to say it was Joshua who murdered Terri."

"What did you tell Miles about Randy Coleman?" Delilah asked.

Casey looked at Delilah. She seemed on the verge of tears. "I didn't mean to lie. Miles told me that I had to say it was Joshua, or Joshua would be acquitted. But I did see Randy that evening. I saw him leaving the boathouse just before I went in."

"You're certain about that?" Larry Birch asked.

Casey nodded. "I know I should have said something, but he was my husband, and Miles. . . ." She looked down again.

"So you saw Randy Coleman leaving the boathouse right before you walked in and found Terri Spencer's body?" Delilah asked.

"Yes."

"And he was your husband and you still had feelings for him, so you decided to cover for him?"

Casey nodded.

"Well that presents us with a whole 'nother problem," Delilah said. "See, Joshua Maxfield says that he made up that story. He says he didn't see anyone running from the boathouse after he heard those screams. There was nobody else there—except you."

Casey's eyes widened. Her head swung back

and forth from Delilah to Birch and Ashley. They were all watching her carefully.

"One other thing, Ms. Van Meter," the detective said. "After Miles was arrested we had a little chat. Know what he told us?"

Casey just stared at the detective.

"He told us that you killed Terri Spencer."

"No, no. Miles would never turn on me," Casey insisted.

Delilah smiled sadly. "You love your brother very much, don't you?"

Casey didn't answer.

"I feel sorry for you," Delilah said. "I shouldn't—you're a cold-blooded killer—but I do. I had a brother. He's dead, but I loved him with all my heart when he was alive. I still love him to this day. People will do strange things for love."

Casey had closed up. Her face betrayed no emotions.

"I bet your heart is beating like a trip hammer, just like it was beating when Terri Spencer told you her suspicions about Joshua Maxfield," Delilah said. "You knew your brother was writing a novel about his crimes. You knew that you had to act fast to silence Terri before she told her suspicions to the police. You were afraid that the police would talk to Maxfield and he'd tell them that he was cribbing from your brother's book. If you'd talked to Miles, he would have told you that he sent the book anonymously, but you couldn't get through to him. So you panicked. You lured Terri to the boathouse and killed her to shut her up."

"Isn't that what happened, **Mom**?" Ashley asked coldly.

"That is pure fiction," Casey said. "None of that happened."

"Then Maxfield walked in when you were crouched over Mrs. Spencer," Delilah continued, ignoring the interruption. "You grabbed the knife again. To confuse him, you shouted, 'Murderer.' That's what Ashley heard from outside the boathouse, wasn't it, Ms. Van Meter, you yelling at Maxfield?"

"This is your story, not mine," Casey answered.

"You hoped that Maxfield would be stunned from seeing Terri's body and paralyzed by your shout. Then you could kill him, too. But he's a trained fighter and his reflexes took over. He blocked the knife and decked you. Poor Joshua. He never suspected that you killed Mrs. Spencer.

He was so guilt-stricken by what he'd done to you that it never dawned on him that you were a murderer. Hell, everyone was real sympathetic to you when you were in that coma. You had us all fooled. We thought you were a victim."

"I was a victim. I didn't kill Terri Spencer."

Delilah sighed. "I guess a jury will have to sort that out. Of course, you could avoid a trial and help yourself by testifying against Miles."

Casey's features hardened and she stared directly into Delilah's eyes.

"That will never happen."

"Then it will go hard for you. You know that draft that Maxfield copied, the one your brother wrote? It has a chapter where the killer's girlfriend helps him torture and murder a hitchhiker. That's where she gets her first taste for blood. There's another chapter where the two lovers break into a house, murder a family, and have sex after everyone is dead.

"The forensic investigators in Connecticut found pubic hairs in the guestroom bed at one of the crime scenes. They thought they belonged to the victim. I wonder what a DNA test would show now?"

Casey didn't take the bait. Delilah hadn't expected her to.

"Henry was a cruel man in his younger days," Delilah said. "I think you and your brother became unnaturally close while you were dealing with his cruelty. There's Miles's vicious attack on Norman Spencer when he learned that he got you pregnant, and there are all these teenage girls he raped and murdered. Do you think he was acting out his fantasies about sleeping with you?"

"That's disgusting," Casey said. She glared at Delilah. Ashley thought that she would have killed the prosecutor if she'd had a weapon.

Delilah shrugged. "My degree is in law, not psychology, but I bet Freud would have had a field day with you and your brother. That kind of twisted love would create an unusual bond. It would explain why you're reluctant to talk about Miles. Funny thing though, it didn't stop him from trying to take you off of life support when you were in your coma."

Casey's features cracked for a second.

"Henry stopped him while he was alive," Ashley said. "When Henry died, Miles filed to be named your guardian. He made no secret of the fact that he was going to take you off life support as soon as he had the power to do it. Coleman wanted you to die, too. I was the only one who wanted to keep you alive."

"I don't believe that."

"It's true," Ashley said. "He had to get rid of you. You were the only one who knew he was a killer. He didn't know what you would say if you came out of the coma. He couldn't take the risk that you'd talk."

Ashley squared her shoulders and stared down Casey Van Meter. "He didn't care about you any more than I do."

EPILOGUE
BOOK TOUR

One Year Later

"I don't care, Howard," Joshua Maxfield shouted into his cell phone. "My contract calls for the **best** suite in **every** hotel I stay in on the tour. This is not the best suite. The view is shit, and the Taj Mahal suite, which has the best view, is bigger."

"I don't know what to say, Joshua," Howard Martin, editor in chief of Scribe publishing, answered. "Margo checked with the hotel. They told her that the Presidential Suite was the best and the biggest. It's the most expensive."

"And there was a bottle of fifteen-year-old scotch in my room," Maxfield continued, ignoring his editor.

"Isn't that what you wanted? Wasn't it the right brand?" Martin asked.

"Yes it was the right brand, but it was fifteen-year-old scotch. I specifically asked that idiot to make sure that the scotch was twenty-five years old. Can't you afford to hire publicists who know their numbers?"

"We're here, Mr. Maxfield," Barbara Bridger said from the front seat of the limousine. Maxfield held up a finger to silence her and continued his tirade. The chauffeur had his door open and was waiting patiently when Maxfield cut the connection. Joshua got out, still muttering to himself about the incompetence of Scribe's publicist.

The back door to Murder for Fun opened, and Jill Lane rushed out to greet her author.

"Mr. Maxfield, you have no idea what an honor it is to meet you. I love your books."

Maxfield plastered a smile on his face and grasped Jill's hands in his. "The honor is all mine. Speaking at your store will be the high point of my tour."

Neither Jill Lane nor Joshua Maxfield saw Barbara Bridger roll her eyes. She couldn't wait for this appearance to be over so she could rid herself of this egomaniacal asshole. She debated whether she should tell Jill how Maxfield had ranted and raved about the indignity of an artiste like himself having to speak at a bookstore that specialized in murder mysteries.

"The store is packed and the press is here. You're our biggest draw since . . . well, since Miles Van Meter."

"I just hope I don't get arrested," Maxfield joked.

Jill laughed and led Joshua and Barbara inside and up to the front of the store. The audience applauded as soon as they spotted the author. He nodded modestly. Jill stepped to the microphone.

"A little over a year ago, Miles Van Meter, one of history's most diabolical serial killers, was arrested in this store on this very spot after giving a reading from his bestseller, **Sleeping Beauty.** **Sleeping Beauty** purported to be a work of true crime, but now we know that it was a work of fiction that falsely accused tonight's guest author of the horrible crimes that Miles and his sister, Casey, committed. Fortunately, the Van Meters are behind bars where they belong. Casey was sentenced to life in prison without possibility of parole in Oregon in exchange for testifying against her brother. Miles Van Meter was sentenced to death in Oregon for the murders of

Norman Spencer and Tanya Jones, and he received other sentences for attempting to murder Ashley Spencer. Of course, Miles and his sister are facing charges in several other states, some of which have the death penalty.

"Our guest tonight, Joshua Maxfield, suffered in prison after he was framed for the Van Meters' crimes, but he turned his suffering into art. While on death row, he penned **Caged,** a work of fiction that details the horrors suffered by an innocent man who is incarcerated for a crime he did not commit. The book was published two months after Mr. Maxfield's release from the Oregon State Penitentiary and it is still on the **New York Times** bestseller list, more than a year after its publication.

"But Mr. Maxfield is not here because of **Caged.** He is here to discuss his memoir, **Framed,** which is his account of the Van Meter case and his years in prison. **Framed** was released this week, and we just learned that it will debut at number one on the **New York Times** bestseller list. And now, without further ado, I give you Joshua Maxfield."

The audience applauded, and Joshua basked in their adulation. He did not want the applause to stop. It sounded so terrific. After all the years of silence his genius was finally being recognized. And he was a genius. A towering literary genius whose works would live forever. He was convinced of it. The years between **The Wishing Well** and **Caged** had simply been a hiccup in his climb up the mountain to the pinnacle of success. His publisher was clamoring for his next book and, as soon as his tour ended, he would begin work on it. Of course, right now, he was too distracted to think about what it would be. In fact, he had no idea whatsoever.

ACKNOWLEDGMENTS

The following people helped me with the research that hopefully made **Sleeping Beauty** believable: Steve Lesser, Brian Ostrum, Dr. Nathan Selden, Dr. Howard Weinstein, Ashley Berman, Bridget Grosso, Mary Joan O'Connell, and Christine Brown. My editor, Dan Conaway, definitely made the book more readable, and I appreciate the help of Dan's intrepid assistant, Jill Schwartzman.

Thanks also to the countless bookstore owners, clerks, managers, and author escorts who have been so kind and supportive during my many book tours. I bet you never guessed that you were unwittingly helping me with my research for **Sleeping Beauty.** Thanks also to Marie Elena Martinez and Elly Weisenberg, who organize my book tours and never get their numbers wrong.

I want to thank everyone at HarperCollins and the Jean V. Naggar Literary Agency for their enthusiastic support.

Last, but definitely not least, I want to thank my family, Doreen, Ami, Daniel, and Chris, for putting up with me.